Dear Reader
If you enjoye
or not! - plea
review on Amaz ..

Helen began writing novels after retirement from teaching. She has just had published her first novel in a trilogy set in Victorian England, but her focus has always been the fifteenth century. She combined this with a love of Shakespeare and achieved a PhD from The Shakespeare Institute, Birmingham University, in 2009. Research for her thesis was on Warwick the Kingmaker in the three parts of *Henry VI*. Later, she wrote a quartet of novels on Warwick's life – *Lodestar*. During research for them, she came across Thomas Malory.

Best wishes

Dedication

Dedicated to my grandchildren: Jack, Mylo, Lewis and Daphne.

Helen Lewis

ROGUE MALORY

AUSTIN MACAULEY PUBLISHERS™
LONDON • CAMBRIDGE • NEW YORK • SHARJAH

A CIP catalogue record for this title is available from the British Library.

ISBN 9781788781039 (Paperback)
ISBN 9781788781046 (Hardback)
ISBN 9781788781053 (E-Book)

www.austinmacauley.com

First Published (2018)
Austin Macauley Publishers Ltd™
25 Canada Square
Canary Wharf
London
E14 5LQ

Acknowledgements

I would like to thank Kate Mcluskie, Lesley Taylor and Carolyn Box for all their help and encouragement. Also Dr Timothy Lustig, whose book *Knight Prisoner* was very helpful in background research and who kindly read part of the manuscript in its early stages. Thanks to Margaret Holland and David Adams for their help reading through the completed manuscript.

Foreword

In My End Is My Beginning

1471: A grey day, just after dawn. Sir Thomas Malory steps out and shivers in the cool, damp March air. Squinting in the gloom, the old knight walks with some urgency towards a pair of ornate metal gates, large and padlocked with a thick chain. He notices immediately that they are in a considerable state of neglect, showing patches of flaking rust. The would-be ornamental figures topping each gate are worn to the point of being unrecognisable, just two incongruous pieces of metal. By the gates stands a small wooden shelter and as Sir Thomas comes nearer, a figure emerges from its interior; a tall imposing man dressed in a dark grey shirt under a black doublet, with black hose and a pale grey hat which standing off his face encircles his whole head.

Spying Sir Tom, he returns to the shelter and brings out a small folding-table, a stool, an ink pot, a quill and a sheaf of papers. Opening the table, he sets out the equipment, seats himself and looks expectantly at his visitor.

'Good morning, Sir Thomas. We've been waiting for you. Can you please confirm you are he?'

'I am indeed Sir Thomas Malory of Newbold Revel in Warwickshire – Knight of –'

'Quite, quite, we know this already but just checking. Now, we need to go through some important procedures.'

'That may well be so, but before anything else, I want you to open the gates and let me in immediately. My bowels are not happy; I need the privy urgently, and I mean urgently!'

‘I sympathise with your distress, Sir Thomas, but, as I said, there are some formalities to be addressed. Perhaps if you concentrate your mind a little on the external, your internal problems may subside for a moment.’

‘That’s all very well, but when a man’s got to go –’

‘Indeed. But first things first.’

Sir Thomas scowls but, in view of the fact that the gentleman holds the keys on his belt and has a determined glint in his eyes, he feels it would be wiser to cooperate, for the time being at least.

‘Now, Sir Thomas, or shall I call you “Sir Tom”? Our protocols demand that we hear how you see matters at this particular juncture of your life – a kind of self-assessment of your performance so far.’

‘Jesus Christ, I –’

The man holds up his hand, ‘Let me stop you there, Sir Thomas. One rule of the House is “no blasphemy”; taking the Lord’s name in vain will do your cause no good at all.’

‘If you say so,’ says Sir Tom sulkily.

‘I do. Now, I’ll just explain our method.’ He takes up the sheaf of paper. Charging his quill with ink, he refers to the top page with a serious face, ‘I have here a list of the Seven Deadly Sins. All I need you to do is to confirm or deny you have been guilty of them – or not as the case may be. By the way, one thing we don’t do here is go over the events of your life one by one. Also, we consider political activities aren’t rooted in the Deadly Sins per se, although of course, they can certainly lead to them – but it’s a moot point among our advisers. You’ll be pleased at that I expect, given your previous heavy involvement in state affairs and your current digestive predicament. No, we simply take the list of the basic Cardinal Sins and ask you to respond honestly. For example – Envy? Would you say that has been a besetting sin or not?’

‘No more than any other man I know.’

‘I choose it, not because it is the most serious, but it comes first if we take the sins in alphabetical order. We like matters to be well-organised, it saves time. I’ll just run through them, in case you’ve forgotten what they are. So: Envy, Gluttony,

Greed, Lust –' Sir Thomas twitches slightly, 'Pride, Sloth, Wrath. We use a sliding scale for your responses; should I record you as being "very envious", "often envious", "hardly ever envious", "never envious" or "don't know"? And if you are envious, is it of anything or anyone in particular?'

Sir Thomas shifts on his feet, 'Well, I will admit to being "often envious". I would've liked more power – to have been further up the social scale – perhaps a baron or an earl.'

'Very well, nothing particularly abnormal there then. But overall, as you suggest, it sounds like an "often"; thank you for your honesty. Now, what about Gluttony?'

'Chance would be a fine thing. I've been in prison off and on for almost fifteen years; the fare's pretty meagre.'

'Yet, our understanding is you've not stinted yourself on food – or wine.'

'Well, I have generous friends – and my wife, of course, who's been most supportive.'

'Ah, your wife; we'll come to her later. I'll mark that one an "often" too, for the moment. Now Greed – we always find this one more difficult. What is the difference between Gluttony and Greed, do you suppose? After much deliberation, our advisers concluded that one is singular to bodily sustenance, the other more general – akin to covetousness. Would you agree?'

'I suppose so. I haven't really thought about it.'

'So, would you say you're a greedy man?'

'Certainly not! And if you were ever uncertain as to its definition, I suggest you put down "don't know" at least.'

'I don't think so, Sir Thomas.'

'Oh – and why not?'

'Because we have a list of felonies committed by yourself, with others admittedly, but all serious and arising out of the Sin of Greed. We had our accountants look at the figures and their reckoning is – let me see,' and he runs down a list using the end of his feathered quill, 'in a criminal spree, over the course of almost two years, you stole £191 4s 8d in cash, excluding the £7 9s 8d you borrowed from two moneylenders and didn't repay; the contents of various coffers and chests, including precious religious items from the monks of Combe Abbey – unfortunately for you, a particularly favourite religious house of the Master – and a rather fine cart valued at twenty-two pounds. What do you say to that?'

'I admit the cart did take my fancy, although it was criminally overpriced on the indictment. But these others were debts – monies owed me and the debtors wouldn't pay up, so I took matters into my own hands.'

'Anyone can say that, Sir Thomas.'

'Are you accusing me of lying, sir?' and Malory bristles; drawing himself up, he looks his inquisitor squarely in the face. His gaze is returned quizzically from a pair of unwavering steely grey eyes.

The man replies gravely, 'I put it to you that these incidents stemmed from the Cardinal Sin of Greed. In the same regard, let us consider the livestock.'

'Livestock?'

'Yes, the cows, calves, sheep and horses you stole; not to mention the six does you took from the Duke of Buckingham's deer park.'

'Fuckingham Buckingham! I was wondering when you'd bring him up.'

The man frowns and tuts with annoyance, 'Our strictures also include the non-use of profanity, Sir Thomas. Now, let's to it. It's noted here that, with others, you drove away quantities of domestic kine and sheep from various neighbours, leaving them short in their herds and flocks. Out of interest, what did you do with them all?'

'Sold them on, of course! I told you, the farmers owed me money.'

'So, you admit to these for-profit crimes?'

'If you have them logged as "crimes" and not "repossession", I suppose I must. But, as you say, I wasn't alone.'

'We're only concerned with you, Sir Thomas. The others will have to take their chances when they appear before us. We pride ourselves on our meticulously fair equal-opportunities policy. Our reckoning shows you have committed enough Sins of Greed to fill a whole catalogue. We have no note of any admission of guilt on your part; no genuine confessions; not even cash in return for indulgences. Indeed, no real remorse according to our records.'

'It was expedient for me to do these things at the time, sir. I told you they owed me and I had need of ready money.'

'Unfortunately, that's no excuse. Greed is apparently one of your main besetting sins.' The man puts two large ticks against "very" and Malory hangs his head, but looks shifty.

'Now, moving on – Lust.' There is a long pause. Malory looks distinctly shiftier and shuffles from one foot to the other. The man studies his script, moving the quill down a list. 'This is where we really come to it, Sir Thomas. We have many shocking incidents logged in this category, including the most serious offence of rape – not once but twice – in the year '50.'

'I was never convicted and she was willing. Everyone knew, including her husband. I was never able to explain that.'

'Now's your chance, Sir Thomas.'

'Look, Joan Smythe was enamoured and couldn't keep her hands off me – why else would I have gone off with the woman, set her up in lodgings and visited her regularly – in Coventry of all places? Her husband cut up rough when he found out I was fu – that I knew her carnally on a regular basis – and reported me.'

'But our understanding is that once you had "lain with her", as you admit you did, you cruelly attacked her husband, Hugh, stole forty pounds worth of his goods and ran off with her.'

'No, hang on just a minute. I didn't abduct her – she suggested we make a bolt for it. We went to Coventry because I had friends there. It was never rape – as I say, she was very willing but, when Smythe found out, in order to stop the gossip, he cried "rape" and tried to have me arrested. It's common practice in cases like that, certainly in Newbold Revel. By the way, let's get it straight, she was the one who took her husband's money and goods.'

‘At your behest, and you sold them and pocketed the cash – we have it on record, Sir Thomas. The fact is you and Mistress Smythe were married to other people at the time, and therefore, even if as you say it wasn’t rape, it was surely adultery – a product of Lust in our Book.’

‘That I cannot deny. We committed adultery – together – willingly and very pleasant it was too!’

‘We’ll take that as a full admission of guilt. Then we also have the dozens of whores you habitually invited to your cells in Newgate, the Fleet, the Marshalsea, the King’s Bench prisons and even in the Tower of London. Your whorelets, as you termed them. Quite a list! And I haven’t included the illicit sexual congress you enjoyed in the Bankside Stews – remarkably lusty activity according to our records. Didn’t they call you “Lusty Loins” down there?’

‘Well, I had a reputation to keep up. I certainly “had them” and treated all of them exceedingly well, there were never any complaints. Look here! A man must satisfy his needs, especially when he’s cooped up in a cell for fifteen years. Besides, you could say I was keeping these poor women from want, they were certainly doing the same for me. It was mut – mutu – what’s the word?’

‘I think the term “mutually beneficial” is what you’re looking for, Sir Thomas. However, it’s no excuse. Your regular use of those women has damned their souls; there’s nothing mutual or beneficial about that.’

‘But I can’t be held responsible for the fate of their souls!’

‘Standing behind every fallen woman is the man who pushed her over, Sir Tom.’

‘I disagree. They made their own choices – they have free-will after all.’

‘Do they? Providence determines otherwise.’

‘No free-will! Do you mean my life has been mapped out for me from the start? I feel cheated!’

‘Indeed; we always had a good idea where you were going, although an element of choice has been built in; hence this appraisal.’

‘So everything depends on my choices in the end?’

'That's the logical way of looking at it, Sir Tom.'

'The divines and the philosophers have got it wrong then?'

'Ah, the philosophers! You know, some of them were on the wrong track altogether. Anyway, why don't you ask them; they're in abundance where you're going. You can have all the teleological arguments you like with them.'

'Teleological? That's a fine word and one I'd like to use myself. What does it mean?'

'You can't use it; it's not available. The philosopher who thinks it up hasn't been born yet. Besides, if you don't know what a word means, you shouldn't use it! But, never mind that; we're truly getting ahead of ourselves. Back to Lust. In all this, we haven't spoken about your wife, Lady Elizabeth. How must she have felt? The rape allegations and then the whoring in various London jails – it was all common knowledge. Your wife's a respectable lady from a respectable family. It must have been very hard on her. Aren't you in the least remorseful?'

'Well, wives must accept this kind of thing. Men are not saints after all; I think –'

'Wrong answer, Sir Thomas! We know plenty of men who *are* saints. According to our judgement, you've treated your wife shamefully. There's no gainsaying it, Lust must come top on the list of your misdeeds.' He takes his quill and with a flourish inscribes three solid ticks on the paper against "very". Then he says, 'Now, let's think about Sin Number Five, Pride.'

'Well, there I can say I have absolutely no pride in me.'

'Hmm. Are you certain about that? What about this perpetual feud with Lord Buckingham? Surely there were many elements of stiff-necked obstinate Pride in your behaviour?'

'Not at all. I had a fair case against him which justified my actions. I refuse to say more than that.'

'We'll come back to his grace the duke later. But you will admit to having a vain approach to your writing. We've noted your refusal to allow anyone to share ownership of *Le Morte*

D'Arthur; Mr Montmorency Pickle, for example. Our understanding is that he has helped you enormously with the work, but will never be acknowledged by you as having the slightest input.'

'I'm not willing to share the praise and acclaim I think the book will deserve. I worked on it for years before I invited Mr Pickle to assist me, and then that was only to adjust and proof-read. He has had no input into the substance.'

'I'm not convinced by that argument. He's acted as an able amanuensis –'

'An able what?'

'Amanuensis – another term which won't come into being for at least eleven decades – it's a rather fine description for a secretary. Mr Pickle was a good one and we feel you didn't give him the recognition he deserved. But in any case, whether you agree or not, in view of the high-handed approach you took with the Duke of Buckingham, we cannot absolve you from the sin of Pride and therefore, must mark our judgement down again as "very".'

'That seems "very" harsh. Is there no appeal?'

'None. But cheer up, Sir Thomas, Sloth looks better for you. We have no record of a time when you were guilty of lazy inaction – wasting time – vacillation. We can honestly credit you with a positive assessment – a definite "never"!'

'Thank Chri – thank you,' says Malory.

'But Wrath is another thing entirely. You are undeniably "very wrathful". This is where your feud with the Duke of Buckingham really lets you down. There is no denying you pursued him, literally; threatened his life and did inordinate damage to his deer park – £500 worth I believe – because you were so angry with him. You had no right to vent your spleen in that way. I don't want to go into detail, but did you have to wreck his dove-cote? All those fluffy babies squawking for their mothers; those poor little squabs were fledging at the time. It was most distressing. However, the point is we're still mystified as to where this great antipathy towards the duke came from. Perhaps –'

'Look here, do we have to continue with all this? I don't want to talk about Fu – the Duke of Buckingham! I'm sick of talking about it. This seems all very unfair to me. I feel I've been denied the right to reply sufficiently.'

'That is clearly untrue, Sir Thomas, and contradictory. The fact is we give you every opportunity to put your side of things, although of course, we've always been fully aware of the truth of events. So far, you have made a very poor case for yourself. Still, we're running out of time so, moving on, when we add up the final figures, we find you seriously guilty of four Deadly Sins and moderately so of one other. In this instance, we'll be generous and write Gluttony off as a "hardly ever"; the management has already agreed that Sloth was never one of your besetting sins.'

'So what does that mean? Are you going to let me in? As I said, my bowels are in a chronic state.'

The man shakes his head, 'I'm afraid not, Sir Tom. It will be The Other Place for you.'

'The Other Place? Where's that?'

'It is how we refer to what you might call "Hell". Our Correctness Committee considers that description oppressive and reactionary. They feel the name "The Other Place" is more appropriate and non-judgemental.'

'Non-judgemental! How ridiculous! Surely you jest? Anyway, changing the name doesn't alter either the substance or the purpose of a thing.'

'A pretty philosophical point, Sir Thomas, and one you might like to present to the Greeks who are all in The Other Place and I'm sure will enjoy debating with you. They are, after all, experts on that kind of sophistry.'

'Are there no Greeks here then?'

'I'm afraid their tendency to polytheism rather ruled them out.'

'But I thought you said you had an equal opportunities policy.'

'Some people are more equal than others.'

'Now, that is an interesting phrase and one I would really like to be able to use.'

'You can't. It's booked for a writer who hasn't yet come into existence. But we've talked for long enough. Come, it's time to leave,' and the man puts two fingers to his mouth and gives a shrill whistle. From out of the grey mist which now descends around Malory, a cloaked and hooded figure pads into view; the apparition carries a scythe on its left shoulder and approaches the pair, putting its free hand on Malory's shoulder.

'GR and on time, excellent!' beams the man in black.

'Always ready to oblige SP!' the deep resonant voice from the hood is very distinct considering it is enveloped in heavy wool. Malory wonders if he doesn't detect a Coventry accent. 'What's the judgement here? Is he in or out?'

'I'm afraid he has been weighed in the balance and found wanting – five to two in favour of the Other Place, with four very serious counts.'

'My money's on Lust being one of them.'

'And you wouldn't lose, Reaper! But it's easy money. Most men fall at that hurdle.'

'What are the others? He's too skinny for Gluttony.'

'Pride – stiff-necked obstinacy! Then there's Greed and Wrath. Envy was an "often".'

'Quite a score! Right! Thomas Malory, you heard what St Peter said. You must come with me.'

Sir Thomas takes a step forward, 'Wait a minute,' and he turns to St Peter, 'are you really saying what I think you're saying?'

'Yes, and I'm afraid it's useless to complain. You've been judged by the highest authority possible. Lucky really, since for years, you've complained so bitterly about not having your day in court.'

'It's not exactly the outcome I was expecting. Look here, are you sure there's no chance of an appeal? All that time I spent in the Confessional – does it mean nothing?'

'We know you didn't mean it when you asked for absolution because the very next day, you committed the same sins and repeatedly. The Master doesn't like that – it's not honourable.'

‘I was always taught He’s a merciful God – that is who you mean when you talk of the “Master” I suppose?’

‘Perhaps. Unfortunately, you’ll never have the opportunity to put it to Him; His Committee’s decisions are irreversible. These gates are forever closed against you.’ St Peter holds up his hand in a gesture of finality.

Malory steps back and shrugs, his face taking on a look of defiance, ‘These gates, yes,’ he says, ‘I’ve never seen anything so – so – what’s the word I’m looking for? Help me out here.’

‘So un-celestial?’

‘That’s it! Un-celestial. They’re distinctly shabby and that gigantic padlock clearly needs oiling. I presume those are supposed to be angels on the top? They look like the discards from a blacksmith’s apprentice; they’ve certainly seen better days. You should be ashamed, especially since you invite in the great and the good! Modern thinking is that everything depends on presentation, people judge things by first impressions, gates and doors are very important. What must the Chosen Ones think? Would they really crave to enter imagining the shabbiness which must lie beyond?’

‘I take your point, which others have often made. They are very unprepossessing, but I’m afraid we can’t get the labour.’

‘Why not? You must have generations of artisans and labourers in there!’

‘We don’t let them in.’

‘Don’t let them in? How so?’

‘It’s all down to money, I’m afraid. The poor don’t pay enough of it into the Church coffers; they don’t have chapels built, pay for masses to be said for the dead or buy indulgences. All the nobility, bishops and archbishops make sure of their places here by donating heavy sums to keep our enterprise on earth in funds. The peasants and labourers can’t afford to pay, so they can’t get in; that makes it very difficult trying to keep everything up here from falling apart, not having a regular labour force. That’s what happens when you’re cash-rich but skills-poor.’

'Why don't you relax the rules and let them in – perhaps on licence until the work's completed; then you could send them to He – the Other Place.'

'A novel idea and one I could put to the Work's Committee on Friday when it sits – on the Master's left hand.'

'Look SP – may I call you that? Here's an idea. I have a quick brain. You've said yourself I never indulged in the Sin of Sloth. Perhaps I could put my organisational flair to some use here?'

'There is logic in that suggestion too but no, I don't think so. It would upset our residents; they would see your presence as a threat to the standards we try to maintain. For a start, the Abbot of Combe Abbey would be incensed – when he eventually gets here. And then there's his Grace, the Duke of Buckingham; he's definitely against your entry. No, we'll stick to the plan. Go off quietly with the Grim Reaper, no fuss.'

St Peter picks up the papers, quill and ink, folds up the table, puts the stool on top, and carries everything back into the porter's hut with undisguised finality. But then, as the Reaper and Sir Thomas begin to walk away, he seems to change his mind and calls them back. 'Wait one moment, Sir Thomas! Because you've given us hours of diversion looking over all your misdemeanours, I'll let you into some secrets before you leave. Firstly, we really liked your book and I can tell you it will delight a great many more people in the future.'

'That's gratifying. But I'm not sure how it will be disseminated. Mr Appleby and Mr Pickle have been given some instructions as to where the manuscript should go, but as for getting it out to a wider public, I never seriously considered how I should go about it. Have you any ideas?'

'Master Caxton – he's your man.'

'I can't say I've heard of him.'

'Well, in about fifteen years' time, he'll take a copy of *Le Morte D'Arthur* and put it through his brand new innovatory pressing system. He'll be able to produce books by the hundreds and I can tell you people will buy them – everyone's books.'

'Geoffrey Chaucer's as well?'

'Indeed.'

'Damn!'

'Your stories will then pass down the ages to come and, I can also tell you this, some five hundred years hence the Master will order a miracle. Arthur, Lancelot, Gawain and the whole pack of the Round Table will appear as moving images on a large white screen which thousands will be able to see all at once, sitting in comfortable seats while making a good deal of noise eating small conglomerates of sticky millet. Don't ask me how it'll work; I'm no good with technology – as it will be called. It's the will of Providence, that's all you need to know.'

'So, my stories will literally "come to life"? That's very satisfying.'

'What you should also know is that by that time, Oxford and Cambridge won't be the only universities in England. There'll be dozens of them. They'll all have departments called Humanities Faculties where professors and doctors will teach a subject called "Literary Criticism" – tearing your work to pieces in desperate attempts to outdo each other in clever explanations of what you really meant.'

'Will they do that to Chaucer?'

'Even more so.'

'So I will be very famous – as famous as Geoff! Will I have a plaque in Westminster Abbey like him?'

'Unfortunately not, and there's another thing. I'm afraid in about a hundred years' time, both you and he will be eclipsed by the coming of one much mightier.'

'You mean Jesus? So the Church is right then? There will be a Second Coming!'

'Not the Lord Jesus; he long since decided once was enough. No, this man will be a writer of plays; I can tell you exactly when he'll appear on earth – April 23rd, 1564; I remember because we have a heavy schedule about that time.'

'Will he be buried in Westminster Abbey?'

'I don't remember all the fine details of his life to come, other than he'll dominate writing for centuries. I must say, you do seem to be rather fixated on the Abbey, Sir Tom.'

'Well, it's this business of Chaucer being there but not me. I find that hard to understand.'

'You'll be a victim of literary whim, I'm afraid. Perhaps they'll think you're just not fashionable enough and, let's face it, Chaucer did get there first with his tales in the vernacular. There's also the problem of your moral decline.'

'Moral decline?'

'Which we have just been discussing. The powers-that-be in the Abbey may not think it appropriate that they laud you in the same place as others with less questionable pasts. After all, that's why you can't enter *our* gates.'

'Mm; Did Chaucer get through – the gates I mean?'

'That's confidential I'm afraid.'

Sir Thomas looks rather crestfallen, then shrugs his shoulders and sighs, 'But I'm sure I'm a more colourful character than Charmless Chaucer the civil servant; everyone seems to agree about that – even you!'

'I do indeed. But there's charm and there's charm, Sir Tom. Now, time is running out and I've kept you long enough. Have you anything else you wish to say – any wise old Malory saws I can include in *my* Book?'

'For the first time in my life, I've run out of words. One question though: is there any chance I could have a second go?'

'A second go at what?'

'Life.'

'I'm afraid not, Sir Thomas. We have a strict "no returns" policy; it's all over for you. Now, no more delays; the Other Place is waiting and they don't hold with unpunctuality any more than we do. I haven't visited since the fall of Lord Lucifer but I've been told his facilities are second to none. Then they would be when you think about it – just my little joke! Apparently, they've money to burn – literally; too much of the stuff from all the "wealthy wicked". But don't get me started on that. GR, make sure Sir Thomas reaches the correct destination. See if you can find which circle Dante inhabits and put them together; they should get along splendidly, sharing literary aspirations as they do. It'll be especially appropriate if it turned out to be the second circle of Lust; Sir Tom will be able to wear himself out!'

'Very well, SP!' The Reaper tightens his grip on Sir Thomas' shoulder, turning him from the gates. As he swings his own shoulder round, the needle-sharp point of the scythe comes dangerously close to Malory's face. 'For fuck's sake!' cries the knight. There is a rustling and a harrumphing from the porter's shed but St Peter stays resolutely where he is, choosing to ignore the lapse. After all, he has discharged his duty, Sir Thomas Malory is no longer his responsibility.

'Careful with that thing!' grumbles Sir Tom.

The Reaper sighs, 'They've given me an upgrade; a new model made of some different material – much lighter than the old one; I'm having to adjust to it.'

'Well, you need more practice then; you could've had my eye out!'

'Sorry!'

The two figures begin to disappear into the mist. But not before St Peter hears Malory say, 'Can we get a shift on? My bowels are moving again.'

***

But that is for the future.

Chapter 1

London, 1469

In which characters are introduced, a contract signed and insults swallowed.

'Come in; close the door behind you. We don't want anyone walking in uninvited; besides Newgate's notoriously draughty.'

'I imagined –'

'You imagined locks and bars perhaps, that I might be chained to the wall, a skeleton for lack of sustenance? We are living in the fifteenth-century, not under the Norman heel.'

'Well, something like that, Sir Thomas – is it he I'm addressing?'

'Certainly is – who else? It is I who sent for you, Montmorency Pickle. The famous – infamous Sir Thomas Malory who has inhabited numerous places of imprisonment – from lockups to manor houses and every London prison you can name. But that's nothing to do with why I've sent for you.' He paused, looked over his shoulder and seemed to speak to the air, 'What do you think of him, Pom? Will he do for us?'

From the shadows in a corner, a middle-aged rotund man with short legs and a long but well-kept beard stepped forward, and looked the visitor up and down. 'Can't rightly say, Sir Tom. We haven't heard what he can do – you so busy talking on as you do. If you give the man a chance, perhaps he'll enlighten us as to his abilities.'

'Enlighten us as to his abilities – I like that, Pom. Let me introduce you both; my servant –'

'Dog's body and scapegoat.'

'My servant, John Appleby gent, otherwise known as Pom. You are Montmorency Pickle – gentleman also I presume – a scribe recommended to us by no one other than the keeper of this place, Master Clyfford. What do we call you, Mr Pickle? A prison is, as you might imagine, a place where formality takes a poor second to the embrace of friendly address.'

'Monty will suit me well, Sir Thomas. Tell me; is it usual for a senior official of the prison to take such an interest in one of his charges?'

'Unique I would say – but it tallies well with my status as a powerful and persistent threat to any government that finds itself in power. But more of that later perhaps, for now, time is pressing and we must get down to business. You know why I've sent for you?'

'Something about assisting you to transcribe a great work – Master Clyfford hinted that your eyes are not as sharp as they once were.'

'The keeper understates the case, Monty Pickle; they gleam but it is with *ignis fatuus*. Years of incarceration in dimly lit cells have rendered them practically useless for transcribing my thoughts to paper over long periods. But I forget my manners. Please sit and take your ease. We have much to discuss.'

It is April, the year 1469; the place a cell – perhaps more accurately described as a decent-sized room – on the top floor of the tower of Newgate Prison in the city of London; not an unpleasant space and set apart from the main cells in the building beyond. It was once used as a base for the prison guards, but they have long-since been moved to more spacious quarters. This room has two small north-facing windows on one side, barred, but which let in a modicum of early-April light and overlook the Greyfriars' Abbey garden across the street. Thick stone walls are plainly whitewashed and the floor spread with rush matting. Four iron sconces for flame torches are embedded in the centre of three of the walls and there is an adequate inglenook fireplace beneath a large chimney which also serves the room below. This being early spring, and one which follows a particularly hard winter, there is a small fire of wood and expensive sea-coal burning in the grate. Furniture is sparse but solid – a single low truckle bed with a supply of blankets and a plain blue woollen coverlet; two wooden arm-chairs and a footstool covered with finely embroidered tapestry – the only nod to femininity in the place, since clearly it has been executed by nimble fingers with skill and bright silks. There is a table of good size equipped with an inkstand; beneath its multi-stained top, two thin drawers hold paper and parchment. Obscured in the shadows of a corner is a roundlet of wine placed on a small trestle. A curtained area for a privy denotes a measure of dignity for the prisoner. For such is Sir Thomas Malory in this year of grace, the beginning of the eighth year of the reign of Edward IV.

And Sir Thomas himself? Nearing fifty-five, he is a tall man and still upright, with a pair of bright eyes, even if their utility is diminished. Hair that was once dark brown is now peppered with grey, but still plentiful, and his once handsome face is now mapped with deep contours which delineate him as rumbustious, roguish and riotous, or heinous, rascally and criminal depending on whose opinion is sought. He has a drinker's nose, broken veined and minutely pitted. He stands in the centre of the room, dressed shabbily for a knight of the realm, but only for want of more careful attention to his apparel; a lack of care which accompanies his state of incarceration and few regular visitors. He wears a patched black woollen doublet which has seen many a summer and winter too; wrinkled hose, like a ship's sails in a breathless sea, and which cling loosely to the masts of his knees and shanks shrunken with age and lack of exercise; boots, scuffed at heel and toe, dusty for want of polish, and a greasy cap of faded black velvet which perches on the dome of a head. But it is his resonant voice which really captures attention; a deep fruity sound emanating from full lips and belying a pigeon-chest, whose lungs seem incapable of carrying enough air to sustain such a volume. Tom Malory is old by any standards, circumstances have accelerated the process. But there still exists an extraordinary zest for life in the rheumy eyes and quick movements of the head, as ideas and mischief circulate inside the thinly covered skull.

His visitor is a man just passing forty, of slim build and medium height. An open unremarkable face which projects honesty, its owner is indeed from a gentle family but whose financial prospects were diminished by his parents who, immediately after their marriage and on an annual basis, produced seven healthy offspring. Monty being second youngest was left in the unenviable position of being almost last in line for any share of the family income. He has, therefore, been forced to make his own way in life on an annual allowance of £2 6s 3d. Therefore, his apparel and general demeanour reflect his status as a "gentle pauper".

At that moment, he is bemused as to why the keeper of Newgate has ordered him to come to Sir Thomas – for it was an order and hurriedly arranged. A messenger from Master Clyfford sent to Monty's lodgings two day previously had insisted he come to assist a prisoner with a task requiring a scribe: "a substantial task which might take some months". Nothing more was indicated. Either Roger Clyfford was not certain of the details of the commission, or Malory had given him nothing to relay. In any case, an order from such an official was not to be ignored, neither was the prospect of long-term gainful employment to be thrust aside. Now as he looked at his would-be employer, two thoughts crossed his mind; the most important being: *How could a man in such a situation afford the expense of hiring a scribe "for some months"?* Second, *What kind of work was it that would take such a time?* Monty's self-employment always concerned official documents which, although sometimes wordy, took no more than a few days to copy or organise.

He cleared his throat and asked, 'You talk of "thoughts of a great work transcribed to paper", Sir Thomas. Can you indicate what kind of thoughts these might be? Perhaps you want me to put your affairs in some order – that is normally the kind of work I do.'

'Certainly not – my wife has complete charge of such matters. I'm rarely available to oversee domestic trifles. No, this is far more important than accounts and land deeds. This is literature, science and history rolled into a distilled form!'

'Literature, science and history – in a distilled form? I see.'

'Evidently, you don't. Otherwise you wouldn't be giving yourself time to think about it. The question is, Monty Pickle, are you up to assisting in transcribing approximately eight hundred pages of fine prose which encompasses these arts?'

Monty bristled slightly at this questioning of his professional ability, but by now intrigued both by the man and the hint of something interesting, he shelved his annoyance and said, 'If you would just describe in more detail what you require, I'm certain I can fulfil whatever are your needs.'

'Arthur – King Arthur! Heard of him? Heard of the French romances?'

'Vaguely, Sir Thomas.'

'Look here, Monty Pickle, for brevity just call me "Sir Tom". I'm disappointed but you're obviously typical of so-called learned men; readers of nothing other than legal and religious fare. The French on the other hand, relish good stories and take time to write them down. This is an epic narrative!'

'An epic narrative, sir?'

'Yes, and I wish you'd get out of this habit of repeating what I say; it wastes time. This will be a narrative with short lines and short sections to satisfy a modern audience with short attention spans. People can't concentrate for very long these days; there are too many distractions – bear-baiting, cock-fighting and dice. Dancing too – what a waste of time that is! There's no dancing or prancing in *Le Morte,* I can tell you! No, this is something very new and in the vernacular!'

'With respect, sir, hasn't that been done already by Mr Chaucer?'

'Don't mention Geoffrey Chaucer to me! This far outstrips his morality fables. Mr Chaucer is out of fashion; no one reads him anymore.'

‘Begging pardon again, sir, but I know kitchen lads who pay pennies for someone to read the saucy bits from *The Canterbury Tales*.’

‘Never mind Chaucer’s “saucy bits”! My work is what a real story should be about – knights, quests, battles, gore, beautiful women, adultery and magic. What could be better? And all in one book.’

‘I see, and you wish me to help you write it?’

‘Edit and proof read with me what I’ve already written – this is strictly my work and will have my name on the cover. But, as I said, my eyes and hands are no longer up to the strain of eight hundred pages of wrist-aching transcription. I estimate it’ll take under two years in all, working five days a week, three or so hours a day. I’ve been told it takes fifteen months to copy the Bible, but that’s at a monkish pace –’

‘And a lot of monks. That’s an awfully long time for me to be involved in one task. Monks have no distractions but I do have other clients, Sir Tom. What am I to say to them? That I won’t be available for two years? They’ll all drift away. Also, if you don’t mind me mentioning it, how do you intend to fund this work? Pay my wages? As I see it you’re not exactly able to provide yourself with an income.’

‘Pots and kettles, Monty! Let’s not pretend. I’ve done some checking and find you’re in desperate need of work. I believe you’ve been “let go” by your last employer, have debts amounting to £2 3s 8d which you cannot hope to pay and are currently behind with your rent to Greyfriars’ next door. That’s how I came to choose you. As for payment, don’t you worry about that? How do you think I maintain myself in this salubrious apartment, when other poor bastards are wallowing in filth in the prison dungeons because they can’t afford to pay for their keep? I’m a man of means; estates and property in the midlands which keeps my wife nicely in furs, and me in relative comfort here. Besides, there’s nothing to stop you continuing your normal work when not engaged with me.’

As far as Montmorency Pickle was concerned, there was something intensely irritating about this man who had had the temerity to check on his private affairs and somehow turn his misfortune to his own advantage. But equally, work was work and Tom Malory was right. Debts were mounting up and prospects of work in the saturated scribal market were slim. Young men were pouring out of the Inns of Court and universities offering efficiencies and charges he couldn't compete with. If, as Tom Malory proposed, he could supplement the task with his regular work, his income would rise considerably.

'If I agree, what are you offering?'

Malory pushed a scrap of paper across the table, 'It's all there. Take it away and think about it. I'll give you a day. Return the same time tomorrow with your answer.'

'I have other questions –'

'Tomorrow, Mr Pickle, your main concern for now should obviously be the cash – if you decide it suits, I'll answer all other queries. Otherwise, it's wasting valuable time to talk of things which will be of no consequence to you if you decline. See yourself out – I'm sure the guard will escort you to the main door and the street. Good day to you.'

And before he realised it, he was out on Newgate Street and walking back to his lodgings on Stinking Lane which ran up the back side of Greyfriars' Chapel. It was all of three minutes' walk to his small set of rooms for which he paid two shillings a week. A woman came in to clean and shop for him on a Saturday; not the most efficient of housekeepers, but unobtrusive and cheap, and she always cleaned round his papers without disturbing them. He shared the premises with a newly-arrived family that occupied rooms on the first and second floors, a noisy and exuberant group – father, mother, two daughters and a son, all of indeterminate ages. Monty had as little to do with them as he could – being especially awkward in the presence of children; not knowing when it was appropriate he should pat them on the head or box their ears. He'd occupied his own rooms for two years in comparative peace since the previous tenant had been a widower with quiet and unobtrusive habits. He was finding it difficult to remember all the names of the newcomers, although he was on nodding terms with the father, Master Talbot, a carpenter with a workshop attached to Monty's living room, from where a great deal of banging and cursing could be heard during working hours. Mistress Talbot was a plain, retiring woman and, thankfully, Monty was never required to exchange more than a few social pleasantries with her, as by silent agreement, they avoided each other whenever possible, both tending to shyness. It was the children who diffused the whole building with a riot of noise; permanently shouting and running across the wooden floor above on the flats of their feet; a constant source of distraction for the cerebral occupation of a scribe. It was one of the reasons Monty Pickle had found himself running short of commissions, since his inability to concentrate by reasons of the thumping above him had resulted in work of a lesser standard than he was expected to achieve. Recently, work produced late, a consequential falling away of clients and a diminished income had led to a worrying situation of two weeks arrears in rent, as well as other debts. Undoubtedly, Tom Malory was right; he was in no position to turn down any work and especially a commission guaranteed for two years. But of course it depended on the terms.

'I may be in great difficulties, but I'll not sell myself cheap. Let's see what Sir Thomas Malory has offered.' He took out the grubby piece of parchment on which a kind of contract had been sketched out:

"Item A commission of two years duration in respect of assisting in the transcription and proof reading of 100 quires of manuscript at 6s .8d per quire . £33 3s.

Item The commission requires the scribe to provide such papers and ink as necessary.

Item The commission requires attendance Monday to Friday, excluding Holy Days after eleven of the clock for no longer than three hours in the winter months and four in the summer.

Item Fees will be forfeited in the event of attendance prohibited by the sickness of either party.

Item The scribe to provide own sustenance and drink.

Item Payment by monthly instalments of £1 7s 6d to the total of £33 3s.

Item Should the commission extend beyond the period agreed then a further contract to be negotiated.

By my hand 4th April anno domini 1469
T. Malory Knt"

Monty did a quick mental calculation; the figures seemed in order, apart from an odd penny or two, in Sir Tom's favour. If Sir Thomas could be persuaded to pay a month in advance, a few of the accumulating debts could be paid off, and the landlord placated with the arrears and an advance of two week's rent, which would offer some security of shelter at least. That is if he was prepared to take the commission. Even though it looked like an offer he could not, or should not refuse, it still required some thought.

Firstly, as he had pointed out to Sir Tom, two years tied in with one client was risky. The man was well over middle-age and clearly not in the best of places to maintain a peak of physical condition. His comfortable arrangements in Newgate Jail notwithstanding, he was still a prisoner and subject to the frequent outbreaks of jail fever and other pestilences which haunted those establishments with notorious frequency. If the man should die, according to Monty's interpretation of the contract, the commission would cease; he would be out of work and his client list obsolete. He would have to start again – posting his availability for trade as he had done when a young man first arriving in the city.

Secondly, was Sir Thomas a man to be trusted? Monty knew nothing of him, despite the man's bragging of his fame. Had he not mentioned infamy also? What was that about? Why was he in jail in the first place? What were these other "escapades" he mentioned – escaping from every known prison in the city? It would surely be sensible to enquire a little deeper into Sir Thomas Malory's past. But who should he ask? Monty had few friends, was unmarried and had little contact with his siblings. His family home was in Wiltshire and he rarely visited such relations as remained there. His small circle of acquaintances in town was limited to those of his clients – for the most part traders and merchants and occasionally, lawyers from the Inns of Court – they would probably know something of the man. But, he reflected, he had little time for deep research since it had been made clear his new client wanted an answer immediately.

After a restless night, while his mind circled round questions which found no satisfactory answers, the following morning as he prepared for the visit, he was still not certain what he should do. Nonetheless, sharp as the Greyfriars' bell tolled eleven, Monty found himself back outside the iron-studded door to Thomas Malory's room. On a peremptory order to "enter", he pulled it open and met almost the identical scene as the day before. This time the servant, John Appleby, was sitting opposite his master in front of a cheerful fire, sipping at a glass of wine; like two old friends passing a pleasant time together.

'Ah, Monty Pickle – and on time! Good; I like punctuality, so let's to business. You've read my proposal? What do you say?'

'I did Sir Thomas –'

'Sir Tom – let's start as we mean to continue.'

'If we continue,' Monty looked Malory squarely in the face, 'as I mentioned yesterday, there are one or two questions I need answering before I commit myself, Sir Tom.'

Malory frowned, 'Questions, questions, what "questions"? It seems to me a perfectly fair offer. No need for quibbling. Is it the money? Not enough for you?'

'No, it's a fair offer. It's more about the security of the work. Two years is a long time to guarantee any such task and especially one of this nature. Will there be enough of it to stretch out that long? What are the outcomes for the project to be? Can I be sure of the monthly payments as you've itemised? What happens if you fall sick and the project ends because –' he faltered.

'Well, let's not be mealy-mouthed about it. Of course, I'm not in the first flush of youth. What you're trying to say is –

because the Grim Reaper has sauntered in and told me my time's up?'

'Well – yes. None of us is immortal, Sir Tom. I appreciate you have comfortable quarters here, but overall you're not in exactly the healthiest of places; fever, pox, the flux could strike at any time.'

'Fever – yes, the flux – probably; the pox – certainly, for I'm well served in that area. But I'm a man who lives life by the maxim *carpe diem*. I'm as likely to die tomorrow as you are, Monty Pickle, and we can't live life simply waiting for the gaunt figure of death to tap us on the shoulder and order us to follow him. As a scholar, do you know the rest of Horace's maxim by the way?'

'*Quam minimum credula postero*. Oxford is my alma mater.'

'I'm impressed; most people go no further than "seize the day". Like Horace, I "trust the least possible to the future". It's a pity your education didn't stretch to the French romances, Monty Pickle, but you'll enjoy them I'm sure. So, it's decision time. Can I count on you to assist me in this great work of literature, which has been burning in my brain for some years and urgently needs setting down in a coherent form?'

'You still haven't fully answered my concerns,' Monty said robustly, 'I accept the financial arrangements, only requesting a month's payment in advance. You're asking me to provide essentials for the work, as well as my victuals. I also have outstanding rent and bills to pay –'

'I'm very aware of your financial situation, Monty. But a month in advance is too much – let's say a week.'

'Two weeks – no less and, should the project fail, payment up to the last page I'm working on, and let's say a courtesy payment of five pounds – to keep me going until I find other work.'

'Five pounds! A courtesy payment? Whatever's that? Never heard of it.'

'It's a legal safeguard,' lied Monty. 'It protects me from the rigours of unemployment in the event of your death or the project failing. It should be entered in your will in the event you die before the work is finished, so there'll be no misunderstanding with your legatees as to what you owe me.'

There was a silence. Tom Malory looked at John Appleby with eyebrows raised so high they almost disappeared under his cap. His steward's mouth twitched as though enjoying his master's discomfort. 'What do we make of him, Pom? Shall we take the malapert wretch on?'

'He appears to me as a man who knows his own mind – could you put up with that for two years?'

'I might if he's able to deliver what we want. We've seen his work and –'

'Sorry, did you say you'd seen my work?' Monty asked with a frown.

'Well, you didn't expect me to hire someone without checking their work was of the necessary standard. No need to translate another favourite aphorism of mine – *caveat emptor*; £33 3s is a lot of money, not taken lightly, especially by me. I sent Pom out to cast around your clients; he returned with the news that by and large, they were happy to show him your abilities with the quill, and mostly satisfied with the quality, although there has been a falling off lately. But overall, we were sufficiently impressed, weren't we, Pom?'

'Indeed, Sir Tom. Stylish, not a blot to be seen and few crossings-out. All in all, it was tidy work.'

'As Pom discovered, your clients were generally satisfied, even if you sometimes took longer than they would wish.'

'Because I'm thorough!' Monty didn't know whether to be angry with the pair of them for prying into his affairs, or gratified for the expressions of confidence.

Malory stood up and pushed back his chair, 'Enough of this vacillation. Are you in or not? It's a simple question requiring a one-word answer.' He poured a glass of wine and pushed it across the desk to Monty, who had been standing all this while because the only two chairs were occupied. 'Come on, man! Make a decision, otherwise I'll withdraw it and look elsewhere. Are we going to drink to a deal, or shall I show you the door?'

Monty looked from one to the other. He had come close to deciding on the way to the jail. He cleared his throat, 'Before I answer, solve one query for me please, Sir Tom?'

'If it makes more complications, then no.'

'Simple question,' he turned to John Appleby, 'why does he call you Pom?'

'Simple answer – Appleby – apple – Pom. I've been Pom to Sir Tom for well over forty years. Does that satisfy you?'

'Indeed, and although some of my other concerns are not yet fully satisfied, it's obvious that your offer will solve many of my problems – as you so assiduously predicted. Therefore, my answer is "yes". I'll take your commission – plus two week's monies in advance on the day I begin – 13s 9d by my reckoning.'

'Splendid! A wise move, Monty Pickle. I suggest this is an appropriate time to drink to success and good fortune for our enterprise,' he raised his glass, and Monty and Pom did the same. 'To King Arthur, his knights, his ladies and his quests. May our quest be as bold and daring as his!'

'King Arthur!' beamed John Appleby through his beard.

'King Arthur!' said Monty, slightly less exuberantly. As he raised his glass, why did the second half of Horace's proposition come back to him?

***

As he left the prison and walked back to his lodgings, he knew he should discuss Malory's offer with a third party; someone with experience to advise him as to whether it was a "good deal" or not. Therefore, the following morning, Monty took himself to Paternoster Row to visit Master Worms, an established and respected stationer and book seller; he was also Monty's supplier of all his materials. What Jack Worms didn't know about the production or circulation of books was not worth knowing.

St Paul's bell was ringing ten o'clock as Monty entered the room off the street which was Master Worms' shop. Although the sun was shining in a weak wintery way, the interior was gloomy with no added light; candles and rush lights were dangerous aids in a room full of incendiary paper, glue and wax, besides the wooden-handled implements used in the production of his books. The proprietor himself stood behind his bench turning the handle of a wicked-looking vice which held the pages of a book he was binding. The astringent odour of hot glue mingled with the smell of bees' wax, and the animal scent of vellum and fine leather. Master Worms' shop counter was piled haphazardly with the goods of his trade. Quills of varying length and colours, priced according to their source: the most expensive swan's feather, the popular goose quill and the cheapest from the crow. Large round containers of ink from which smaller quantities could be ladled into the customers' own containers left their historical imprint on the counter in the form of many coloured circles. Reams of paper and vellum of differing sizes and thicknesses were tied with string, and stood in piles on the floor. Other materials necessary for the production of books were hidden in a dove-cote of small boxes behind the counter – blocks of wax, quill-cutting knives, small, precious bottles of expensive coloured inks, string; everything one could need for the translation of ideas into words on paper and finally into books. Master Worms had no need of labels; he could lay his hand on anything requested, blindfolded if necessary.

'Good day to you, Master Worms, you're in good health?'

'Good day to you, Mr Pickle. Indeed, I keep tolerably well.'

By any standards, Jack Worms was a young man to be as well-established in his trade as he was. Apprentice to his father, he had taken to the book-supply business with a will and, on the early demise of that good old man, had inherited the premises at the age of twenty-two. He immediately set about modernising and improving the business's reputation; now at twenty-eight, he had increased the number of his customers five-fold. Monty Pickle was one such and considered loyal, although not totally reliable when it came to payment. Indeed, he owed Master Worms a long-outstanding sum of 2s 6d and the shop-keeper was on the point of withdrawing supplies until the debt was honoured. Therefore, he met his customer's gaze with narrowed grey eyes and a half-smile, but also a slight frown as he anticipated the man's disappointment when he had to refuse any further request for credit.

'I bring good news, Master Worms! Later today, I'll be able to pay my debt.'

'Excellent news, Mr Pickle, your fortunes have changed then?'

'They have indeed. I am at this moment on my way to begin a new commission – a rather peculiar one.'

'Peculiar – funny or strange? How so?'

'Strange – that is why I've come – to speak to you and seek your opinion; that and to gather supplies for the task.'

Master Worms groaned inwardly. He knew it! The man wanted more credit and he certainly wouldn't get it this time. But for the moment he nodded and simply said, 'I see.'

'I wondered if you would be prepared to leave the shop for half an hour and take a drink with me.'

Jack Worms frowned and for a moment was going to decline. Leaving the shop, even at a quiet time, was not good business. But there was something in Monty's face which struck him and the word "peculiar", to anyone involved in the literary world was intriguing.

'Very well, just one.' He took off his apron, did up his doublet and gathered his cloak from the back of the shop door. As they passed into the street, he called his young apprentice to mind the place, and the two men strolled down Paternoster Row towards Cheapside and the first available tavern. The place was quiet, but warm from the few bodies about and the waft of heat from a smoky fire. Monty paid for their ale and they found seats at a small rickety beer-stained table in a corner.

'I'll come straight to the point, Jack. I have a customer who wishes me to assist him in transcribing – well, proof-reading as well – a deal of pages – a two year-contract. He's made me what I consider a generous offer,' Monty looked over the rim of his pot and grimaced, 'particularly given my circumstances.' Worms nodded encouragingly, hoping the story would be short. Monty went on to describe his visit to Newgate, and the terms and conditions of the arrangement with Thomas Malory.

'Tom Malory – now there's a name I recognise,' said Jack.

'Really, I'd never heard of him.'

'Well, I'm surprised since he's one of the more notorious felons locked away in Newgate. As a literary man, I'd describe him as a "colourful character" who's been involved in all sorts of escapades.'

'That's what he said. He described himself as "infamous", but I thought he was exaggerating to make himself more interesting. He seems that kind of man.'

'I don't know all the details, but he's been a thorn in the side of the authorities for years. It's well known he was mixed up in the Yorkist and Lancastrian disputes – and now in prison on the orders of King Edward himself. As I say, I don't know what he's been involved in.'

'This disturbs me. I was hoping he was reliable – banking on his money.'

'Me too, Monty. I was looking forward to you clearing your debt.'

'He says he has property in the Midlands and a wife he keeps in furs.'

'That may well be true, but did he show you any cash?'

'Not as such, but he obviously has means since he lives better than I do. Meals, coal, candles and evidently some excellent wine. That costs, Jack. The question is can I afford to turn him down? Now you tell me he has a dubious reputation, I'm not so sure. Perhaps I should. Besides, I've no materials to work with and I'm due to start at eleven this morning,' his voice tailed away and he looked at Jack for a response.

Master Worms obliged, 'If you want my opinion, I'd say go and make a start, but make sure the money's in your pocket before you put any ink on your quill. That way you can be assured of two week's work, even if it all goes horribly wrong.

In those two weeks, you'll have chance to find out more about him. If he's the scoundrel I've heard he is, he'll try and weasel out of paying you with some trick or pretext. Don't fall for it.'

'That does sound like good advice. If I put him on the spot, I'll be able to tell how genuine he is.'

'Well, good luck with it. Now, I suppose you want me to advance you the materials? I'm taking a risk here and so are you – increasing your debt by a shilling at least. If I provide the stuff, I'll expect you back in my shop by five o'clock with all the money – 3s 6d. Your debt's gone on too long, Monty.'

'Thanks, Jack. Let me shake your hand to seal my promise to you.' Having duly reached their agreement, by silent mutual consent they drained their pots and made their way back to the stationer's shop. The apprentice was sitting on a stool in the street guarding the outside counter which was piled with papers and pamphlets. He was in fact thumbing through a most lurid and suggestive-looking ballad sheet, and Master Worms caught him such a buffet round the ear that he fell off his stool and papers scattered onto the muddy footpath,

'I pay you to mind the place, not browse the stock! Now, take Mr Pickle inside and give him what he says he needs – no more than a shilling's worth – and mark it down on his account.'

The boy picked himself up, rubbed the side of his head and red in the face, led Monty inside. Within five minutes, the scribe was back on the street, equipped with several sheets of paper, a dozen goose quills and a small, very small, bottle of ink.

'When you come back, you can have more – once you've paid me. Good luck!'

As Monty walked away, Jack Worms shouted, 'Don't forget to ask him for the money before you even sit down!'

Waving his hand, Monty strolled off into the maze of back-alleys radiating from St Paul's, some of them leading to Greyfriars and Newgate. Besides his writing materials in his leather satchel, he had a piece of two-day old bread, some mouse-trap cheese and a withered apple. He wondered whether Sir Tom would be generous with his wine, otherwise he would have to take his chance with the prison water.

***

Malory's desk was set out for work. Manuscripts in small neat piles, the inkwells charged and quills sharpened. Monty Pickle was surprised at this representation of an ordered mind, for Tom Malory had not struck him as the organised type. His employer was sitting at the desk squinting at a loose page; he looked up as Monty entered.

'Ah, Mr Pickle, and on time. Good! We can make a start.' There was no sign of Pom.

Remembering Master Worm's last exhortation to him, Monty drew breath and said, 'Money first, Sir Thomas, I think it will be well to start as we mean to continue. You're a man of your word, I'm sure. The payment was agreed "in advance" and there's no better time than now – in advance of my setting to work; 13s 9d as we agreed.'

Tom Malory stood up, frowning heavily, 'Come, Mr Pickle, this is all very hasty. I must have time to collect such a large sum of cash.'

'You mean you don't have it?'

'I do have it, but not to hand.'

'Well, there's no more to be said.' Monty felt a deep stab of disappointment. He had envisaged the feel of the money in his pocket, the pleasure he would give Jack Worms when he settled his debt and the security of the roof over his head when his landlords were paid off. Nonetheless, he wouldn't stay to argue; he turned on his heel and headed for the door.

'Send Mr Appleby to my lodgings when and if you can produce the money. Until then, good day to you sir.'

'Don't be so hasty, Mr Pickle. I said I couldn't lay hand on it immediately. If you give me a few minutes, I can satisfy our agreement. But I must ask you to leave the room whilst I do so.'

Standing outside just beyond the heavy oak door, Monty could hear movement of furniture, heavy grunting and much muttering and cursing, 'Fuck the man, doesn't he trust me?'

After a few minutes the door opened and Malory inclined his head for Monty to re-enter. On the desk, had appeared a small, interesting-looking leather purse,

'Come in, you reprobate. You've made your point,' he growled.

Picking up the purse and throwing it at Monty, he said, 'It's not in my interest to try and cheat you, and I must say I resent the implication that I might. I was always going to give you the money –'

Monty broke in, 'But perhaps not today, or tomorrow? My understanding of the word "advance" in our context is "to supply beforehand". There should be no equivocation about it.'

'Indeed, and I don't need a lecture from you on etymology, Mr Pickle.' Malory's tone had become sharp, his eyes narrowing with annoyance. Then, like the sun peering out from the corner of a storm-cloud, his face began to clear and his fleshy lips formed a wide smile showing good teeth.

'Look, Monty, let's not get off on the wrong foot. You have your money, you're here and I'm ready to start. Shall we shake hands and start again?'

Feeling satisfied that he had won at least the first small battle with this perplexing man, Monty took the proffered hand and shook it, before opening the purse and spreading the coins out on the desk and counting them. 'All here, Sir Tom! Thank you.'

Malory scowled momentarily, but then composed his face into a look of resignation. Monty felt pleased with himself; he was certain there would be other skirmishes, but at least he had the upper hand for the moment.

Sir Tom began to bustle, 'Please sit – a glass of wine perhaps? Pom's out gathering stores. He's promised to steer clear for at least two hours while we get down to business.'

'I'll take a glass with you, Sir Tom, to show no hard feelings.'

'Good! Before we embark on anything practical, it's obviously necessary that you understand what we're about here.'

'You've already described a little of what you're working on, but as you say it would wise for you to share your main objectives.'

'For the last few years or so, I've been working on redefining the old French romances – *Suite du Merlin,* the *Tristan and Léonois* and *Lancelot* among many others. I'm also introducing the English *Morte D'Arthur* and ballads in the tradition of romantic adventure. But look, there's no time for a lecture on my Arthurian sources – you can always go away and find out about them for yourself. What you need to know is that I've already begun to compile the work in these manuscripts,' and he waved his arm expansively at the piles of papers on the desk, 'They're mostly in the order I wish to present the work, but rough drafts and possibly full of errors: probable repetition and even some anomalies. I require a second pair of professional eyes to iron out all such wrinkles. Working together, we should produce a work of significance – with my name on it,' he added hastily.

'May I ask to what end the book is being produced, Sir Tom?'

'For people to read and enjoy of course!'

'What people? How many would buy such a manuscript and at what cost?'

'Very practical questions, Monty. But let me tell you, great men are beginning to extend their learning and thereby their libraries. I know this as one who has rubbed shoulders with them. The latest thing is that the greater the number of books in a nobleman's library, the greater his status with his educated peers. Did you know the king's brother-in-law, Anthony Woodville, who has a house not far away, has a great library? I have a friend with access to it and who has, on occasion, slipped me the odd book unbeknown to the earl.'

'A loyal friend to take such a risk!'

'I have friends in places you've never heard of, Monty Pickle. In any case, it's unlikely Anthony Woodville even knows what he's got on his shelves. I've been told he's the most ignorant and badly educated bastard in the king's court. I think the books are just for show and it's my pleasure to put them to proper use! But, let's not digress. You asked about a market for my book; I can assure you there'll be one and a profitable one too. And don't forget the new printing processes on the continent are sure to find their way here very soon.'

'Printing? What's that?'

'You don't know what printing is? I'm amazed. It's surely something you should take note of because scribes like you will soon find themselves out of work once these machines take over.'

Monty's eyes widened, 'Whatever do you mean, "out of work"? What are these "machines"?'

'They're called printing presses. Some German wizard has developed a complicated apparatus that will press out pages of writing repeatedly at speeds you couldn't imagine.'

Monty's mouth gaped, 'You jest! Nothing will ever replace beautiful script and handwritten manuscripts. Surely, the art of fine quill-man-ship will always find a place in the market; it's been tried and tested for centuries.'

'Not in the commercial world where books will be produced at speed and in great quantities – at least that's what I've been hearing from my friends on the continent. There's already been a Bible produced in a matter of days – not the fifteen months hundreds of monks take to copy one. But don't worry – I'm sure you'll be below ground before it affects you. Now, let's get on. I want to complete a few pages, at least before the bells ring again.'

Monty sat back in his chair most distracted. If Tom Malory had wished to put him off his stroke – literally – then he couldn't have done a better job. He took another pull at his wine and stared at the papers before him. Malory, ignoring his colleague's clear deflation, proceeded unabashed. Pushing back his chair, taking up a page and standing four-square in front of Monty, he said, 'These are my opening lines – the lines I must hook the reader in with; those that will make him want to read on. Listen and tell me what you think.'

Holding the sheet at arm's length and in a voice resonant with emotion he declaimed:

"It befell in the days of Uther Pendragon, when he was king of all England and so reigned, that there was a mighty duke in Cornwall that held war against him for a long time and the duke was called the Duke of Tintagel. And so by some means King Uther sent for this duke charging him to bring his wife with him, for she was a fair lady and passing wise, and her name was Igraine."

At the same time, waving his free arm with abandon, as though propelling the words forward into the world to shift for themselves. As he concluded, and red in the face with excitement, he looked expectantly at Monty and said, 'You see what I mean; the reader is immediately plunged into infinite possibilities – we have a king, a duke, a beautiful duchess and a war. Doesn't this whet your appetite, Monty Pickle? It certainly does mine and there are eight hundred more pages of such excitement to come!'

Monty forced his mind from the fearful possibility of professional superfluity and wrenched it back to having his appetite whetted. 'I see this section is headed *Merlin* so I presume it introduces one of the French Romance characters.'

'It certainly does. But never mind that, what do you think of the style? It is, of course, in the vernacular – no French or Latin; good plain English for good plain Englishmen – like Chaucer, I will admit.'

'Well, as it goes, it seems to have some merit,' Monty hardly knew what to say, or what he was expected to say. In truth, he was still reeling from Malory's stark predictions of unemployment.

'Fuck me, Monty Pickle, show some enthusiasm. We'll be working on this together for two years. If you can't be more positive, we're going to struggle here.'

Monty winced; Tom Malory's ribald language was not something he was used to, other than from Master Talbot cussing in his workshop.

'You can't expect me to make a judgement about a piece of writing only – what,' and he quickly counted, 'just over seventy words.'

'Very well,' Malory pursed his lips and sat back in his chair, 'Let's get on. I'll try to ignore your negativity.'

'That's hardly fair, Sir Thomas. I'll be able to assess the work further as we go along – I'm sure you've researched both the content and the market for it. I'm just here to help.' Feeling this was as placatory as he was prepared to be, Monty picked up his quill and looked expectantly at his employer, 'How should we proceed – have you a plan?'

Malory grunted and shuffled in his seat, 'I thought we could go through it page by page, reading and amending as we go. I'd like you to take a quire of pages home each evening and read them through, and bring back your suggestions to discuss on the morrow.'

Monty immediately saw the snag in this. Malory was paying for his presence here three or four hours daily. Twenty-five sheets were a lot of reading and working from home had never been mentioned, let alone itemised in the contract. The man was a rogue – trying to get extra work out of him for nothing. He bristled, 'I take it these extra hours will entail suitable pecuniary arrangements? I'll have to buy candles and extra materials.'

'Pecuniary arrangements? Oh I see – extra payment? As Pom would say – there's no flies on you, Mr Pickle. I had considered this after I wrote the contract and I would have discussed it with you when we signed – but it slipped my mind.'

I bet it did! thought Monty, but did not say so. Instead he asked, 'And what financial arrangement did you have in mind?'

'Say every quire you take home to work on, I pay you sixpence. It won't be every night but should average out at about 1s – 1/6d a week. Besides that, we'll forget the clause in the contract about you supplying materials and I'll supply you with four candles a week. How does that sound?'

The scribe was in no mood to argue. A shilling a week and candles sounded reasonable; the extra cash would cover some of his rent and Malory's offer to supply all the materials himself meant no further outlay on Monty's part. In any case, his evenings were long and lonely; once darkness came, he could afford no more than three candles a week and would retire early to bed, which, in the winter particularly, was the warmest place in his rooms and saved on fuel. He nodded and said, 'Very well, I accept.'

'You realise I'm placing the highest level of trust in you, Monty – letting the work out of my sight for a night and in the hands of a virtual stranger?'

'Well, you'll just have to trust me, Sir Thomas,' said Monty stiffly. He was still annoyed at Malory's deviousness.

Not so crass that he couldn't detect resentment in the air, and realising that they were to work together for a very extensive period, Sir Thomas cleared his throat and said, 'Look here, Monty – I apologise if you thought there was anything untoward in my not mentioning this extra work. I meant nothing by it – and also I do welcome criticism of my work – from someone I respect that is. Once again, can we forget it now we've come to a mutual understanding?'

Until the next time, thought Monty but again did not say it. Instead, he nodded and said, 'I think we'll eventually become tuned to one another and settle to a routine of working which should suit us both. Now, having heard a little of what you intend, I'm looking forward to reading the rest of it.'

'Good, that's settled!' and Tom Malory smiled – as a man satisfied he had won the day – and picked up another sheet of paper.

***

They worked for an hour until the Greyfriars' bell rang the half hour, when they stopped for a break. Monty was relieved to see the claret jug returned as he took out his meagre rations from his satchel and laid them on the table. Malory raised an eyebrow when he saw the poor fare, but said nothing. Pom had left his master a chicken leg and some bread which he tucked into with gusto. As Monty began to chew on his apple, Malory asked him to tell him a little about himself. *More out of politeness than interest,* thought the scribe. It was obvious to Monty that Malory was the type of man who would not be particularly engaged by the details of a stranger's life, therefore, he made his history as brief as possible.

'I was born in Wiltshire, a younger son with one brother and five sisters; my parents are deceased; my brother, the inheritor of the farm and tenant of the earl of the county, John Stafford'. There was a severe reaction from Tom Malory, who jumped in his seat when Monty mentioned that noble name.

'Stafford! Fuck me!'

Ignoring the cussing, Monty said, 'Yes, do you know of him? Have you had dealings?'

'No, not him particularly. Just something in my past – it's of no consequence; go on.'

'Well,' and Monty continued, 'my history's soon told. I was forced to make my own way in the world, my brother taking on the estate and having to provide my many sisters with dowries. He paid for me to attend Oxford, as I told you, where I completed my degree in law. But I had no desire to follow that profession. I felt I couldn't and didn't want to compete socially with the young bucks haunting the Inns of Court – with their obsession with dress, women and fighting the apprentice-boys! But I still came to London, where I considered I could best sell my talents. I've been a scribe for fifteen years or so earning an honest living.'

'Unmarried?'

'I've never been fortunate and found the right lady.'

'What about fornication?'

Completely taken aback by this line of questioning, Monty hesitated and then said robustly, 'An impertinent question, Sir Thomas, and one you've no right to ask.' Unfortunately for a man in his middle-years, he blushed pink.

‘Fucking is important, Monty – no point in being shy about it. I’ve always found ways to enjoy myself in that regard. Perhaps, that’s what you need!’

‘I beg your pardon?’ Still taken completely by surprise, and incensed at the turn of the conversation, Monty pushed back his chair, picked up his satchel and prepared to walk out.

‘Don’t get huffy. I only speak the truth. A man must perform what God and nature intended him for. Otherwise he might run mad.’

‘You might, I’m prepared to wait for the right woman at the right time.’

‘At forty years old? You’ve left it a bit late, haven’t you? Are you a virgin?’

Monty was completely taken aback. ‘This is intolerable, Sir Thomas. You’ve no right to question me so. I really don’t know what to say to you except I can’t continue in your service if this is to be the level of our professional relationship – and that’s how I see it – a professional arrangement. I would be grateful if you could rein in your salacious remarks and concentrate on what we are supposed to be doing! Otherwise our contract must come to an end.’

‘Oh, so touchy! I can see I’m going to have to be careful what I say to you, Mr Pickle, otherwise I will be “in a pickle” – there I’ve said it; I’ve been waiting for the chance since we met, but I promise I won’t make light of your name again. Neither will I pry into matters of a carnal nature.’

This really is too bad, thought Monty. *The man’s clearly a law unto himself, with a mouth that runs away with him; it has obviously got him in much trouble throughout his life, or else why is he here?*

And yet – and yet. There was something so open and uncomplicated about Sir Tom that was almost attractive. Clearly, he would get to know the man more intimately as time progressed and could make a judgement based on experience rather than the gossip which embraced him.

Perhaps, it would be good for me being around such a man, he thought, *the complete opposite in temperament and outlook to myself. His rackety life may have landed him in jail, but at least it's probably been a full life, unlike mine.* Suddenly, Monty felt grey and tired beside this force of nature, which now sat opposite him paring his fingernails with a small dagger and looking at him quizzically. Monty drew a deep breath and said, 'Keep your promise – on both counts for, since a boy I've had enough of jokes about my name – and I'll stay and help you complete your project, and try not to take offence when you insult me.'

'Good man! I like a man of mettle who doesn't take offence –'

'I didn't say I wouldn't take –'

'Whatever's passed between us, we'll forget it now and return to the task. Leave chewing on that apple and take another glass of wine.'

At that moment, John Appleby appeared struggling with a large basket of supplies – cheese, bread, fruit and balanced on the top, a substantial red sausage. Tom Malory picked it up, looked over to Pom and back again to Monty, and suddenly gave a great bellow of laughter. Within seconds, the scribe looking on in bewilderment, the two men were holding their sides in uncontrolled mirth.

Montmorency Pickle's education had begun.

Chapter 2

Monty learns more of his employer and suffers the penalties of drinking in the afternoon.

Four days later, a Sunday, found Monty walking home from mass at St Martin le Grand, just around the corner off Newgate Street. This church was closest to his lodgings and one where he easily merged with the large congregation, going unnoticed and ignored. Therefore, he was surprised to hear his name called and fast footsteps padding after him, 'Mr Pickle, sir! Wait a moment!'

Turning, he saw John Appleby hurrying towards him, pink in that section of his face not obscured by his beard and evidently keen to attract Monty's attention. As Pom caught up, he said breathlessly, 'Good morning, Mr Pickle. I saw you in church – we obviously worship in the same parish.'

'Good morning, Mr Appleby. I can't recall seeing you here before, but then it is a large church and a large congregation.'

'I've been attending St Martin's since Sir Thomas was confined to Newgate eight months ago. Of course, he has a priest who visits to say mass in the prison chapel.'

'I don't imagine the authorities are so lax, they let every prisoner out to attend church.'

'You would be surprised. Sir Tom has the opportunity for worship at St Martin's, but prefers a private mass.'

Wouldn't we all! thought Monty, but did not say it.

'I wondered if you would walk with me a while. We've never had chance to speak alone and there are things I would like you to know – things you're probably curious about anyway, but not yet prepared to ask Sir Thomas.'

'That's certainly true, Mr Appleby –'

'Pom, please. It's what I'm used to.'

'Perhaps, we could walk to my house and take our ease out of this chill wind. I can offer you a little wine – purchased with my advance!'

Pom grinned and nodded, 'It was nicely done, Mr Pickle.'

'If we are to eschew formality then please call me Monty.'

'Monty; you certainly set out your stall and I'm sure for once you had the measure of my master; that's not easily done I can tell you! But, as I said, there must be many things you wish to know about him.'

'It's not my style to speak of a man behind his back, Pom.'

'Indeed no; but Sir Tom has a notoriety which means his name is as often traduced as it is lauded. Once it's put about you're associated with him, you'll be open to the speculation and gossip that has always encircled his name. Before that occurs, I'd like to give you some facts; particularly how he has come to be presently in Newgate.'

By this time, they had reached Monty's front door which led directly off Stinking Lane. He knew the house would be quiet, the family upstairs having decamped for a few days to visit Mistress Talbot's mother in Highgate.

'Come in and take a seat.'

Pom looked round the room which described the life-style of a typical middle-aged bachelor-clerk. There were no feminine touches here; the place was a litter of paper and writing materials. Monty had to clear a pile of velum sheets, which he was ruling up, to make way for a tray with glasses and a jug of undistinguished cheap wine. The fire was almost out but, with the judicious use of a pair of bellows, it was soon brought to life and throwing out as much heat as kindling and small mean lumps of sea-coal were capable of. He moved two chairs to either side of the fireplace and set the tray down on a table between them. As the flames grew higher, they reflected on the glasses; the room took on a more cheerful atmosphere and both men suddenly felt very much at ease with each other.

Pom sipped at the wine, inwardly grimacing, but nodding as though appreciating the finest vintage.

'As I said, I expect you're curious as to why Sir Thomas is incarcerated. You've been polite in forbearing to ask him and he noticed. "Either the man's totally uninterested in other people or he's hopelessly shy, Pom," he said to me after you left on the first day, "isn't he the slightest curious why I'm here? I would be!"

"I think it's natural delicacy, Sir Tom," I said.

"Delicacy my arse!" he said – you'll have observed that my master is free in his use of profanities. It's something you'll have to get used to.'

'Hmm, it seems many allowances have to be made for Sir Thomas's behaviour. So, what is the story behind his imprisonment? Does he know you're here by the way?'

'It was at his suggestion. He's happy for you to ask me any questions you like. He says he has no time to waste telling you his life story – as eventful and astounding as it is, but has deputed me to provide as much as you want to know.'

'If it's with his consent, I'm all ears, Pom!'

'It's a long story, but I'll keep it to the bare bones. Sir Thomas Malory is in Newgate on the specific order of King Edward.'

'Master Worms said as such. Sir Tom claimed he is infamous – but I didn't realise –'

'He's that important? Well, even you must have heard of the Cornelius plot last June?'

'Wasn't it some sort of conspiracy by the Lancastrians against the king?'

'John Cornelius, one of Margaret's emissaries, she who *was* queen and would like to be again, was caught coming in on the coast of Kent from France, searched and found to be bearing incriminating letters to "various Lancastrian supporters". They took Cornelius to the Tower where appropriately, given the man was a shoemaker, they applied hot irons to his feet, which must have made him hop. He succumbed and gave the names of a dozen prominent London citizens – and one was John Hawkins.'

‘Who he?’

‘Baron John Wenlock’s servant; I take it you’ve heard of *him*?’

‘I don’t move in such exalted circles, Pom. I lead a quiet life.’

‘Excessively quiet if you ask me, Monty! Still, Lord Wenlock’s a diplomat and great friend of Richard Neville – you’ve heard of the Earl of Warwick I presume!’

‘Of course – he has lodgings in Greyfriars. I’ve actually seen him on occasions – certainly heard his troops and horses in the fields behind the abbey.’

‘That’s something I suppose. Anyway, when Hawkins was questioned he incriminated Sir Thomas Cook – our former Lord Mayor – who, while the screws were tightened to stretch the rack on *him*, told the inquisitor that men close to Lord Wenlock were all “up to their necks in Lancastrian plotting”. The king had anyone connected to the baron rounded up immediately, and our mutual friend Sir Tom, being an old and loyal acquaintance of Wenlock was included.’

‘So how does he come to be in Newgate for so long?’

‘The case went to court and as legal wrangles are inclined to do, the hearings dragged on and on, and it wasn’t until late into the autumn that the court came to its conclusion. No solid evidence of a Lancastrian conspiracy was uncovered, but Hawkins, a draper and another man were all three condemned to death; the rest suffered heavy fines or were imprisoned; Thomas Cook was pardoned. Wenlock pleaded for Hawkins but to no avail; he was hanged, although the draper was spared at the last minute. Lord Wenlock himself was soon back in the king’s favour with no charges to answer; too valuable a diplomat; but Sir Tom was still confined in Newgate.’

‘Why wouldn’t they let him go?’

‘I think mostly because he’s so well-known to the authorities and considered a troublemaker, and “tainted by association”. We think they were looking for any excuse to incarcerate him again. At any rate, he’s still waiting for a hearing.’

‘But it’s ten months since! Shouldn’t he be properly sentenced? Has he even appeared in court?’

‘He has, once or twice. The problem is he always pleads to be heard by his Warwickshire peers – as is his right – but none of them are willing to make the journey to London.’

‘He must be very angry? No wonder he’s so abrupt with people.’

‘That has nothing to do with it – that’s his way as you’ll discover – and part of his problem. But he’s less angry than he was because he realises this is a golden opportunity to devote time to *Le Morte D’Arthur*; no distractions of duties or responsibilities to his estates; he leaves all that to his wife, Elizabeth. They have a son, Robert, who’s thirty and here in London – quite a gentleman by all accounts, but he doesn’t visit.’

‘Sir Tom did tell me how he keeps himself in the manner he does with money from his estates.’

‘Yes, and Lord Wenlock.’

‘Wenlock? Is he that friendly?’

‘Indeed; and when he’s in London he always visits. Where do you think Sir Tom’s good wine comes from? Wenlock’s lieutenant of the Calais garrison, and has gallons of the stuff, mostly pirated from French and Spanish ships. It gives Sir Tom a great thrill to think he’s sipping illicit wine.’

The thought flashed across Monty’s mind that he too had enjoyed such bounty. But now he knew it was appropriated through piracy, he didn’t quite know how he’d feel about drinking it next time it was offered.

‘His wine is certainly excellent, Pom, although I’m no expert on fine vintages. But tell me, Sir Thomas certainly doesn’t act like a prisoner; for a start, he’s not locked in. Does he actually have any contact with the rest of the inmates of Newgate?’

‘None; he’s self-contained in his tower – has a separate entrance. His room used to be the old guard room. He can’t leave the building unless under escort and when he does, it’s only for an hour or two a month but he rarely leaves the place. Apart from that, you wouldn’t know he’s a prisoner at all.’

'How very odd!' murmured Monty, 'So, what you're telling me is that our friend has been incarcerated on orders of the king for possible treason, but isn't too concerned because he has time, privacy and space to complete a book?'

'Summed up beautifully – I understand you did train in the law – perhaps you should have taken it up after all!'

'And you, Pom. How do you fit into the story? How long have you been with Sir Tom?'

'Man and boy about forty years. I was – am – his steward. He's not exaggerating when he says he has lands in the Midlands. The Malory family is extensive and holds offices in all the shires of that part of the country. Sir Tom has been everything and everywhere – a soldier, knight of the shire, member of the king's commissions – every shire office you could think of. His father was Sheriff of Warwickshire at one time – and Escheator. He has a very respectable background.'

'So, where did it all go wrong?'

'If I were to begin that story, we'd been here a' twelve month! Believe me, it's one worth the telling. I don't believe there's anyone else I know of who's life has been so – so –'

'Colourful?'

'Exactly. I've thought of writing it myself, but admit, I don't have the literary skills like my master. It's a pity; I think more people would be prepared to read the real-life adventures of Sir Thomas Malory than will want to plough through eight hundred pages of French flim-flam! But of course, I would never say that to *him*. He's obsessed with his project; spends hours poring over his old French romances and appropriating what he calls "choice phrases" to insert into his book; talks about it in his sleep sometimes.'

'So you share the room with him? But you're clearly not a prisoner yourself?'

'Oh no, but I spend most of my time there, and occasionally take a blanket and sleep in front of the fire – when he's particularly anxious about how the work's going. He often gets himself into a state of panic that he won't have time to finish it, and then I have to be on hand to soothe him with Wenlock's good wine and the purchase of a whore or two – or three even!'

Monty thought he would go no further on that track. Instead he asked, 'And when you're not sleeping at the prison, where do you live?'

'Not far from you, Monty. I have a small room at the back of the Greyfriars' stables. It's a three minute walk to the prison, and if there's an urgent need, one of the guards will always come over and fetch me.'

Monty fell silent as he absorbed what John Appleby was telling him. Here was a man steeped in loyalty who evidently revered his master to the point of devoting his whole life to his service. He wondered what the relationship between them was – man and servant? Friends? Why had Pom never married? Evidently, Mr Appleby was there for the duration and prepared to serve Sir Tom as long as the man survived. They could go on in this way for another twenty years. From what Pom had hinted, Sir Tom's appetites had not diminished in any form. But surely the authorities would want to see his case concluded. Although it was apparent the prisoner had a great deal of freedom and was given little supervision, he was still using up space in an official jail which would surely be needed for more egregious felons.

That led him to another line of questioning. What exactly was the status of Sir Thomas as a prisoner – why was he allowed visitors to his room at will – and the door unlocked? Monty knew nothing about the prison system, although he had heard rumours. He determined to ask Pom for details, but as he drew breath, his guest said, 'Thank you for the drink. It's been pleasant talking to you and I hope you're a little clearer about the man you'll be acquainted with for at least the next two years. I must say, I'm very pleased he's taken on some help at last and that he's chosen you, Monty. I feel you'll suit him well. But I must get back to him to prepare his dinner now, now he'll have made his confession and returned from mass.'

'I can't think he has much to confess, confined as he is,' observed Monty.

'You'd be very surprised, Mr Pickle!' said Pom with a wink as he pulled on his cloak.

***

Chronically conscientious, Monty spent Sunday afternoon reading through two dozen pages of the first section of *The Tale of King Arthur*, which opened the series of twenty-one books making up the whole work. By five o'clock, the light became so bad he was forced to draw a halt, just at the point where King Arthur and the six kings were about to do battle with each other. As he laid down the last page, he thought, *This is a story like nothing I've ever read. Sir Tom's right; it's a saga of tribal warfare, knightly deeds and artful adultery in a highly readable form. Any literary man would appreciate the quality of the prose and an illiterate peasant would enjoy having it read to him.*

He found many mistakes: misspellings and a few anomalies, but mostly he was impressed with the liveliness of the text and the fact that it held his attention for almost four hours of solid reading. He made careful notes of questions and suggestions he would put to Sir Tom the next morning, and as he laid down his quill, he began to anticipate the coming task with more pleasure than when he had started it.

As he sat in front of the dying fire, disinclined to leave its warmth for his chilly bedchamber, he considered Pom's description of Thomas Malory as an angry, emotional man. Monty had found him somewhat abrasive, even tetchy; but with a sense of the ridiculous – reference the sausage – something which Monty thought he could share. Pom had talked about "being called when he was needed urgently" and Monty wondered how often and under what circumstances that would be. Pom's reverberant phrase, "a colourful past" was intriguing and the scribe wondered too what that meant exactly. No doubt, all this would eventually come out as they worked together – like a penitent and his priest in the confessional.

That led to another link in his chain of thought – Sir Tom's confessions. Pom had hinted they were the opposite of mundane; perhaps the mention of whores would make them memorable. Monty thought of his own, so tediously uninteresting that he sometimes wondered if the priest grimaced when he recognised his voice. Monty's small catalogue of dreary misdeeds must have seemed small beer as they came through the grill, and he felt certain the priest wished he'd make haste and leave the confessional for someone with a more salacious set of sins.

My vices are mostly concerned with the sin of gluttony – or the absence of anything decent to be gluttonous about, he thought. Food was fittingly an all-consuming element of his life. A meagre diet, prepared by his own hand which lacked the culinary skills of a wife or housekeeper, led to a permanent craving, particularly for more meat and decent bread. The sight of Sir Tom tearing at the leg of a plump capon had made his mouth water excessively and he wondered how often he could stand to watch that daily performance. It would be ironic if he had to pull out of the arrangement because he couldn't bear to watch his employer casually tearing at pieces of spiced meat every day.

He sighed, extinguished the candle, poked the fire into oblivion and went to bed.

***

'Well, here we are, Monty. Have you read the section?'

'Good morning, Sir Tom. Indeed I have.'

'And?'

'I enjoyed it very much.'

'Excellent, so we can proceed. Have you made notes for me?'

Monty took a sheaf of papers from his satchel and handed it over. 'I'll look through it and then we can set to work incorporating your suggestions if I think they fit.' Malory sat back in his chair and, squinting as ever, very quickly scanned the sheets, sometimes nodding, sometimes sighing and sometimes frowning.

'You seem to have been thorough – I must say I reject some of your comments, but accept others – so I'm not displeased. Now, quill to the ready and we'll work through these pages together.'

Monty drew his chair to the table. There was no sign of Pom and when he asked Sir Tom where he was, he said, 'I told him to make himself scarce – he's apt to fiddle about tidying up and finding useless things to do – all very laudable for a servant, but not when we're working. We need complete peace to concentrate properly. He'll be back in an hour to make up the fire when we break for dinner. You've brought something I suppose? The same as Friday's?' Monty nodded. 'You know, Monty, a man can't subsist too long on bread, cheese and an apple. Can't you do better than that? What you need is a wife!'

For someone who had seemed anxious to begin work, Sir Tom had become easily distracted by a trivial issue. He also seemed fixated on his scribe's marital status. Determined to return to the business in hand, Monty cleared his throat and said, 'I'm quite content, sir, shall we get on?'

'Very well. It really is none of my business, I suppose.'

'Hmm,' Monty took up his quill. 'Shall we start with the second page, the line beginning "I shall tell thee" said the king, "I am sick for anger and for love of fair Ingrain".'

And so they worked on the text for a full hour and a half, at which point, as the abbey bells chimed, Pom returned with Malory's dinner. From his basket, he took a wooden platter covered with a cloth and set it on the desk which Malory had cleared. Out of a corner cupboard came three glasses; Pom poured generous measures from a jug filled from the roundlet and handed them round. As he drank the good claret, Monty considered how he felt about drinking the fruits of piracy; but it was too good to quibble over and he felt he could at least offer a genuine sin to the priest the following Sunday.

'Pom, bring another plate and set it before Mr Pickle. I can't sit here chewing on a fowl while he picks at cheese for which a church mouse would have turned up its whiskers. He can share my dinner – but tomorrow make sure you bring enough for two.'

'But the terms of the agreement, Sir Tom?' protested Monty.

'Fuck the agreement; it does my digestion no good just watching you. You can eat at my expense – perhaps do half an hour extra in return. How does that suit?'

Monty hesitated – but only for an instant, 'Very well, sir. I must say this is excellent wine, Sir Tom. Mr Appleby – Pom – tells me it's a gift from Baron Wenlock.'

'Yes, indeed. A good man and a useful one; great friend of the Earl of Warwick who lives next door. It's something when one can say one lives next door to an earl – don't you think?'

'Yes, I suppose it is. Do you see him often – the earl, I mean?'

'Only when he's in London – he's a man who moves about constantly; never in one place for long.'

'You sound as though you know him well,' said Monty.

'Off and on for about twenty-five years. But that's another matter – finish the food and we can get on.'

It appeared that there was going to be no time for idle chat and Monty's curiosity about Sir Thomas's relationship with his near-neighbour would remain unanswered for the time being. They worked steadily for another two hours until Sir Tom suddenly put down his quill, stretched his arms above his head and said, 'That's enough for today, Monty; I think we can be satisfied with our achievement. Pom, tap the roundlet and let's *round* off the day's work!'

Pom obliged by pouring them each a large glass of claret from the tiny barrel in the corner.

The wine was liberally circulated and within a very short space of time, Monty had helped polish off at least two large jugs. After the second, he began to feel very light-headed, and was soon anxious to make his way home and lie down for an hour or so. But Sir Tom was having none of that, 'We'll make an afternoon of it. Pom, fill the glasses again.'

Monty waved his hand in protest, 'Really, Sir Tom, I'm not used to drinking in the afternoon – not used to drinking so much at any time.'

'Fucking nonsense, man – you're not going to tell me you can't hold your drink?'

'As I say, I'm not used to it and I want a clear head to carry on reading your – your –'

'Excellent romance, I know. But I often crave the conversation of educated men. Pom here's not bad company, but doesn't have an idea in his head other than dice and whoring – isn't that so, Pom?'

'If you say so, Sir Tom!' Monty thought he saw Pom winking at him with both eyes, but by this time, his head was so fuddled he couldn't be sure of what he was seeing. Suddenly, he was hit by a wave of dizziness and all he knew was he had to get out of the room before he was sick.

'I don't think I'm in a fit shtate for any kind of convershashion; I rather feel I should gesh out into the fresh air before –' and to his acute embarrassment, he vomited into the fireplace.

'Fuck me! Shot Monty – I had no idea you literally couldn't hold your drink. Fetch a bucket, Pom, and clear up the mess – although perhaps you'd better see our friend home first. I don't think he has it in him to carry on. A pity, for I had a fancy to make an evening of it – get a couple of women in.'

'Very well, Sir Tom,'

And Pom took an unresisting Monty by the arm and led him out of the door, and with great gentleness and some skill, helped him negotiate the stone steps. Thoughtfully, he took him to the prison well-head just outside the main gate and offered his companion several ladles of water. Monty gulped the liquid down, wiping his mouth with the cuff of his doublet, then shaking his head. 'I'm shoe shorry, Pom. I feel wreshed – drinking that quantity ishn't shomething – shomething I'm ushed to. How many glashes?' Monty was having the inebriate's common problem with sibilants.

'Only ten, Monty. But you're probably wise to escape. I can see Sir Tom has the taste and will continue well into the night.'

'And wo – wo – women? Whash'e mean?'

'What do you think he means?'

'Whoresh?' whispered Monty, faintly.

'Of course.'

'Arc they allowed? Whoresh in the prishonsh?' The elusive sibilants remained unbound by tongue and lips.

'It's the way of things. Besides, it keeps the prisoners docile – cheaper than paying wages to keep them chained and under guard. Now, no more questions; just be grateful you're on your way home. I'm not sure you're ready for one of Sir Tom's evenings of pleasure!'

They'd reached Monty's front door and, to his further discomfort, the three Talbot offspring were clustered on the pavement playing knucklebones. They looked up, as Pom helped Monty through the door, and well-accustomed to seeing their father in a similar state, the eldest girl giggled and pointed, 'The old Pickleman's soused!'

Pom gestured with his arm as if to box their ears, but they dodged him and ran away down the street, still laughing and poking out their tongues. 'Little bastards! I'll catch them next time,' laughed Pom, who seemed to be in a permanent good humour, 'I'll leave you now. My advice is to get yourself to bed for a couple of hours and then have some food. I'll see you tomorrow.'

Monty hiccoughed, 'Thank you – er – er – Pom,' he said meekly, beginning to feel sick again. 'I'm – I'm shorry about the messh – and everything, putting you to sho mush trouble – I'm shorry about the fire and the washted coalsh.'

'There's nothing that a rinshe in a bucket of water won't put right! Believe me, that's not the worst I've seen!' and laughing, Pom walked off up Stinking Lane back to Newgate.

***

Thumping! There was a thumping somewhere close by. He dreamt it was from the workshop next door: Master Talbot wrestling with yet another ill-made and useless article of furniture. But no – there was no rhythmic cussing, no repetitive profanity which were the constant accompaniment to the carpenter's labours. Flat-footed children perhaps, but he would recognise that immediately. Then where was the source of this regular banging in his ears and the top of his head?

Monty turned over in his bed, painstakingly opened one eye and closed it rapidly. The noise was closer now, very close – thump, thump, thump. 'It's in my head! Jesus Christ, it's in my head. If it doesn't stop, I might explode!' The torrent of noise engulfed him again and he put his head under the pillow, stuffing his fingers in his ears at the same time, but to no avail; the thumping was magnified.

Throwing off the pillow, he turned over on his back and slowly began to come to his senses. Stirred into action, unfortunately those senses reminded him cruelly of the events of the previous afternoon. The whole episode came flooding back and overwhelmed him; unwanted memories chimed with the unwanted thumping and Monty lay back in his bed reliving the nightmare from start to finish. The last time he'd been that drunk was fifteen year ago at his sister's wedding.

Fifteen minutes later, he had roused himself, immersed his head in one of the two buckets of water he paid a boy a penny a day to fill, dressed, and chewed on some bread and cheese. He heard the abbey bell chime eleven, and in a panic, picked up his satchel and made for the door. He would be at least five minutes late, but perhaps, if Pom was right and Sir Tom had "made a night of it", then his employer was likely to be in a worse state than he was – probably still in bed. He reached the main gate and the warden on guard duty nodded and let him in. Now recognised as having "regular" business with Sir Thomas Malory, he was allowed in unquestioned. Indeed, he made his unaccompanied way up to Sir Tom's room, where he found the door ajar and heard voices.

'What kind of a fucking state did you leave him in, Pom?'

'Not very good, Sir Tom. In fact, I'd be surprised if we saw him today.'

'Christ! He'll have to do better than this. I'm amazed a man of his age can't take his drink.'

'As he said, he's not used to it. I don't think he can afford bottles of wine on a regular basis. He did buy some gut-rot with his advance, but he seemed to think of it as a rare indulgence.'

'Poor bastard. He's evidently in dire straits – for a gentleman. Surely, he has other sources of income than what I'm giving him? What about his family?'

'My family is none of your business, Sir Thomas!' Monty stepped into the room. Having overheard most of this conversation, his gore was rising. There's nothing worse than a gentleman's poverty being recognised and discussed by strangers. Pom looked abashed; Sir Tom shrugged, 'There you are, Monty. Pom here says you were in a bad way and unlikely to make it this morning.'

'I'm five minutes late and I apologise. But I would like it known that I take it amiss that people I know little about should discuss my affairs behind my back.'

'Now don't get tetchy because you have a headache, Monty!'

'How do you know I have a headache?'

'Because I've been there so many times myself. Now, are you up to working today?'

Monty was silent; he would have like some recognition of the validity of his complaint and looked at Sir Tom for an apology. But his employer looked back, shook his head and raised his eyebrows. 'You're here so I presume you can work, yes?'

Monty nodded, 'I haven't read through any of the most recent text – for obvious reasons.'

'Because you were fuddled! Well, let that pass. We'll read the next section together and see what we can do with it. We've reached an important event in the story; how Arthur was shown to be the son of Uther, but raised by Sir Ector. There is an interesting passage about how Queen Ingrain was fooled into believing that her first husband, the Duke of Cornwall, had lain with her, when it was Uther himself. An old trick and often cited in romances – adultery without consent, but nonetheless in this case enjoyed by both sides.'

Monty frowned and made his headache worse, 'Some people call that rape, Sir Tom. Is it a feature which should be included in a romance?'

'As I say, she enjoys it. Believe me, this will be as close to real life as I can make it, give or take the inclusion of plenty of magic.'

'Surely you must experience those things for yourself if you're writing to reflect truth.'

Malory and Pom exchanged looks, 'Christ! We've no time for a debate about truth and fiction, Monty Pickle. We'll just follow my text so far and discuss it as we go. You know the terms of our agreement. You're here to correct language and sniff out any contradictions, not re-write the book. Now let's get on.'

They worked steadily for an hour and a half. There were the odd differences over matters of style, but mostly they avoided any clashes, probably because Sir Tom generally had his way. As the bell chimed the half hour, they broke for dinner. Monty was aware that Sir Tom showed no sign of the previous day's heavy drinking – indeed he seemed sharper than ever. Monty still had a headache and a stomach that was rolling like a heavy swell in the North Sea. He had very little appetite, which was a shame, since Pom set out a decent meal of a cold pie, slices of beef and Pease pottage which he warmed on the fire. Master and servant tucked in with a will, but Monty picked at a piece of pink beef which he swallowed down with a little water.

'No appetite, Mr Pickle? You really should learn to take your drink better,' said Sir Tom gulping down his wine. 'To my mind, it's the mark of a gentleman that he can take an afternoon's drinking without getting nauseous. To be blunt, you disappointed me, Monty. I was looking forward to a convivial afternoon and evening. Instead, you left a stinking mess in my fireplace and no possibility of us sharing any other activity.'

'I suppose you mean your whores?'

'Yes. As I say, I had it in mind for us both – at my expense of course. But there you are – a missed opportunity.'

'For my part, I'm glad I missed it. I have no wish for that kind of "activity" as you call it.'

'Jesus, Monty! What a dull fellow you are! I told Pom I thought you were a virgin and –'

Along with the churning in his stomach and the ache in his head, Monty felt anger rising in his mind, and the beat of his heart beginning to pound in his ears. He was in no mood for Sir Tom making free with his assumptions; the man's obsession with fornication was too much. He stood up and reached for his satchel, 'Enough, Sir Thomas, I'm not in the mood! I'm going home now, you can subtract whatever hours I've missed. I'll continue reading the next section this afternoon and return, on time, tomorrow – as long as I have assurances from you that the tenor of this conversation ceases as from today. I don't find it funny, or appropriate.' And he walked out of the door, closing it firmly behind him.

Before it shut, he caught Malory saying, 'Well, fuck me, Pom. I didn't know he had it in him!'

***

Returning to his lodgings, Monty went back to bed for a couple of hours and woke refreshed. Then, finding himself ravenously hungry, he strolled down to the nearest pie shop and bought a large, hot meat pie; an indulgence which he took back to his rooms, and enjoyed in front of a fire liberally banked-up with wood and sea-coal. *To hell with the expense!* he thought. Then he settled down to read the next section of *The Tale of King Arthur*.

He had taken a dozen pages of the manuscript back with him and as he read on, he became increasingly immersed in Malory's world of chivalry and gore. 'Where does he get his ideas from?' he asked himself. 'They can't all be from the

French sources? I believe there are many references to Malory's own life here. When I mentioned the need to experience things in order to write about them, it seemed to resonate with him and Pom. There's much more to Sir Thomas Malory than I know of presently.'

By the end of the day, as the light was waning and his eyes were straining to catch the script, he had decided to seek Pom out and ask the man directly to share what he knew of Sir Tom's life. 'Pom mentioned something about it being worthy of recording. Perhaps we could work together on it, if Pom's memory is sufficiently sharp after forty years.' Monty felt a sudden buzzing of excitement in his head – perhaps he could also write an account of a life – not as a romance and certainly not in the form of chronicles or annals, as was the general custom, but picking out those elements which would make an interesting story.

Later, as he lay in bed, he began to sketch out how he would set about it. He might even tie it in with *Le Morte D'Arthur*. Reliving the text in his mind, he became absolutely convinced that there were elements of Malory's own life-story embedded in it. He would consult Pom as soon as possible. Providence had thrown him a bone of opportunity; Malory was a man out of his time in action and words – what the astronomers would call "an eccentric". Perhaps, perhaps he could make something of his own talents – throw himself into uncharted territory – become a commentator. There were evidently coming possibilities with these new printing machines Malory had described.

Monty drifted off to sleep and dreamt he was in Master Worm's workshop being pressed in a vice between two pieces of wood; the bookseller was leaning over him saying, "Just a little more, Mr Pickle, just a little more. Keep still while I sew up your spine." He woke in a sweat and pitch black with no idea of the time. Now wide awake, his mind returned to the possibility of recording Sir Tom's life. His first move would be to canvas John Appleby as to his willingness to be involved.

***

'Fuckingham Buckingham! We can expose the bastard for what he was. We'll bring it all back, Pom! This fellow Pickle has the right idea. I wish I'd thought of it myself – my own story writ large for everyone to read and Fuckingham Buckingham stuffed! Excellent!'

Three days after Monty had dreamt of his demise in a bookbinder's vice, Pom was discussing the scribe's suggestion for a commentary on the man with the subject himself.

'Mr Pickle wanted me to speak to you first, sir. He's nothing if not scrupulous in demanding you know exactly what he proposes and where I fit into it.'

'So, lay it out. How is he to proceed? I hope you told him I can give him very little of my time. My priority must be THE WORK and I say that in capitals!'

'Well fortunately, as you know, ever since I came into your service, I've kept short notes of dates, times and – shall we say – situations we've found ourselves in. I kept them for the court – in cases where I was called as a witness, or as evidence for my own defence, as happened on a time. When I told him that, Mr Pickle became very excited, as near emotional as I've ever seen him.'

'It's gratifying that the thought of putting my life-story down on paper should energise him so. Fuck me, Pom, it doesn't take much to get his juices going! So, what's his plan? When's he going to find the time to carry it out? Don't forget I'm his priority.'

'That's the beauty of it, sir. He intends to pin-point aspects in your romance with actual details of your life. For example, he says you identify one of Arthur's knights as Sir Hervis de Revell – a reference surely to your own estate of Newbold Revel.'

'Yes I did. I described him as "a noble knight" I believe.'

'And as one of the older knights of the round table too.'

'It suited my purposes to have him so.'

'Perhaps you were thinking of yourself, sir?'

‘Well, one has to be realistic. But never mind that; I don’t want this enterprise impacting on my own work, that’s all. When do you intend to consult together?’

‘We both pray at St Martin le Grande and thought Sunday afternoons would suit us both. You’re generally asleep by one o’clock – with or without company – and I have some free time then. I’ll stroll around to Mr Pickle’s lodgings, taking some dinner with me for us both as I don’t fancy his fare at all.’

‘It won’t stop you getting my dinner, will it?’

‘I can assure you there’ll be no inconvenience to yourself, sir. I’ll be back by lock-up and remember we’re doing this for your immortality.’

‘Making me immortal, eh? I’m hoping *Le Morte* will do that, but I suppose doubling up the opportunity to stay memorable to all generations down the line is even better. Jesus Christ! It’s a genius of an idea. Go to it, Pom!’

‘Perhaps, you should tell Mr Pickle yourself when he comes this morning. It will give him confidence to hear you agree.’

‘Well, I still need to know how he intends to approach the work. You know how some of these annals can be extremely biased; the Lancastrians are painted as devils incarnate by Yorkist chroniclers and vice versa. We want everyone to know what really happened. I’ve never had my day in court for twenty years, so no one’s heard it from our point of view. But do you think he’s up to writing something with imagination and flair? He comes across as a bit of a dullard to me. It’s my only concern, that it might turn out to be so tedious, no one wants to read it!’

‘I think you should insist you have an editorial role to play – look over the text from time to time. Obviously I’ll be relating it, so there should be few discrepancies. I know you say you’re too short of time to be involved, but in truth you have plenty of hours in the day.’ Pom looked round the room and the barred windows, ‘It’s not as though you’ll be going anywhere,’ he said airily.

***

'Where shall we start?' Monty asked.

'The year of our Lord 1441. That was a good year, Mr Pickle,' replied Pom opening his notebook and peering down at the relevant page.

The two men were seated in Monty's room on the third Sunday in April. They had come spiritually refreshed from St Martin le Grande and Monty was in the process of spreading out the items of provender which Pom had brought along in his wicker basket.

'I've brought a skin of wine – courtesy of my master, who wishes our enterprise "God speed".'

'He makes it sound as though we're about to embark on a sea-voyage,' laughed Monty, testing the liquor and even his uneducated palate appreciated it as an expensive vintage; one of Sir John Wenlock's finest and presumably the proceeds of incorrigible Channel piracy.

'In a way we are; the journey through the life of Sir Thomas Malory knight of the realm and one-time member of parliament.'

'Member of parliament? I didn't –'

'Let's not get ahead of ourselves. I said '41 was a good year because it was then Sir Tom became a knight; he was twenty-five.'

'Why was it a "good" year, Pom?'

'After his father's death in '34, Sir Tom came into some nice little properties in Northamptonshire and Warwickshire. The income from both Winwick and Newbold Revel allowed him to take up his knighthood. I told you once that Sir Tom's father was a local worthy – but was only an esquire. He never became a knight.'

'Is this when Sir Tom became interested in stories of chivalry?'

'He told me that started when he was a boy.'

'Oh, I see! Well, how did you become connected with him, Pom?'

'We met when we were boys. I'm of gentry stock from Appleby manor in Leicestershire. Unfortunately, like you, a younger son and one of many. The network of gentry families in the midlands is huge, like a giant spider's web and we're all caught up in it. I was Sir Tom's saving grace when we were lads.'

'How so?'

'Well he was the only boy in a family of four: two elder sisters, Philippa and Isobel and a younger one, Helen. He was what's nowadays called "spoiled", certainly by Philippa and Isobel, Helen and he fought most of the time. It hasn't surprised me that she's become a real tartar! Their mother indulged him too. Mistress Malory was a proud lady from a wealthy family, the Chetwynds, and very obsessed with her ancestry. In fact, in a way, that was how I first met Sir Tom.'

'You talk about this network of families, are you related to Sir Tom in any way?'

'Funny you should ask that because we probably are, from the mists of time. Anyway, as I say, Sir Tom's mother was very keen to trace her forebears. She knew she came from a knightly family which existed in Shropshire and Staffordshire, and went back to early Norman times.'

'So, Sir Tom's family goes back many generations?'

'Everyone's does that, Monty,' Pom laughed, 'otherwise we wouldn't be here.'

'I know that of course, but significant families can actually identify where their line comes from.'

'It certainly makes them more interesting. Sir Tom's mother consulted the gentry in our region, including my father and discovered a common ancestor – or a common name among them – Antekil. They reckoned there were Malorys and Applebys with the Normans at Hastings, and discovered this mutual name – which, as they subsequently found, seems to have been very common among all our local families.'

'But that doesn't explain how you came to meet Sir Tom.'

'We were about fourteen and the Malory family had come to Leicestershire to visit distant relations. We were invited to a general gathering of gentry and that's where we met. Two young boys bored with adult chat, not yet interested in eyeing the ladies and looking to relieve the tedium. We walked outside, and threw stones at the carp in the manor pool, until we were spotted by the bailiff and had to run for it. That's when it all began.'

'So you've been friends ever since?'

'Yes. The upshot of all this research was that our families became very friendly. Not knowing quite what to do with a wayward son with no prospects, my father agreed I would go to Newbold to be companion/servant to Tom Malory. I would have a roof over my head and he would have a "brother". We've hardly been parted since, although once he took knighthood, I've become more of a steward –'

'And dogsbody, as I remember,' laughed Monty.

'Sir Tom's not one to be refused, as I found out oft times later. But that's for another day. I take it you now have sufficient background to begin your story?'

'I'm sure there are many more interesting details you could give me regarding your boyhood together.'

'If I go down that track, we'll be here until Michaelmas and still not started on the really interesting stuff. Next time I'll tell you about – but no, you'll have to wait a week for that. I promised Sir Tom I wouldn't be too long. He likes to play me at Hasard for as long as the candles and his money last.'

Monty put down his quill and looked over the pages of his notes. There seemed to be background enough to make a start at pulling it all together into some coherence. He was tempted to begin as soon as Pom had left, but, conscientious as ever, he put the papers aside and drew Sir Tom's quires toward him. Soon, he was deep into discovering more about Arthur's battles with the Roman Emperor Lucius.

***

Before setting off for Newgate on Monday morning, Monty walked round to Master Worms' shop. This would be his first visit since he'd paid the man his dues. He needed more supplies but it was also in his mind to ask the book-seller what he knew of Sir Tom and to catch up with the latest news of the city. Generally, Montmorency Pickle took little interest in politics. He had long held the view that it was best to keep his head down and not take sides in any dispute, local or national, both of which were outside his control.

Times had certainly been volatile during the fifteen years he had been a resident of the capital. The throne had been occupied by three different arses, if the old Duke of York was included. The nobility, which should have known better, had made a slaughter-house of the country: father against son, brother against brother. London had seen much violence – starting with Jack Cade and his rebels twenty years before. A blood-thirsty Kentish mob, they had arrived on the south shore of the Thames, and then streamed unhindered across London Bridge with the intention of disrupting the good governance of the country and instigating what they called "reforms". From then on, there was sporadic violence in the capital for several days and, when it became most serious, Monty had stayed indoors, shuttered his windows and kept a dagger under his pillow, for there was much blood on the streets, and not the usual kind from the shamble's slaughterhouses.

This was not the first or only time he had taken defensive action. There was regular and often vicious violence between different factions: groups of lawyers of the Inns of Court and the 'prentice boys – the former, young bucks full of their own self-importance, the latter young lads out for bloody excitement; both sides relishing the idea of cracking heads and worse. Other groups, mostly young males, were scapegoated in concert by these hotheads, especially the immigrant Italians and the Flemings who were seen as a persistent threat to native commerce; not to mention the Jews who were a perennial target for every group. London violence was endemic and he had learned to live with it by avoiding it.

Monty entered the gloomy space of Master Worms' shop and peered around until he spied his quarry bending over reams of paper which he was sorting into piles.

'Good day, Master Worms.'

Jack Worms stood up, 'Good day to you, Monty. Let me see, you're off to do the bidding of that rascal Sir Thomas Malory, no doubt?'

'That is so. I'm interested you should call him "rascal", Master Worms.'

'Tom Malory's well known to us book-sellers. Everyone's aware of his project and your involvement. The word on Paternoster Row is that it won't be finished before the man's either hanged, released or dead. Have you any idea how long he's been in prison?'

'He told me fifteen –'

'That's right. He's been incarcerated in all the London prisons – the two King's Benches, the Marshalsea, the Fleet, Ludgate, the Tower and now Newgate. They say no one has been kept locked up for so long without trial.'

'Yes, he's tried to explain that to me, at least his servant, John Appleby has. I still don't understand how the law can allow such a situation. But I admit, the man himself is remarkably sanguine about it and shows no urgency to obtain his freedom, or even to be heard. Appleby's certain Sir Thomas wishes to remain in Newgate until his work's finished – it's a matter of peace and quiet I believe, and it's not as though he's living in bad conditions, quite the opposite.'

'There's some sense in that I suppose, given the volatile times we live in.'

'Ah yes, the times we live in. What's been happening? I'm out of joint with recent events.'

'Complaints mostly; you've lived in London long enough to know how the people love to carp. It's the old story and I hear it in here every day – resentment as to how the country's governed, especially how taxes are misused; money, titles and land lavished on the undeserving. Now there's real anger against the court and, as usual, the Woodvilles are blamed. King Edward just doesn't seem aware how people dislike his in-laws.'

'I've not been aware of any disturbances round here.'

'It's mostly round the Steelyard where the Flemings are, and, as usual, the Inns of Court, round Lincoln's Inn and the Inner and Middle Temples, haunts of the young lawyers; they should know better. Many of my customers are from there and they regularly walk about in threatening groups, fully armed regardless of the city ordinances about carrying swords. As usual, it's mostly fuelled by drink. But you've no need to worry, after all, you couldn't be anywhere safer than Newgate!'

'The irony isn't lost on me, Master Worms! But I'm surprised how much freedom Sir Thomas seems to enjoy. It's almost as though he has the run of the place.'

'The rule of prison is the more you pay, the less your discomfort. Sir Tom must have profitable estates and rich friends to maintain the level of life-style he apparently enjoys.'

'I believe he has a great friend in Sir John Wenlock.'

'Baron Wenlock, you mean – Knight of the Garter no less – a man at the top of honour! Yes, I'd heard that too; a useful man to have on your side.'

'Well, he certainly keeps Sir Tom in regular stocks of fine wine. I've never tasted better, although my palate isn't tuned to the good stuff,' Monty added hastily, in case Master Worms got it into his head that his customer might be trying to live beyond the means of a humble scribe and wondered how he could afford to.

'The proceeds of piracy I've heard,' said Master Worms cheerfully. Monty said nothing, but was curious as to how Master Worms was so well informed about his employer's domestic arrangements.

'I only met Sir Tom two weeks ago and it's difficult to get his measure, I'll admit.'

'He has a shocking reputation, you know. A man isn't locked away in prison for so long without trial unless there's good reason. But you're now on the inside – literally – you can find out for us what the man's about; we've never been able to get to the bottom of it.'

Monty could see where this was leading and immediately decided he wouldn't become an espial for the local book-sellers' brotherhood. He was always scrupulous about gossip – trying neither to listen to it nor pass it on. As for being a source, his life was so devoid of interest that he was never canvassed by any of his acquaintance on the grounds they knew they would be disappointed. But to his alarm, he could see how his new connection put him in prime position to furnish his neighbours with all the details of this mystery man and his "shocking reputation", for which they had obviously been thirsting.

'I'm very busy with his "great work" as he calls it, Master Worms.' Monty said nothing to the book-seller about his venture to chart the life of Sir Thomas; that would open the floodgates to enquiries he wasn't prepared to answer.

'Ah yes! The *magnum opus*. You know Pom Appleby comes here for Malory's supplies – and a great deal of it there is too. I deliver to him sometimes. The man gets through reams of paper and numerous bottles of ink in a month. He's made my profits rise and I'll feel it when the work's completed. No chance of you editing it so that he has cause to use more materials?'

Monty shook his head, 'I'm hardly editing the work, just making suggestions and correcting scribal mistakes. I've only been working on it for two weeks.' Monty was keen to disabuse Master Worms of the idea that he had any hand in the actual composition of *Le Morte D'Arthur*.

'Is there any chance of me being able to bind the manuscript for him when it's finished? Will you put in a word?'

Monty wouldn't be drawn, 'I daresay you'll have as good an opportunity as anyone, especially as you supply him already.'

Jack Worms shrugged his shoulders and then proceeded to probe Monty on the subject which interested him most, 'What I want to know is what was it the man did years ago to be so long incarcerated? We've heard rumours, but nothing definite.'

Monty recognised Master Worms was determined to change the conversation back to the realms of speculation and he felt it was time to withdraw. But just before he made a move to leave, he said, 'Jack, what do you know of this new process of printing? Sir Thomas seems to think it will spell the end of handwritten manuscripts. He has me worried.'

'Of course, all in our trade have heard about the German pressing machine which has been talked about for more than twenty years, although no one in England has ever seen it, as far as I know.'

'That long? I'd never heard of it until Sir Tom mentioned how a Bible had been produced in days. I can tell you, the idea has given me some sleepless nights and it must concern you too.'

'Well, yes and no. According to what I've been told, once these pages are pressed out, they will still have to be sewn up into books – so our trade can only prosper. They'll be many more books than there are at present, so demand for materials and binding will greatly increase. But I think scribes will have more of a problem. I have no idea how this machine works, but I haven't heard that it necessarily needs exquisite quill-man-ship or beautiful monkish illustrations.'

Monty looked very downcast and his friend sought to reassure him, 'Don't worry, Monty. As I said, this process has been talked about for decades and nothing has really come of it, certainly not in England.'

'Malory thinks it will.'

'Even if it does, don't forget, people will always want someone to write things down for them – the sort of work you do already with legal papers – wills, deeds – things like that will still have to be written out by hand. It will only be the large works – the Bible, chronicles – *Le Morte D'Arthur* – those epic works which will be pressed out, sewn together and bound, and grace the libraries of the filthy rich! And think about it, someone will have to set them down by hand in the first place. I guarantee you'll still be needed, even when the first printing press finds its way into Paternoster Row! It's my view that it'll be the monks and copyists who'll suffer from the new process most. There'll be no need for them; they'll be the ones who are put out of work.'

Monty nodded and looked relieved, 'What you say makes sense, thank you, Jack. You've gone some way to putting my mind at rest.'

At that point, he heard the Greyfriars bell chime the quarter. 'Is that the time? I must be off, Master Worms. I'll leave this list of my requirements and collect it this afternoon, if that's all right?'

'Payment on collection, Mr Pickle!'

'Absolutely, Master Worms!' and Monty jingled some coins in his pocket reassuringly.

***

"It befell when King Arthur had wedded Queen Gwynyvere and fulfilled the Round Table, and so after his marvellous knights and he had vanquished the most part of his enemies, then soon after came Sir Lancelot de Lake unto the court, and Sir Tristram came that time also, and King Arthur held a royal feast at the Round Table."

'Now we introduce our hero-in-chief, Monty Pickle.'

'I thought King Arthur fulfilled that role, Sir Tom?'

'Ultimately yes, and certainly in this section about his war against the Roman Emperor, which I hope you've taken careful note of?'

'I spent all last evening on it after Mr Appleby left.'

'Ah yes! Your session on my life story. What do you think?'

'Well, we've just begun to scratch the surface.'

'Scratch the surface? A strange choice of words, as though you're relieving a flea bite.'

'Well, when you consider what might be to come, we might even draw a little blood – to continue the analogy. I'm excited about the project.'

'Well, Pom's already told me how my early life has set your juices flowing. I must say, you look as though you could do with livening up. But wait until he really gets going. I'll be interested to hear what you think.'

What is it about your story that excites so many? thought Monty, but did not say it. Instead, he took the quire of *Le Morte D'Arthur* from his bag and laid it on the table.

'How far did you get?' asked Sir Tom.

'Well, I had a little trouble with the speed of the return journey you send the Roman senators – all the way from Carlisle to the port of Sandwich, which Arthur tells them to accomplish in seven days. I asked Pom how far he thought it was and he said the route you send them – Carlisle to Shrewsbury at the top of Watling Street, and then down to the south-east coast, was over four hundred miles. Now, I'm no horseman, but even I know a single skilled rider with change of horses, good tracks, good weather and good light can just manage fifty miles a day unrestricted by companions. It's unlikely they'd do it in so short a time'

'God's bones! You're too scrupulous, Monty. But, if you remember, I make sure they hired hackneys from town to town and we're only talking a couple of days here or there. Believe me, there'll be many times the reader will need to suspend their disbelief; pedantry has no place here! Shall we get on?'

Monty sighed inwardly. He had realised from the start Sir Tom would always have his way. If anomalies were to be ignored, was it worth him researching for corrections? Editing legal documents was simply a matter of format and custom. This work was completely different; a figment of a man's imagination. His chain of thought took him to the story he was proposing to write. Who would he ask to cast his eye over it to detect his own errors and anomalies? Under the circumstances, Sir Tom would be the only appropriate candidate – not something to be relished. If only –

'Pickle, are you listening?' Malory's sharp tone cut through his meanderings, 'Jesus Christ! I'm not paying you to wool-gather. Can we get back to Section 4 of Book 5 and Arthur's dream: "…a dreadful dragon did drench much of his people." What do you think of the alliteration? Good, eh! And then the explanation of the dream by the philosopher; that's like Pharaoh consulting Joseph, I would say.'

'Indeed and it's very good, Sir Tom,' and Monty tried to look enthusiastic again. 'You clearly have a way with words. I can't say I've ever read anything which compares with it. But then, as I told you, my reading experiences have been of the purely legal variety. I've never read Chaucer – not for want of interest, I simply couldn't get my hands on a copy.'

'You have to know the right fucking people, Monty Pickle! But I suppose I was lucky too. During our war with France, I was there for a short time with my cousin, Sir Philip Chetwynd – as a soldier, just after I took up my knighthood. We were in Gascony, Bayonne to be exact, where he was the mayor. While there, I became friendly with one of the locals who, I found out, shared my interest in the French romance stories. I'd heard them as a boy from one of my many relations, I forget which one. He'd served in France under good King Harry and then his feeble son, Henry VI, and come across these accounts of courtly love and knightly deeds. He filled my head with them and ever after, I've been fascinated. This local acquaintance in Bayonne told me about a collection of manuscripts that had been recently left to the Church; he'd been told that among them were copies of the romances. He also knew exactly where they were – hidden in a nunnery "out of harm's way". So, slipping away from soldiering duties for a while, I got on the scent and discovered this convent, where I found the sisterhood was more than hospitable – you know what nuns are like, Monty,' he said with wink.

Completely taken aback by these obvious hints, Monty shook his head; his eyes widening.

'What I mean is, they were anxious to share the contents of the nunnery library with me. Jesus! What did you think I meant?'

'I'm not sure, Sir Tom. But why would they do that? Why would they believe you were interested in French romance? It's rather unusual for a soldier, surely? How did they come to have them there in the first place? It seems an odd thing to happen.'

'I simply told them I was interested in old documents and I understood they'd recently been asked to store some.'

'So they let you look at these books?'

'Look at them and take them away on a long-term loan. The Mother Superior herself had no idea what they were concerned with; neither was she interested. It was a matter of her having agreed to the bishop's request to provide storage space for a pile of old manuscripts. I think my Bayonne friend was right; the bishop, being a sly old fox had them placed there rather than with the monks at the abbey down the road, who would have been forbidden to even touch them; but that order in itself would have made them mad with curiosity.'

'Are they considered to be so profane in France then?'

'In some quarters – all that adulterous fucking will only titillate young men already suffering the dire effect of celibacy. No doubt, the bishop thumbed his way through them a few times once he realised what was there. Anyway, I had to sign for them, of course; the Mother Superior wasn't that fucking hospitable. I think the nuns liked the look of me – I was a handsome devil in those days, just twenty-six and full of young energy; it was oozing out of me and they scented it, like mares on heat.'

Monty suddenly had a mental image of black-habited, wimpled women in their cells in the pitch black of night, all lusting after this young Englishman with a strange relish for bundles of musty manuscripts.

'So that's where you started writing *Le Morte D'Arthur*?'

'No, it never entered my head, that came much later. But look, you've managed to side-track me again. We must get on. Where were we?'

Monty consulted his page, 'We've transported the senators back to Rome with Arthur's answer that he refuses to do homage to Lucius; rather he'll take possession of the empire through feats of war.'

'I like the next bit particularly, when the senators impress upon Lucius that Arthur is "the most manly man that lives and likely to conquer all the world" etc. etc. I think we have him in a nutshell there, don't you? The reader can't be mistaken as to his qualities.'

'Indeed not. Although, we have been assured of it many times. But what about these fifty giants engendered by fiends who were ordered as Lucius' bodyguards? Are they very large men or proper giants? Would a description help?'

Malory frowned, 'Jesus Christ! Does it matter? It's all in the head of the reader what they look like. If they want them to have two fucking heads, so be it. The fact is Lucius is surrounded by these fifty colossal guards, as well as having this enormous Roman army at his back, stuffed with warriors from all over the empire. Who cares what the giants look like! By the way, do you like the way I leave the reader guessing what happens next? By moving the action back to York and leaving Lucius straddled across western France ready "to destroy the realm of Little Britain"?'

'A clever device,' agreed Monty. *And one I may use myself,* he thought but did not say it.

They pressed on, and by dinner time had managed ten pages without distraction and with little dissension. As the abbey bell chimed the hour, Tom Malory leaned back in his chair and said, 'We've done well and deserve a drink.' He turned to his servant, who was seated half-dozing next to the fire, 'Stir yourself, Pom! It's dinner-time.'

The good man stood up, and placed glasses and a jug on a wooden tray. 'Excellent! What are we having today?'

'Being as you are to set the next part of the tale in Burgundy, I thought it appropriate to serve it this morning. Another of Wenlock's finest. I know its origins – the *Katarina*, a Spanish carvel taken a month ago off Bordeaux by Lord Warwick's men; she was crammed with silks, pewter and wine. The baron has sent us three roundlets of the stuff – beautifully casked and stored safely at the right temperature in the prison cellars where it keeps well, guarded by – well, the guards.'

'This is the life, eh, Monty?' Malory stood up and turned to warm his arse by the fire, holding up his glass and letting the light from the window shine through the purple liquid,

'Good wine, good books, a warm fire and good companions. All we need are some women – in short supply here most of the time, but procurable for ready money. Pom, see if Meg's available later today – usual rates and free drink.'

'Very well, sir, I'll enquire. She may have other business, but I'll do my best.'

'What about you, Monty? Fancy it?'

'No indeed, Sir Tom. I'll make my own arrangements, thank you,' said Monty primly, extremely discomforted as he always was when Malory touched upon the subject of sexual congress, which seemed to be almost daily.

'Make sure you do, Monty Pickle! Make sure you do! A man can't do without it or he'll run mad, as I've told you. Now, Pom, dinner, what do we have today?'

To Monty's great relief, the conversation was closed and alimentary matters took precedence. The food was brought out, the wine poured again and conversation revolved around the rumours of trouble in the wilds of northern England, a place totally unknown to Monty and in his mind unimaginably bleak and dangerous.

'We've been there you know, Monty,' Sir Tom scratched his head with both hands, making his short, greying hair stand up on end like a stable grooming-brush, ''63 to '64 wasn't it, Pom?'

'Indeed it was, sir. And a real time we had of it.'

'Hmm, well perhaps we should leave that for another day. That's the sort of tale you can describe to Monty here for his account of my life. There's plenty of action and will be of great interest to my readers I'm sure.'

My readers? thought Monty. *Is he planning to take ownership of my project when it's finished?* From that moment, he determined to keep his work well separated from his employer and discuss it with him as little as possible. There was no doubt Montmorency Pickle was going to have to tread carefully around this slippery customer.

Chapter 3

Monty hears tales of Sir Tom's first adventure; Jack Worms has a worrying encounter; Sir Tom reveals more about his past than perhaps he should and Monty is confronted by a stranger.

The following weeks took on a similar pattern, although the terms of the original agreement were breached many times, Monty's hours having become increasingly "flexible". From his arrival at eleven o'clock, he and Malory worked at a frantic pace for a good hour before they broke for "refreshment". Then the old knight gave Monty the benefit of his wit and wisdom on many topics for at least half an hour, before grumbling that the scribe had deliberately distracted him. They would return to their labour for another hour, stop for dinner and then continue until approximately four o'clock when Sir Tom always retired for a nap, and Monty went home. Thus, Monty's hours had been extended by these crafty means, but he made no complaint. After all, Sir Tom was true to his word and fed him well. In truth, Monty enjoyed listening to the old man who he quickly recognised as someone with excessively colourful opinions.

On occasion, Malory would begin to discuss current matters concerning the king and the court, as though he was fully involved in the affairs of the royal council. Monty wondered where his authoritative comments came from. But given the laxity of Malory's supervision, perhaps he had visitors of whom Monty was unaware. After all, he spent only five hours a day with the man; who knew what he was about the rest of the time?

It was the second Sunday on which Pom visited Monty's lodgings to continue the account of Malory's life. Anxious to get down to work immediately, Monty recapped, 'We left it where you'd become his companion and he'd inherited his father's estates and taken up knighthood.'

'What I omitted to tell you was that in '37, Sir Tom married a Leicestershire woman, Elizabeth Walsh of Wanlip. Not a bad match, except her uncle who held the estate was barking mad. His brother-in-law ran the place but bled it dry and was forced to relinquish control. Lady Malory's father Richard took it on as the heir. But mad old Thomas Walsh didn't die until twenty years later and, when Sir Tom married Elizabeth, Richard Walsh was not a wealthy man; she brought little to the Malory fortune. I've always assumed it was a love match and that Sir Tom waited until he was of age, and married despite his family. He rarely discusses it, even with me, so it's only conjecture. His son, Robert, was born nine months to the day of the wedding in '38. He always said he went to it "with a will". I think I told you, Robert's here in London but never visits; perhaps he's embarrassed having a father in prison, I don't know. Anyway, moving on, I understand Sir Tom filled in a little of his story of his time in France with Sir Philip Chetwynd – the time when he came across the romances?'

'Were you with him then, Pom?'

'Man and boy, Monty! Where he went, I went and so it has remained ever since. Some say we're like the "Scottish brothers", the ones born joined at the head ten years ago. Still alive I believe and exhibited; people pay to see them. Well, if we weren't actually joined at any places, Sir Tom and I were brothers-in-arms on many occasion and brothers in other escapades also. But I'm getting in front of myself. The French expedition only lasted a few months, and we came home at the beginning of '43 with no money and balking at the idea of settling to a life of estate management and farming. We were twenty-seven and in our prime; both good horsemen, swordsmen and lusty when it came to women; too lusty on occasion.'

'Did you come back to Warwickshire?'

'Yes, back to our roots and our families, which had now grown with nieces and nephews, as well as young Robert Malory who was six or thereabouts. Lady Elizabeth put her foot down for a while, and insisted we stay and did our duty to the family. There would be no more wandering off on foreign adventures.'

Monty, painstakingly getting all this down, looked up and asked, 'Did Sir Thomas start on *Le Morte D'Arthur* then, Pom? When did he actually start writing them down?'

'He didn't really set to work on the manuscripts until last year. But the tales have always been in his head, Monty. Everything we did, he would relate to something in the stories which was akin to it. He became particularly obsessed with Sir Lancelot of the Lake – I believe you're in the process of writing him up?'

'We are. He seems a remarkable character. By my estimation, he should have been dead of his wounds three pages in! I've never known a knight sustain so many injuries without succumbing to the inevitable.'

'As Sir Tom advises – suspend your disbelief, Monty Pickle! They are only stories of magic. But they did have an effect on our friend and he often spoke about "going on quests". Unfortunately, he began to act out his fantasies and we were in our first real trouble in '43.'

Monty leaned forward, 'So, what happened?'

'It was the old story, we were short of money and he had a grievance against a man called Thomas Smythe who lived in Spratton Northamptonshire. The combination of the two was irresistible. Sir Tom became convinced Smythe had used insulting language about Lady Elizabeth. He was sufficiently exercised to recruit myself and his brother-in-law, Eustace Burnaby, Philippa's husband, to ride the twenty-five miles to Spratton and take the man hostage for a while.'

'Hostage?'

'Oh yes, we waylaid him on a quiet lane as he was riding home, pulled him from his horse, blindfolded him and took him to a barn. We had to handle him roughly – he put up quite a fight, but Eustace laid into him with a will, threatening Smythe with all sorts unless he sent word for his wife to give us money.'

'Was Smythe an old man? Young man?'

'Fortyish, overweight, red in the face and certainly out of condition; anyway, there were three of us. Sir Tom was as free with his words as Eustace was with his fists and feet. While Eustace punched and kicked him, Sir Tom called him the foulest names, and insulted his wife to his face. The aspersions levelled at Lady Elizabeth had really got under his skin. In the end, Smythe caved in, and I was sent to his house with a demand for forty pounds in cash and goods. I admit to menacing the lady of the house – briefly – for she soon paid up. I rode back to the barn with various domestic items, trinkets and ten pounds in cash. Sir Tom and Burnaby released Smythe, threw him over his horse, slapped its backside, and sent the man home with two black eyes and some broken ribs. We went home and shared the spoils three ways.'

Monty was silent; shocked at this frank revelation of violence, whether deserved or not. It was all very unedifying to him. This was no way to sort out differences. However, he was a realist, and knew that in this day and age, many people took matters of personal justice into their own hands, the courts being either unwilling or too slow to act, not to mention juries packed with placemen. However, Pom's tale was shocking to Monty. The idea of kidnapping and menacing a man – and his wife – until they agreed to pay up was well outside his experience.

'There's nothing chivalrous about this, Pom. Nothing which we could relate to the exploits of the Knights of the Round Table. I'm sure Sir Lancelot never asked for money with menaces!'

'I disagree. I think Sir Tom put his wife's honour above everything, just as any of Arthur's knights were trained to do. And, let's face it, none of us "*stove in his head with his sword and cleaved him to the paps*". I believe I'm quoting correctly?'

'But the money? That shouldn't have played any part in it.'

'Compensation, Mr Pickle!'

Monty digested this explanation before asking, 'Am I to include this in the commentary? Will Sir Thomas want it widely known?'

'I don't think he'll give it two thoughts and there's far worse to come, Monty. This is just the beginning. It's all common knowledge anyway – written up in various indictments.'

'Oh!' said Monty faintly, 'I see. Dare I ask, did Smythe complain?'

'Of course, he did! A writ was served pretty quickly afterwards and we were all to appear in court on various charges. But somehow it didn't come to anything. I wondered if Sir Philip Chetwynd pulled some strings. But Sir Tom didn't get away with it completely. Sir Philip called him in when he heard the rumours of what had happened. In sharp tones, he told Sir Tom to stop degrading the family name and settle down to managing his estates, or else he'd no longer support him. But I think Sir Tom managed to charm him somehow and Chetwynd mellowed. In any case, he was a fair man and recognised Sir Tom had energy which should be channelled more positively. He helped him to get elected Knight of the Shire for Warwickshire and guaranteed him an annual income of forty pounds – I was never sure whether that sum was a coincidence or not!'

'From kidnapper to Knight of the Shire! That's a leap, Pom!'

'Well, yes and there was further irony; once he was elected, he was sent on a royal commission to confirm tax exemptions to poor towns in Warwickshire – in other words, providing them with extra cash, which made him very popular. As the burgesses were shaking his hand, he was imagining himself as Robin of the Hood! However, I'm afraid involvement in this form of official philanthropy soon began to pall and it wasn't long before he was seeking further excitement.'

Suddenly, Pom sat back in his chair and began to pull on his boots, 'But look, Monty, I don't want to outstay my welcome. I've been here some hours and in any case, Sir Thomas will want feeding. This is a good time to stop so let's leave that story for next Sunday.'

Disappointed, Monty nodded, wiped his quill on his sleeve and tidied up his papers. 'I shall look forward to the next set of stories, especially if they're even more shocking.'

'Wait 'til we get to Fuckingham Buckingham,' laughed Pom, 'I guarantee you'll be vastly entertained!'

'Can't wait!' said Monty shaking Pom's hand as his friend walked through the door and out onto the street.

***

The book-sellers' quarter, Paternoster Row, was a quiet but busy street in London to which anyone with any literary interest must eventually find their way through a maze of back allies around St Paul's. Two rows of small shops crowded one on another with a narrow, cindered walk-way between, their proprietors selling materials and books; everything required for the circular process of committing thoughts to paper and paper back to thoughts.

Paternoster was mercifully empty of the detritus and stink which other City streets accumulated. Many surrounding areas were named specifically to their trades; thus, curds, sour milk and greasy butter-waste invested Milk Street; Bread Street likewise exhibited aspects of its products; the ground beneath peppered with thin grey powder, the air above infused with the more agreeable smell of yeast, malt and new loaves. Above all, there was the appalling reek which rose from the streets of Eastcheap and Poultry, the butchering centre; otherwise known as the Shambles, where offal and bones thrown casually into the street from the slaughterhouses mingled with the everyday excrement of the citizens.

Thus, a blind man might identify where he was in London through his sense of smell. But he would have had difficulty in Paternoster Row where the air was suffused with a variety of unusual scents, although it was always the faint smell of glue which dominated. There was hardly any waste thrown into the street, for paper, quills, ink, wax and glue were expensive, and all carefully measured and accounted for. Paper hardly ever casually discarded, but reused where possible; the remnants of ink poured back into their original source of gallon jars and the empty containers rinsed thoroughly with water; quills used almost down to the feathers.

Worms' Books' was at the end of the Row which backed onto St Paul's churchyard; quieter than the east end, which was very close to the noisy business of Cheapside. Its proprietor, Master Jack Worms, liked to think he supplied a better class of customer than his east end competitors. The young man prided himself on the quality of his work and that of his patrons. He supplied their needs and bound their finished works with skill and devotion, for he was an avid reader who believed in the power of words. Jack took every opportunity to peruse all the material which came across his counter; he considered it a perquisite of the job since he couldn't afford to buy books himself. His heart always leapt when a customer walked into his shop carrying a bulging bag and brought forth a thick manuscript, laying it with pride on the counter. He felt himself fortunate that he was living in an age when men were beginning to record their times again, like the monks of old had done. He'd had several sections of these new London Chronicles to bind and became engrossed in their accounts of not only his own times, but even further back. They were not unprofitable, but rare, so there was no escaping the need for bread-and-butter work – pamphlets, ballad sheets, legal documents – which on a day to day basis kept him in business.

He was sufficiently busy to require an apprentice; a dull boy who came cheap because his father was desperate to get him out of the house. At the age of thirteen, Dickon Puddledock, so called because that was the family domicile, was a lanky, unappealing lad with a permanent dew-drop on the end of a sharp nose and thick blonde locks which flapped over his face, like disordered damp stockings on a washing line. Jack Worms was not necessarily kind to the boy, calling him Dick Addlepate to his face and applying a good number of buffets to the lad's head on an hourly basis, often for no other reason than he felt a surge of general irritation at the youth's lack of useful wits. Dickon was in the second year of a seven-year apprenticeship and had made little progress in the trade. Jack despaired of him, particularly his inability to handle anything liquid without spilling quantities in awkward places. He could never successfully fill a bottle of ink without it dripping down the sides onto something expensive; as for the glue, Jack had forbidden him to go near the barrel, let alone trusting him with decanting the stuff into bottles. Nor was there any question of him being introduced to the finer art of book-binding. The book-seller's wooden vices had minds of their own, seeking out careless fingers and hands to nip and press. Master Worms anticipated Dickon Puddledock was an accident waiting to happen.

It was Friday morning; a thin stream of weak sunshine had fought its way through the dust of the shop and settled on a corner of the counter on which Master Dickon was leaning on his elbows; hand cupped round his chin and his eyes gazing vacantly into space. Master Worms had taken the opportunity of a lull in trade to visit the privy for a shit. Suddenly, the sun was obscured by a shadow and Dickon looked up to see an extremely tall, rangy and well-dressed gentleman looming in the doorway. As he approached the counter, the lad could see he was accompanied by a squat, swarthy man, unshaven and bald, dressed in leather jerkin and grubby breeches. Both were carrying swords. Uncertain as to whether he should attempt to serve them, or ask them to wait until Master Worms returned, Dickon wiped the snot off his nose with the back of his hand and forced what he considered a welcoming smile, 'Good morning, gentlemen, can I help you? My master is –'

'Jack Worms, yes I'm aware of that. Where is he?'

'In the privy, sir. Will you wait?'

‘It seems as though we’ll have to.’ Even Addlepated Dickon knew the sound of menace when he heard it and he looked round nervously.

‘I’ll go and hurry him up, sir.’

‘You’ll stay right here, lad,’ the tall man gave a signal to his companion who immediately leaned over, took the boy by the scruff of his shirt with one hand and heaved him in one go over the counter. He then proceeded to pinion Dickon’s arms behind his back, still holding them with one hand, as though to make the point that any further effort of restraint was quite unnecessary, which was true since the boy had gone completely limp with terror.

At this point, Master Worms emerged from behind a curtain at the back of the shop, which concealed the closet. ‘By Christ, lad! Pickled herrings don’t please my bowels.’ He was in the process of pulling up his hose when he became aware of a gangling, red-headed man approaching him with a thin smile. Jack looked round and saw his apprentice captured and held. ‘God’s bones! What’s happening here? Who are you? What’s to do?’

‘There’s no harm in you knowing since we’ll surely be having dealings in the future. My name is Sir Jasper Percy and I’m after information. In truth, I’m seeking an acquaintance of yours. All I need for the moment are directions to his lodgings.’

Jack Worms had never considered he was a courageous man, but then he had never been tested. This assault on his apprentice and, more importantly, the sanctity of his business riled him and he felt his fists clench. ‘Well, rough-handling my apprentice is not the usual way to obtain information. You could have just come and asked nicely like anyone else. Now, get out of my shop!’

On a nod from Jasper Percy, the bald individual gave a vicious twist to Dickon’s arms, which made the boy squeal. Jack made the fateful mistake of moving towards him in a vain attempt at rescue, but was forestalled by Percy who, taking a knife from his belt, grabbed him and held the blade to his throat.

‘Now, I’ll make this easy for you, Master Worms. Just give me the information and we’ll leave you. As I say we may be back, but no harm will come to either of you if you cooperate.’

By now, Jack’s gore was rising. What would happen if he refused? Surely the man wouldn’t really slit his throat in broad daylight. With a surge of courage fuelled mostly by anger, he shook his head defiantly and the next thing he knew he was being dragged across the floor by his neck, the knife still pressed to his Adam’s apple. Within seconds, Jasper Percy had Jack’s hand in the largest vice screwed to the binding table, its wooden jaws gaping wide and its screw, as he knew, well-oiled and efficient.

‘Now, Master Worms, I’m gambling that you’re right-handed, most of us are; you have no sinister tendencies I take it. In a few seconds, I’ll make sure you never work again – a crushed hand is of no use to anyone.’

He nodded to his companion who, still holding Dickon’s wrists, dragged him across to the vice. With his free hand, the man held the screw and began to turn it. Percy held Jack’s wrist in an equally vice-like grip. The jaws of the machine were closing and Jack could feel the wood brushing against his flesh. He caved in, ‘Very well, very well! Let us both go and tell me what you want?’

The accomplice released the screw and Percy took his blade from Jack’s neck. On a nod, his companion let the apprentice go. Dickon Puddledock was by now a trembling mess and his legs went from under him. His captor dragged him to a stool and sat him down.

‘Now, Master Worms, having established that you’ll cooperate with me, I want to know the whereabouts of one of your customers – Mr Montmorency Pickle.’

For the first time, Jack Worms could look his interrogator fully in the face. Here was a man with the clear and awful blemishes of the smallpox. Under a thatch of bright ginger hair, his face was pink, pitted and scarred. He had scanty eyebrows, a pointed nose and full mouth. But it was his voice which had caught Jack’s attention from the beginning. An extremely tall man and, although thin, the expectation would be that he would produce a solid manly sound. Instead, what came out of that florid mouth was a high-pitched sinister whine, with little volume and an unattractive timbre. The thought raced through Jack's head that either the man's balls hadn't dropped, or he had lost them somehow and he was a eunuch. But surely, they ran to fat?

'Why on earth would you want to know that? What business would you have with Mr Pickle?'

Percy fingered his knife again, 'That's for me to know. As for business with Mr Pickle, you should mind your own. Just say it's a matter of great importance to me – and others.'

Here was a dilemma. Jack considered Monty a friend as well as – now – a good customer. This caitiff, whoever he was, clearly meant him harm. As far as he knew, Monty led the most blameless of lives. In fact, Jack considered him the dullest man he knew and one with whom sharing an evening's drinking was never relished. 'You mean him some harm, I suppose? Does he owe you money? He has none, you know.'

'No, he doesn't owe me money, he may just be able to help me – us.'

Jack drew a deep breath and said, 'If you could tell me a little more, perhaps I could be of help too?'

'I don't think so, Master Worms, At least not at present. But, as I told you, I'll probably be visiting you again. For now, just tell me where he lives.'

Jack considered his options. He was never going to get rid of these men unless he cooperated. In recompense for involving his friend in what was clearly a mess of trouble, he decided that once they'd gone, he could dash up to Newgate and warn him, for Monty was presently at work with Sir Thomas.

'Number 3, Stinking Lane. You'll find him there,' he added.

'That wasn't hard, was it?' Percy squeaked and clipped his knife back onto his belt. He gestured to his silent companion that they should leave, and to Jack and Dickon's relief, the two men walked out of the shop into the spring sunshine, as carefree and unobtrusive as if they had just been shopping for ink.

Jack's legs were also going and he found a chair. 'Well, what was that about?' he asked. Dickon was still speechless and Jack noticed an unfortunate puddle on the floor around the lad's stool. 'There was no need for that, Dick!'

Dickon looked abashed, but recovering himself said, 'Did you notice the knife, Master Worms?'

'Not really. It was hard to see it pressed up against my throat!'

'It was shaped like a set of bollocks. Honestly. It had two balls on the hilt and then the blade between them. When he clipped it back on his belt it hung down between his legs like a set of – of –'

'Yes, I believe they're called bollock knives for that reason. I've heard they're very sharp and very expensive. One thing I did notice, he was a well-dressed villain. He obviously has wealthy connections – well he said he was a knight. Who knows? Now, I've no idea what this is all about, but you'll have to forget changing your breeches for now, and stay and mind the shop. Just mop up the puddle and don't let any more vicious strangers past the door! I'm off to Newgate to warn Mr Pickle immediately!

***

Percy and his accomplice, Robert Costello, strolled casually round to Number 3, Stinking Lane which was but two minutes from Paternoster Row.

'A grubby street for a gentleman, Bob,' observed Sir Jasper, curling his lip.

'Perhaps that's why they call it "Stinking Lane", sir.'

'Very likely, but you'd think the monks of Greyfriars would insist on something more salubrious on their doorstep. Here we are – Number 3.'

He stopped outside Monty's front door, carefully taking stock as to who might be observing them, for neighbours in any class of street are notoriously nosey. Hearing only a rhythmic banging and repeated imprecations from somewhere at the back of the property, Jasper was satisfied they were not observed and tapped on the door. There was no reply. 'It seems our friend is not at home.'

'Then who's doing the banging and cussing, sir?'

'I've no idea, but I don't imagine it's Mr Montmorency Pickle who has a side-line in manual work.'

'Will wc wait, sir?'

'No, Bob, we won't. We now know that Mr Pickle doesn't travel far. He'll probably come back for his dinner at mid-day – which must be about half an hour's time; we'll come back then and wait for him.'

Robert looked disappointed, as though he thought he had been cheated of more strong-arm tactics. Reading his thoughts, as he always did, Jasper laughed and said, 'Don't worry, Bob. You'll be able to stretch your muscles again very soon I'm sure. Now, let's get back with the news that we have at least tracked the man down!'

***

Hard at work in Malory's room, Monty was busy transcribing some extra notes which his employer had decided should be included. 'I've decided to liven this scene up – the one where King Arthur deals with the giant of Brittany – needs something other than simply describing the king loping off his head, I think we need some meat on the bone and I mean literally. Listen to this:

"Arthur went by a crest of a hill and saw a giant sitting at supper gnawing on the limb of a man, baking his broad limbs by the fire, and breechless. And three fair damsels turning three spits whereon were spitted twelve young children like young birds."

We must put this in for it will conjure all kinds of images in the reader's head and make them read on.'

'Does it have to be so graphic? A giant without his hose? And why include little children and put them to such a grisly end?'

'Monty, you have an unfortunate tendency to mawkishness. Tell me, why is sentimentality like porridge?'

'No idea.'

'Because like porridge, it causes constipation; not of the bowels but of the mind; it's a shackle to action. These are people's worst nightmares – their offspring carried off, roasted and eaten by giants. They'll be captured by the thought. But if you are concerned with justice, I have a very grisly end for the giant too:

"Then the glutton started up and took a great club and smote at the king until his crown fell off. And Arthur hit him again in the belly and carved off his genytrotters."'

'Genytrotters?' Monty said, now very curious.

'Old English country word for bollocks. I like it, it has a ring to it – "genytrotters", yes, we'll include it. As we will –'

But just as he was about to explain his next good idea, there was a bang on the door which was then pulled open; a guard put his head round and said, 'Visitor for you, Sir Tom, and he says it's very urgent he speaks to Mr Pickle.'

Malory looked annoyed; he disliked being interrupted while working and, at that particular moment, he felt he was on the verge of composing something spectacular. 'Jesus Christ! Nothing can be that important; tell him to visit Mr Pickle at home and not use my time for social calls.'

'This isn't a social call, Sir Thomas,' and Jack Worms came into the room, red-faced and breathing hard, having run the few hundred yards from Paternoster Row to Newgate, and then up the stone stairs to the top room. 'I must speak to Mr Pickle immediately; it's very important.'

'Very well, I'll give you five minutes and then you can clear off. What's this all about anyway?' Malory remained disgruntled at this unwanted intrusion, but sat back in his chair, put down his quill and looked from Master Worms to Monty, his eyebrows raised.

As briefly as he could, Jack described the visit of Percy and his accomplice, their strong-arm tactics on himself and his apprentice, and their desire for knowledge of Monty's home address.

'Do you know anything of this man, Monty?' asked Jack Worms.

'I've never heard of Sir Jasper Percy.'

'I havc,' Tom Malory looked at them both with a frown, 'I've come across him before now, but can only guess at his interest in you, Monty. You say you don't know him, but he evidently knows about you and has taken some trouble to find you.'

'But for what reason? What possible interest could he have in me?'

'I rather think,' said Sir Tom, 'that his interest may be in me.'

'You? Why you?'

'Because I've had dealings in the past with the Earl of Warwick, and Jasper Percy is his enemy and a staunch supporter of Margaret of Anjou and Henry VI.'

'That doesn't explain anything.'

'Fuck it! I'll make it as simple as I can for you both. It can't have escaped either of you that there are various plots and schemes to put sad Henry Lancaster back on the throne. Like me, he's a prisoner of Edward's government – in the Tower as we speak. There are people in the city conspiring to have him rescued and Edward deposed as a tyrant.'

'I'm still not clear where I come into this. I've never plotted or schemed with anyone, certainly not anyone of note.'

'Christ! I know you haven't, Mr Pickle. You are, after all, a quiet retiring man.' Monty wasn't sure whether Sir Tom meant it ironically or was speaking genuinely. Malory continued, 'My explanation is that Percy has been sent to find you as a link to myself. Somehow, they've found out you're working for me. There are no secrets in Newgate; everyone knows I'm here and the guards will sell any information for a groat or two.'

‘Why would my working for you be of interest to Lancastrian plotters?’

Jack Worms was beginning to see daylight, ‘Sir Thomas, are you involved in any conspiracies to replace the lawful King Edward, fourth of that name, with Henry Lancaster? There! Addressing a man I’ve been told likes plain speaking, I can’t be plainer than that.’

‘Fuck me, Master Worms! I do like a man who comes to the point. And I can’t answer it.’

‘Which means you are involved in some way. Otherwise you’d deny it straight out and tell me to go to the Devil!’

‘You may interpret it as you like, Master Worms, I’m saying nothing.’

‘But where does that leave me, Sir Tom?’ asked Monty wide-eyed and apprehensive.

‘To put no finer point on it, deeply in the shit, Mr Pickle!’

‘Sir Tom’s right, Monty. These men clearly meant business and consequently I’m afraid I had to tell them where you lived. Undoubtedly, they’ll be back when they think you’re at home.’

‘Marvellous! I’m a man totally bereft of any fighting skills. I don’t even own a sword – well, not one that works.’

Shrugging his shoulders, Tom Malory said, ‘Perhaps you could try explaining to them that you have no idea of any of my business and that you aren’t involved in anything. After all, that is the truth. If they don’t like it, tell them to go to hell!’

‘Oh yes, that’s very good advice! Two armed men, one a fighting knight, the other a cut-throat, waiting on my doorstep to murder me.’

‘Jesus Christ, how you exaggerate! They probably only want to talk to you about me.’

‘And what am I to say?’

‘Refer them to my room at Newgate and say I’ll be delighted to discuss any matters they want to raise – at my convenience. On the other hand, perhaps not; if possible, I’d like my name kept out of it.’

‘It isn’t possible. You’ve already admitted this is about you, so what am I to tell them?’

Jack Worms intervened, 'How's this for a suggestion, I come back with you and we face them together in a civilised way. Find out what they want from you and then decide what to do.'

'You can take one of the Newgate guards with you if you like – I'll arrange it – no charge,' offered Sir Tom.

With as much sarcasm as he was capable of, Monty said, 'Thank you, Sir Tom, that's very generous of you!' He was becoming increasingly enraged by his employer's insouciance. Thomas Malory had no thought other than for himself. It was clear to Monty that he was now embroiled in his employer's business in some unfortunate way, but Malory was hardly over-generous in offers to support his employee. However, the presence of an armed prison guard sounded comforting. There was clearly no way out other than to confront these strangers who had taken a sudden interest in his life. He sighed and said, 'Very well, if you're sure he can be released.'

'No problem at all. The keeper, Master Clyfford, is in my debt over a wager. I'll call it in. Now, I suppose you wish to discontinue our work here for the rest of the day. A pity; I was relishing those dozen children being turned on the spit. Never mind, they'll keep – although they'll probably be a little charred by the time we resume!'

***

There appeared to be abnormal activity around Number 3, Stinking Lane. Normally, a street where neighbours closed their doors on each other and only passed the time of day when forced to, it was unusual for strangers to lurk, particularly such an odd couple as Sir Jasper Percy and Master Robert Costello presented; the one very ginger and gangly, the other very swarthy and squat. Both men gave off an air of intimidation which evidently worked well on the Talbot children who, occupying their usual spot playing in the road, warily regarded the strangers. Jasper gave the signal to Bob Costello to make enquiries of them as to the whereabouts of

Mr Pickle. The eldest girl, more malapert and braver than her siblings, had asked him what such information was worth. Bob had raised his hand to give her a clout, but Jasper intervened, setting a more conciliatory tone.

'All we want to know is when Mr Pickle is expected home.'

'Don't know,' was the unhelpful answer.

'Well, is it before or after dinner?'

'Could be anytime.'

Jasper felt he couldn't afford to waste any more of his time and took a small coin from his pocket, holding it up enticingly in front of the girl, 'This is yours if you'll try to be more helpful. If not, Master Costello will encourage you by other means.'

The girl looked defiant and her siblings giggled – but nervously. However, she was cheated of her reward and Bob relaxed his striking arm as three figures appeared at the top of the lane. The girl pointed and said, 'There he is; there's old Pickleman! And he's got friends – Wormwood's with him!'

Jasper replaced the coin in his pocket and Bob made a move towards the girl, but she side-stepped him, and the three ran off laughing and gesticulating in the way only defiant children can. There was also a measure of defiance in Monty Pickle's stride as he entered the lane, and saw Sir Jasper and his accomplice waiting outside his door. He was comforted by the presence of Fat Gregory, the Newgate guard, who was armed with a cudgel and trying out an unfamiliar resolute expression. Jack Worms had drawn himself up to his full height and stuck out his chest. Jasper Percy stepped forward, 'Good day, Mr Pickle. I'm glad to see you at last; I've been waiting sometime. I'm sure Master Worms here informed you I was seeking you out?'

Monty drew a deep breath and tried to control his trembling legs, 'Yes, and I'm curious to know why and why you used such bullying tactics on my friend here.'

'Perhaps we could go inside. I have important and confidential matters to discuss with you, and the pavement is not an appropriate venue.'

Jasper Percy's emollient approach gave Monty increased confidence, 'You may enter my house, but I would ask you to take off your sword – and knife – and for your friend to do likewise, and hand them to the guard here.' Jasper hesitated. He had no intention of causing Monty any physical harm and he was always loath to part with his weapons, especially in neighbourhoods with which he was unfamiliar. But he could see that Monty Pickle presented no physical threat to either of them and, as for the guard, he was a pudding-faced overweight donkey who Bob Costello could easily overcome if it came to it.

'Very well!' and he took his sword from its scabbard and the knife from his belt, and handed them to Gregory, nodding to Bob to do the same. The guard took the weapons gingerly by their hilts, uncertain as to which way round he should maintain them.

'Stay outside, Master Gregory and come in if you are called,' Monty suddenly felt as though he was in charge. Unlocking the front door, he walked into his living room, closely followed by the three men who squeezed themselves into the available space. Jasper wrinkled his scarred nose; there was a musty smell of paper, ink and dusty books, as well as damp. He could smell genteel poverty in the air and immediately saw possibilities.

Monty wasted no time, 'I would be grateful if you could tell me as briefly as possible what this is all about. What is your interest in me and, as I already asked you, why use such intimidating tactics on my friend here?'

'I would rather speak to you alone, Mr Pickle. What I wish to discuss are matters of a highly sensitive nature – matters of state.'

Master Worms was particularly impressed and wondered what on earth Monty could be involved in. There had never been any hint of his friend and customer being a man of any significance, let alone embroiled in "matters of state". He hoped he could stay and discover more, but, to his intense disappointment, Monty nodded his head and said, 'Very well, if you insist. But I insist my friend and the guard remain within calling distance, and that you send your companion away likewise.'

Jasper Percy could see he had no option and indicated to Bob Costello that he should wait with the others outside the door. Crowding out the way they came in, Master Worms and Bob Costello left reluctantly to join Fat Gregory on the cindered street.

'Now, Mr Pickle, let's not waste any more time. I've spent enough hours looking for you. I believe you are working for Sir Thomas Malory? Is that correct?'

I knew it! said Monty to himself, *Malory is definitely mixed up in this.* There was no point in denying it; Monty could see that Sir Jasper Percy knew all about him. 'That is correct, although what it has to do with you, I don't know.'

'Well, you will shortly. Anyone connected with Thomas Malory is of interest to me and many others. Look, I come in peace and with a proposal. Why don't we sit down and take our ease?' And Jasper pulled up a chair, sat down, and stretched his long legs in front of him, looking Monty full in the face. Monty stared back, shrugged his shoulders and took the chair opposite.

***

'This proposal, what exactly was it?' Sir Thomas Malory had abandoned his usual studied carelessness and was now leaning forward in his chair, all attention.

'That he would pay me to arrange for him to visit you.'

'A visit? For what purpose?'

'I asked him that and he just said he wanted to talk to you about a serious matter. I did try to press him but that's all he would say. When I'd arranged the meeting, Percy would then explain everything to you. He has no access to you in Newgate unless you invite him in. I'm to be a sort of conduit for him, for which he'll pay me – quite well, I must say.'

'This is all very annoying, a great fucking distraction from what I'm about. I have no time and no inclination to play politics.'

'How do you know this is about politics, Sir Tom?' asked Pom.

'Jasper Percy's up to his neck in conspiracy. Damn the man for disrupting my quiet life, but if I don't hear him out, he'll persist. I know enough about him to believe that.'

'You seem to know a lot about Sir Jasper,' said Monty, 'how so?'

'Through my friend, the Earl of Warwick.'

'I didn't realise you were on those kind of terms, Sir Tom,' Monty sounded surprised.

'It's true. As I told you, we go back more than twenty-five years. I count him a friend.'

Pom looked doubtful, 'Shall we say an acquaintance, Sir Tom? I agree you've known him a long time, but you were never in his intimate circle.'

'Well, perhaps not, but I think we could have been convivial if circumstances had been different. I'm sure the man would take a drink with me now.'

Monty felt he needed to wrest the discussion back to current considerations, 'So what do you know of this Jasper Percy?'

'When I rode with the Earl of Warwick, I talked with his friends and acquaintances, and they told me about him; how he had been at Middleham Castle with Warwick as a boy and how they disliked one another. Percy claimed to have direct links back to that great hero warrior, Henry "Hotspur" Percy. Jasper was always bragging about it. Warwick gave him a hard time I believe, but he probably deserved it; got on everyone's nerves – especially that awful voice.'

'Do you think your acquaintance with the earl has something to do with this?'

'I'm certain of it. Percy's a Lancastrian to his sword-tip – I heard he's been in France with Margaret of Anjou these last few years. There's something in the wind and he's involved. Now it seems he wants to involve me.'

'Are we talking treason here?' asked Pom frowning. Monty started at that. It was just beginning to occur to him how deeply he was becoming implicated in business which he had no interest in nor experience of and he didn't feel at all comfortable.

'I rather think we are. The combination of Percy, a Lancastrian, seeking a meeting with a staunch friend of the Yorkist Warwick smacks of some kind of plotting.'

'You could take this directly to Robert Stillington, the Lord Chancellor, and have Percy committed to the Tower and then the block.'

'And tell Stillington what, Pom? Even if I could get access to him, what can I say? That I'm expecting a visit from a pock-marked, ginger-haired zealot with a squeaky voice and think he might be up to no good? Not sensible. Fuck it! I can't even get to talk to anyone in Stillington's office about my own cases.'

'Perhaps, he wants some kind of accord between the Lancastrians and the Yorkists – patch things up?' said Monty hopefully.

'I wouldn't believe a word of it if he suggested it. There's so much mutual hatred between Warwick and Margaret's Lancastrian followers, that if they were in a room together, you could gather up the loathing and weave it into a blanket, it's so palpable. No, Percy's misled or being deliberately devious, with some other plan in mind by which he wishes to implicate me. I'm sure this is directed at me personally. I've made a lot of powerful enemies in my time; ever since Fuckingham Buckingham. He's at the bottom of all this, Monty, I'll bet my wife's honour on it.'

Pom shook his head in exasperation, 'The old Duke of Buckingham's dead, Sir Tom, and has been these nine years. His son Henry's only – what – sixteen, married to the queen's sister and a staunch supporter of King Edward. As for any plots against you, that was over and done with years ago.'

'Why am I still in prison then? No trial, no court appearances.'

'Mostly because you like it here and have made no serious moves to get out, sir.'

'Hmm. But getting back to the business of Percy and his proposal, I better see him and find out what's on his mind.

Jesus Christ, I could do without all these interruptions! What arrangement did you make with him, Monty? What's he paying you, by the way?'

'A crown.'

'That much? It must be important!'

'He said he'd call again this evening.'

'So it's Tuesday today, collect your money and tell him to come with you tomorrow morning. You can get him in through the gates. In any case, I'll tell the guards to expect a pox-marked lanky fucker to be accompanying you.'

'Indeed, Sir Tom,' said Monty with a sigh. This persistent cussing irritated him intensely at times.

Thomas Malory turned in his chair, picked up his quill and said, 'Now, can we get back to work? Those scorched infants should be done to a turn!'

***

Sir Jasper Percy was closeted with Sir Thomas Malory for a good hour. Monty had been sent away and told to return when Pom came to find him. That good man knocked on the door of Number 3 looking unusually serious.

'Percy's left and Sir Tom wants you back.'

'Is anything wrong, Pom? You look worried.'

'I am indeed, but it's not my place to talk about it and in any case, better you don't know.'

Monty was now thoroughly alarmed. The talk of plots and conspiracy had unnerved him enough; the worried countenance of his friend increased his anxiety. They hurried together down Stinking Lane and up Newgate Street to the gates of the prison.

'Should I enquire what's gone on, Pom?'

'Best see if Sir Tom wants to share it with you. I must say, it's all a great surprise – something I would never have expected in my wildest thoughts. These are dangerous times, Monty, dangerous times. I –'

He broke off as they climbed the stairs one behind the other and came to Malory's door.

'Look, before we go in, let me warn you, my master's in a foul mood. Try not to upset him further by asking questions.'

Monty nodded, increasingly apprehensive as to what had put his employer into such an angry state. The door opened revealing Sir Thomas sitting at his table, a frown on his face, his hair upright where he had been rubbing it repeatedly with his hands. He looked up and scowled even more when he saw Pom and Monty enter. 'I should have told you to tell that caitiff Percy to go to the devil! I should never have allowed him in.'

'Well, Sir Tom, you didn't and you can't undo what's happened.'

'Indeed not. As you say I can't un-know what I know, the question is what to do about it? Have you told him?' and he glanced from Pom to Monty.

'No sir, I wasn't sure whether you wanted him included.'

'He's implicated already by having contact with that ginger-pated bastard.'

Monty really didn't like the sound of this. Implicated in what? He opened his mouth to ask, but then, heeding Pom's advice, closed it and waited for Sir Thomas to explain.

'The man's suggesting – demanding even – that I act as conduit for letters between the Lancastrians and the Earl of Warwick plotting the removal of King Edward, and the return of the simple-minded priest-king, Henry Lancaster. That's it in a nutshell. It's pure treason. I'm sure you find it unbelievable, I can hardly believe it myself. As if Warwick would have any dealings with Margaret of Anjou. As I said the other day, they all hate each other – Lords Somerset, Devon, Exeter, the whole pack of them have long-standing grievances with Warwick, Oxford and Clarence, and likewise. Fathers and sons executed and killed in battles during the last fifteen years. Is it likely they'll suddenly kiss and make up? Another grand Loveday in St Pauls? We all know how that ended!'

Monty vaguely recognised this last reference but his knowledge of the complexities of the civil strife which had wracked the country for decades was patchy. He drew a deep breath, 'The conduit business. What would it entail? Surely, he's asking you to take a terrible risk? How does he know he can trust you not to report him?'

'If I could trot round to the Lord Chancellor's office and tell Robert Stillington to his face what's in Percy's mind, it would be his word against mine and I'm a prisoner of the state. They'd most likely have me on the rack to see what else I knew. The question would be asked, "Why Malory? He must be sympathetic to the cause". No, I'm stuffed.'

'As I understand it, the Earl of Warwick's in France anyway, so Percy can't contact him.'

'Percy has ways and means far beyond imagination. Anyway, I know the earl's due back in Sandwich at any time. He's having his ship, the *Trinity,* re-fitted. He'll come to London soon after. Then there's all this trouble in the north which must bring him back; it's on his patch after all.'

'What trouble?' asked Monty?

Malory tutted, 'Don't you take notice of anything? Christ, everyone knows there's been trouble in the north. The peasants are revolting. They have a new champion, Robin of Redesdale, who's leading a mob and has threatened the city of York.'

'York's far off, Sir Tom. I'm not sure what it has to do with our current problem. What does Percy want you to do exactly?'

'Pass letters from his Lancastrian conspirators directly to the earl and then bring his response to Percy who says he'll collect them from you. Also, you're to pick his letters up and bring them to me.'

Monty's mouth fell open, 'Me! That's unreasonable! Oh no, I'm not getting involved in treason. I'm a reasonable man, not a treasonable one.'

'It's amazing how the addition of a single letter can seriously alter a meaning. Reasonable or treasonable – it has a ring to it. I think on this occasion, you'll be both – you have no choice now you know these facts – which are of course, strictly confidential!'

'You make them sound like legal documents which can't be shared. We're talking execution here – heads lopped off and not by a knight on a quest. I'm definitely not prepared to be one of your Arthurian characters, Sir Thomas.' Monty felt the blood in his head, a rushing in his ears and his heart banging in his chest. He had never been so worked up. 'No!' He clenched his fist and brought it down on the table with a bang.

'Steady on, Monty!' grunted Sir Tom, 'No need to get so excited. It's only a matter of carrying some letters. You won't know the contents.'

'So what happens when someone gets suspicious, a nosey neighbourhood spy? Even I know the king has plenty of those all around the country. Percy's hardly commonplace. If they notice him hanging around my house, they'll be curious and before I know it, they'll arrest me to find out what's going on. I'll be on "Exeter's daughter", stretched to – stretched to –'

'Stretched to sodomy, yes I know. But he won't be coming to your house. The exchange will take place at Worms' Books –'

'Jesus Christ! Are you saying Jack Worms is involved too?'

'He doesn't know it yet. Perhaps he doesn't even need to. Percy suggested it was the perfect cover; a bookshop where papers and manuscripts change hands every day. No one will suspect a thing.'

Monty caught a change in tone. 'Sir Thomas, have you agreed to this?'

'I had no fucking choice, Monty. I'm sorry to say.'

'Everyone has a choice, Sir Thomas. You could report him, even if it meant difficulties for you. Who knows, the king might be so grateful, he'll give you a pardon and you could be freed.'

'Hmm!' For once, Sir Thomas seemed disinclined to respond. Fleetingly, it crossed Monty's mind that his employer had not told him everything. For a man who seemed to know his own mind inside-out and back-to-front, he seemed to have caved in to Percy's request very quickly.

There must be more behind it. He thought he knew Sir Tom well enough now to detect when he was keeping something from him. But how to prise it out of him was another matter.

'As it seems, you've signed me up to this. Can you tell me exactly how it will work since I'm "implicated" as you so worryingly put it?'

'There's very little for you to do,' said Sir Tom with a casual shrug. 'Just collect and deliver some packages to me, and I'll arrange for them to be taken to Greyfriars when the earl's in residence. We're not involved when he's elsewhere. Percy's making other arrangements.'

'So, Sir Percy has some other poor bastards woven into his web?'

'I imagine so, I didn't ask for details. The less we know the better.'

'All the more reason for them to tighten the screw on the rack!' Monty shuddered at the thought.

'Percy will drop the package off at Master Worms' shop and you're to call in there every day on your way here, that is when Lord Warwick's in residence next door.'

'Jack Worms has a right to know what's going on, Sir Tom. Anyway, he'll be very suspicious of Sir Percy given the treatment he received from the man. He'll know he's up to some kind of funny business, he's not stupid.'

'I never thought he was,' said Malory airily, 'I'm just not sure about his mouth running away with him, among his customers that is.'

'I hardly think he'll make it known that he's now up to his neck in treason and that his head could be parted from it.'

'I'm sure he won't. So, if you insist, we'll tell him. Shall you tell him, or shall I?'

'I'll do it. I'll be more – more circumspect than you.'

'Circumspect, a goodly word and one I might incorporate somewhere.'

'Somehow I don't see your knights of the Round Table exercising circumspection, Sir Tom. Like the author, they generally seem less tactful, more tactile.'

'Tactile, that's a new one for me. I'll probably use that too. What does it mean?'

'You're trying to deflect me here, Sir Tom. We were discussing the ramifications –'

'Ramifications, now there's another good –'

And Monty gave up.

***

As Monty expected, Jack Worms' reaction was one of horror as the plan and its means of expedition were explained to him. 'You mean, I'm involved in a plot against King Edward? Me, who's always supported the Yorkists? Whose father fought at Wakefield for the old Duke of York?'

'I didn't know that. What happened to him?'

'He was lucky. Unlike the duke, he survived. But let's get back to this plan of Jasper Percy's. Explain to me again what we're dealing with and what Sir Tom says is my part in it.'

And patiently, Monty went through it once again, this time pointing out their invidious position of already being guilty by association, although having yet done nothing wrong. Hearing it all a second time seemed to make Jack even more anxious and he leaned heavily against the binding-table. 'Is this likely to take place very often? Are we talking daily? Weekly? Monthly?'

'As I understand it, Percy will drop packages off when the Earl of Warwick is in residence in Greyfriars. I've no idea how often. But you're to pass them to me in the shop and no other, even if they come flashing warrants from the Lord Chancellor's office.'

'Jesus Christ!' and Jack crossed himself, 'Is that likely?'

'It will be if we go talking about it. For all our sakes, we must keep our mouths shut. There can be no gossiping with customers. If people ask about Percy – and he is very distinctive, let's face it – then he's become a regular customer for some special commodity which only you can get him. Let's hope the earl makes his stay at Greyfriars short. Sir

Thomas once told me the man spends most of his time on his horse galloping up and down the country.'

'Perhaps, he'll be engaged with the trouble up in York. I hear his brother, Lord Montague, has been sent to put it down.'

'Let's hope so. I have no wish to be involved in this for any longer than can be helped. God knows what's really behind it all. I dread to think!'

'So, I'll wait to hear from Percy with his, er, package and then from you with another, is that right?'

'Indeed it is!' and Monty held out his hand, 'No hard feelings, Jack?'

'This is none of your doing. I resent these so-called great men involving lesser men in their plotting. Look what happened to that poor bastard shoemaker who had his feet burned with coals! I'm sure he didn't deserve that.'

'Who knows! All I know is that Sir Thomas Malory has embroiled me in matters which don't concern me. Until I met him, I was leading a quiet life, many would say dull. But I oversaw my own destiny, at least in my head. It now seems both our fates are in the hands of scoundrels!' and with a rueful smile, he shook his head and took his leave.

***

The following morning, Wednesday 3rd May, having slept very badly, Monty decided to leave for Newgate half-an-hour before his normal time. He had lain in bed worrying over various aspects of the business, not least whether he should confess it all to his priest. The thought made him even more worried. What if the priest thought this so serious, he decided to go to the authorities and report it? What if the seal of the confessional didn't count in sins of treason? But was treason a sin? Or was it simply a political crime? After all, moving against Edward IV would, now, certainly be considered treasonable. But what would it be if Henry VI was returned to the throne? Then Monty's actions wouldn't even count as sedition because he would be on the "right side". At present, confessing all to the priest was extremely risky. Perhaps he could confess directly to God – bypass his agent on earth and make his own absolution. But that was akin to Lollardry, for which he could be burnt at the stake. Profoundly confused, eventually he fell asleep and dreamed that he was passing a package to the pope whilst apologising profusely.

His intention the next morning was to revisit yesterday's conversation with Sir Tom, in case he'd dreamed it, although he knew he hadn't. There seemed to be so many things which could go wrong. He thought it would be wise to ascertain if Sir Thomas viewed the matter with as much trepidation as he did, although in his heart he knew by now the knight's insouciance was immutable.

He reached the prison, where the guard idling at the gate gave him a cheery "Good day" and waved him through. He mounted the stairs and reaching Sir Tom's door, saw it was half open. Coming from it was the distinct sound of a woman's voice – a laughing and coaxing voice, 'Oh Sir Tom, are you asking again? You're a naughty boy!'

'Fuck it, Meg, come on! I can manage –', and at that point, Monty pulled open the door.

The sight of Tom Malory, his hose round his ankles and his shirt disarrayed, his grey withered buttocks heaving in the air, and clasped round his thin shanks and torso, the bare legs and arms of an unidentified body which writhed beneath him. They were perilously occupying the truckle bed which, had it played host to more substantial individuals, would have surely given up and cracked its legs.

Monty stood, mouth agape, in the doorway. Sensing a presence in the room, Sir Tom looked over his shoulder and with a throaty chuckle, said, 'You've come too early!'

A voice of indignation came from the body beneath, 'Never in my life, Sir Tom! I'm a professional.'

Her paramour laughed and said, 'Not you, Meg, not you!'

Having no experience of what was the correct etiquette in such circumstances, Monty prepared to withdraw discreetly, take his leave and seek a draught of fresh air, preferably several miles away. The look of absolute horror on his scribe's face as he backed out of the doorway seemed to initiate in Sir Thomas immediate mischief and he determined to embarrass Monty as much as he was able.

'Don't go! I'm nearly done here.'

'And so am I,' a voice squeaked, and a face struggled to find its way to the surface and out where Monty could see it. It was a brown-eyed, regularly featured visage surrounded by an incredible mop of dark curls, or perhaps not curls at all, but simply hair which stood in want of a good combing, circling its owner's face like a sweep's brush looking for a chimney.

To compound the awkwardness, Pom appeared in the doorway and brushed past Monty with his customary basket of provender. Totally unfazed, he said, 'I see you've come too soon, Monty!'

'We've already played that line, Pom, but I trust you're talking of Mr Pickle here and not me. If not, I resent the implication,' and the two men went off into gales of laughter which discomforted Monty even more.

'And me!' cried Meg, who by this time had extricated herself from Sir Tom and moved from the supine to the upright. As she hastily scrabbled for her shift, breasts awry, she asked, 'Are we all done here, Sir Tom? Sure there are no extras today? I could use the money.'

'No, my little whorelet, I have work to do,' Slapping her backside, he made a move towards the table but, with his hose still round his ankles, he was forced to hop and shuffle to reach a pile of ready money which he placed in her outstretched hands. His flanks and genitals were all exposed and Monty tried to avert his gaze, but became transfixed by the now shrivelled appendages. The last time he had seen a man naked was when his brother and he had decided, on a whim, to take a swim in the local lake. But that was his brother and they had been young men; this was his employer and it was a gross sight. Fortunately for everyone, Sir Thomas began to pull up his hose as Meg made for the door. Monty's attention was then diverted to the woman, and he noted she was a sturdy creature, of medium height and whose face was rather pleasing – open and spirited; he judged her to be about sixteen, although he was no expert in such matters. He surprised himself by having the presence of mind to hold the door open for her and wish her “good day”, at which she giggled and curtsied. He heard her laughing as she ran down the steps and out towards the main gate.

By this time, Sir Thomas was dressed and exploring the contents of Pom’s basket. He selected a slice of cold beef which he wrapped between two pieces of bread and proceeded to gnaw at voraciously. Pom obligingly produced a jug of claret and poured three glasses. ‘Not for me, Mr Appleby,’ said Monty stiffly, ‘It’s too early.’

‘Mr Appleby? Since when has that been the order of things?’ Malory frowned at Monty and chewed heavily on his breakfast. ‘You’re not piqued, are you?’

Monty was silent, feeling cornered. ‘I must say I was taken by surprise. It was certainly not what I expected to find at this time of day.’

‘By “it”, I suppose you mean me fucking my whorelet? Pom was right, you came too early,’ he couldn’t resist it, ‘unlike me!’ he said with a laugh.

‘At ten in the morning, one doesn’t expect to walk into a room and find a man in – in –’

‘In bed fucking a woman? Does it frighten you? I imagine there are a great many men “in bed with a woman” at this time if they have nothing better to do. What finer way to work up an appetite for breakfast. Personally, I’m at my best first thing in the morning. I find a little physical pleasure sharpens my wits, although I admit at my age I require a little sleep in the afternoon. But, never mind that, you’ve come to work, I take it, even though you’re early. That’s very useful. We’ve missed time for the enterprise with this Percy business –’

‘That’s why I came early. I wanted to ask you a few things about this “business”.’

‘I thought we discussed all this yesterday – it’s simple, you collect and deliver – from Master Worms to me and from me to Master Worms. That’s all you need to do.’

‘But what if the authorities already suspect Jasper Percy? Jack Worms seems to think he’s probably known to them as a Lancastrian supporter.’

‘Probably, yes. There are hundreds of them in London, all going about their business and causing no trouble. He’s just another – although his appearance is unfortunate and could draw attention. Never mind that. I’m sure Sir Jasper Percy can take care of himself. Now, to business. This section on –’ and he sat down, picked up his quill and drew a sheet of text to him, squinting at it closely.

But Monty was not to be diverted, ‘I’m sorry, Sir Tom, but I’m extremely put out about this whole conspiracy business and where it might end.’

Sir Tom threw down his quill and stood up, becoming red in the face. ‘Listen, Mr Pickle, I won’t repeat myself. We’re in this whether we like it or not! We can’t go to the authorities and report Percy for fear of being arrested and tortured ourselves. We must grin and bear it – like Sir Lancelot and – and – Sir Tristram –’

‘I keep telling you we’re not in an Arthurian legend, Sir Thomas.’

‘No, we’re in the shit and have to flow with it. Best we just get our heads down and do as we’re asked, quietly and discreetly; that should suit your temperament at least. Now look, I’m on the verge of losing my temper and you wouldn’t want to witness that.’

‘No indeed, Mr Pickle!’ said Pom; having briefly left the room he had now returned, ‘You wouldn’t want to be at the receiving end of one of Sir Thomas’s rages. However, putting that aside, I have some news, something which might put us all out of temper.’

‘What’s that?’ asked Sir Tom sharply.

‘The Neville standard – the bear and ragged staff – is flying from the flagpole in his lodgings next door. The earl will be back in London tomorrow!’

***

Feeling distinctly shifty, and certain there were hundreds of pairs of eyes seeking him out, Monty opened the door of Jack's shop and looked around furtively. Master Worms appeared from the workshop at the back, wiping his hands on his apron, and said perfectly politely and calmly, 'Good day, Mr Pickle, what can I do for you?'

Monty had no idea what his response should be. Considering the shop was empty – not even Dickon Puddledock was in evidence – there was no risk at all of being overheard or overlooked, but he was still extremely nervous; his hands trembled and his voice shook, 'Er, er, have you any news? Anything to say?'

'No, not really. We've had some new inks in – rather fine –'

'Inks? I wasn't thinking about inks.'

'I know you weren't but we must act normally. This spying business requires a certain air of assurance and – and –'

'Shh! Don't talk about "spying"; subterfuge is the word you're looking for I think. We must be underhand and stealthy; not in my nature that! This whole business is a nightmare for me. You must be worried too. If it gets out that we're passing secrets, we'll be in the Tower before you can say – before you can say –'

'Turn the screw three notches, jailer! Yes, I understand that, but all we're doing is passing packages. We've no idea of their contents.'

'I don't know which is worse, not knowing and having to suffer endless torture as they try to stretch it out of us, or knowing and suffering the inevitable punishment for treason after we've caved in and admitted it.'

'That's not going to happen, Monty, not if we're careful. Anyway, you can stop worrying. Nothing came today. There was no sign of Jasper Percy, I certainly wouldn't have missed him if he had been about, not being that tall and with that hair and that voice!'

'You seem remarkably calm about all this, Jack.'

‘We mustn’t be anything else, otherwise people will become suspicious. As Percy rightly said, this is the perfect place to exchange documents. If we don’t know what they contain, we should be all right.’

‘Hmm,’ Monty sighed with relief, ‘Well, if there’s nothing for me to collect, I’ll get off to Newgate. Sir Tom will be waiting for news I’m sure.’

‘Call tomorrow, Monty. My feeling is that Percy will be organising things as we speak and is likely to drop something off today.’

***

The whole morning and early afternoon was taken up with *Le Morte* as it was referred to. Despite distractions, Sir Tom expressed the fruity view that, ‘We’re making good fucking progress.’ In fact, they had reached the point in *The Tale of King Arthur* where the king, Herod-like, thought fit to destroy every baby born to lords and ladies on May Day, and who:

“Were put into a ship to the sea; and some were four weeks old and some less. And so by fortune the ship drove unto a castle and was all riven and destroyed for the most part, save that Mordred was cast up and a good man found him and fostered him until he was fourteen year.”

‘You do seem to be obsessed with killing small children, Sir Tom,’ observed Monty, ‘is it necessary to the plot to drown week-old babies?’

‘You’re getting sentimental again, Mr Pickle. Of course, we need this in the plot. Arthur was forced into this action to save himself. Life’s full of expedient death.’

‘Don’t remind me, Sir Tom, as one who fears for his head.’

‘Please don’t keep mentioning the business until it’s necessary. It’s not a subject for casual conversation and I find it a great distraction. Can we just move on to Two-swords Balin?’

‘In a moment. I agree and there’s nothing casual about it. May I ask if there are things you’re not telling me about Lord Warwick and Sir Jasper Percy?’

Sir Tom heaved a sigh and began to flush pink, ‘Look, Mr Pickle,’ Malory always addressed Monty formally when he was exasperated, ‘When I have any information which directly concerns you or your welfare, I’ll tell you. For now, as far as you are concerned, ignorance is bliss, it’s folly to be wise as they say!’ He picked up his quill and said, ‘I’m starting the next section with:

“After the death of Uther, reigned Arthur…”

‘You’re going to ask me why I have repeated what we already know.’

‘No, actually I wasn’t.’

‘It’s a literary device to wake up the lazy reader and proof reader, who might have drifted off and lost the thread of the plot.’

‘They’re not likely to forget that Arthur’s king. You’ve been writing about his exploits as such for the last forty-odd pages.’

Malory huffed, ‘I’m just following the French version for a time. Their readers evidently have even less powers of concentration than we English. Can we get on?’

Monty realised he was going to get no more out of Sir Thomas on the subject of Lord Warwick and Jasper Percy, so bowed to his employer’s wishes. The morning’s work continued in a quiet and studious atmosphere; Pom, making himself scarce, the two men remained undisturbed. The story of Balin, the damsel, the two swords and the Lady of the Lake began to take shape under Monty’s quill, following Sir Tom’s direction.

They stopped for dinner at the point in the story where Balin “smote off the head of the Lady of the Lake”.

‘A suitable place to stop,’ observed Malory, ‘We will consider how to express the outcome after a couple of glasses of wine.’

The three men shared a good meal washed down with some passable liquor. Monty had by now become used to midday drinking and found he rather enjoyed it; to the point where his spirits rose when he heard the jug being filled from the roundlet. Any qualms he had about sharing pirated goods had long since disappeared. By two o'clock, as the Greyfriars' bell sounded, Malory said he was weary and would take a nap. Pom asked Monty if he would stay and play Hasard with him, but his friend was in no mood to while away the time at dice and said he would take his leave. On his way home, he was determined to call in on Jack Worms and see if there had been any developments. There had not and relieved but apprehensive of what might be there the following morning, Monty walked back to Number 3, Stinking Lane, where he spent a nervous evening and another sleepless night.

***

There was one customer in Worms' Books as Monty entered the following morning. He hung about waiting for the man to complete his purchase, which seemed to the scribe to be a shipping order for paper and inks, and took a vast amount of time. Eventually, Jack and his customer shook hands on their deal, and the man walked out of the shop into the warm May weather.

'Thank goodness! I thought he'd never go. Is there any news? Is there anything for us?'

'There is, Monty. I have it in the back, along with some money for you. Sir Jasper seems to be a man of his word, he's left you a crown as he promised and says there'll be more next time.'

'Blood money!' said Monty, 'I'm not sure I should take it.'

'I'll leave you to struggle with your conscience over that. Talking of consciences, are you going to confess this to the priest?'

'Are you?'

'I've thought long and hard about it. You do realise we share the same father confessor. If we both confess the same thing, he'll know there's a conspiracy between us – which would make it worse if we're caught. We could never back each other up by concocting the same story.'

'I hadn't thought of that, but I have already made up my mind not to confess. Who knows, Henry Lancaster might be back on the throne next week – the way things change so quickly – then we wouldn't have committed treason at all, but have been loyal subjects to the new king.'

'Good thinking. I agree, we should both keep our mouths shut. Anyway, I don't trust priests. Now, I'll go and get the package.' He disappeared into the workshop, and almost immediately, emerged carrying a small pack of papers bound with string and heavily sealed. 'Here you are; to be delivered into the hands of Sir Thomas Malory and no other.'

Monty took the parcel with a shaking hand and immediately placed it in his leather bag. Once it was out of sight, he felt a little better, but still dreaded the walk from Paternoster Row to the prison, for who knew what spies there were about? The word may have already got out that he was spying for the Lancastrians – although he wasn't, since he considered himself neutral in all these matters. That wouldn't save his head if he was caught.

'I'll go straight to Newgate and hope no one follows me!'

'I've seen no strangers hereabouts, apart from Jasper Percy who arrived here about nine o'clock and left immediately after he'd delivered the letters.' Monty headed for the door,

'Don't forget your money!' shouted Jack and threw him the coin. Monty caught it and put it in his jerkin pocket, still uncertain as to whether he should keep it or not.

Walking towards Newgate Street, he felt as though his leather bag weighed a ton and was as hot as smouldering coals. He was so self-conscious, he kept his head unnaturally erect and his eyes fixed on the gatehouse of the prison as it loomed nearer. In this position, he failed to see three armed soldiers coming up Paternoster Row from the Cheapside end and approaching Jack Worms' shop. When they arrived, two went inside and closed the door behind them; the third stationed himself in front of the door, his halberd across his chest, and standing legs apart barring all would-be entrants.

***

Monty climbed the stairs slowly and heavily. As he neared the top, he heard voices coming from Malory's room and breathed a sigh of relief when he realised it was only men speaking.

'No whorelets today?' He knocked cautiously on the door which was opened by Pom.

'Come in, Monty! We have a visitor and he wants to meet you.'

The small room seemed to be crowded with bodies and as Monty perceived, many roundlets of wine which took up a great deal of the available space. Sitting in one of Malory's two chairs was a large man, clearly of some height when standing and with a bulky girth. He had a completely bald head, an open, friendly face, weather-worn and with skin lined with great age. Monty estimated he must have been at least seventy, but the man rose to his feet with an agility which defied longevity.

Malory said, 'Ah! Mr Pickle, let me introduce Lord John, First Baron Wenlock, Knight of the Garter; one whom I count as among my most honourable friends! Lord John, this is Mr Montmorency Pickle, my secretary.'

Monty started. He had never been addressed as such before and wondered what Sir Tom meant by it exactly. He bowed as low as he thought it correct before a First Baron, that is almost touching the floor with his nose.

Sir Tom took him by the elbow and pulled him upright, 'No need to grovel, Monty. We're all friends here, isn't that so, John?'

'Indeed it is, Tom. I understand you are of great assistance to Sir Thomas in his enterprise, Mr Pickle?'

'I – I do try to help, my lord.'

'I believe there are other ways you're helping us?'

'"Us"?' Monty picked up the nuance immediately. *What does he mean "us"?* he thought, but did not say it.

Sir Tom intervened, 'Perhaps we should all have a drink before we settle to discussion. I'm sure we could all do with one, eh, Monty?'

'If you say so, but it is rather early for me.' Sir Tom glanced at Lord Wenlock and raised his eyebrows as much as to say, "I told you he was something of a milksop!"

'God's bones, man! We've important matters to discuss. I'd have thought it was never too early to lubricate our words with suitable liquor. With his usual generosity, Lord Wenlock has brought with him six roundlets of excellent wine from his large stock in Calais.'

Monty did a quick mental calculation, *One roundlet – eighteen gallons – 144 pints; six times one roundlet – 864 pints. Jesus Christ! Where will they store it all and how long to get through that quantity?* he thought, but did not say it.

'I knew your own stocks must need replenishing, since you received the last consignment some month ago. As I was in London, I thought I'd bring them personally,' and he waved his hand towards the roundlets on the floor and stacked against the wall.

Taking a glass of rich-red Burgundy from Pom, Monty shuffled from one foot to another feeling distinctly out of place. The two men opposite him exuded the confidence which came from their mutually privileged background and status, increasing his feeling of inadequacy. But after a few gulps of Wenlock's excellent wine, he started to feel more comfortable and seated himself by dividing the cheeks of his buttocks on the top of two roundlets, stretching out his legs to keep himself balanced.

'Let's get to the point,' said Sir Tom, 'Was anything left with Master Worms this morning, Monty?'

With great care lest the roundlets toppled beneath him, Monty shuffled to reach his bag and took out the bundle of papers.

'No trouble, I take it?' asked Wenlock, 'Did you see Percy at all?'

'No. Master Worms had the letters safely in his workshop and just handed them to me. You have them exactly as Sir Percy left them.' He spoke with some asperity, wanting to make it quite clear that he was at no time tempted to break the seal and read the contents. Lord Wenlock took the papers from Sir Tom and to Monty's disappointment, put them away in a large pocket in his robe.

'These will go immediately to Lord Warwick who's waiting for them. I'd like to stay and talk with you, Mr Pickle, but it is a matter of urgency that I now return to Greyfriars. Perhaps, at some time soon we can meet on more relaxed terms? I'm sure there are questions you would like to ask me and I would like to know something of your life.'

Monty was immediately flattered by this invitation and was suitably self-effacing in his reply, 'My life would be extremely uninteresting to a man who has achieved such a high status, a diplomat and soldier, my lord. It must have been – be –' he corrected himself, not wishing the man to think he was writing him off as a dotard, 'very – very –'

'Fucking exciting are the words you're searching for, Monty, Eh, Lord John?' Monty flinched as usual when Sir Tom's language became ribald. He wondered how this senior nobleman would react to such barrack-room speech. But then, of course, Lord Wenlock had been in active service all his life and would have lived among soldiers for decades; his reply confirmed it.

'Indeed, Tom, it has been "fucking exciting" at times, also "fucking nerve-wracking" and "fucking dangerous". But never underestimate the simple life, Mr Pickle. Men like you are keeping the country stable and believe me we're going to need all the stability we can muster. There's a wave of great turbulence coming and we're all involved, whether we like it or not.'

Monty didn't like the sound of the phrase "we're involved whether or not"; use of the noun "turbulence" was also worrying. He opened his mouth to ask Lord Wenlock what he meant, but Sir Tom forestalled him and said, 'Well, Lord John, good to see you. I suppose you'll be back quite soon?'

'Once Lord Warwick has read these and decided on his reply, I'll bring it to you for delivery by the now established means. We're expected to ride to Windsor to join the king in a few days, but our base will remain Greyfriars.'

'Very well. We wish you good day and please pass on my regards to Lord Warwick.'

'I will indeed,' and with that he was out of the door and on his way down the stairs.

'Good man! Good man!' Malory sighed.

'How long have you known him?' asked Monty. 'He seems to be well-acquainted with you, Sir Tom.'

'Almost a decade.'

'How did you meet? Under what circumstances did you become friends?'

'Not now, Monty. Let's save that for another day. We've jumped the first hurdle safely, and will wait and see what the next one will be when the reply comes; my guess, that will be tomorrow. Now, let's get to work,' he picked up a sheaf of papers, 'As I remember it, Balin had just struck off the head of the Lady of the Lake and was in deep trouble with Arthur.'

Deep trouble, how appropriate, thought Monty, but did not say it, 'Yes, according to my notes we have got to Sir Lanceor, son of the King of Ireland, who was an orgulous knight.'

'Good word, "orgulous" – means proud you know.'

'Yes, you told me yesterday. Merlin is just about to tell of Lanceor and how he asked King Arthur that he be allowed to go on a quest to find Balin and avenge the Lady of the Lake for the loss of her head.'

'Yes, that was it. And Arthur says:

"'Do your best,' said Arthur, 'I am right wroth with Balin; I would he were quit of the despite that he hath done me and to my court.'"

'You know, Monty, there's something in that which resonates with me. When I read those words aloud, it reminds me of King Edward and the Earl of Warwick.'

'In what way?'

'Just the way things are, Monty, just the way things are!' and he would say no more.

***

Monty felt it was incumbent on him to report to Jack that the mission had been achieved. Not only had the letters been safely delivered, but into the hands of the great Lord Wenlock himself who would see they were handed directly to Lord Warwick. With more jauntiness in his step than he had shown hours earlier, he made his way round to Paternoster Row. To his disappointment, Worms' Books was shut and there was no sign of the owner, or his apprentice. He wondered where they might be; it was still within the shop's trading hours and unlike the owner to close his shop completely. He decided to walk round to Jack's lodgings, a house in Gutter Lane, off Cheapside. *He must have decided to take some time off,* he thought, *I'll stroll round and bring him up to date with events.* As he walked the length of Paternoster Row, he couldn't help but notice that other shops seemed to be closed, and through the doorways of those that were open, apprentices could be seen overly busy with mops and brooms.

'Perhaps it's a stationer's ritual spring-clean,' was the only explanation he could offer to himself.

Within a few minutes, he was picking his way through the filth of Gutter Lane. Half-way down, he was outside the door of a shabby building with a large upper storey overhanging the street. Knocking on the door, he waited for some time before it opened a crack and a voice whispered, 'Who is it?'

'Is that you Jack? It's Monty, Monty Pickle. Are you ill?' There was a shuffling and movement of furniture. *Jesus! He's barricaded himself in,* he thought. Slowly, the obstructions were moved away and the door opened wide enough for Monty to squeeze through, 'God's Bones, Jack! Whatever's the matter?'

'Were you followed? Is there anyone about looking suspicious?'

‘No, not at all. What’s happened? You look scared to death.’

‘I look as I feel, Monty, believe me. Did you walk past the shop? Was there any sight of Dickon?’

‘Yes and no. But Paternoster Row seemed to be a hive of extraordinary activity. The shopkeepers seemed to be doing a great deal of clearing up. What’s all that about?’ Monty looked round the room and noted the presence of a broadsword lying on a table, unsheathed, rusty and notched. ‘My father’s,’ explained Jack seeing Monty glance at it, ‘I thought I might need it.’

‘It’s hardly adequate to splice an apple!’ observed Monty, ‘What are you going to do with it, wave it about and hope for the best?’

Jack ignored the jeer, ‘Almost straightway after you left, three soldiers arrived, two entered the shop and one stood outside guarding the place. They were fully armed – halberds, short swords and mail. I was completely stunned.’

‘So, what did they want? Surely, they weren’t after searching the place for our documents? Christ! Are we to conclude the authorities know about Jasper and –’

‘No! And I thank Jesus Christ for it,’ and Jack crossed himself and muttered a short “Ave Maria”.

‘Who were they? Who sent them?’

‘The Lord Chancellor’s men. Stillington sent them.’

‘Jesus! No wonder you were scared.’

‘The fact that they came into the shop immediately after you left, I could only think the two things were connected – their visit and Percy’s letters.’

‘And you say they aren’t?’

‘No. They were looking for something altogether different and a right mess they made of the shop too, turning everything over and going through every piece of paper they could find.’

‘And what were they looking for?’

‘You won’t believe it! I couldn’t myself. They showed me a paper with foul accusations against one of the highest in the land written on it.’

‘Yes, so there are always plenty of those posted on standards and ale-house doors.’

‘Not like this!’

‘So, what did it say?’ Even the equable Monty Pickle was becoming impatient.

‘That King Edward can’t be king because he’s a bastard!’

‘A bastard! Wherever has that come from?’

‘They say that his mother Lady Cecily, Duchess of York, had an illicit liaison with a lusty English archer, one Blabourne, when she accompanied the duke while he was campaigning in France. I managed to pull off a copy from a post, one they’d overlooked. It’s scurrilous. Listen, here’s a taste:

“Question: Where does an English long bowman store his arrow?

Answer: In a duchess’s quiver.

Question: What happens when he takes it out?

Answer: She still has a quiverful.”

‘I won’t go on. It’s also said the dates and everything fit the story, according to gossip anyway.’

‘Surely, no one will believe that of the duchess! A more pious woman couldn’t be found.’

‘Guilt! That’s what they’re saying. She’s spent a lifetime making amends for her “lustful sin”, to quote the paper.’

‘But why did they come to you?’

‘It’s obvious. Such writings must have an origin somewhere. They were looking for more copies, and the place where the paper came from and copies made. You’ve no idea how frightened we were, Dick Addlepate and me! He wet himself again.’

‘Where is he now? There was no sign of him when I went to the shop.’

‘I left him clearing up and told him not to open the door to anyone. When they came in, they didn’t say anything at first, and I was sure the game was up and I’d be carted off to the Tower. But then, as they were ransacking the shop, they showed me the paper and asked me if I knew who’d copied it or had I done any myself. If not, had I provided materials? Of course, I said "no" but they carried on – paper, ink everywhere; at least they stayed away from the barrels of glue – didn't want to get themselves sticky!'

'I'm sure you weren't the only one searched. As I came down Paternoster Row, I saw other stationers cleaning up their premises. They must have all been visited too.'

'Thank Christ for that,' and Jack crossed himself again. 'It seems it has no connection with – with our business,' and his voice fell to a whisper.

'Indeed not and I share your relief. I think it would be a good idea to return to your shop, business as usual. If you appear to be unusually put-out by this visit, it might cause suspicion that you really have something to hide.'

'I think you speak sense, Monty. Will you walk back with me and examine the damage? I don't know where we would go for recompense?'

'There will be none. Lord Stillington will say it was on the king's business. The soldiers had warrants, I suppose?'

'Well, one of them waved a paper in front of me, but I didn't have chance to examine it thoroughly. There seemed to be a seal dangling from it. I had to take their word for it since they had halberds in their hands. I wasn't prepared to argue.'

'Neither were the other stationers from what I saw. Let's go back, you can compare notes with your book-binding fraternity. That should give you comfort that this is a matter of sedition and rumour, nothing to do with Jasper Percy and his plots.'

They walked back together and as they came into Paternoster Row, Jack stopped occasionally to speak to other stationers, all of whom told of similar treatment by Stillington's men. Everyone was grumbling about the damage and questioning how they might obtain reparation. When they arrived at the door of Worms' Books, at first Jack couldn't gain access. True to his orders, Dickon Puddledock refused to let him in, until Jack cussed so vehemently and threatened dire treatment, which the lad immediately recognised as peculiar to his master, that he opened the door. As they entered, Jack shook his head. Monty could see the string around reams of paper had been cut and their contents scattered over the wooden floor. There were pools of ink from bottles which had been upturned in the search. Dickon Puddledock had gone back to half-heartedly pushing a broom about with little effect. As his master came in, he wiped his nose on his sleeve and quickened his pace,

'You don't seem to have made much progress, Dickon!' observed Jack with a scowl. 'Have you been able to assess the damage?'

'Not really, sir, it's taking me all my time to collect up the paper. What should I do about the ink?'

'Mop it up, we'll have to write it off and order more. This is going to cost me real money, Monty. I'm furious, the business was showing a good profit too.'

'Well, at least you'll have money to cover the costs then,' said Monty, 'I imagine others in the trade aren't so lucky.'

'Well, that's their misfortune. I had plans for that money.'

Monty thought it would be useful to move away from Jack's problems with profit and loss, 'What do you make of this rumour, the accusations in the ballad?'

'I don't know. There must be a purpose to it, which means someone important is behind it. It must be the Lancastrians. You don't suppose Jasper Percy has a hand in it? God's teeth, I hope he's not dragging us into seditious libel as well as treason!' Monty looked anxiously at Dickon and put his fingers to his lips to shut Jack up.

'Careful what you're saying!' he mouthed.

Fortunately, Dickon seemed to inhabit a world of his own as he mechanically and ineffectively pushed papers about at the end of his broom; Jack nodded his understanding.

Monty wanted to get away and think things through. He wondered if he should visit Sir Tom, and tell him what was happening, but he knew the man would be taking his afternoon nap and not want to be disturbed. He thought he might chance a visit in the evening, but then caution made him think again. There was a good chance Sir Tom would have a whore with him. He turned his thoughts to Pom. When Sir

Tom was "resting" in the late afternoon, John Appleby usually went back to his lodging for an hour or so. He might be there now.

***

'This is an unexpected pleasure, Monty! Come in, I'm just about to eat, why don't you join me.'

Suddenly aware he's had nothing to eat since the morning, Monty nodded, 'Thank you Pom, I'd be grateful for something.'

The "something" turned out to be a substantial early supper – meat and cheese, a game pie and sweetmeats. 'We always live well when Lord Wenlock has visited!'

'I'm very intrigued as to the great friendship he shows towards Sir Thomas and how it has come about.'

'A long story and perhaps better told during our Sunday afternoon meeting. We are going to resume, I hope?'

'Do you think it's appropriate? At this time, with – with –'

'With what I call the "PB"?'

'"PB"?'

'Percy Business.'

'Yes.'

'You really are so little involved, I can't see why your life shouldn't go on as normal; neither can Sir Tom. He's very keen on the idea of you writing his life story. Keeps on about it!'

'I'm not sure I'm in the right frame of mind, Pom. Particularly after what's happened today.'

'Why, what's happened today?'

'You obviously haven't heard. Lord Stillington –'

'The Lord Chancellor?'

'Yes, he sent his men to raid all the stationers' shops in Paternoster Row this morning. Master Jack Worm's shop was first on the list.' Monty proceeded to relate the events and how terrified Jack Worms had been, considering his involvement with "PB". 'I wondered if you've heard anything about these rumours concerning the legitimacy of King Edward and where they might have come from. Has Sir Tom said anything? He seems to have friends in high places?'

Pom was unusually silent for several moments, 'We had heard something. Lord Wenlock mentioned it when he visited this morning, but I think he would be surprised to know the king has taken it seriously. These sorts of libels are not uncommon.'

'Not about the king, surely? Why would someone put this kind of thing about?'

'Someone or some people. It's a political device to unsettle people's minds. This accusation is particularly sharp because it would mean Edward Plantagenet is not of the "full family" – never mind a duchess for a mother, the fact of having a common soldier for a father and born out of wedlock would eliminate him from all claim to the throne. It seems particularly hard on the duchess. If she demeans herself by denying it, it looks as though she has some knowledge of what's behind the accusation. If she remains silent, then people will think she's guilty anyway. There's an expression "mud sticks", and the king can only take a very hard line with the rumour and crush whoever is behind it – if he can catch them.'

'Are the Lancastrians likely to be the culprits?'

'Who can say; best not to speculate.' Monty sensed unease in Pom and although he would have like to discuss it more, suddenly felt pursuing the subject would not be productive. In fact, Pom moved the conversation on rapidly by asking general questions about Jack Worms' welfare and whether the soldiers' actions would cost him much. 'It must have come as a blow to him and the other stationers. I imagine they aren't best pleased and will consult their Guild about any action they can take for redress.'

'Jack didn't mention the Stationers' Guild but certainly he's talking of recompense, although he's doubtful there'll be any. Those who have made enquiries have been told it was "official king's business, carried out under a warrant".'

‘Isn’t it always!’ said Pom with a smile, ‘It’s a pity Jack’s not here with you. I have something which would have cheered him up. Lord Wenlock has brought with him from Calais a rare treat: pure French brandy-wine. Have you ever tried it? You’ll never taste better,’ and with that, he brought the conversation to a close.

***

‘So Pom, Monty Pickle and Jack Worms are aware of these rumours?’

‘As is all of London, Sir Tom.’ Malory and John Appleby were taking breakfast together the following morning as Pom related the details of Monty’s visit the evening before.

‘You said nothing of their source, I hope?’

‘Certainly not, sir. I personally want to keep an arm’s length from the whole business.’

‘That’s not going to be easy, knowing what we both know.’

‘Mr Pickle asked me whether Lord Wenlock would be visiting again.’

‘What did you tell him?’

‘That it is unlikely as he rides with the earl to Windsor today and doesn’t know when they will return to Greyfriars.’

‘These are such fucking unstable times, Pom. All this trouble in the north.’

‘I believe Lord Warwick has been summoned to Windsor to report on the situation to the king.’

‘Well, Yorkshire’s far away – and so much the better for us. It’s probably unlikely that Jasper Percy will be forwarding any further letters while the earl’s absent from here – even though he’s only a day’s ride away. It will be a relief that we’re not to act as go-between for that carrot-topped caitiff for a while.’

‘Can I ask if you have any knowledge of what those letters contain, sir?’

‘Best you don’t know, Pom, for your own safety.’

Pom was not comforted by that statement. He knew he was up to his neck in Sir Tom's affairs and would not escape the king's inquisitor if any suspicions fell on his master.

'There is one piece of good news. Lord Wenlock, may God bless his good soul, has promised to ask Lord Warwick to intercede with the king on my behalf.'

'To be released?'

'No, that will never happen. But I might be given leave to walk about the city for short periods, under escort, of course, but it would give me a change of scene. I've been shut up here for a year and although it has suited my purpose to complete *Le Morte*, it's becoming irksome not to be able to feel regular sun on my face. Remember, we've always enjoyed the outdoor life, Pom!'

'We certainly have, Sir Tom!'

'What I really want to do is go down to Southwark and visit the Stews, have a hot perfumed bath and be rubbed down by the ladies there,' and he gave a leering wink.

'I get your meaning, sir.'

'You know, with this trade war we're waging with Burgundy, their nationals are right out of favour. I've heard, the Flemish women who've tended the Stews for generations have, for their own safety, been replaced by English women, such is the hostility towards all Flemings, all foreigners if it comes to that.'

'The streets are certainly dangerous for them, sir, and for the rest of us. Are you sure you want to be abroad in them? I suppose you'll not be allowed to go armed?'

'No, but I'll be well protected with a guard and you can arm yourself. We have to consider that a man soaking in a bathtub and being sponged by a comely woman is probably at his most disadvantaged!'

'Indeed, sir,' and Pom wondered how he would be able to take advantage of Sir Tom's licence to roam and enjoy the comfort of a good hot bath.

'This talk of "comely women" has made me itch. Send down to Gropecunt Lane and ask Meg to come up. I need something to take my mind off our current business, which weighs heavily on me, Pom, very heavily indeed!'

***

'Sir Thomas delights in calling him "Fuckingham Buckingham" but his full title was Humphrey Stafford, 1st Duke of Buckingham, 6th Earl of Stafford and Knight of the Garter. Dead of course – executed after the Battle of Northampton in the year '60.'

'So why this great antipathy towards his grace?'

Monty Pickle and John Appleby were spending Sunday afternoon together in Monty's lodgings in Stinking Lane. It was 8th July, a month after the ransacking of Jack Worm's shop and three weeks since Sir Jasper Percy had left his last package for delivery to the Earl of Warwick. Lord Warwick and Lord Wenlock were by now on their way to Calais, according to Sir Thomas Malory's intelligence, so there was unlikely to be any more covert action required by either Monty or Jack – for the time being at least. A fact which made them both significantly more cheerful.

"You can get on with my story, Monty!" Sir Tom had said, more cheerful than he had seemed for some time. This was not only because Percy's looming presence had disappeared and his noble friends had sailed for Calais, but because Sir Tom had been granted leave "to go abroad under escort for four hours a week" by the king. The earl himself had successfully craved the king's clemency for the prisoner who, as he pointed out, had still not been tried for any crime.

'Four hours of bliss in the Stews, Pom. You have no idea how fucking magical it is – like – like – I don't know what it's like; even I don't have the words. But those hands, Pom, those hands! What she does with the soap is not to be decently described; it's even better when she loses it! I certainly couldn't put that in the *Le Morte*!'

So after some weeks' absence, Pom was back with Monty trying to piece together the significant moments in Malory's life, with which the scribe could continue to weave a coherent account.

'As I remember, we broke off after I told you how Sir Philip Chetwynd, Sir Tom's cousin, had remonstrated with Sir Tom over the Smythe business, but mellowed and assisted him in becoming a Knight of the Shire.'

Monty looked at his notes, 'Yes, that's as far as we got. So, what happened then?'

'Something I didn't mention was that Sir Philip was part of Lord Humphrey's affinity and was very loyal to the Earl of Stafford, as he was at the time. That meant that, as Sir Philip's close kin, Sir Tom was seen as an important man in Warwickshire, not only because he was a Knight of the Shire but because he owned land. Unfortunately, the land produced less than half the income required for knightly status – £40.'

'But you said that Sir Philip Chetwynd gave Sir Tom an annual income with which he could maintain himself as a knight.'

'Indeed, but that was after the £40 we stole from Thomas Smythe went into the pot to pay for Sir Tom's knighthood in the first place.'

'I see. But it still doesn't explain Sir Tom's hatred of Buckingham.'

'I'm coming to that. A year after the Smythe affair, in '44, Humphrey Stafford was created first Duke of Buckingham. Five years later, young Henry Beauchamp, first and last Duke of Warwick, died, and was succeeded by the present earl, Lord Richard Neville. Now it's impossible to have two cocks crowing on the same dung-hill, and there was instant rivalry between Buckingham and Warwick for precedence in the midland counties. As I told you, the Malorys had long-standing connections with Buckingham, but more profitable ones with the Duke of Warwick and when he died, Sir Tom received a pension from him of £4 15s. When Richard Neville became Earl of Warwick, he continued to honour it and still does. Sir Tom has a great deal of respect and admiration for the earl, which we will come to by and by.'

‘So, how did this rivalry affect how Sir Tom saw the Duke of Buckingham? I’m still not clear.’

‘You’re almost as impatient as Sir Tom, Monty. We have to take this slowly as it’s complicated.’

‘There must be a simple way to tell it. Feuds generally start with a single incident, not a general feeling of antipathy.’

‘True enough, but it’s difficult to pinpoint one single event in this story. There were antecedents.’

‘Good, perhaps we can get to one of them.’

‘Malory says it all started over the Harcourt affair.’

‘And what was that?’

Pom consulted a small notebook in which he had faithfully recorded major events of his life which was so closely bound to Sir Tom’s. ‘In the year ’47, Richard Stafford of Grafton in Worcestershire, kinsman of Buckingham, was killed in a fight by Sir Robert Harcourt of Stanton Harcourt in Oxfordshire. Robert was a very close friend of Sir Tom, but this was a particularly bloody attack; Harcourt “stove in the man’s head with a great stroke of Stafford’s own sword”, according to the indictment. It’s a description worthy of *Le Morte*!’

‘And what was the fight about?’

‘Long standing grievances over a woman I believe, a matter of honour, Harcourt maintained. But his action produced a particularly vicious response from Lord Buckingham, who immediately took a goodly number of soldiers, and chased Harcourt and his men, including Sir Tom and myself, into Oxfordshire. They caught up with us in Stanton Harcourt and set fire to the church where we’d taken sanctuary – we all escaped through the vestry door; it was fortunate it had been left unlocked. Personally, I think that was the root cause of Sir Tom’s hatred for the duke – that he was prepared to burn a dozen men without a thought. He knew we were in there but didn’t hesitate to give the order. His soldiers then proceeded to ransack Sir Robert’s manor and did much damage – the place was almost burnt out. Anyone involved on Harcourt’s side was immediately in bad grace with his grace. Like all great men, Buckingham held loyalty to him and his house above everything.'

'So what did Buckingham do? Have Sir Tom arrested?'

'You might have thought he would but perversely at this point, wider events took over. Buckingham's priorities changed and suddenly he needed all the support he could get in parliament. This was to get rid of the over-mighty subject, the Duke of Suffolk. Lord Humphrey, therefore, had Sir Tom elected to his safe seat of Great Bedwyn in Wiltshire.'

'That seems strange, if Sir Tom had upset him so much?'

'This was a time of complicated and vicious politics – who knows what was going on in the duke's mind. Sir Tom became tied into the duke's scheming again – for a short while – but I know the Harcourt business continued to grate on him. Sir Robert and Sir Tom maintained close contact, even joining forces to take some Leicestershire men to court over land deals. I believe, Sir Robert egged Sir Tom on to the next and most remarkable event in this tale – but with other more significant figures.'

'Who were?'

'For next time!'

'Why do you always break off at the most interesting point?'

'The art of good story-telling, Mr Pickle, as Sir Tom tells me: "Always leave them wanting more!"'

***

The weeks between Pom's visits to Number 3, Stinking Lane continued as normal. Saturday afternoons were now taken up with Malory's visit to the Stews, carefully escorted by a prison guard and sometimes accompanied by Pom – "for a bath, not casual congress" – he would insist when Monty enquired.

They were making good headway with *Le Morte D'Arthur,* and had reached a point in the story where Monty was reintroduced to the characters of Sir Lancelot of the Lake and Sir Tristram de Lyons.

'We have some background to fill in before we get to either's full story, Monty,' explained Sir Tom. 'We haven't finished with Sir Balin yet, who does great deeds for Arthur in North Wales against King Rience. We also come to Merlin's prophecy that Balin will strike the "dolorous stroke". I'm particularly pleased with that description; it rolls round the tongue sweetly – like a maiden's –'

'Let me stop you there, Sir Tom,' said Monty, holding up his hand and turning his head away. He was by now well use to Malory's predilection for unsavoury references to a lady's nether-regions. 'Can we just stay with the script? I grant you "the dolorous stroke" will, I'm sure, become a memorable phrase, but shall we move on?' Over the weeks since he first began the task, Monty felt he had successfully tamed Sir Tom into concentrating on the matter in hand. The knight's digressions had become less intrusive and he felt the work was taking shape well.

Life for Sir Tom remained as it had always done, without any seeming hope for release. No lawyers visited, no writs were served and there were certainly no appearances at the court of the King's Bench. However, Malory remained unperturbed; as he said, 'Where else would I find such peace and quiet to finish my *magnum opus*. Who will disturb me here? I think I shall see out my days in Newgate, God willing.'

As far as events outside the prison were concerned, Malory was kept in regular touch with those by means of one of Lord Wenlock's servants, who made brief and occasional visits to Newgate with letters or verbal reports of happenings across the Channel.

At first, these were general matters concerning the sea-crossing, life in Calais and general gossip. Monty asked Malory why Lord Wenlock, a busy man, took it upon himself to keep a poor prisoner informed of his doings. 'It seems very generous of him to give you so much of his time in this way, Sir Tom. That and all the gifts you receive from him. He must hold you in some esteem.'

'Why does he bother with a fucking old reprobate like me, is what you really want to ask, Monty.'

‘If you say so, sir.’

‘Lord Wenlock and I have a long history. Indeed, we’ve fought battles side by side; more than that I’m not prepared to say, at this particular moment anyway. Now, can we get back to the Castle Terrable and Arthur’s battle against King Lot? I like King Lot of the Orkneys, I consider him an honourable man. He reminds me of –’ he stopped. ‘But no more digressions, Mr Pickle. Write as I dictate:

“‘Alas,’ said King Lot, ‘I am ashamed, for by my default there is many a worshipful man slain, for and we had been together there had been none host under heaven that had been able to have matched with us.’”’

King Lot’s right: strength through unity, Monty! The old Aesop fable about the bundle of sticks comes to mind. Let’s hope that lesson has been learned in certain quarters.’ But again he refused to explain this enigmatic desire.

***

Monty looked forward to his Sunday afternoons. Until he had become so well acquainted with Malory and John Appleby, this time had been spent working on dry legal or church documents; a lonely existence. His only social activity had been at Mass in the morning and his weekly confession, which was hardly worth the bother since his level of sin was so low he often thought himself “in credit”.

Now, as the time came for Pom to visit, he busied himself setting out the small table with glasses and wine – the same bottle appeared and reappeared each week, since Pom always brought at least two with him and insisted he opened them, ‘Save that one for yourself, Monty. Sir Tom has plenty.’ Monty had long since worked out that this was a polite gesture on Pom’s part to avoid drinking an unpalatable vintage; he had also given up feeling any embarrassment.

'Now, we have reached a point in Sir Tom's story when things really "hot up" as the young bucks in the Inns of Court would have it. Remember the tale of Sir Robert Harcourt?'

'Indeed, how he stove in the head of Richard Stafford and Lord Buckingham took his revenge.'

'At this time, as I mentioned, there was great rivalry between the Duke of Buckingham and the new Earl of Warwick – both anxious to make their mark. As Sir Tom put it, "It's a matter of who can piss highest up the tree". My master's instincts were with Lord Warwick – because of the pension he was being paid and the vicious attack by Buckingham on his friend's manor. I wasn't privy to all the details, but, following a "request to visit" from Warwick Castle, Sir Tom returned and summoned together myself and twenty-five others: a mixed bunch of gentlemen, yeomen farmers and labourers. Sir Tom told us he had been commissioned to waylay, and kill the Duke of Buckingham for crimes and misdemeanours he had committed against "certain noblemen and gentry, including me".'

'An execution?'

'Most certainly, and it shows the level of loyalty Sir Tom achieved from his friends and neighbours, and the trust he had in them. We were all sworn to secrecy and at the time none of us knew the identity of the commissioner of the deed. I found out later who it was.'

'And who was it?'

'The Earl of Warwick, of course.'

'Was Harcourt among this group of executioners?'

'No, it was mostly local Warwickshire men loyal to the new earl.'

'So, what happened?'

'On 4th January in the year '50 – a bitterly cold day as I remember – we hid up in the woods around Combe Abbey in Warwickshire, waiting for the duke who we knew was to visit the abbot. Our intelligence was good and along came Humphrey Stafford all unawares, but unfortunately for us, with a unit of fifty or so men. We had less numbers, but did have surprise on our side. Most of our men were in the trees ready to drop down on the duke, and despatch him there and then. But when they saw the small army he had brought with him, they changed their minds and remained where they were, trying desperately to hide themselves. Unfortunately, being winter, the trees were bare and despite the precaution of us all wearing indistinguishable jerkins, we were spotted and the alarm raised. The duke, realising an ambush but not knowing he had the advantage of numbers, chose to avoid a skirmish, and ordered his unit to wheel about and retreat.'

'So did the duke know that Sir Tom was behind the ambush?'

'Not, 'til one of our men sold us out many months later and gave him our names. Sir Tom was then a wanted man.'

'An outlaw?'

'No, he'd not been tried and found guilty of any crime against the king, but Buckingham was after his blood. Humphrey Stafford had a very bad temper. But there were other attempts on the duke's life which had nothing to do with Sir Tom. That same year, eight members of Lord Ferrer's affinity banded together to assault him; I think it concerned debts – certainly money was involved. Buckingham must have been ready for them because they were all caught and indicted of the crime the following year. He was an unpopular man. Later that year, Sir Tom and I laughed 'til our sides might split when we heard how a hundred armed man had raided Buckingham's deer park in Kent. It was said they had long beards and had painted their faces with charcoal – claiming they were "servants of the queen of the fairies". I have no idea what that was all about, but I'm sure the duke was not as amused as we were!'

'So, what happened to Sir Tom? Was he arrested? What happened to the traitor? Was he found out? Was Sir Tom still a member of parliament?'

'Too many questions, Monty!' laughed Pom. 'The traitor was dealt with the way all informers are – he had his tongue cut out; Sir Tom saw to it personally. After the ambush, my master came to London to attend the parliament – yes, he was still a Knight of the Shire. There was so much going in

Westminster – the Duke of Suffolk had been dismissed and his enemies were closing in. Nobody was much interested in Buckingham's inconsequential county affairs. But there were concerns about rebellion, particularly in the south of the country, and so King Henry and his parliament moved to Leicester. Sir Tom was summoned to attend the opening session on 29th April. This was fortunate because we didn't have to pay much for lodgings; we could travel to and fro mostly – Sir Tom's property was in Newbold Revel, just twenty miles away from the city.'

'So that was the end of the matter? He got away with it.'

'Not quite. A person doesn't spend over fifteen years in prison for no reason. There were other – shall we say "events" – which occurred and were considered extremely serious by the authorities, although Sir Tom knew the truth.'

'I can see we are coming to the point when you tell me "That is for next time"?'

'No, I'll go on, because the timings of these matters were closely connected. But let's open another bottle and you should try this Dutch Edammer cheese I brought with me – Edam for short. It was popular last century but sadly went out of favour in England; I like it!' and he cut off a generous wedge of the bright yellow curd and placed it in front of Monty.

'But I digress; the parliament had been sitting exactly a month when Sir Tom decided to take some time off and visit, shall we say, a "friend"?'

By now, fully able to recognise both Sir Tom and Pom's abilities to load a word with extra-meaning, Monty said, 'I suppose by "friend" you mean a woman?'

'Yes, indeed, and a very comely one too. Her name was Joan Smythe; an innocuous name, but a beauty.'

'Miss Smythe?'

'That was the problem, she was Mistress Smythe, married to one Hugh Smythe of Newbold Revel.'

'So, a member of Sir Tom's own community?'

'Yes, although he and Master Smythe had never been anything other than acquaintances. Sir Tom thought him a fool and a wastrel who could never hang onto his money. That was how he met Mistress Smythe; she came to him for help over a debt and –'

'You're going to say "and one thing led to another" aren't you?'

'Something like that,' laughed Pom, 'It seemed they fell instantly in love and it didn't take Sir Tom much persuasion to get her into a bed – I say a bed – both were married and there was no question they could make love illicitly in their own lodgings.'

'So where did they go?'

'They came to my lodgings and I kept look-out.'

'So you were complicit in this enterprise?'

'I confessed it every time, I don't take the sin of Lust lightly.'

'Mm, how long did this go on for?'

'Months, until they made the rash decision to run off together; he's always been one to listen to his loins rather than his head. I counselled him against it, but he told me to –'

'Yes, I can imagine what he said; so what happened?'

'Exactly a month after parliament opened, 23rd May, Sir Tom and three friends: William Weston, a gentleman from the village, Adam Brown, a weaver from Coventry and Thomas Potter of Berangle, a husbandman – he was the muscle – were let into Hugh Smythe's house by his wife, who was ready with her bags packed.'

'Where was Hugh Smythe?'

'That was the problem. He was supposed to have gone off on some farming business, but at the last minute changed his mind. I always thought he was suspicious of his wife and sensed she was up to something – I'm told married people can read each other's thoughts – although neither you, nor I can confirm that! Perhaps someone in the village tipped him off. Anyway, she didn't know it but he had hidden himself away in an outhouse. When Sir Tom and his friends turned up, he confronted them and there was a scuffle. Thomas Potter gave Hugh such a clout round the head that it knocked him out. Sir Tom and Joan Smythe made a run for it to the horses which I had ready, and they galloped off to Coventry to stay at the weaver's house until they could make other arrangements. It was all very romantic – very Arthurian!'

'You don't think he was living out some kind of fantasy – he was Sir Lancelot; she was Queen Guinevere?'

'She turned out to be more like Morgan la Fay! After a week of passion, Sir Tom left her in lodgings in Coventry, and he and I rode back to Leicester and took up permanent lodgings while the parliament was in session. It was obviously not appropriate to return to Newbold Revel where the heavily-bandaged Hugh Smythe was looking for us and with his four brothers.'

'So Sir Tom left his lady languishing, not in a castle but in a lodging house in Coventry?'

'That's it, and it didn't suit the lady, although he visited her whenever he could. After six weeks, she sent him a letter telling him she was in danger of being found by her husband, who had been spreading his money about in search of information. It seemed Hugh Smythe was as much exercised by the fact that his wife had taken forty pounds of his goods and chattels with her as he was disturbed about the assault on his honour. I told you, he wasn't a man who managed his money well.'

'So how did Sir Tom respond?'

'During the first week of August, he visited Joan for the last time and, as he reported to me, "The gloss has gone off, Pom. I think I made a mistake. She's turned out a shrew. I did kiss her a passionate goodbye and told her our parting was more painful for me than she would ever know, but that we must do the right thing for the sake of our immortal souls! I've told her to go back to her husband and stop writing to me. She kicked up a real racket as I was leaving".'

'That's very harsh,' said Monty sighing slightly, but nonetheless enraptured by this story of passion and soured love.

'That was very Thomas Malory, Mr Pickle. He loved them and left them.'

'But what about his wife, Lady Elizabeth? She must have known about this?'

'She did, but acted with great dignity. She's a real lady and he doesn't deserve her. She carried on as though nothing had happened and throughout all Sir Thomas's escapades, she has kept tight-lipped and uncomplaining. She's always managed the estates with the help of a steward – that should have been my job – but I chose instead to follow the man, not the profession.'

'So what happened next?'

'That is a story for another time. I can hear the Greyfriars' bells ringing for evening prayers. I must get back and see to Sir Tom's supper.'

'I have enough material here to write a two-volume book! Thank you, Pom, and thank you for the wine and the cheese, which I enjoyed too, by the way.'

'It's a real pleasure for me to reminisce about the old days. I don't want to make them sound too singular, but it was an extraordinary period in Sir Tom's life. And I haven't told you all of it!'

'I shall look forward to that next Sunday, Pom!'

***

'You had a successful afternoon, Pom?' asked Sir Tom, stretching his skinny arms above his head and then scratching his crotch with a sigh of pleasure.

'Yes, indeed, Sir Tom.'

'So, what did you tell him this time?'

'The story of Mistress Smythe and the "elopement" from Newbold Revel.'

'Ah yes! That was a night, Pom. It's a pity it didn't turn out so well for me. Still, that was then – we are where we are – locked up!'

'It could be worse, sir,' said Pom as cheerful as ever. 'You could be down stairs in the cheaper cells!'

'I suppose so. But before you set out the supper, I have news.'

‘Good news?’

‘I’m not sure. It concerns our friends across the water. There have been serious developments.’

‘I see, sir. Are these “developments” something you should share with me?’

‘I have to tell someone and I only trust you. Wenlock’s been in touch again and from what he tells me, it’s the beginning of serious business, Pom – as serious as I’ve ever known.’

Chapter 4

In which London welcomes Lord Warwick in the heat;
Sir Tom is confronted by a visitor in the Stews;
Monty welcomes Pom for more tales from the past.

London – July 1469. An abnormally hot summer brought flies in abundance to the butchers of Eastcheap, where the insects settled on the slabs of meat laid out in the sunshine, sometimes depositing their eggs which then lay like a circlet of tiny seed pearls on the wrinkled flabby throat of an elderly duchess; the sickly smell of hens' entrails from Poultry; a foul stench of sour milk which had gone "off" in Milk Street; a sluggish Thames even more congested with rubbish and excrement than usual, and giving off noxious fumes which penetrated well beyond the city walls, into the small hamlets and green fields which surrounded them. The citizens inside those walls were ill-tempered and inconsiderate of each other. Some took delight in emptying the contents of their privies in the street to splash, or even cover, unlucky passers-by. This was out of kilter with the way things generally were; there was an accepted neighbourly protocol that nothing was discarded through windows which might discomfort anyone underneath, or at least a warning was given first. It took little for what began as small irritations to expand quickly into physical confrontations. All good manners were suspended as the citizens struggled with the heat. Timber houses were at risk from fires, and extra care was taken with lanterns, braziers and candles. Anyone deemed to be careless with fire was at best castigated publicly, at worst taken into a dark alley and given a hard, painful lesson. Neither was there any respite at night, for the temperature was hardly cooler. Lack of sleep only served to increase the sullen discontent festering in the airless streets and houses.

But the weather in the streets was not the only cause for bitterness and disquiet. The rumours circulating for weeks, concerning riot and rebellion in Yorkshire had done much to stir up angry feelings in the citizens against their noble lords. The king had seen fit to leave his capital and wander towards the north with the vaguely-expressed intention of "dealing with the rebels". The people understood that, during the journey, Edward would undoubtedly divert his army to some decent hunting-grounds; he could never go a week without indulging in the chase. Money had been raised through taxation to equip his men to tackle rebels and northern caitiffs, not to provide resources for the hunt. Word got back to London that tactlessly, on arriving in Norfolk on 18th June, Edward immediately ordered a substantial quantity of banners, coat armour, over one thousand jackets in York colours and other jackets "in rich materials" as it was reported. Many people in London were hungry, and the idea of damask and velvet jackets for a sortie against wild northerners went down badly.

Murmurings on this score were but little to the continued dislike and outspoken contempt for the noblemen who surrounded King Edward; these were mostly members of Queen Elizabeth's family, and a large brood the Woodvilles were too; all needing land, titles and offices, not to mention good marriages. The queen had so many siblings of marriageable age that soon after she had been wedded to Edward, the marriage market was emptied – of anything of value at least. This, of course, alienated many others of the nobility who felt cheated of their birth right and struggled to find a place in the first circle around King Edward, elbowed out as they were by his in-laws. Therefore, the incendiary atmosphere at court matched that in the streets, where it was magnified by the relentless sunshine.

Saturday morning saw Monty Pickle striding towards Jack Worm's shop. He had cleared out of his lodgings to allow his housekeeper room to work. In any case, being outside was slightly more comfortable than being in and he also craved some company. Outside his shop, Jack was also taking the air, such as it was, and discussing a purchase with a customer. Seeing his friend, he waved him to the stool which was placed on the street for customers who wished to browse in comfort.

'Good morning, Monty. Just give us a minute and I'll be with you.'

'Good morning, Jack. I'm happy to wait.'

Soon the purchase was made and a deal struck with the shake of hands; the customer walked off and Jack gave Monty his full attention, 'Good to see you, after our excitement!'

'I've been look at some of your new bindings. They're very attractive with the gold leaf tooling on the red leather. Expensive, I suppose?'

'They are the best I do, Monty. Now, what can I do for you?'

'I just wanted some company that's all. I wondered if you would take a pot of ale with me.'

'Are you sure you want to walk the streets at the moment?'

'Why not?'

'Monty, I sometimes think you must wear blinkers. Have you no idea what's going on – this heat for a start – it's making everyone thoroughly bad tempered, especially towards foreigners.'

'People always look for scapegoats when times are hard. But you and I can safely walk the streets; we're not foreigners after all!'

'It's not only them; some people are out for trouble at all costs. There have been some nasty incidents, especially near the Inns of Court where the 'prentice boys are at their perennial war with the law students. But today, that's not the problem. You must be the only person who hasn't heard that Lord Warwick is on his way, riding up from Canterbury, collecting men as he does so. He's expected to cross London Bridge sometime this afternoon, and with an army of ten thousand.'

‘Ten thousand! However will they all squeeze into the city?’

‘A good question. This is a dangerous business; the whole city’s already seething in the heat. The man I’ve just served said he couldn’t remember things being this bad since Jack Cade and his rebels streamed across the Bridge twenty years ago. This morning, my customer was attacked on his way here by two villains after his purse. He was walking down Cheapside which was crowded even more than usual, with these rumours of Lord Warwick making his appearance. They jostled him into a doorway and threatened him. He managed to fend them off with the help of a bystander. He was shaken up but not surprised. It’s happening all the time; you must have heard similar stories?’

‘My life seems to be confined to Newgate prison and Stinking Lane. That’s one of the reasons I wanted a change of scene.’

‘I must say, Monty, this is a desperate time to decide to roam abroad! Still I never say “no” to an offer of drink. I’ll get that blockhead Addlepate to mind the shop. I’ve only had two customers this morning, trade is hardly brisk with these rumours flying about. But we must take precautions; I see you aren’t wearing your rusty sword! Have you any weapon about you?’

‘Only my eating knife.’

‘Then I better prepare for us both,’ and he dived back into the shop and reappeared carrying a weighty leather-covered cudgel. ‘This was my father’s. We can at least try and make a good account of ourselves if it comes to a fight.’

By now, Monty was wondering if he’d made the right decision. He had an urgent instinct to return home and put up his shutters, no matter the heat. But, as Jack stuffed his weapon through his belt with a determined look, Monty was comforted that his friend appeared to have enough confidence for them both.

Within minutes of Jack organising his down-trodden apprentice with dire warnings of condign punishment if anything “went amiss”, the two men were pushing their way through the crowds which thronged in Cheapside. Jack suggested they visit a "decent tavern", *The Hog's Head,* which was half-way down Eastcheap and half-a-mile from Jack's shop. The crush of people held up their progress considerably and a walk which normally might have taken them five or six minutes, took them half an hour.

'What's to do, Jack? Why are there so many people abroad?'

'Besides the fact there was trouble in the night because no one can sleep and people came out onto the streets – liquor was taken and fighting broke out. Now they are fuelled up to meet Lord Warwick and his army.'

'But even I know the earl's a very popular man.'

'Precisely. They're heading to the Bridge to welcome him. The only people he's not popular with are the City worthies.'

'If they're expecting trouble, where are the constables – the guards to ensure law and order?'

'The councillors have gone very quiet. The only action has been from the Mayor, Sir Richard Leigh, who issued notices two days ago, forbidding the armourers to send out arms from the city without a special licence. He has no liking for the idea of Lord Warwick billeting his men here. It's obvious the streets can hardly accommodate ten thousand men and in this heat! There's bound to be trouble.'

They continued to push their way through the crowd which fortunately seemed to be flowing their way – down Cheapside to Poultry where Jack, like most citizens having a sound knowledge of the back alleys of London, veered off and led Monty through a maze of small lanes, too small to walk two-abreast, until they came out at the top of Eastcheap, and re-joined the main throng. After another exhausting few minutes of pushing and squeezing, they reached the entrance of a tavern; the sign of a hog's head gave it away as their destination. It was difficult to gain the entrance as, mugs in hand, people were spilling out onto the street which was permanently sticky with the remnants of slaughtered animals.

'We'll just have to push our way in, Monty!' shouted Jack, 'If we can get to the counter, I'm sure Mistress Pegge will recognise me and we'll get served quickly.'

It took a great deal of pushing and shoving with elbows to gain access to the large table on which stood the jugs of ale and numerous pots. A large, handsome woman, pepper-coloured hair under a woollen cap, stood supervising the allocation of ale and ensuring a strict protocol of first-come, first-served. Monty noticed she also had a cudgel lying close to her hand – evidently, she was prepared to deal with any wayward customer. She looked rather harassed, as indeed the press in her bar was becoming overwhelming. Two young men were serving as fast as they could and Monty, who had an eye for detail, noted that they made sure money changed hands before the tankards were filled, a wise precaution in such a crowded place. He also noted that most customers had brought their own drinking vessels.

'Should we have brought pots, Jack?'

'I think Mistress Pegge will trust us, Monty,' laughed Jack and he caught the innkeeper's eye and she nodded in recognition. 'Two pots of your best, Mistress Pegge, please!'

'Good to see you, Master Worms. Have you ever seen such a crush?'

'No, indeed. I believe it's all because we're expecting Lord Warwick and his men across the Bridge.'

'Some time this afternoon. Most of these will be too drunk to notice by then! Perhaps, they'll have gone home to their beds. There's been precious little sleeping in the city, no one's taking any notice of the curfew.'

'How will London cope with an influx of ten thousand soldiers?' Jack shouted above the general din.

'As it always does, Master Worms. We'll just have to suffer it.'

'This is my friend, Mr Montmorency Pickle. Mr Pickle, this is Mistress Peggy Pegge who I count as a friend also.'

She nodded at Monty, 'My knowledge of Lord Warwick is that he'll keep his men under control. He doesn't want to lose any of the support he has. He's still popular here, despite the City Councillors who apparently don't trust him.'

'Mistress Pegge knows more about London politics than anyone I know, Monty,' laughed Jack. He turned to Peggy and said, 'It's a pity you're so busy, we would have like to ask you your views on what's been happening.'

'There's no time for gossiping today, Master Worms, you can see how it is. All I'll say is that I've always been a great supporter of Lord Warwick and especially his kinsmen. We went through the Cade rebellion together and have been friends ever since. The earl's a generous man to the London citizens. It's well known that anyone can visit his kitchens in Greyfriars, and be carved as much roasted and boiled meat as he can carry on his knife. That's been the case for years now, he's never wavered in his generosity. So I welcome him back and hope he can bring some order to London – and the country.'

Customers were pressing behind them, some tutting with impatience. Jack felt he shouldn't distract the landlady any further, so he and Monty pushed their way back outside, tankards in hand.

'This is hopeless, Monty. I suggest we drink up, go home and have dinner at the shop. If you have a mind to come out onto the streets later today, we may see Lord Warwick and his men pass over the Bridge. It won't be comfortable, but memorable I'm sure!'

By now, Monty was thoroughly intrigued by the thought of the Earl of Warwick coming into London arrayed for – what? Not war, certainly, for he would never be allowed to cross from the south bank at Southwark if the authorities thought that was in his mind. But there was undoubtedly an air of expectation; the crowds were waiting to see what he would do. Monty's curiosity was also roused. He would risk the crowd and return.

***

'Pom, I have urgent business for you!' At the same time as Monty and Jack were forcing their passage through the narrow streets of the city, Sir Tom was sitting at his table with a thoughtful expression as he toyed with a small but weighty bag of coins.

'Is it a delivery, Sir Tom?'

'Yes, and to the usual place; usual people. Tell them these are to be distributed as soon as possible,' and he handed Pom a sheaf of small papers, 'Your contact will know what to do with them and where to put them. Now, the most important thing is secrecy – as usual; at all times keep your mouth shut –'

'Really, Sir Tom, That's not necessary!' protested Pom.

'It is. I have to be certain none of this is discovered. Fuck it, Pom! You know the risks as well as I do. The money is exactly the amount agreed; there'll be no arguing. So, is that all clear?'

'Certainly, sir!' said Pom stiffly; he was still smarting from the assertion that he might not be trustworthy.

'On your way then!'

'What will you be doing, sir?'

'Me? I'm going down to the Stews for my weekly, er –'

'For your weekly relief, sir?'

'You may say that, Pom, I wouldn't put it quite that way! I have other business there and I don't just mean losing the soap!' He took from a drawer a tiny package, two inches square and deep, wrapped in a sealed paper. It all looked innocuous enough, but its contents were designed for mischief. Malory's eyes brightened as he looked at it. There was nothing he enjoyed more than mischief.

***

Pom's journey to Mincing Lane was hampered by the crowded streets. It was clear many were making their way to London Bridge to view the coming of Lord Warwick who, it was rumoured, would cross the bridge in the late afternoon. The heat was intense and he was sweating profusely under his beard. *Perhaps I should shave it off,* he thought – but he had had the same idea for years every time the weather had been excessively hot. By the time winter came, he'd been glad he'd discarded the thought. Now he pushed and prodded his way through the throng until he arrived at a low door in a small two-storey house on the corner of Great Tower Street. Hearing Pom's gentle tapping, the occupant opened the door and his visitor made his way inside. Few words were spoken as Pom handed over a leather bag containing the papers. The small purse was also delivered. Within a minute, Pom's business was completed and he was back outside on the street.

In view of the fact that the whole area was so tight-packed with people, rather than fight his way back to Newgate, he thought he would try and hail a wherry from the quayside at the Bridge. This would take him across the river directly to its south end. Like Jack and Monty, he had a mind to catch a view of the Earl of Warwick and his followers as they came up through Kent to cross the bridge at Southwark – the only means of crossing the Thames into the city. It was evident the bridge had been cleared in anticipation of this event, for no one was allowed on it. Others had the same idea and it took him almost half-an-hour to find a free wherry-man. Normally, a row across the river would be accompanied by a talkative oarsman, but this one seemed abnormally taciturn and Pom was reduced to staring over the side of the boat at the fluvial mass of solid detritus moving sluggishly along the great water-way. He never ceased to wonder how the whole width of the river didn't become a permanent walk-way; there was so much rubbish accumulating that one might attempt to stride across it from bank to bank. The wherry-man had to work hard against both the barrier of rubbish and the flow of the water. Paying his sixpence, Pom alighted on the south shore of the river and made his way towards one of the two gatehouses which defended the entrance to the bridge. Many others had already arrived, having prior intelligence that Lord Warwick's "army" was on its way. He found a small grove of ash trees which lined the road to the bridge and as luck would have it, he was able to claim a viewing spot which not only gave him clear sight of the road, but also provided some shade from the glaring heat. With his back propped against a trunk, he sat and waited.

***

While Pom dozed in the shade of the ash tree, Sir Thomas Malory was luxuriating in a small wooden bathtub in the Stews of Southwark. He had been accompanied across the river by his guard, Fat Gregory, a man whose soubriquet suited him perfectly. Gregory Hapgood had been a good and steady soldier, but age and lack of agility had seen him pensioned off to become a Newgate prison guard, where continued absence of physical activity and the sin of gluttony had broadened his physique to extremes. But Sir Thomas was especially grateful to "Fat Greg" for the fact that the narrowness of his intelligence matched his conversation. He could guarantee that nothing spoken of in the privacy of his Newgate room would ever be disclosed elsewhere since Gregory had neither the wit nor the capacity to remember anything other than his last meal. In gratitude for this happy arrangement, Sir Tom kept his guard well supplied in all his bodily needs – and this now included specific services available exclusively in the Stews on a weekly basis.

Malory's brothel of choice was the *Unicorn*, a large "inn" managed by an experienced whoremaster for an absentee landlord, who happened to be the Bishop of Winchester – Bankside had been church land for centuries. Now, having been greeted in a most friendly way by Plump Poll, Malory's regular whorelet, he lay back in the hot water while she administered her usual skilful service. "Hunt the soap" had become Malory's favourite activity and he sighed with pleasure as her small podgy hands did their work. The rose petals floating in the water had cost him an extra thrupence, but the extravagance was justified by the experience of something exotic, something "Arabian".

The room was tolerably clean; the *Unicorn* was expensive in comparison with the other fifteen or so similar establishments which stretched along Bankside, but well worth the money. He had a bath and water to himself – there was no sharing here – and the room was airy and light enough, although the barred windows were small. There was also less chance of being robbed since the whoremaster employed a bunch of cut-throats to protect his clients. They made a discreet but determined presence outside the place. Now having been here half-an-hour, Sir Tom was really enjoying himself, 'Just a little more, Poll!' he muttered when he felt her hands growing tired.

'They don't call you "Lusty Loins" for nothing, Sir Tom!' sighed Pauline, for the most-part a good-natured woman, but well able to take care of herself when it came to awkward customers. Everyone knew she carried a poniard in her undergarments and kept a cudgel close by, both of which she had been known to use judiciously. The range of customers at the *Unicorn* spanned the whole social stratum – from artisans to an archbishop on occasion. Everyone was treated as an equal. As Poll wisely observed, 'You're all the same to me with your dicks showing! Who am I to tell whether you're a duke or a drover?' Anyone of note would come disguised and usually retain the services of a particular whore to whom they were partial, for safety reasons as well as familiarity – but which never bred contempt here.

'How's Fat Greg, Poll? Well served as usual?'

'As usual, five minutes and he's on his back snoring. He's not an easy client. Bessie finds it very difficult to keep him going. She says she needs three hands – two to hold back the fat and the third to find –'

'Never mind the details. He can sleep as long as he likes for the next hour; as long as I'm not disturbed. Now, Poll, what about some more hot water?'

'I'll fill the jug, sir,' and she got up from her knees and walked to the door. Malory lay back again with a sigh. It had been a stroke of genius for John Wenlock to persuade Lord Warwick to get him this weekly release. The bath was a pleasure, but was nothing to the rest. He heard her come into the room and closed his eyes in anticipation of the stream of hot water from the jug, and a further, perhaps more intensive application of Plump Poll's skills.

But instead, there came a deluge of cold water from above his head, enveloping his skinny body which convulsed in protest. He sat bolt upright, 'Fuck it! Pauline, you whore!' he shouted while attempting to turn around and deal her a hefty blow. But it was not Plump Poll who had delivered the shock. A firm masculine hand came down onto his left shoulder and he felt the prick of a knife on the right-hand side of his throat, exactly where the pulse in his scraggy neck could be seen pumping wildly.

'I advise you not to move, Sir Thomas!'

***

It was the noise which struck him first. It was too far away to identify the source, but Pom could just detect the faint rhythmic beat of hooves, feet and drums. Then he was aware of a small cloud of dust in the distance; far off and rising from the dry, bone-hard Borough High Street, the main road passing through Southwark which led directly onto the bridge. A murmur went through the crowd, which had in the past hour grown large and restive in the heat. Hawking their fly-blown wares, pie-sellers took advantage of captive potential customers. For the most part, the hawkers kept their goods covered with a cloth, but directly they were removed the flying creatures were back in force, covering the pasties until the pie-crusts were indiscernible under a heaving mass of black insects. Hungry as he was, Pom decided to avoid a purchase, although he noted that others were not so particular.

The noises were more distinctive now and Pom could hear cries of "À Warwick! À Warwick!", the familiar greeting whenever the Earl of Warwick appeared. The man was evidently on his way and with a large following. Some said ten thousand men were with him, but Pom knew, as an old soldier, that these numbers were always exaggerated. Still, it would not be many minutes before he would find out. People were become animated and a few nearer to him were beginning to make the familiar shout. Then, the man himself appeared in the distance, leading his army – for it was an army, definitely not a rabble as had been at Jack Cade's back twenty years before.

Now with a clear view, Pom could see a tall figure dressed in black armour and bareheaded. The man sat very upright on a grey warhorse which bore all the trappings an earl should display. As horse and rider came closer, he recognised Lord Warwick, having seen him many times before, but he noted how much older the man looked – a weather-beaten, time-worn face which belied his forty years. He rode slowly and deliberately, stopping every so often to acknowledge a hand rising to him in greeting, or bending low over his saddle to accept a flower from a pretty girl. It was the stock response of a triumphant general returning from war. Although, Lord Warwick was not returning from war – perhaps he was arriving to make one.

Alongside him rode the Duke of Clarence. George Plantagenet was shorter than his cousin Lord Warwick and Pom could see his face in detail. King Edward's brother was weak-mouthed and sulky-looking, as though he had never received what he thought he was due. He tried to smile and acknowledge the crowd, but their attention was all on Lord Warwick, which must have added to his air of distain. *They don't like him,* thought Pom. Behind Clarence rode another George, George Neville, Lord Warwick's younger brother and Archbishop of York. He was a popular figure, not least because his reputation for largesse was almost as great as his brother's. Everyone knew the details of the feast George had arranged after his enthronement as Archbishop; it was said no one in York had gone hungry for days afterwards. Like his brother, he seemed genuinely to enjoy the adulation of the crowd and he also stopped to acknowledge well-wishers. There were others in Lord Warwick's party, some of whom Pom knew and recognised from earlier days. They all streamed behind their leader, and behind them came the retainers and followers. All displayed the badge of the bear and ragged staff in some form or another – the Warwick symbol worn by all who acknowledged the earl as their lord; pennons and banners decorated likewise. On they came, wave after wave as their leader moved off the road and onto the bridge. He began to make his way across at a very slow pace; those behind began to shuffle into files of three or four abreast to suit the room available – a narrow walkway between the numerous houses and shops which occupied much of the span. Pom watched them go by; there were huge numbers, too many to count. None of the soldiers were armed, apart from their swords and knives. There were no halberds, spears, crossbows or longbows in sight. Clearly, this was to be a signal of Lord Warwick's intent – he was not arrayed for warfare. If there were weapons and Pom was certain there must be weapons, then they would be brought separately in carts at the back of the army – for Pom was also certain, this was an army.

Some in the crowd around him were beginning to move away. The notable attraction had long since passed by and people were ready to return to their homes, for it was almost seven o'clock. Pom knew he must return to Newgate soon, for Sir Tom would have left the Stews by now and would be waiting for his supper. He fought his way back to the bank side and waited for a wherry. But others had the same idea and it would be a long wait, and he would be in bad grace with Sir Tom for being late.

***

'What are people saying, Monty? Can you hear above this racket?' Jack was squeezed in between his friend and a young carpenter's apprentice who stank obnoxiously.

'It's difficult to hear and I wish we hadn't bothered to struggle here. I can't see a thing,' grumbled Monty, who hated being hemmed in by strangers, 'I think we should try, and get out and go home.'

'I don't think that'll be possible, we'll never be able to push our way through this mob. We'll have to stick it out. What a waste of an evening!'

'At least the crowd seem good natured! Lord Warwick's a popular man in the city and people are unlikely to turn nasty. Just watch out for thieves and cut purses.'

Monty's hand automatically sought his belt to check. With relief, he found his purse was still attached, so he undid it and clutched it tightly in his hand. Since he could see nothing, other than the back and shoulders of the people in front, he began to listen to the conversations around him. He heard a man behind him ask his neighbour, 'If there are ten thousand men with him, where will they all be billeted?'

'Across the city, I suppose,' a voice replied, 'Which will make it bloody uncomfortable for the rest of us. I hope he's given a strict order for his men to remain in their quarters while they're here.'

'One thing you can say about the earl is that he won't want to offend the city worthies. I've heard he's come looking for money too. He's got to feed these men somehow.'

'Somebody in the front of the crowd said the mayor and aldermen had stayed in the guildhall, hadn't come out to greet his lordship as they usually do when an earl turns up like this.'

'I suppose they're worried he'll bring more trouble.'

'Why has he brought an army anyway?'

'I've heard he's planning to follow the king to the north, to help him deal with the rebels up there.'

'So he won't be in London long then?'

'Probably not. They say the king's in Nottingham.'

'Hunting in the forest, I suppose!'

'This is all costing a deal of money, neighbour. Where's it coming from?' asked a third observer.

'Poor bastards like us!'

'Careful what you say, too many strangers around for loose talk. You never know who's listening these days. I've heard the king has as many spies as soldiers.'

Jack called across to Monty, 'I wish he'd hurry up; I want my supper. We should have come earlier and got a better view; it's hardly worth standing here. I can't see a thing!'

Likewise! thought Monty, but Jack's observation was correct – they couldn't move in any direction. They would just have to stand and wait.

***

Malory sat and waited, while the poniard quivered just above that tiny throbbing vessel in his neck. He gulped and hoped the movement wouldn't result in the spilling of blood – his blood.

'Caught you unawares, my friend!' said a voice with a laugh and the dagger was removed, as was the hand on Sir Tom's shoulder. Malory breathed a sigh of relief and heaved himself onto his feet, his skinny frame illuminated by the light through the open door. He was thrown a rough towel, 'Cover yourself up, Tom, you scraggy wretch! You're not a pleasant sight bollock-naked.'

Malory stepped out of the bath folding the cloth round his loins. 'Of course, I wasn't fooled! I knew it was you, you bastard! After all, wasn't I expecting you?'

'Of course, but, admit it, you were still surprised.'

'The cold water didn't help, you caitiff! Now, let me get dressed, Tony, then we can get down to business. I haven't much time, I have to be back in Newgate within the hour.'

Anthony Tanner was a man in his mid-twenties, extremely handsome according to verbal testimonials from numerous young women – and in his own opinion. It was undoubtedly true that he displayed a mop of luxuriant black hair, a pair of deep blue eyes and a physique envied by many of his peers – long-legged, tight-buttocked and well-proportioned where it mattered most. Brimming with natural energy and youthful vigour, he made a stark contrast to the worn-out specimen presenting to him by the side of the bathtub. Resentfully, Sir Tom felt the full force of the young man's presence and wished it made him feel less tired. But he comforted himself with the excuse that Plump Poll had just drained him of his manly strength, although – as he admitted inwardly – it had not been much of a performance on his part – Polly had done most of the work.

Also known as "Six-toed Tanner", Anthony was a soldier, courier and spy; his paymaster identified through the small silver ring worn on his little finger which was engraved with a bear chained to a staff. His soubriquet came from the fact that he had lost two toes on each foot to frostbite while campaigning in Northumberland eight years previously; the consequence being, he walked with a very slight limp. The rumour soon got about that he had bitten the affected digits off with his teeth, a "feat" marvelled at by his brothers-in-arms, as he was only eighteen at the time. Whether this was true had never actually been confirmed by witnesses, but for many, the story was so outlandish that it was thought it could not possibly be made up and the toes had truly been detached in this way. From then on, he was viewed by his fellows as either a freak of nature, or a man without fear. He was popular, but not always trustworthy as far as women and money were concerned. He had loved and left many of the former, and salted away much of the latter; sometimes neither was actually his. But Anthony would undertake any task for the Earl of Warwick, who he revered as a father-figure, not being entirely certain of his own paternal origin.

'So, what's the news from France and the earl? You didn't see anything of our friend, Jasper Percy?'

'The Lanky Lancastrian? No, thank God! But listen, there's plenty to tell, Tom. Some of it will surprise you, some won't. I rode ahead of the main party with the news. The shock of the month is the Duke of Clarence married Earl Warwick's daughter a week ago in Calais!'

'Jesus Christ! Does his brother the king know?'

'He certainly knew it might happen. Their mother, the Duchess Cecily, made the journey to Sandwich some weeks before to try to persuade George out of it. Harsh words were said between them, I heard, but surprisingly, Clarence stood firm. Anyway, there was never any suggestion that Lord Warwick or Clarence would wait for the king's permission – which he would never have given in any case.'

Malory frowned, 'This puts a whole new light on Lord Warwick's visit here – with this damn great army – ten or twelve thousand men I've heard and he's collecting more as he rides up from Sandwich.'

'We can dispute the figure, but he has a fair-sized following. It doesn't take much working out, Tom, the earl's been very clever. Fuck me, he's put himself in the way of becoming a king's father-in-law! King Edward has produced no male heir –'

'For the moment. He has two daughters but the law of averages tells me, he must be due a son next.'

'Yes, but for now, the Duke of Clarence is still the next male in line; which means Isobel Neville could become queen.'

'And your point is, Tony?'

'Lord Warwick has fallen out with the king's relations, it's common knowledge they hate each other. Clarence is like a sulky school-boy – never really grown up and, if he were to become king easily managed by Lord Warwick – which would make the earl the most powerful man in the kingdom. Perhaps, he'll make a bid for power before Edward can father a son.'

'Wenlock hasn't given much away when I've seen him and he's as close to Lord Warwick as anyone. He certainly didn't let anything slip out about this wedding. Were you there?'

'In the shadows, as usual. It was a muted affair. I took ship for Sandwich immediately afterwards and a bad crossing it was; filthy food!'

'That's the price you pay for too much travelling, Tony! As for this business, we'll have to wait and see what comes out of it. In the meantime, we have affairs of our own to conclude,' and he picked up his doublet, felt for a pocket and drew out the tiny, sealed package, 'Here's some real work for you. The instructions have been written on this paper, but you must memorise them and give it back to me to be burned, it's too risky for you to take it with you.' He broke the seal and unwrapped the parcel, handing both the paper and box to Mr

Tanner. 'I warn you, Tony, if you're caught with this, you can consider your tongue separated from the rest of you and the detachment of more useful parts of your anatomy. You'll see the box is sealed also, on no account be tempted to open it,' and he crossed himself – an unusual gesture for Sir Tom.

'Intriguing!' said Anthony. He took the paper and sat down on a stool, 'Any chance of a drink while I'm here? Any chance of anything else?'

'Yes and no. I'll get Poll in with some wine, it's not bad quality here.' He called Pauline who arrived with a jug and glasses. She became completely flustered when she saw Six-toed Tanner perched on the stool, his long legs stretched out before him. Pink in the face, she poured the wine and almost curtsied as she handed him his glass.

'Thank you, Poll. Still performing then? How's trade?'

She waved her hands in the air in what she hoped was a casual worldly gesture and in her confusion almost knocked over the jug.

'Careful, Poll!' grumbled Malory. Pauline ignored him, giving her best attention to this devilishly handsome young man; such looks rarely seen in a whorehouse. She drew a deep breath, 'Very good, sir. There's nothing I can do for you, sir? On the House?'

'Tempting, Mistress Poll, but no time, I'm afraid, not even for a quick one. Besides, I like to take my time, especially with a beauty like you!'

In truth, Plump Poll was past her prime and had never really been a "beauty", but Tony Tanner could never resist the reaction flattery brought when he laid it on thickly with any woman. He always wondered why they chose to believe what he said, when a glance in a mirror would tell them he was lying. Pauline withdrew with another sigh and thoughts of what might have been.

By now, Tom Malory was becoming irritated with Six-toed. *I'm paying for the woman's services; she should be giving me her full attention!* he thought. He was also annoyed that Poll had obviously been party to Tanner's trick with the cold water; she would have filled up the jug in the first place.

It was time to bring matters to a close, 'Right, Tony, read and digest the instructions; then drink up and fuck off!'

Anthony looked up from the paper, 'Beggar me, Tom! These instructions are very precise. It's a good job I have an efficient memory, one must have one in my line of work. I suppose matters are in hand here too?'

'Of course. You don't have the monopoly on efficiency. Now, on your way out, send Polly back in; I have a payment to make. I wish she did home visits, but fortunately I have young Meg for that.'

'Have I met Meg?'

'No,' said Sir Tom firmly, 'Good bye, Tony, and good luck!'

***

The crowds had departed. Lord Warwick had dispersed his followers with strict instructions to his captains as to how their men should disport themselves; a six o'clock curfew was ordered and no liquor was to be taken while any soldier was within the city walls. Then the noble earl made his way to the guildhall, where he asked for "a loan" of a thousand pounds and was granted it – grudgingly according to rumour.

It took Jack and Monty thirty minutes to reach the latter's lodgings as they pushed their way through the throng.

'Let's hope Lord Warwick's orders are respected,' said Jack, 'otherwise, it'll be a noisy night.'

'Despite the heat, I'm putting up my shutters,' said Monty, 'I shall answer the door to no one.'

'I'm heading for the shop to see what state Addlepate has left it. I don't suppose we've had any customers today, the whole of the city seemed to be out on the streets.'

'You're very welcome to come in and share my meal, Jack.'

'No, thank you. I'll get back home and do as you are, lock my doors and shutter my windows. Will I see you in church tomorrow for matins?'

'Indeed, and I hope to see Pom there too. We have our usual appointment afterwards.'

'What point are you at with Sir Tom's stories?'

'Pom is just about to tell me more concerning his hostility towards the Duke of Buckingham.'

'The old duke's long dead. How does Sir Tom feel about the new one?'

'I'm not sure, but it will all probably come out as Pom reveals more of what he knows. I must say, John Appleby's been a true servant and loyal friend to Sir Tom. The man's lucky to have him, I think.'

'Probably takes him for granted. Sir Tom seems a law unto himself! But Pom does have a secure livelihood from it, so there's something in it for him.'

'Yes, but as he tells me more about their past together, I can see Pom has implicated himself in some serious crimes and misdeeds. It's a wonder he hasn't been imprisoned on his own account.'

'One thing's for certain, if you're ever able to put it into stories – like Master Chaucer – then I'm sure they would sell. I'll certainly promote them in my shop! What should you call them? *The Newgate Tales*? *Tales from Newgate*? *My life with Buckingham,* perhaps?'

'We've reached half way through the year '50 and I believe we're not yet halfway through the narrative. But remember, we have stories concerning the present which are unfolding as we speak. The involvement with Jasper Percy and Lord Wenlock; the passing of secret messages. They all make for a good tale if I can write it adequately. The trouble is, I'm too used to copying legal and church documents, that has definitely cramped my literary style.'

'I'm sure you'll improve with practice, Monty. It's not as though you're short of material. You know I'll always help you out, read it through and comment.'

'That would be very useful, Jack, and an offer I shall take you up on, if the work ever comes to fruition. For now, I'll continue taking notes from Pom's stories, which makes for a very pleasant Sunday! Look here, why don't you join us tomorrow? Pom always brings plenty of food and wine; enough for three certainly.'

'That's an offer I can't refuse. Thank you, Monty.'

***

'Well, gentlemen, this is pleasant,' and Pom Appleby stretched out his short, stumpy legs, leaning back in his chair, nursing a full glass of Wenlock's best Burgundy. 'I believe Monty has given you an outline of events so far, Jack?'

'Indeed he has. I'm sure I can make sense of things as you go along.'

'Good! Now, where had I got to?'

'Hugh Smythe has accused Sir Tom of rape after our friend ran off with his wife to Coventry.'

'Ah, yes. Well nothing came of that for a while. The accusation was noted, but neither Sir Tom nor I were apprehended. At that time there were two more minor scores for us to settle, concerning old debts which, according to Sir Tom, had been outstanding for "too long" and so he took his own steps to procure the cash. The first took place in the middle of the Smythe affair – a week after Sir Tom and Mistress Joan had run off together. She had taken her husband's forty pounds, but much of that was in goods which they had to sell. In the meantime, Sir Tom was still short of cash so he tried to call in a debt of five pounds, which, with a little persuasion, we retrieved from Mistress Margaret King and her brother, Master William Hale, who owed him the money. They lived in Monks Kirby, a few miles from Newbold Revel.'

'When you say "persuasion", I presume you mean "threatened"?' queried Monty.

'They would say that. In fact, later, they accused us both of using "oppression" and "threats".'

'And did you?' asked Jack.

'Well, if you think tying the lady to a chair, and giving her and her brother a scare with a small knife and a pair of pincers is oppressive, then I suppose it was, but really it was only gentle playfulness on our part!' Monty and Jack looked at each other doubtfully.

'You said there were two minor scores; what was the second?' asked Jack.

'That was similar and it took place in –' and he took out his small notebook – 'in August of that year. We had the same response from Mr John Milner, who also lived in Monk's Kirby; later he accused us of using force to obtain just one pound from him. I still don't know what all the fuss was about; we frightened him for a short while, that's all; roughed him up a little. He knew he owed Sir Tom – he just wouldn't pay up without making difficulties for himself. Anyway, these all went down on the charge sheet, although again, we were never arrested at the time.'

'Sir Tom does have a habit of taking the law into his own hands, Pom, and taking it to extremes,' said Jack, filling his glass to a generous level.

'Have either of you ever tried going through the courts to get redress – either justice or cash?' He looked from one to the other, 'No, I thought not. It's the most time-consuming, expensive and frustrating experience. It was simple; they owed Sir Tom the money, he needed it, they wouldn't pay up even when we tried being nice. So we had to adopt other methods.'

'I see,' said Monty. 'What happened next?'

'Well, this was when Sir Tom really became involved with the old Duke of York. I won't go over the details of how that nobleman was trying to take the crown etc., etc. It's all common knowledge, but Sir Tom was by now deeply in the pay of the new Earl of Warwick, Richard Neville, he whom we all saw safely across the bridge yesterday. The earl was the duke's nephew by marriage. The Duke of York heard how Sir Tom had done the earl some service –'

'You mean, the attack on the Duke of Buckingham?'

'That's it. Buckingham and York were enemies, just as Sir Tom was Buckingham's enemy. On the assumption that "my enemy's enemy is my friend", the duke took Sir Tom into his service for a short time and got him a seat as the Knight of the Shire for Wareham in Dorset. This was all at the time the duke was making his bid for power and needed supporters in the Commons. Of course, we never went to Wareham, I couldn't even tell you where Dorset is! But he became its representative with a fee attached, which helped our finances at the time. Things became much quieter for Sir Tom for a while. Of course, there had been great excitement in London with the Cade riots and everything back in July, but that never touched us and life after September '50 was rather dull for us both. Until – until –'

'This where he always leaves us hanging. I can tell by his voice!' said Monty.

'I certainly am. Let's forget Sir Tom for a time, open another bottle and talk about the events of yesterday. What did you think of the Earl of Warwick?'

Monty shrugged, 'Neither of us saw him, we were in the middle of the crowd!'

'I had a good view from the Southwark end of the Bridge. He had a warm welcome from the folk around me at least! I think he's a great man,' Pom said approvingly.

'But why has he come, and with an army?' asked Jack.

'There are many theories about that. The only person who really knows is probably the man himself.'

'You must know more than you're telling us, Pom,' said Jack Worms. 'We all know Sir Tom's involved in plots with Lord Wenlock – and there's Jasper Percy as well – he's mixed up in all this. What aren't you telling us?'

Pom frowned and paused; then he said, 'Sir Tom keeps some matters closer to his chest than his whorelets! I think he does it as much for my safety as for any security for himself; the less I know, the less I'd give away if I was taken for torture.'

Monty definitely didn't like the use of that word. He knew that deep in the bowels of the Tower were instruments of devilish cunning which could extract information even before they were applied – just the sight of them could turn a strong man to jelly; willing to spill everything he knew – true and false.

‘I hope there’ll be no more visits from Sir Jasper,’ said Jack, reading Monty’s thoughts – his friend’s face always exposed what he was thinking. Montmorency Pickle would make a poor conspirator.

‘Who knows? What I do know and can tell you is, that things are coming to the boil. You may have heard by now that the Duke of Clarence is married? No?’ and Pom relayed the news which he had heard from Sir Tom the previous evening, after he had returned late from Southwark and Sir Tom was back from the Stews.

‘Of course, you can work out the implications of such a match for yourselves,’ and he looked hard at them both. Jack, who was more sophisticated and knowing than his friend, immediately grasped what Pom was suggesting. Monty looked bemused and Jack said, ‘I’ll tell you later.’

‘Yes, and I must be getting back to Sir Tom. We’ll see you tomorrow, Monty? My master is anxious that the work resumes despite all “the effing external distractions”, as he puts it. He says be sure you’re up to date with your reading!’

***

Dawn on Monday morning. Monty was awakened by the sound of men shouting, horses whinnying and hooves clattering on the dry streets around his lodgings. Pulling back the shutters, he looked out to see a mass of men on horseback in his street, manoeuvring themselves into small units which could safely negotiate the narrow streets out of the city. It seemed those of Warwick’s army billeted in the fields behind Greyfriars were on the move.

Lord Warwick’s strictures to his men had evidently been carried out to the letter. There had been little evidence of their presence, certainly around Newgate Street and Stinking Lane; neither had there been much noise. The only sounds he was aware of, were the yelping of the camp dogs which were let loose to patrol the perimeter as the sun went down. All he could see through the cracks in his shutters were the gleams from small fires, which burned in the camp throughout the night.

He waited a couple of hours before venturing onto the street, by which time, it was as though there had never been an army at all. Still relentlessly hot, everything was quiet and undisturbed. Before he made his way to Newgate, he called in on Jack Worms. His friend was taking down the boards from the front of his shop; Dickon Puddledock was leaning on his broom regarding a bucket which he'd just filled with horseshit.

'What shall I do with it, sir?'

'What you do with all the rubbish, you empty-headed boy. Take it to the midden and dump it.'

'My father always puts it on his vegetables,' said the much-put-upon lad.

'Does he? Well, I prefer mine with a little salt!' Young Dickon didn't get the joke and Jack turned to Monty and sighed, 'Wit's wasted on a boy with no wits!'

'I must say it's a relief now Lord Warwick's cleared out of the city. Do you know where he's gone?'

'To the midlands, to join the king at Nottingham. At least, that was what he told the Lord Mayor, when he asked for a loan.

'You haven't seen or heard any more of Sir Jasper Percy, I suppose?'

'I would have certainly told you if I had. As Sir Tom told us, Jasper supposedly left the country and is somewhere on the continent with Queen Margaret.'

'Should you call her that? After all, we have a Queen Elizabeth on the throne. It's all so confusing, Jack.'

'It's all politics, Monty. It's my belief we'll be hearing a lot more of both – conspiracies and queens!'

'I only wanted a quiet life, Jack!' Monty sighed. 'Being around Sir Tom has put an end to that for sure.'

'As I see it, we can have excitement or safety – never both. Perhaps, you should follow Sir Tom's maxim of *carpe diem* and do as he does with his whorelets – lie back and enjoy it!'

‘If I could be sure of where it’s leading, then I would. Everything revolving around Sir Thomas Malory is unstable and uncertain. It’s transitory, like trying to catch feathers.’

‘You like the work though? And the money?’

‘Yes, Jack, I suppose so. There’s certainly enough work to keep us going for at least another year. He must have taken years to assemble it all and put it in order.’

‘Well, as he keeps reminding us, he’s had fifteen years of incarceration. There’s nowhere more peaceful than a prison cell!’

‘Unless you’re directly above the dungeons, I suppose, or worse if you’re in them!’

‘Don’t even joke about that! The thought of “Exeter’s daughter” is a constant presence in my mind. Now, I have some orders to make up and you don’t want to be late for Sir Tom; he’ll only swear at you.’

***

Settling to work that morning, it occurred to Monty that the tales of Sir Tristram, on which they were working, seemed inexorably long. Although he only occasionally questioned Sir Tom on matters of content, he did feel that 164 pages of smiting, hurtling, hewing, beheading, clipping and kissing were excessive, and that was only the first book concerning that particular knight errant.

‘There seems to be a great deal of repetition, Sir Tom,’ he finally observed, after taking a deep breath.

‘What do you mean? What are you saying – too much repetition?’

‘Well, just that it goes on and on – and on the same theme: Sir Tristram, questing, finds a knight at a well – or sprawling outside the walls of a castle or some such – and seeks to “have a do” with him for no other reason than he feels he must. Then they “fewter their spears”; what is “fewtering”, by the way?’

‘Fixing their spears before they fight.’

‘Oh I see. Then one “smites the other and his horse to the ground” and then “voiding their horses”, the pair “lash together, rasing and tracing, foining and dashing many sad strokes" until one gives the other such a "buffet on the helm" that his opponent "falls down upon his side". This goes on knight after knight. We must be into double figures and Sir Tristram hardly gets a scratch –'

'Wait just a minute, that's not true! Early in the story, if you remember, Sir Marhaus gives him a great wound in the side –'

'But as remember it, Sir Tristram gets up immediately and gives out yet another buffet; this time with his sword, slicing through the helmet so that bits of the weapon are lodged in Sir Marhaus' brain. That's most improbable.'

'Of course, my hero can't be killed off within the first few sections and he must always show his mettle, otherwise he wouldn't be a –'

'Yes, I see that!' interrupted Monty spiritedly, 'But what about all these thirty knights he beats at the joust over a couple of days? Any man would be exhausted after two bouts, surely? He hardly ever gets to rest.'

'For fuck's sake, Mr Pickle! As I keep telling you, suspend your disbelief for a time. We're not writing chronicles of our island history. This is *Le Morte D'Arthur*, just stories. The French in particular like to exaggerate – that's why they lost at Agincourt – overestimated their numbers, underestimated our valour. Take Sir Tristram for what he is – a true and perfect knight.'

'I thought that was Sir Galahad.'

'Well yes, but the description fits them both. Look, can we get on? We've still got a way to go before we finish with Sir Tristram.'

Monty sighed inwardly; he knew he was right – there was too much repetition. If he was honest, over the last few weeks, he'd begun to think the work was becoming a trifle tedious. The love scenes were more interesting and often quite tender, but why had Sir Tom chosen to call the two most important women in Sir Tristram's story "Isolde"? A pretty name to be sure, but very confusing for the reader. Perhaps, he would try and persuade him to always use their full name to distinguish them. But for the moment, he decided he would distract Sir Tom no further, picked up his quill and followed the dictation. They worked solidly for an hour before Pom appeared with food, drink and information.

'Fresh news from the midlands, sir. On the way here, I met with one of Lord Warwick's officials coming from his lodgings in Greyfriars. There's been a battle at place called Edgecote. Don't ask me where it is –'

'It's in Oxfordshire somewhere,' said Sir Tom. 'Don't ask me how I know; it's one of those snippets one picks up over time. Anyway, what was this battle about, who was it between and who won? Is there anything of interest I can put into *Le Morte*?'

'It was the northern rebels led by so-called Robin of Redesdale fighting William Herbert, Earl of Pembroke and Humphrey Stafford, Earl of Devon for the king.'

'Ah, Stafford –'

'Just a cadet branch of Buckingham's family, Sir Tom.'

'Still, a noble earl of that cursed line – first Earl of Devon, I hear. He was killed I hope?'

'He escaped. Have some patience, Sir Tom, and I'll tell you briefly what happened. From what I was told, there was nothing glorious about it, it was more of a skirmish than a battle. Pembroke and Devon had sent an advance guard of two thousand cavalry which attacked the rear guard of Redesdale's army, but were chased off back to their main army. But listen to what happened next – apparently, while waiting three miles off in Banbury, Stafford and Herbert fell out over a barmaid! Stafford went off in a pique because he couldn't have first go and took his six thousand archers with him.'

'Typical Stafford response!' snorted Sir Tom, 'Where was Lord Warwick while this was going on?'

'Billeted in Northampton Castle where he heard that his nephews, Henry Neville and Henry Fitzhugh, had been captured and executed by William Herbert at this place called Edgecote. But in the end, the rebels won, and Lord William and Sir Richard Herbert were captured themselves. Lord

Warwick took his revenge and they were executed next day. There was plenty of smiting and beheading, Sir Tom!'

'Does anyone know what happened to Stafford?'

'Last seen heading west I believe, sir.'

'One question no one seems to have considered, where was the king while all this was going on?' asked Monty.

'Good fucking question, and one I was going to ask,' nodded Sir Tom.

'King Edward was still in Nottingham. He'd no idea of Pembroke and Devon's defeat, let alone the executions. On 29th he decided to leave the castle and ride to meet them at Northampton. As his army came closer to the city, they heard the news and immediately, it's said, Edward was deserted by a significant number of his men. That's all the news Lord Warwick's servant could tell me.'

'How frustrating! I wonder what Lord Warwick's next move will be, sir?' Monty posed the question they had all been musing on.

Malory said nothing; unusual for a man who always had an opinion about everything. Monty watched him and immediately sensed the man knew much more than he was prepared to reveal.

Chapter 5

Where more momentous events unfold; Six-toed Tony reappears;
Monty has an encounter with A Very Important Person and spends some sleepless nights.

Early August in the year '69 and the weather had broken. Storm clouds appeared for three days before the longed-for rain covered the dusty streets and turned them into streams of fine slippery mud. As always, some people are never satisfied and they grumbled about the sticky mess. But overall, there was much relief as the marshes, springs, wells, aquifers and conduits were filled again, and the citizens' water supply replenished. It rained solidly for two days; sheets of water ran off roofs into the channels in the streets, meandering their way through the city until they poured into the River Thames.

Monty was particularly relieved to get a decent night's sleep. The air had cleared and the stifling, sticky atmosphere was replaced by a cool breeze. At work, being at the top of the Newgate Tower, Sir Tom's room was comparatively airy, although, of course, the windows could not be opened; but for the most part, the door remained permanently ajar and a welcome draught found its way inside.

It seemed to Monty that Sir Thomas was in a state of no little excitement and expectation. He asked Pom many times if there had been any letters; had he met anyone with "news"? Monty did not pry – Sir Tom's response to unwelcomed questions was always robust, 'None of your fucking business!' The scribe knew his master's agitation was connected to the business in the midlands and that he waited on further news from "his sources", as Pom once described them. As the weather broke, so did the silence when Malory received a long-awaited visitor. They were working hard on a section of text telling how Sir Tristram slew Queen Morgan le Fay's paramour and took the queen's shield.

'I particularly like the way I end this section, leaving the reader guessing,' said Sir Tom:

Then Sir Tristram took that shield and promised her – Morgan le Fay that is; I think I make it clear enough – *and promised her to bear it to the tournament at the Castle of Hard Rock. But Sir Tristram knew not that the shield was ordained against Sir Lancelot, but afterwards he knew it.*

Monty was doubtful as to how much suspense this would generate, but he was not prepared to argue the matter. Sir Tom was not in a receiving mood.

'I think it flows well, don't you, Monty?'

'Yes, indeed,' Monty lied.

'Now, let's press on to the section where Sir Kay –'

But before the words were out, there was the sound of panting and feet running up the stairs outside. The door was pulled wide open with a firm hand and Monty was aware of a tall, good-looking man entering the room in somewhat of a lather.

'Sir Tom, what news!'

'Fuck it, Tony! You shouldn't be here!' and Sir Tom looked at Monty and then to Pom, who had been quietly busying himself with domestic matters, 'It's too dangerous for us both!'

'There's no danger, Tom. Lord Warwick's done it!'

Malory raised his eyebrows, 'Are you sure you want to discuss this now – here?' and he looked at Monty again and back at the stranger with alarm.

'There's no need to worry, we can speak freely,' he turned to Monty. 'This is your scribe, I presume? Aren't you going to introduce me?'

Reluctantly, Sir Tom nodded towards Monty, 'Mr Montmorency Pickle, this is Mr Anthony Tanner –'

'Let me stop you there. It's Sir Anthony as of three days ago. Lord Warwick was kind enough to elevate me "for great services rendered"!'

'Congratulations,' said Sir Tom drily, 'I suppose the earl knows what he's doing. You can provide the necessary cash to keep you in that state of chivalry?'

'As much as you can, old man,' smiled Sir Anthony, 'Now, from what you've told me of this fellow here – Mr Pickle – he's to be trusted?'

'Certainly, but I was trying to avoid involving him any further. I'm not sure how he would be under torture.'

By now, Monty was feeling considerable hostility towards the two knights, who saw fit to discuss him as though he was absent. Sir Tom's last slur on his honour was too much. Drawing a deep breath, he said, 'Excuse me, I am in the room. Whatever it is that's going here, either trust me fully or excuse me and I'll leave with my mouth shut! But please don't talk above me; it's most – most –'

'"Fucking unchivalrous" are the words you're looking for, I think!' said Sir Anthony, 'I beg your pardon, Mr Pickle, but these are dangerous times for us all. We can't afford to share confidences with anyone we aren't certain of. But if Sir Tom vouches for you, then that's all right with me. Now, let's get down to what's happened.'

'First, Pom, organise some wine for our guest! And Mr Pickle, you'd better stay to listen, after all, you've been involved in much of this business.'

Within minutes, the four men were seated – Pom found a couple of three-legged stools from somewhere, and Monty and he perched on them precariously, while the two knights sat comfortably in the only available chairs; all were well-served with full glasses of claret. Six-toed Tanner wasted no time. 'You know, of course, about Edgecote, and how afterwards Lord Warwick executed Lord Herbert and his brother; oversaw it personally?' Sir Tom nodded,

'Well,' continued Tony, 'You also know that the king was in Nottingham and had no idea of what had taken place. He was so slow in moving out to meet Stafford and Herbert – who by this time was dead – that he was still on the road to Coventry when the fun started.'

'Fun?' asked Monty.

'When Lord Warwick made his move, he sent his brother George Neville to "collect" the king, who was staying the night in some manor house in Olney, twenty miles from Northampton. Edward's brother, Richard Duke of Gloucester and Lord Hastings were in the place with him. I know all this because I rode with George Neville and was present.'

'So you were witness to it?'

'Indeed, and it was all too easy. King Edward was in his bed, although he woke when he heard us clatter in. Young Gloucester tried to put up a fight, but Edward stopped him. George Neville was excessively polite, invited the king to be escorted by him to Coventry to meet his loyal servants, Warwick and Clarence. We left Gloucester and Hastings to go whither they would. As I say, it was all too easy.'

'So the king went just like that! No fuss?'

'No, he rode along with us as though we were on some official business. George Neville remained courteous, not a hand was laid on the royal personage.'

'So what happened when you arrived at Coventry?'

'After he had seen that the king had all he required for his comfort, Lord Warwick spoke to him privately. The earl told us afterwards that there were no recriminations on either side and Lord Warwick told him he remained his most loyal servant, and if Edward would use him as a guide and mentor, his rule would be embellished with wisdom, which would reassert the popularity he enjoyed when he was first crowned. Lord Warwick would ensure the esteem of the people would be brought back to him and they'd love him as they did the earl. You see, Tom, I have a keen memory for detail!'

'Did the king accept this?' asked Sir Tom.

'Well, they appeared later at supper together and as far as I could tell, the king was compliant to the point of geniality. They were laughing and joking together – again, as far as I could tell. I wasn't on the top table, you understand!'

'So what happened then?' asked Pom.

‘I was sent from Coventry to bring the news to my contacts here in London, you included, Sir Tom. But my understanding is that Lord Warwick has by now personally escorted Edward out of Coventry and deposited him behind the walls of Warwick Castle; which is where he remains, according to the last piece of intelligence I received while on the road.’

‘Jesus Christ! So who knows about this?’ asked Sir Tom.

‘If I’ve arrived after an especially swift journey, you can be sure others are arriving too. The senior noblemen and court officials will have the news by now, and given how fast rumour spreads in this city, the Commons and the people will know of it by supper time. I’d put money on it.’

The four men fell silent as they absorbed Anthony Tanner’s words. Then Monty said, ‘So, who is exactly in charge of the country, now, as we speak?’

‘Good question!’ Thomas Malory paced the room. ‘We knew this was a possibility, but in all honesty, I never thought he’d do it. Take the king captive!’

‘Are you saying you’ve known this might happen?’ said Monty incredulously.

‘Well, as I say, not exactly.’

‘Is this what all the plotting’s been about?’

‘Let’s just say “connected”.’

‘So, I’m up to my neck in treasonable activities with men who would lead us all into the Tower to suffer God knows what kind of pain and agony?’

Tony Tanner held up his hand, ‘Don’t get over-excited, Mr Pickle! As long as we keep calm, and just wait and see what happens, no one can implicate us in this particular event –’

Monty broke in, ‘You’re hinting there are others, Sir Anthony.’

Sir Thomas broke in, ‘Fuck it, Monty. You have to understand we’re in the middle of great change and upheaval. Of course, we support Lord Warwick; always have done and always will. Anything we can do to help him!’

'But treason? By Christ, I didn't sign up for that!' protested Monty.

Six-Toed Tanner held up his hand again, 'Sir Tom's right, Mr Pickle. Sir Tom and I are involved in several matters which will give assistance to Lord Warwick in his aims.'

'Yes, but what exactly are his aims?'

'It's complicated –'

'That's what everyone says when they don't want to speak the truth.'

'For now, it's better you don't know, for your own safety.'

'I'd quite like to know so that I can tell the authorities immediately before they tie me to the rack!'

'Another good reason not to tell you!' said Sir Tom cheerfully, 'Now, if I were you, I'd calm down and listen. Lord Warwick wants what's best for the –'

'For himself!' said Monty.

'For the country,' intervened Tony smoothly, 'King Edward has surrounded himself with arse-lickers and no longer listens to his true advisers. You've heard what they're saying in the streets. He's becoming unpopular. Lord Warwick simply wants to be able to give his majesty good advice; get him to listen to the people through him. Nothing wrong with that, is there? He just wants the king to be well regarded, as he once was.'

Monty conceded with a shrug and Tony went on, 'Your question as to who is running the country at this precise moment is very relevant. There will be a breach in governance –'

'Good phrase that, Six-toed. I might use it in –'

'Never mind the *Le Morte D'Arthur,* Tom. If we don't concentrate, it'll be *Le Morte du Thomas, Le Morte d'Anthony and Le Morte du Lord Warwick.* As I say, there'll be some initial upheaval, so I'm not sure who'll be in charge until we receive direct orders from Warwick.'

'Well, I know who should be in charge,' said Monty with asperity.

'Oh yes, who's that?'

‘I studied Law and as I understand it, when the king is “indisposed”, that is ill or mad, or captured in the cells of some castle –’, and he looked hard at Sir Anthony, ‘the Lord Chancellor immediately deputises for him while other arrangements are being made.’

‘That’s true enough!’ said Sir Tom. ‘So, my friend, Lord Robert Stillington will be in charge for the moment. I suppose he knows?’

***

The man knew well enough. He’d been informed some three hours previously in the early hours of the morning, when he was rudely wakened by his servant to admit a sweating and panting rider with the news from the midlands. Now he sat at his desk in the half-light of morning, several grubby and water-stained sheets of paper spread across his desk. These were his second problem, but totally outweighed by information that his majesty the king was now under lock and key, and in the power of a renegade nobleman with ideas above his station.

Robert Stillington was a fat, squat man just fifty, with an unprepossessing face dominated by a drinker’s nose. Currently, he was as bald as an egg; the consequence of an outbreak of lice in his thinning grey locks. Too embarrassed to advertise the fact with herbal treatments which would clearly give away the condition to any onlooker, he had taken the drastic step of having his head completely shaved in the hope the little bastards and their offspring would be swept away in the pile of greasy hair left on the floor. His judge’s velvet hat was currently being enveloped by smoke from the fireplace, in the expectation that any unwanted little visitors remaining within its lining would choke themselves to death, following the principle which jackdaws adopt when divesting their wings of pests in the fumes from chimney pots.

He had to admit, this infestation was his own fault for frequenting the Stews where he was certain it had originated. His weekly visits were covert and carefully managed. Heavily disguised, he was known only to his particular whore of choice and he paid her handsomely to keep her mouth shut. In turn, she recognised a good deal when she found one – the Lord Chancellor was a catch for any harlot and he paid well for her discretion. But for Lord Robert, there were risks other than being recognised; he ran the gauntlet of numerous diseases and in this case, the infestation. He had been able to keep it hidden from his long-term mistress, otherwise known as his housekeeper, who, at her time of life was completely uninterested in her lover in matters of the flesh – hence, his recourse to the Stews. In his eyes, she had become slatternly and gluttonous; in hers, he'd become pompous, overweight and bibulous; she had no further carnal interest in him. The pair lived out their separate lives comfortably enough, but Lord Robert could still remember happier days in the relationship and he sometimes felt a fleeting, but generally insignificant prick of conscience when he was lying with whores.

'Thinking of insignificant pricks, where's that caitiff Crosby?' Lord Robert said to himself, and as though thought was father to the deed, the man knocked and entered. A slim and well-groomed young man of four and twenty, while Peter Crosby viewed the office of Lord Chancellor with respect, he was also fully aware of its incumbent's weakness and vanity. His approach to his master was without guile or unctuousness, on the grounds that, since everyone else around the great man fawned on him, Crosby's would be refreshingly candid.

Stillington nodded as his secretary entered, 'Ah, Crosby, is there any further news from Warwick, the Castle or the Lord?'

'Nothing yet, although we've had further confirmation that it is so, that Lord Warwick has his majesty under his control.'

'Damn the man and his ambition! But we've now other things to concern us also. I want you to look at something; I'm certain it's connected,' and he pushed one of the mud-spattered papers across the desk towards his secretary. 'What do you think of that? Read it back to me,' and Mr Crosby read aloud:

'"Duchess Jacquetta, you should have known better,
And not become a witch – you bitch!"'

'That's absolutely appalling!'

'Yes, anyone writing that about a duchess –'

'No, no, sir! The rhyme, it's doggerel, my lord. Whoever wrote it has no sense of proper metric construction or style! I fancy myself as a bit of a poet and –'

'Yes, yes! Never mind poetical structure. This is an appalling slur on the Duchess of Bedford, the king's mother-in-law! It's all over London apparently; these are just a few copies which have been brought in for me to see. Christ knows how many more there are. I've sent men out to hunt them down, but I'm very much afraid it's too late.'

'Do we know if it's true, my lord?'

'True? The Duchess of Bedford a witch? I could have you whipped for that!'

'Indeed, but they say there's no smoke without fire. By the way, my lord, speaking of fire, is that your hat smouldering in the hearth?' and they both looked across at the Lord Chancellor's velvet cap which, through lack of attention, was rapidly losing its nap in the heat. Mr Crosby neatly retrieved it from the embers, gently brushed it down and hung it back on the peg above the fine silk gown of Lord Robert's office.

'This mischief has come from somewhere and I've a very good idea where!' said Lord Robert.

'Oh yes, sir, where has it come from?'

'That nest of espials, the Stews.'

'And what makes you so sure, my lord?'

'I have spies of my own, Crosby.'

Now, Mr Crosby knew that Lord Robert was a visitor to that notorious part of Bankside – and Stillington knew he knew; but the fact was always left unspoken. Crosby was loyal to his master because he enjoyed one of the best and most interesting jobs in the government, and which gave him a great deal of power among his peers. Not highly paid, but worth it for the deference it brought him, especially from those seeking audience with the great man. Peter Crosby was the gate-keeper and made a nice little nest-egg with bribes from those seeking preferential treatment in the way of access to his master.

'Have we anyone in mind, my lord? Anyone you wish to have – interrogated?' And he rolled his tongue round the word with some relish.

'That caitiff, Thomas Malory, for a start! I'd wager a year's salary he's involved.'

'As I understand it, he's in Newgate. How can he possibly organise the distribution of such dogger – of such scurrilous libel as this?'

'The king's allowed him out once a week and Malory visits the Stews to indulge his vices!'

'And what vices would they be, my lord?' asked Crosby with his tongue firmly in his cheek.

'You know as well as I do why a man visits Bankside, Crosby. Now, tell me what you know of Malory, his friends and acquaintances. We must have intelligence on the man; after all, he's been a guest of the Crown for upwards of fifteen years or so.'

'Well, we do know he's hired a secretary. I can't remember the man's name offhand, but he's been visiting Sir Thomas for some months. Then there's John Appleby –'

'Yes, I know all about Appleby. He's Malory's partner in crime and has been for forty years. They're two of a kind.'

'Why have they never been brought to trial, my lord?'

'Long story and I won't go into details. Originally, it was in the interests of a certain great nobleman to keep Sir Thomas under lock and key. It's become a kind of tradition now!'

'Tradition, my lord?'

'We're really colluding with the man. Believe it or not, he wishes to stay in Newgate to "finish his book", as he says.'

'What book's that, my lord?' asked Peter Crosby, 'I fancy myself as a writer –'

'As well as a poet?'

'One does one's best.'

'I know little of Malory's book and care less. What I do care about is Malory's relationship with the Earl of Warwick. It's common knowledge he's been in his pay and service for years. He must be involved in Richard Neville's latest bid for power.'

'Is that what it is, my lord?'

'Of course, it is. Now, we've wasted enough time. I want you to find out all you can about this secretary and bring him to me for questioning. Also, make a note of everyone who visits Sir Thomas; have Appleby followed – discreetly – and tell me where he goes and who he sees.'

'And what will you do now, my lord?'

'I shall be busy running the country on behalf of our absent monarch.'

***

On a fine Saturday afternoon in late August, Monty was in Jack Worm's stationers' shop. He had been in a state of agitation since he heard how the king was now under the care and control of Lord Warwick, and that Sir Thomas Malory was fully implicated in these momentous events. He had immediately confided his fears of imminent arrest to Master Worms, who had been sympathetic but initially wary of offering too much comfort. The maxim, "He who sups with the devil should use a long-spoon", came into the shop-keeper's mind and he had no wish to be considered guilty by association. But, seeing his friend's agitation, his conscience told him Monty was a loyal companion, an innocent in the business and deserving of his support. So he listened attentively to everything Monty said, although advice was easier to give than concrete assurances that "everything would be all right".

'Should I break my contract and contact with Sir Tom? Perhaps, I should flee the country, go to France or Burg –'

'I think you're getting ahead of yourself here, Monty. What have you done that's so bad?'

'I passed secret messages between Jasper Percy and Sir Thomas, who then passed them onto spies in Greyfriars Abbey.'

'Under duress, just as I did.'

'I don't think they'll worry whether it was "under duress" or willingly when they come to put me on the rack.'

'Christ, Monty! Brace up, man! I'm sure they would have been after you by now. Lord Robert Stillington has king's spies everywhere.'

'Indeed, and they know I'm a frequent visitor to Sir Tom.'

'In the capacity of scribe. They'll also know he's visited by whores, has a washerwoman who cleans for him, and Pom comes in and out all the time. They can't arrest everyone on the grounds of association. I come into that category and I have colluded with Jasper Percy too, under serious threat though. But I'm not necessarily worried about it. I'm a business man who supplies Sir Tom with his writing materials.'

'Well, have you thought what those materials were used for? You can't have failed to see those accusations about the Duchess Cicely. Can you be certain the paper didn't bear your supplier's water-mark and can be traced back to you?'

'Why on earth should I be involved, any more than any other stationer?'

But Jack Worms fell silent for a moment. Monty had a point. If Stillington's officials were charged with looking into every aspect of anyone suspected of colluding with Lord Warwick, then they might dig very deeply indeed. He shook his head, 'I think you're worrying unduly, Monty. Let's wait and see what develops. Besides, if Lord Warwick is totally in charge, the likes of Sir Tom and Six-toed Tanner are perfectly safe, and more likely to be awarded an earldom. Look on the bright side, you and I could even get a knighthood apiece!'

Monty wasn't comforted. He was a simple man with a set of simple principles. One of these was, that whoever the man was anointed with the holy oil in the sight of God, he should be recognised and obeyed as the king. Edward IV was such a man and the idea that his most senior nobleman should have seen fit to have him unceremoniously placed in a dungeon somewhere in the midlands, was anathema to him. He felt most uneasy; his life had been turned upside down. It may have been mundane, but it was at least safe. He had started looking over his shoulder whenever he went out, to check he wasn't being followed. Unfortunately, being the guileless man he was, he did not detect the two men who were walking the street some yards behind him and who then loitered casually just beyond his front door.

***

There was no loitering for Tony Tanner, although, on his way back to Warwickshire, he had reigned in to rest a short time for the sake of his horse. Half way from London, he had been caught up by one of his brother agents riding the opposite way. This man had two pieces of news. The first was that Thomas Herbert, younger brother of William and Richard had been taken prisoner, and immediately hanged by a baying mob in Bristol. The second was, as far as Tony Tanner was concerned, unsurprising. A Northampton man, Thomas Wake of Blisworth, had come to Warwick Castle and asked to see the earl "on secret business". That business revealed that the Duchess of Bedford, her Grace, the Lady Jacquetta was practising witchcraft.

The messenger gave Tony details, much of which he was aware of already, but he feigned surprise as he listened to the tale.

'I was there when Lord Warwick questioned Wake about his source, Tony. The man rummaged in his purse and brought out a filthy cloth. Wrapped in the middle was a small lump of dull grey metal which I could see quite clearly. It was a roughly moulded lead figure, about the length of my middle finger, broken in the middle and held fast by a wire.

'"This is a strange object, Wake," said my Lord Warwick, "But how is it linked to the duchess? Who found it?"

"Someone in the village of Stoke Bruerne, a few miles from Northampton, sir. This man Harry Kingston found it in the church after Earl River's men left. He said it was left on the altar in a small box," and Wake crossed himself before he continued. "They'd been billeted in the village. The earl's the duchess's husband after all and must have known of it."'

'Did Wake say how he got the object?' asked Tony, hoping to hurry the man up.

'He said Harry Kingston took it to the parish clerk who gave it to the parson. It's said it was even sent to a nunnery for their opinion; the Mother Superior said it was definitely the Devil's work. The thing was passed round the villagers and came into Wake's possession. He thought Lord Warwick should know of it. He told Lord Warwick there were two other images made by her grace, one of the king and one of the queen, but no one has seen them yet.'

'You said this object was held together with wire, friend?' asked Tony.

'Yes, it was a piece of grey metal forged in the Devil's furnace. I'm sure it was some kind offering to the Dark Lord,' and he shivered and crossed himself.

Tony breathed a sigh of relief. That lump of grey metal was in the small box Sir Tom had put in his charge ten days before. Riding to Northamptonshire where he knew Lord Rivers' men were camped, as ordered, Tony hid it in the church at Stoke Bruerne. He'd set the wheels in motion for it to be found and when that had been accomplished, everything else had gone to plan. The metal image was now in the hands of Lord Warwick who would send it to the Bishop of London. The fact that the figure was the product of an alchemist's mortar and pestle, heated in a crucible over his garret fire in Cripplegate was of no importance; it was the outrage its appearance would prompt when it was shown in the right quarters. Word would soon spread across the country via chapmen, tinkers, soldiers and other sundry travellers that King Edward's mother-in-law was a witch who had commissioned the making of a relic of the Devil, which could be seen and felt – if anyone dared. That, coupled with the rhyme which was circulating throughout London, would be sufficient to inflame even further hostility towards the queen's side of the royal family and especially the haughty duchess.

Wishing his companion "God speed to London", Sir Anthony Tanner spurred his horse on towards Warwick; certain, his master would reward him handsomely for his work.

***

In London, Sir Thomas and Monty Pickle continued their work. Despite the imminent possibility he might be exposed as a traitor, the old knight was remarkably insouciant. 'The bastards will never be able to trace anything back to me.'

Monty wasn't so sure. He continued to feel very uneasy, and found it hard to concentrate on the doings of Sir Tristram and Sir Galahad. Sir Tom was aware his scribe was abstracted.

'Buck-up, Mr Pickle! I don't pay you to wool-gather. We've reached a point where I need an honest opinion.'

Monty dragged his mind back from the prospects of red-hot metal pressed against his flesh and said, 'Indeed, Sir Tom. What is it?'

'Just to remind you where we are, as you clearly haven't been listening, we've got to the point in Book 10 where Arthur and Tristram fight, and the king is wounded in the side.'

'I notice that all your knights are wounded in the same place, Sir Tom. Is there any reason for that?'

'Weak point in a man's armour.'

'Is it? I thought full body armour gives full protection, Sir Tom.'

'Fuck it, Monty, but you can be so – so – what's the word I'm looking for?'

'Literal, Sir Tom?'

'Indeed, literal. I keep telling you this is a story not a martial handbook.'

Monty sighed inwardly, then said, 'What is it you want me to consider, Sir Tom?'

‘This section with the damosel in it. I have a great many damsels scattered throughout the tales, but mostly they go unnamed. Do you think I should identify these maidens with a Christian name each?’

‘How many are we talking about?’

‘I haven’t counted, but probably twenty or so in the whole work.’

‘Unless they play a significant part in the story, then I wouldn’t bother; if they’re a serious part of the plot, then of course they should be recognisable.’

‘That makes sense and comes as a relief since I don’t think I can find twenty appropriate damosel-like names! Right, we continue. Take this down.’

And so they went on. After an hour, Monty decided he would do what he had wanted to do for some weeks. He put down his quill and sat back in his chair. Sir Tom raised his eyebrows, but saw the determined look on Monty’s face and said, ‘You want to speak to me about something on your mind, don’t you?’

‘How do you know?’

‘I’m not entirely insensate. You’ve been distracted for days, ever since Six-toed arrived with the news about the king and Lord Warwick. So what is it?’

‘Aside from being in a permanent state of fear that I’ll be arrested and thrown in the Tower, what I really would like to know is this, what is your true involvement with the Earl of Warwick? How long have you known him and are you part of his retinue, despite being in jail?’

‘So many questions, Mr Pickle. I’m not sure you’ll want to hear some of the answers. My connection with Lord Warwick goes back almost twenty-five years. I don’t hide the fact that I’m totally loyal to the man and would do anything in my power to preserve his noble status.’

‘So, have you been in his service that long?’

‘Yes, he has been a good friend to me in return; saved me from the spite of that renegade nobleman, Fuckingham Buckingham.’

‘Yes, Pom did tell me you carried out an attack on that noble lord. He told me it was at the behest of Lord Warwick. So what was behind the hostility between the two lords in the first place?’

‘At bottom what it always is, land and money which together always equals power. But look, I’m not paying you to enquire after details of my past life; we have much work to do and I seem to be constantly interrupted, either by you or Six-toed Tanner; or Pom fussing about money, which is running low, by the way. I may not be able to pay you the full amount this week.’

All thoughts of delving further into Sir Tom’s past flew away as Monty absorbed the implications of this casually-made statement. ‘I see. How much will you be able to give me of the 13s 9d you’ll owe me on Friday?’

Sir Tom put his hand in the small drawer in his table, felt round it, then brought out a handful of coins which he counted out carefully as he piled them up. ‘4s 2d is about all I can manage for the moment.’

‘But that’s less than a third of what you owe me!’ protested Monty, ‘When am I likely to get the rest?’

‘Calm down, Mr Pickle. I’m temporarily frustrated financially. Pom cleaned me out at Hasard the other night, but I can assure you all will be well when Anthony returns from Lord Warwick. Six-toed will bring me my annuity which is due. His lordship never fails to pay it and on time. As I told you, he’s an honourable man.’

While Sir Tom was explaining, Monty was doing some swift calculations. He concluded that he would have to ask his landlords, through the Treasurer at the Greyfriars’, for time to pay. There was also the matter of having to buy more materials for his other commission; for he knew, he was getting especially low on paper. He was certain both Greyfriars’ and Jack Worms would be patient, knowing the money would be forthcoming from Lord Warwick – and soon he hoped. ‘Do we know when Sir Anthony is likely to return?’

‘Things are moving very quickly. It’s my guess he’ll be back with fresh news within a week.’

'Very well. I'll just have to accept your assurances. But I would like the arrears as soon as possible. I have bills to pay.'

'Don't we all, Mr Pickle?'

'By my reckoning, you'll owe me 9s 7d.'

'Noted, Mr Pickle,' said Sir Tom stiffly. 'Now, can we get back to work?'

'Am I to hear nothing more of Lord Warwick and yourself in the old days?'

'No, the story is too long and complicated. I suggest you ask Pom to tell you on one of his Sunday visits. There's nothing he doesn't know about me, Lord Warwick and Fuckingham Buckingham. Pom will probably tell it better than I. I'm a written-word man, not one for sitting round a fire telling yarns. Ask Pom!'

'I will!' nodded Monty.

***

The opportunity for an explanation of Sir Thomas' relationship with Lord Warwick was missed for the simple reason that from Friday evening onward, Monty found himself unusually "unavailable" and "not at home to visitors".

His lack of observational skills became telling when he returned to his house unaware he had been followed from Newgate by two men and a man-at-arms. Now in fairness to Mr Pickle, soldiers in the streets were a familiar sight in those unstable times and Monty had thought nothing of it, neither did he connect the two plainly-dressed young men to the soldier. As he approached his front door, one of them stepped out in front of him, taking him completely by surprise.

'Mr Montmorency Pickle?'

'Yes,' Monty said cautiously.

'By order of the Lord Chancellor, Lord Robert Stillington, I have an order for your arrest,' and he waved a paper with a substantial and important-looking seal dangling from it.

Monty's first reaction was one of strange relief. He had been rehearsing this possibility for days. But that feeling disappeared immediately, and was replaced by an overwhelming sense of panic which made his stomach churn and his bowels turn to water. His knees buckled and the man took his arm firmly, grabbing Monty's key which he was about to place in the lock.

'I'll take that and we can all go inside,' said the young man and wrestled with the lock while they all stood in a huddle outside the door. The man-at-arms made a great show in preventing the few onlookers from approaching, which by now included Master Talbot's children, to Monty's shame. The soldier brandished his halberd at them and looked appropriately menacing. The two younger ones stared back wide-eyed, but the eldest girl put her hands on her hips and looked challengingly at him. 'What's the old man done then? Have you come to chop off his head?' and she gestured with her arm as though bringing down the axe. 'My ma's always said he was strange. She said, a man not married by his age wasn't right. She said –' and to Monty's delight, one of the men caught her such a clout round the ear that she fell back into the road and didn't recover herself until the three of them were safely inside.

'Little bitch, she should have more respect for the king's officers!' grumbled her attacker. 'Now, let's get down to it. Show us your desk and any papers you have in the house.'

So they were after proof from documents. He breathed a sigh of relief. He had never secreted any letters or papers in connection with Jasper Percy, neither was he implicated in Lord Warwick's affairs in the midlands. They would find nothing in his small house, however they might disrupt it. And they did – turning drawers, tables, chairs, his one cupboard and even the bucket in his privy upside down.

'You'd be surprised at the number of people who hide things in their own shit, Mr Pickle!' said one of the men cheerfully as he emptied its fortunately small liquid content over the floor. 'But there's nothing here. In fact you seem to lead the dullest of lives, you poor bastard! However, the Lord Chancellor has ordered your arrest and you are to be brought before him –'

'In the Tower?' squeaked Monty.

'Not yet, although it may come to it. No, our orders are to take you to his chambers in Westminster immediately. We'll take the wherry we came by, it's a short-ish walk to the quayside. Now, let's get off!'

'But the mess?' The fact that he was not going to the Tower came as a great relief to him. Monty was not particularly meticulous in his housekeeping, but the thought of the contents of his privy lying unattended on the floor for God knew how long, was almost as worrying as the thought of the rack.

'We're not barbarians, Mr Pickle. I'll call up your neighbour and ask them to arrange someone to come in. I suppose, you have money to pay them?'

'A sixpence will cover it. There's one in my pocket, if you'll allow me to find it,' said Monty faintly.

'Very well,'

The man went outside to find one of the Talbot children who were still loitering in the street; the girl now silent and resentful, nursing her ear. He collared the youngest by the scruff of his neck, 'Tell your mother I wish to speak to her, you brat!'

He ran off as fast as two stubby legs could take him, and very soon Mistress Talbot arrived and agreed to arrange matters. As he handed over the money, Monty could see there was a look of sympathy in the woman's eyes. She took the key from the man, promising her neighbour she would take care of his property "for the time being".

That's the problem, thought Monty as they made their way to the quayside, *How long is that likely to be? Will I ever see my house, my friends – this river again?* Strangely, he thought of Sir Thomas' strictures against sentimentality. What would the old man say under these circumstances? Something like: "Tell them to fuck off, Monty! Don't show them you're soft. Let them do their worst. You've nothing to hide."

No, that was most unhelpful. He didn't want them to "do their worst"! He wanted to stay alive and pain-free!

***

Feeling very much alive while wallowing in his bathtub on Saturday in the Stews, Sir Thomas mused on the latest turn of events. Despite his incarceration, or because of the length of it, he had discovered numerous ways of gaining information about what was happening in the world outside his Newgate cell. Admittedly, some of it came from unreliable sources. For example, his whorelets never really had a grasp of the finer points of statecraft and politics. They were more interested in people than events. Take this latest business with the Duchess of Bedford. They were agog with the news that the king's mother-in-law was into witchcraft and Plump Poll took great delight in reciting the poem which Sir Tom had written himself. Unbeknown to him, Lord Robert Stillington's secretary, Peter Crosby, had recognised the work for what it was – pure doggerel. But that had been Malory's intention. No one on their right-mind would associate this "trash", as such literary rubbish was only lately described, as his work. Malory – the man of letters and fine words could never be guilty of such an offence against the vernacular!

Things had gone as smoothly as Lord Warwick intended and Malory expected to be rewarded when Anthony Tanner returned from Warwickshire. He would be able to pay Monty Pickle what he owed him and then purchase a new batch of wine to replenish the stocks. But, on consideration, perhaps in future he should retrench; be less extravagant. He would desist from long evenings of Hasard with Pom – for a while at least. The man was having devilish good luck lately and Sir Tom wondered if his servant had found the "holy grail" of the game of dice: a fool-proof system.

He wrenched his mind back from his own pecuniary difficulties to the latest news, which mine host of the *Unicorn* had passed to him while he was enjoying a pre-bath drink with the man.

'The Earl of Warwick must be running the country, Sir Tom. He's ordered the next parliament for 23rd September and it's to be held in York. He's also made Sir John Langstrother

Lord Treasurer, in place of Lord Rivers. You heard what's happened to his lordship?'

'No, Master Roberts, I haven't been in the way of much news today, other than the witchcraft business.'

'Yesterday news came about Lord Rivers and his son, John Woodville.'

'Ah yes, they'd escaped from this last battle in Northamptonshire.'

'Yes, well they were caught soon after hiding up trees near Chepstow in the Forest of Dean, although Rivers' eldest son, Anthony Lord Scales, escaped. Rivers and John Woodville were brought back to Coventry, and Lord Warwick had them exhibited in chains in the great hall of the castle.'

'I can guess what he did next, Master Roberts.'

'I'm sure you can, Sir Tom. He chopped off their heads without a second thought. The king's father-in-law and brother-in-law! Who'd of thought it? You've got to admire the earl. He doesn't do things by halves, does he?'

'He's always been a man of energy, no one can deny that.'

'He's generous too; his kitchens are always open to anyone who's hungry. I think they have some kind of test and don't hand out food to anyone, otherwise people would be filing up all day long! But he does take care of the poor folk of the city, no doubt about that. That's why he's popular, Sir Tom.'

'Some doubters would call it what Juvenal described as: "bread and circuses". Throw the people a little bread and give them entertainment, and they'll forget their grievances. The old Roman talked bollocks, Master Roberts, the people never forget their grievances. Jack Cade should remind us of that! Londoners love Lord Warwick because he's straight with them.'

'Well, I don't know anything about this Juvenal and his circus, but Lord Warwick certainly hates the Woodvilles, but then most of us Londoner's do. Parvenus and arse-lickers the lot of them,' and he spat a gobbet of Burgundy-coloured phlegm onto the wooden floor.

‘Talking of arse-lickers, where’s Plump Poll today? She knew I would be here. Fuck it, Master Roberts, it’s your job to arrange it!’

‘She sent a message that she’s not too well. Has an ague!’

‘Well, I’m not paying her to be ill. Is there anyone else handy? What about Bessie?’

‘Bessie’s busy –’

‘Clever use of alliteration, Master Roberts!’

‘She’s busy alliterating someone else, I’m afraid. If you’re prepared to wait, she’ll be free when the cathedral bell chimes.’

Now, Sir Tom lay back in his bath tub as Bessie’s hands did their work. Smaller and not as skilful as Poll, yet adequate to make him feel as happy as he had done for some days. He was secretly trying to brush aside the prospect of an inquisition by Robert Stillington’s henchmen and hoped his anxiety would not be passed onto anyone other than Pom, from whom he could hide nothing. Montmorency Pickle was clearly agitated and such agitation could be dangerous if he couldn’t keep his mouth shut. He fervently prayed that his scribe would go unnoticed by the authorities. He comforted himself with the thought that Monty was a nobody – an insignificant little man of no interest to anyone except himself.

***

Robert Stillington didn’t agree. He had this “insignificant little man of no interest to anyone” sitting on the opposite side of his desk in the Lord Chancellor’s chambers. He viewed Monty rather as a lazy hound viewed a worn-out fox; there wouldn’t be much fun in the kill. Long experience told him immediately that his quarry probably had no valuable information to impart – either willingly or under duress. No, his value lay elsewhere. But first, he would learn a little more of this scribe who seemed to have got himself embroiled with some very dubious characters. They were of far more interest to him than Mr Montmorency Pickle.

Lord Robert had taken pains to set an official atmosphere to show his captive he meant business. He had dressed himself in his official silk robe in the shade of red he'd become attached to and he wore his velvet cap. Although showing the scars from the heat of the fire, he remained fond of it and reluctant to replace it. His vanity was such that he would always now cover his bald head. The lice had fortunately met their end in the fire, along with their offspring. There had been no further signs of infestation and Lord Robert took pains now to wear a hat at all times while participating in casual congress in the Stews.

He looked across at Monty, and with a critical eye, noted the man's well-worn doublet and hose. He'd also noticed his footwear as he'd walked across the room; they clearly needed attention. This was a man short of money. Perhaps that would be helpful, perhaps it wouldn't. He would see. He cleared his throat and pretended to read a long document that stretched the full width of his desk. After what he considered sufficient time to put his victim fully on edge, he looked up and said, 'Mr Montmorency Pickle of Number 3, Stinking Lane in the parish of St Martin le Grande. Is that correct?'

'Yes, my lord,' replied Monty faintly, 'I'm not sure why I'm here.'

'That will be revealed shortly. Firstly, I want to know what your connection is to Sir Thomas Malory.'

'I'm his scribe, my lord. He's writing a great work – *Le Morte* –'

'Yes, I know all about his book. Today, I'm only interested in your part in his writings, Pickle.'

'My part, my lord?'

'Don't play for time; time is something we're short of. Just describe to me the type of work you do for him. Let me help you a little. Take a look at this,' and he pushed across one of the scraps of paper his soldiers had retrieved from the streets of the city. Monty took the paper with a trembling hand and cast his eye over it. Of course, he had seen it before; a copy had been posted up on the door of the tavern at the top of his street. It was the verse concerning the Duchess of Bedford.

'It's terrible, my lord!' Monty whispered hoarsely.

'If you're going to tell me it's appalling verse, don't bother. My secretary has already pointed that out.'

'No, my lord, it's terrible to write such a thing about a lady – any lady. It's scurrilous!'

'Ah, I see you have a wider vocabulary than most; then I suppose Sir Tom would find that particularly useful. Tell me about the work you do for him,' and Monty proceeded to explain his function in Malory's writing process.

'That seems straightforward, just making suggestions and copying out. Is that all? Does he ever ask you to do other work for him? Write letters?' He leaned forward and waved one of the scraps of paper on his desk in Monty's face. 'Or these verses, for instance?' His voice had taken on a note of menace. 'Tell me, Mr Pickle, what other work do you do for him?'

'Nothing for him at all. I do other work for other people – lawyers mostly – to provide myself with an income. I –'

'I'm not interested in "other people", only Sir Thomas. Besides, we know who you work for – all their names. I must say, it wasn't difficult to find out. There aren't many of them, are there? In fact, you seem to be remarkably hard up for a trained lawyer. But we'll come to that later. Another question for you,' and he leaned forward in his great chair and almost whispered, 'we're interested in Sir Thomas' friends and acquaintances – his visitors. Who are they and what have they to do with him?'

'He's in prison, my lord, and does not have visitors.'

'That is clearly a lie, Pickle,' Stillington had become more robust and threatening and, in Monty's eyes, seemed to grow in his chair, 'You visit regularly –'

'Yes, but that was on the request of Master Roger Clyfford, the Newgate Keeper. It was all authorised and from this office too, at least I was told so.'

'I grant you that, but others have been seen entering his cell. What about Master Jack Worms, the stationer?'

Monty was taken aback. He never imagined his friend would have come to the attention of the Lord Chancellor. He must have spies everywhere. 'Master Worms supplies Sir Thomas with writing materials. He has a shop in Paternoster Row and is highly thought of –'

'I'm not looking for a reference for Master Worms, Mr Pickle. I just want to know what you and he talk about when you're visiting Sir Thomas. I'm sure it's not just the weather.'

Monty was becoming confused. 'Talk about?' he said almost inaudibly.

'Yes, talk about – discuss – chew over – any of those three! I told you, don't play for time here. I have numerous methods of extracting information from you and immediately.'

There was a definite change in Lord Robert's tone and a wave of fear ripped through Monty, starting with a tingling in his feet to a crawling sensation at the top of his head. This was it, his worst nightmare. In the following seconds, he imagined the door opening, and two bulky soldiers bursting in and covering his head with a bag. Then taking him by the arms and dragging him off, down to the riverside, onto a wherry, and then the long pull to the quayside of the Tower, where he would be rowed through Traitors' Gate and unloaded to his tormentors.

Robert Stillington noticed immediately he had hit the mark with his victim. He used this method of terror only on the most susceptible of them. It was wasted on bolder characters who would always try and bluff it out; he wasted no time in that situation but sent them straight to his experts. Monty Pickle was the perfect type to reduce to a state of terror by suggestion in less than five minutes. But he would take matters slowly and reinforce the notion in Mr Pickle of the state's power to cause pain. He sat back in his chair and smiled stiffly.

'I think we've gone as far as we can today, Mr Pickle. We intend to lodge you in the Tower while you are with us – you must sleep somewhere and we cannot allow you home. My men will escort you.' And he rang a small hand bell on his desk. As his secretary entered he said, 'Arrange for Mr Pickle to be escorted to the Tower for the night. See he has all he needs, Crosby.' He turned to Monty, 'You see, we're not barbarians, sir!'

Why did Monty consider that phrase had a ring of threat in it? It was exactly what the officer had said when he'd arrested him.

***

Once Mr Montmorency Pickle had been dealt with, the Lord Chancellor had two more potential culprits to interview. The fact that his majesty was festering in some kind of habitation in the midlands and out of reach had caused Lord Robert the greatest of concern. It was all most inconvenient. Who knew what that bastard Earl Warwick intended? An order to convene a parliament had been sent, out of the blue and was supposedly authorised by the king. "Under duress, no doubt", was Lord Robert's comment to Peter Crosby. Now he had just learned that Lord Rivers and his son were without their heads, which were surely on pikes, and being mocked by bastard peasants, somewhere in the benighted county of Warwickshire.

'The king's close relations decapitated before breakfast; spies and agents everywhere, toing and froing,' he complained to his secretary, 'I can't be certain they've not infiltrated Westminster itself.' He looked at the large gilded wooden box which contained the Great Seal – apart from the crown regalia, the highest symbol of royal power and which took pride of place on his desk where everyone could see it. *Well, I can only do so much,* he thought, *It'll be a matter of setting a thief to catch a thief. I haven't the manpower to trail every would-be agent in the city. Now, Mistress Pauline Fisher, let's see how you can help us.*

Plump Poll sat waiting outside Stillington's chamber. She had been summoned, not arrested, but given clear instructions to "wear something decent and cover up with a veil; preferably come attired as a respectable widow".

'Bring Mistress Fisher in!' and Mr Crosby went outside and soon returned with a curious Poll. 'That's all, Crosby. I'll ring when I need you!'

Now, Peter Crosby was no fool and knew his master was up to something secretive. In the secretary's experience, whenever there was a woman involved, then it was all about sex. He knew of Lord Robert's predilection for whores and had a suspicion that the Widow Fisher was not the innocent she seemed. Peter knew a worldly woman when he met one.

Once inside, Polly divested herself of her veil and was about to make a convivial comment, but the Lord Chancellor held up his hand and said, 'Mistress Fisher, I have brought you here on official business.'

'Well, my lord –'

'No need to call me that here; I'm just "sir" to you.'

'It always sounds so special when I call you "My Lord". You know you like it; how it makes you excited!'

The Lord Chancellor could see immediately that he was going to have difficulty separating his official responsibilities from his whoring activities. Plump Poll was also struggling to reconcile in her mind the scarlet-gowned official staring at her from the other side of his highly-polished desk, with the bare-buttocked, minutely hung and flabby body which graced her four-poster in the Stews once a week.

'Let's get down to business!'

'That's what you always say!' she laughed uproariously.

Lord Robert was becoming highly irritated, 'Will you be quiet? This is a serious matter!'

'You always say that too, especially when you're "having trouble",' and she whispered the words behind her hand.

'Can I remind you, Mistress Fisher, I am the Lord Chancellor and currently in charge of the country.'

'Indeed, and a very good job you'll do, I'm sure!'

'I don't need your approval. I asked you here to question you and was kind enough to make it on your own volition, in view of our – of our –'

'In view of you fucking me every week?'

Stillington inwardly shuddered, but remained outwardly smooth, 'I could have just as easily had you arrested and brought in chains, and don't make any facetious comment about being tied up!'

Poll settled her face into seriousness and sat with her hands in her lap trying to look like a demure widow. 'What is it you want from me, Lord Robert?'

'That's better. I want information about Sir Thomas Malory. I know he is your client every Saturday morning –'

'And he won't be best pleased I'm not there today!'

'I'm interested in who visits him when he's in the Stews and any other information you have via your numerous professional friends. You have many of those I know.'

'Many of them know you too, my lord!' said Poll cheerfully, 'As for Sir Thomas, I just give him his weekly bath, and a few extras if he has the money.'

'Does he talk to you about what he's been doing?'

'Oh no, sir. By the time I've got to work on him, he's not fit to talk!' The visual imagery became too much for Lord Robert and he decided to tack to a different route. 'I know he has visitors, can you remember any of them?'

'Well, we had one recently who I could hardly forget. Such a handsome young man – bright blue eyes, black hair like – like – soot! Oh, I would have given him a free one, but he said he didn't have the time.'

'His name, did you get his name?'

'It was a strange one, something about toes!'

'Toes?'

'That's all I can remember, I was too busy taking in his body, my lord. A finer young man I've yet to meet!'

Stillington felt a tinge of jealousy, 'This man, this "fine young man", you're sure you can't remember his name?'

'No, my lord, it's gone completely out of my head,' and she gazed at him with an unusually innocent expression.

'Did he have a long conversation with Sir Thomas? I take it they were alone?'

'I'm not sure how long they were together. When he came out, he was very attentive to me.'

'Never mind that, did you overhear anything of what they were saying?'

'The doors are very thick in the *Unicorn*, which is a good thing, considering the amount of noise you make sometimes!'

He sighed with frustration. Whatever he said, Plump Poll was never going to let him forget he was her client. *This is going nowhere. I'll have to move on to my next option,* he thought.

'Now, Poll, listen. It's obvious you have little relevant information to give me now, but you will be useful to me in other ways –'

'Oh I know that, my lord. After all, you're always telling me so!'

'Just keep your mouth shut for a few minutes and listen to me. This is what I want you to do.'

***

'Should I start marking the walls to remind myself how long I've been here?' Monty Pickle had been in his cell in the Tower all of twenty minutes, but it was beginning to feel like a lifetime. Who knew he was there, apart from the Lord Chancellor and the guards who had escorted him through Tower Green, past the king's menagerie – he hadn't liked the sound of those lions – and inside the building to the first floor. He looked around his room, for it was more of a room than a cell. Not badly furnished, with a bed off the floor – a mattress and blankets. He had a table and chair. The only item he baulked at was the bucket in the corner; there was no separate privy. Perhaps, he would be out of here before he needed to use it properly, but his bowels were not in good shape since the shock of his arrest.

He then began to ponder what Robert Stillington really wanted from him. After all, Monty was a simple scribe with a nondescript life. Of no significance to the state at all, other than his connection to Sir Thomas. Sir Thomas! It all came back to him, and Monty knew much more about the man and his dealings than was healthy for anyone. It was not just the delivery of treasonable letters from Jasper Percy, but a more serious threat from just knowing of the existence of Sir Anthony Tanner, master spy in the pay of the Earl of Warwick. That Sir Tom and Six-toed were colluding in mischief was a certainty. That would be what the Lord Chancellor would want to know and would take pains – Monty's pains – to find out. That thought brought him to imagine "Exeter's daughter", the incongruously named rack, inspired by its cruel originator, Henry Holland, 3rd Duke of Exeter, who had once been constable of this very place.

As night drew in, and all candles and flames were summarily extinguished, he lay on his bed staring into the dark. He had never felt so alone. As a solitary man by inclination and circumstance, he mostly enjoyed his own company. But that was when he had the choice of sociability – he could seek his friends or not, according to his whim. Now he had no choices and no one to consult or advise him. He wondered whether Sir Tom would miss him; perhaps take steps to find out what had become of his scribe when he didn't appear on Monday morning. For Monty felt certain his incarceration would be a long one, if he wasn't dead from torture within days.

Torture! The very word made him feel sick. How much could he withstand? He thought of all those tender parts of his body which could be attacked – from toe to head: nails, toes, genitals, fingers, tongue, eyes; especially sickening thoughts crowded his brain as he thought of red-hot needles – and pokers. Hadn't they been the instrument of choice on two occasions, when a monarch and a noble lord had died in such a devilishly horrible way? Red-hot, and stuck up the fundaments of Edward II and the old Duke of Gloucester. He must shut his mind to these images, but once they were in his head, he could not get rid of them. He knew himself to be a weak man, physically; he'd never been robust. He had once overheard his father refer to him as "the runt of the litter" and when he asked his sister what that meant, she laughed and said, 'He's right! The weakest of us all and just like a piglet!' After that, he was bullied unmercifully by the girls who would grunt and snort at him. He knew he would fall at the first painful hurdle, give the whole thing away; make up things Lord Robert would want to hear. Anything rather than face the continual threat of agony in some dark and secret place where no one could hear his screams.

***

'You're back early, Pom!' Malory observed, 'Has Monty grown tired of hearing of my misdeeds?'

'No, Sir Tom; he wasn't in church this morning and neither was he at home. I've just come from Stinking Lane and there's no sign of him.'

'Well, that is certainly strange. Mr Pickle is a creature of habit; something's up, Pom!'

'I was hoping Master Worms would know more, but he wasn't in church either. His shop's closed, but then it is a Sunday.'

'Did Monty's neighbours have any idea where he was?'

'They're never there on a Sunday. They don't attend our church. Monty told me they visit relations elsewhere in the city and worship with them.'

'The trouble is Mr Pickle seems to have few friends and acquaintances who might know the answer. We'll have to hope he turns up here tomorrow morning. Fuck it, Pom! I have a mass of work to catch up with and I don't pay him to go wandering.'

'Well, Sir Tom, you won't pay him if he doesn't appear, according to the contract.'

'You don't think he's ill and couldn't hear when you knocked?'

'No, I knocked hard and yelled, but there was obviously no one in.'

'What's happening to everyone? Plump Poll wasn't working yesterday; she had the ague.'

'I'd walk round to Master Worms' lodgings and enquire, if I knew where he lived.'

‘Well, that’s not much help. Better see to our dinner, Pom. If Pickle doesn’t turn up tomorrow, you can enquire at Worms’ Books as to where he might be,’ and Malory sat back in his chair and continued to peruse his manuscript. But Monty’s disappearance had rattled him.

***

Monty was equally rattled. He’d spent two nights in the Tower; heard what he thought were cries of agony and desperation from unfortunate bastards below his room; had imagined every kind of pain and insult which could be inflicted on his own body, and had finally been released on Sunday evening and told to “find his own way home”. Admittedly, he was in one piece.

Having spent Friday night in abject terror of what Saturday might bring, he had been almost relieved to be brought back to Westminster and the Lord Chancellor’s chamber again. Robert Stillington had resumed the same stance and attitude he displayed the day before: that is one of calm superiority and dignified expectation of cooperation on the part of his captive.

‘Good morning, Mr Pickle. I trust you had a comfortable night? Were you fed properly this morning?’

Monty was taken aback by this apparent concern for his welfare and relaxed slightly. Of course, Stillington could be softening up for something unpleasant, but better to see how matters unfolded and remain calm himself.

‘Indeed, my lord, but it wasn’t the place I would have chosen to spend the night.’

‘I’m sure! But, as I said, we need to keep you safe from unhealthy influences.’ Monty knew he meant Sir Thomas and chose to remain silent. Stillington leant forward in his chair to indicate he wanted to get down to business. ‘Now, yesterday you explained your function as far as Sir Thomas Malory’s – shall we say secretary – is concerned. Today, I really want to press you about his visitors and how he spends his time.’

'There is nothing I can add to what I told you yesterday, my lord.'

'I don't think that's quite true, Mr Pickle,' said the Lord Chancellor smoothly, 'Mr Worms visits, we've already established that –'

'But Jack Worms' visits are connected with his business. I explained that already, my lord.'

'But Mr Worms deals in paper and we have some evidence that the paper he deals in has been misused, for instance,' and he pushed a scrap of manuscript across the desk, 'This has been in circulation for some weeks.'

Monty read the libel concerning the Duchess of York. Stillington continued, 'This is even more serious than the nonsense in the verse I showed you yesterday. This is a gross and treasonable slurring of the king's mother, and thereby, the king himself. Whoever was responsible for its composition and dissemination is a traitor to England, and must suffer the severest penalty.'

'Of course, my lord, and I entirely agree. But I fail to see what that has to do with Master Worms.'

'It was his paper it was written on, as was the rhyme.'

'How can you possibly know that, my lord?'

'The water-mark, you fool. It came from a supply with the same mark we found in his shop.'

'But he doesn't make the paper. He imports it from a paper mill in Holland! He told me he has to get his supplies from abroad because we don't make paper in England!'

'So you say, but nonetheless, the paper came from his shop. You said yourself, Master Worms is the only visitor from the Row who supplies Sir Thomas directly. Therefore, it must have been paper from his shop which was used to write this filth!'

For the first time, Monty felt angry rather than intimidated and said robustly, 'My lord, you're wrong to assume that these were written by Sir Thomas. Didn't you search the other shops in Paternoster Row? I believe they all buy from the same supplier. It's impossible to identify a single source since the stationers sell this paper to all the scribes and legal men in London. What evidence do you have that it was Sir Thomas?'

'You're not here for me to reveal my sources to you, Mr Pickle,' retorted Stillington, 'You're here to help me get to the bottom of plots and conspiracies, which I believe emanate from Sir Thomas Malory in his Newgate cell.'

Confidence immediately deflated, Monty reverted to being terrified. How much did the Lord Chancellor and his henchmen know? What was the source of their information? Who else had been arrested and interrogated? Perhaps, Pom was also in the Tower by now – even Sir Tom himself. Should he confess what he knew – that his employer had been in several conversations with a spy in the pay of the Earl of Warwick? But the Earl of Warwick was now officially in charge of the king and issuing orders to Monty's interrogator. Who was in the right? Wasn't it the right thing to do to support the earl who was doing his best for the country and trying to get the king to mend his ways? These thoughts flashed through his mind as Lord Robert regarded him through narrowed eyes, 'Well, have you anything to tell me?'

Monty decided to play for sympathy, 'My lord, I am a simple scribe, as you have discovered, I'm sure. I lead a simple life trying to earn a decent living and causing no offence to anyone. I've been placed in a situation not of my choosing, whereby the man I work for is now under suspicion for actions which I can neither confirm nor deny. I have no knowledge of who might have written these – these – libels. All I can tell you is, Sir Thomas has treated me fairly and I have no reason to doubt his integrity –'

'Integrity! Do you know how long the crime sheet is for this man and how long it's been increasing? For fuck's sake!' and Monty jumped in surprise at this unexpected profanity, 'The man's been in jail for years for felonies which are eye-watering. He's capable of anything!'

'But that's because he's never been brought to trial in all those years, my lord.'

'He's been a thorn in the side of many a great nobleman –'

‘Lord Buckingham, I suppose you mean? But he’s dead now.’

‘Him and others. The man’s a menace and should have been dealt with years ago.’

‘But isn’t that up to this office and whoever was Lord Chancellor before you?’

‘Don’t get malapert with me, sir. Remember my office and what it is capable of!’ Stillington was becoming rattled himself and decided it was time to show Mr Pickle his teeth, ‘I think it would be better you are returned to the Tower for a while. If I need you again, I will call you back.’ He rang his little bell and Peter Crosby came in. ‘Have Pickle taken back to the Tower. I have no further use for him. I’ll give instructions as to what to do with him when I have considered the matter.’

Monty was propelled out of the room by two burly soldiers without ceremony. Returned to the Tower, he found himself in a room on the ground floor and much less salubrious than the one he had occupied the night before. *Was this to be the system?* he asked himself. *Each time I’m returned, I’ll be incarcerated deeper and deeper, until I reach those parts of the Tower more closely related to Hell itself; places where the real experts get to work on my pathetic body.* The food was also worse – meagre portions of cold pottage and rye bread. How long could he withstand this treatment? What would be his breaking point? He had never felt so miserable and alone in all his life. His sisters’ bullying had been painful and of long duration, but this short, sharp terror was far in excess of that. He had no sleep on Saturday night, and as dawn broke and he saw chinks of light through the holes in the shutters which covered the bars, he wondered what Lord Robert would have in mind for him today. But then, he realised it was Sunday and a blessed day of rest. Hadn’t Sir Tom told him Stillington was Bishop of Bath and Wells? The Lord Chancellor must have a day off to conduct services or whatever a bishop did on a Sunday. At any rate, he would have time to refresh his soul and afterwards he might look kindlier on his prisoner when he had cleansed it through confession. But perhaps, he wouldn't see him today at all and that would mean another twenty-four hours of solitude in which his imagination could run free.

However, the Bishop of Bath and Wells, having "cleansed his soul" and assisted with Mass in St Paul's, felt ready to confront Mr Pickle once more. His intentions had always been clear to him, for he knew exactly what kind of a man he was dealing with – a weak and conscientious one who was too honourable to be bribed but could be manipulated by terror – or by kindness. Having given Mr Pickle a taste of terror, he decided he would try the alternative.

'Mr Pickle, first let me apologise for the inconvenience you have suffered these last two days. It has never been my intention to cause you harm or embarrassment.' Monty was completely taken aback and sat speechless in front of Lord Stillington. The Lord Chancellor continued, 'I know you are a good and loyal servant of the king – that is his royal majesty King Edward IV – and are as appalled as I and the rest of his servants are at this attempt by scurrilous knaves to undermine his authority, and disrupt the country through sedition and treason. I know also that you would do anything to help in both rounding up all the villains involved and safeguarding the person of his majesty – as much as it is in your power to do so.'

'Of course, Lord Robert!' Monty visibly relaxed in his seat, which was the response Robert Stillington was looking for. *Got him!* he thought, and went on, 'There are, of course, certain things we can all do in these troubled times, like keeping our eyes and ears open.'

Immediately, Monty was on his guard again. This was where Stillington would come to the point of the last two days and Monty quickly surmised what it was. *Jesus Christ!* he thought. *He wants me to spy on my friends and neighbours.*

'I want you to report to me anything untoward which occurs in Sir Thomas Malory's cell in Newgate. Write nothing down, but I will arrange for you to visit my private quarters in complete confidentiality once a week, regardless of whether there is anything of note to report. I'd be interested in anything Sir Tom has been doing – even how his book is progressing, although it's probably not to my taste. How is it coming along, by the way?' Stillington really had no interest in any nonsensical stuff about knights and their damsels – women's stories! But if an interest in such trash generated a reason for discussion with Mr Pickle, then so be it. Lord Robert would put up with a full exposition of *Le Morte D'Arthur* if it meant he was able to sift out a single nugget of useful gold from the rest of the dross.

'I see, my lord,' said Monty faintly. He had knowledge of Sir Thomas' involvement in certain questionable projects, but he had managed to keep them to himself throughout the interrogation. To start revealing things now would make him seem shifty, to say the least. It was better to remain silent about what he knew. But how to deal with this suggestion – or order as it really was, however nicely spread in honeyed words. All he wanted to do was get out of this room, out of this man's presence, out of Westminster and back inside the four walls of his house.

He drew a deep breath, 'Very well, my lord. I'll do my best. But, as I've told you, I am a simple man, just an agent commissioned to help a writer. My experiences as a spy are non-existent and I'm sure there are others who could do better.'

'I'm sure there are, Mr Pickle, but they're not so well placed as you. Besides, I don't like the word "spy"; it's so – so – underhand and almost dishonest!'

Well, you of all people should know of that! This office runs more spies than any other official department of state! thought Monty, but did not say it. Instead, he just nodded and said weakly, 'As I said, I'll do my best, Lord Robert!'

'Good. Now, you can go back to the Tower as I may want to speak to you again – I may not. You may wish to talk to me – about anything. My door is always open!'

Which is more than my cell door will be! thought Monty.

***

Monday morning found Sir Tom and Pom, in their Newgate cell, finishing a hearty breakfast washed down with several glasses of Wenlock's finest, 'Any sign of Mr Pickle, Pom? He's late.' The Abbey bell had just struck eleven.

'Nothing yet, sir.'

'Go down and ask Fat Greg if he's heard anything unusual happening in the district. I'm as concerned as to Jack Worm's whereabouts, almost as much as our scribbling friend.'

Pom went outside just in time to hear footsteps on the stairs and to see a flushed and panting Monty taking the steps two at a time. 'Ah, Monty, we were worried.' Monty nodded and entered Malory's room.

'Sorry I'm late. I had a bad night, Sir Tom.'

'Thank Christ you've arrived at last! Where have you been? Pom tells me you weren't at home yesterday.'

Monty had been rehearsing his reasons for absence throughout the night and now simply said, 'I was called away. Relations on the other side of the city suddenly turned up and expected me to meet them. They wanted some work doing on legal documents.' It had all sounded very plausible in the middle of the night, but now Sir Tom's face showed a certain unwillingness to be deceived.

'Relations? Who are these fucking relations? You've never mentioned anyone before. As far as Pom and I are concerned, you don't have any!'

'We've all got relations, Sir Tom. Sometimes we don't talk about them.'

'I see.' But evidently Sir Tom was still suspicious, 'What was their business; what did they want you to do?'

'I think that's my business, Sir Tom,' said Monty stoutly. 'You really shouldn't pry –'

'Pry? Who's prying? I'm taking an interest that's all. Still, if you want to be secretive, so be it! It makes no difference to me. All I want is for you to be reliable and attend on me as we've agreed.'

'I'm here now. I've never let you down, have I?'

'No, I suppose not. But another thing have you heard anything from Master Worms?'

‘Jack Worms? No, nothing. I presume he’s the same as when I saw him last.’

‘He wasn’t in church yesterday, Monty,’ said Pom, ‘I even went around to his shop.’

‘But that would have been closed anyway. Did you go to his lodgings?’

‘I don’t know where he lives.’

‘It’s not like him to miss the church services,’ said Monty with a frown.

‘Probably gone off to visit some fucking relations!’ growled Malory, ‘He’s bound to be back in his shop this morning.’

‘As soon as I’ve finished here, I’ll go to the shop,’ said Monty, ‘I’m sure there’ll be a simple explanation.’

‘Can we set to with our tasks this morning, Mr Pickle?’ said Sir Tom sternly, ‘We’ve wasted enough time on absent friends! I want to examine this passage which starts us off on the quest for the Holy Grail.’

Monty was also glad to change the subject and said eagerly, ‘This is a major part of the story I believe, Sir Tom.’

‘Yes, and has to be handled well.’

Monty felt he had handled an otherwise awkward situation well. Sir Tom had lost interest in Monty’s “lost weekend”, to the scribe’s great relief and it seemed that he would be questioned no further. Thankfully, he turned his attention to the work in hand – the Holy Grail. *Thank Christ we’ve finished with the tale of Sir Tristram!* he thought, but did not say it. Instead, he asked, ‘Well, Sir Tom, how do you intend to begin this section?’

‘It’s going to take place at the feast of the Pentecost – everyone will be in Camelot, Arthur and all his knights. A strange woman on a sweating horse gallops in and asks that Sir Lancelot accompanies her to King Pelles.’

‘Who he?’

‘Really, Mr Pickle! I wish you’d keep up; we’ve mentioned him previously. King Pelles is the father of Elaine, the mother of Galahad –’

‘Who hasn’t appeared yet. Really, Sir Tom, there are so many characters in this book. Wouldn’t it be an idea to have a list of them all at the back – who they are and who they’re related to?’

‘Well, you know all about relations, Monty! We’ll consider your idea when it’s all finished.’

‘But if we’re going to do it, wouldn’t it be another idea to take a note of them as we work on the text? That way we’ll be sure to include them all; obviate mistakes.’

‘If you wish to take on that burden, I won’t stop you, but it will be in your own time and at your own expense.’

Sly old dog! thought Monty, *getting me to do the work for nothing! Still, it would be interesting to try and keep track of who’s who in this massive work, which grows by the day.*

Sir Thomas went on, ‘Now, quill ready – the title is “The Departure”, have you got that? Good, now let’s continue without any interruption, I hope.’

Monty worked mechanically that morning. Fortunately, Sir Tom had already mapped out what he wanted to take down, and it was just a matter of listening to his voice and recording his dictation. Monty never had a problem with Sir Tom’s diction which was clear and sharp, and delivered at an easily recordable speed. As he worked, circling in his head were the events of the last three days. How on earth was he to carry out the Lord Chancellor’s order? Last night, back in his own bed, he had lain awake trying to decide which the better of three available options were. The first was to come clean about what Sir Tom wanted him to do. The second was to obey the Lord Chancellor’s command and report everything the old knight was up to. The third would be to do nothing and report bland, useless information until the noble lord became tired or bored with listening. That was quite a dangerous option. Stillington was no fool and would soon gather he was being fed nothing of significance. He might become frustrated enough to throw him back in the Tower – into its lowest depths! Along with this necessity to make a firm decision, there was now another problem – where was Jack Worms? Monty hoped he had not taken sick and was alone in his lodgings untended by anyone. Monty knew Jack had a sister somewhere in the city, but they didn't meet that often. Immediately he had finished at Newgate, he would walk round to Worms' Books and reassure himself his friend was well.

'Are you awake, Mr Pickle? Did you get that last sentence? Read it back to me please!' And Monty wrenched his mind to the matter in hand:

"'As God me help,' said Sir Lancelot, 'A gentlewoman brought me hither, but I know not the cause.'"

'And I know not the cause as to why you are seven lines behind, Mr Pickle! This won't do. We have ten pages to complete this morning. Please do me the courtesy of paying attention! So help me, Pom. What is the matter with the man this morning?'

'That's what comes of spending Sundays with relations, Sir Tom; it addles the mind!'

***

Addle-pated Dickon pushed his broom idly across the shop floor towards the door where he would deposit the dust and rubbish collected in its bristles into the street beyond. He was just about to give the brush an almighty heave when it was blocked by a pair of boots.

'Steady, Dickon!'

'I'm sorry, Mr Pickle, didn't see you there.'

'That's because you weren't looking! Is Master Worms in the back?'

'No, sir, he hasn't come in today!'

'Oh? Do you know why?'

'No, sir, he wasn't here on Saturday either. It's a good job he trusts me with the keys, otherwise I wouldn't have been able to open up. We've had four customers in this morning, but I couldn't serve any of them as they all wanted "specials".'

Not necessarily keen to know what "specials" were, Monty pressed Dickon for anything he knew of Jack's possible whereabouts. All the time he was talking to the lad, he was distracted by the presence of a dewdrop which was dangling precariously from the tip of the boy's nose, like a fledgling undecided as to when to launch itself. Eventually, to Monty's relief, Dickon wiped his nose with the cuff of his jacket, sniffed to recall any future droplets making a bid for freedom and put down his broom.

'Was your master well on Friday, Dickon?'

'Yes, sir, nothing wrong with him. Although, he was in a bad temper over some money he said was owed.'

'That was all?'

'Yes, sir.'

'Have you thought of going around to his lodgings? He may be unwell.'

'I can't be in two places at once, sir. I thought it better I stayed here with the customers.'

'I suppose you're right. Never mind, I'll walk round now and see if he's there. Will you be able to manage alone until I can find out where Master Worms is?'

'I suppose so, sir,' said Dickon unpromisingly. The lad put up his broom and returned inside. Monty set his face south and headed for Jack's lodgings ten minutes' walk away in The Wall, just off Ludgate.

***

'Jack! Jack Worms!' Monty yelled up at the first-floor window. The house seemed quiet and deserted, but not willing to give up, Monty continued to bang on the door. To his relief, after a minute or so, he heard a shuffling and finally the door opened to reveal Master Worms with a bandage round his head and his left arm in a sling.

'Oh, it's you, Monty. I was in bed.'

'Christ, Jack! What's happened to you?'

'Come in, old friend, I'm not so bad, but I do feel rather sick and giddy.'

Monty went through into Jack's living room where he had evidently made up a bed on the floor, rather than attempt the stairs. The curtains were pulled and the atmosphere unhealthy for lack of fresh air. Monty surmised that Jack Worms had lain unattended by anyone for some time.

'Jesus! How did things come to this, Jack? How did you get these injuries?'

'Lord Robert Stillington –' said Jack faintly, as he ushered Monty to a chair and sat down himself, holding his left arm protectively.

'The Lord Chancellor? Christ, has he had you interrogated – tortured?'

Jack raised a feeble hand and was about to speak, but Monty, horrified that his friend had clearly undergone some terrible experiences at the hands of Stillington villainous torturers, wanted to express his understanding through his own.

'You know, Jack, I've been in the Tower too – and for the whole weekend. I was picked up on Friday evening and then let out yesterday afternoon.' Monty plunged into an account of everything that had happened to him and how he was now in the situation of having to spy on their mutual acquaintance, Sir Tom. He looked with great sympathy at his friend, shaking his head, 'You poor thing, Jack. At least, I didn't have to face the instruments of torture. Did they get any information out of you? Were you able to resist the hot irons? Clearly, they've broken some bones; was it the rack? It must have all be excruciatingly painful. I'm amazed you got out alive!'

Jack had, for some seconds been trying to intervene, but Monty was so incensed at what he could see had been the physical maltreatment of a great friend, that he continued to share some of his own terrible experience which might perhaps ease his friend's memories. 'I heard some frightful noises coming from the cells below me – perhaps it was you, Jack. Good God! – I'm glad I didn't know that; it would have made it much worse. I'm so sorry –'

As he stopped for breath, Jack waved his hands and said, 'No, no! Monty, it's all right! I didn't get these injuries in a torture chamber. I slipped on the steps on Westminster Wharf on my way to Lord Robert's office. You know how slimy they are, like ice. Anyway, I went arse-over-tit from the top to the bottom, cracked my head open and hurt my wrist. The soldiers on duty were very kind and escorted me to the Lord Chancellor's room where he personally organised a surgeon to tend to my wounds. He was most convivial and –'

'Stillington helped you! Why were you going to see him?'

'He asked me to go and see him. You don't ignore a "request", however polite, from the Lord Chancellor. Anyway, I thought it might be something to do with business. Perhaps, he wanted me to supply his office –'

'Don't be naive, Jack. The Lord Chancellor doesn't lower himself to procure materials! He obviously wanted to talk about other matters,' and Monty could make an accurate guess as to what they were.

'Of course, I know that now, Monty. I was rather confused at the time, although I felt much worse later. Anyway, once the surgeon had patched me up, Lord Robert was most kind, and talked to me about paper and water-marks. I can't remember too much. He wants me to go back and see him again in a week, when I feel better.'

'I bet he does!' said Monty vigorously. 'Do you know what this is all about?'

'Well, having heard your experiences in the Tower, I can begin to guess. As you said, it's all concerning Sir Thomas.'

'Right! Stillington knows Sir Tom is mixed up in these rumours which have been put about concerning the two duchesses. You know he thinks they originated from Sir Tom because you supply him with the same paper they were written on?'

'I don't remember much about what was said, but water-marks did come into it, as I told you.'

'His agents have obviously purchased paper openly from you and made the connection.'

'But everyone sells this paper –'

'I told him that, but he didn't seem convinced. I think he knows much more than we think he does – about Sir Tom's visitors, for instance. One of them he didn't mention was Baron Wenlock who comes and goes freely when he's in the country.'

Jack was silent for a while and then said, 'Perhaps, because Lord Wenlock does it so openly. Besides, everyone knows he's a staunch supporter of the Earl of Warwick, he makes no secret of it. Lord Warwick hasn't been accused of any treason as far as we know. He may have the king under his control, but he's not made a bid for the crown. Have you heard anything more about what's happening in the north? Has Sir Anthony Tanner visited lately?'

'He's gone back to Lord Warwick. God knows where he is. Sir Tom's short of cash and is waiting for Six-toed to return with money from the earl. We're all out of funds until he comes back! But returning to Lord Robert. You say he's asked you to visit him again. I'm sure he'll want you to do what he's asked me to do, spy on Sir Tom. Are you willing to do that?'

'Of course not! I don't dishonour my friends – or my customers!'

'Noble, but perhaps foolhardy. It seems to me the Lord Chancellor has spies spying on his spies. He's a very shrewd man and not to be underestimated.'

'What are you going to do, Monty? We're both in the same position. How do I know you won't go straight to Stillington with stories about me?'

'You don't. That's where the man is so clever, set one friend against another. It all comes down to trust in the end, Jack.'

'I can't take all this in, my head's throbbing and I haven't even had a drink.' Monty noticed that Jack had gone very pale and immediately insisted he returned to his mattress.

'Look, don't worry. I'll go back to the shop and tell Dickon you won't be in for the rest of the day. I'm sure he can manage.'

Jack groaned and not from pain, 'That young fool will probably ruin the business in a few hours. It would be better if you could pin a notice up telling everyone the shop's closed today because of illness. My customers are very loyal and will understand, I'm sure. I'll be better tomorrow.'

'Let's hope so, Jack, and let's hope Stillington doesn't insist you visit him until we've had time to discuss what we're going to do!'

Chapter 6

Six-toed Tanner experiences politics in the north;
King Edward returns to his capital; Pom continues his story;
and the Newgate Four share a memorable Christmas.

Reaching Warwick Castle on 15th August, Sir Anthony Tanner found the king was still a "guest" of Lord Warwick, and according to castle gossip, was cooperating extremely well and causing no trouble. In fact, it was said he had enjoyed a few days hunting in Charlecote Park with his lordship and the two seemed to be rubbing along together nicely. However, the earl had been discomforted by news from London that the royal council were not so composed. In fact, they were livid that their king was being held under effective house-arrest. In order to placate them, Lord Warwick had sent his brother, George, the Archbishop of York and the other George, now his son-in-law, the Duke of Clarence, to the city to stiffen the resolve of the council to cleanse itself of the parvenus which habitually surrounded King Edward. He wanted them to listen instead to those with the best interests of the country at heart. The two noblemen were also charged to deny rumours that the king was dead.

At the same time as his kinsmen rode to London, Lord Warwick decided it would be expedient to house his "guest" further away from anyone who might try to "rescue" him. Even more pressing was the threat from the north of another uprising said to have been plotted by the Lancastrians lurking there, and who seemed ready and able to make a challenge at whim. Therefore, on a cool August morning, his lordship assembled everyone in the castle bailey, including the king and declared they were all riding to his beloved castle of

Middleham in North Yorkshire. Sir Anthony was included, and made ready for this tedious ride which was all of 170 miles and over some desperate country. He had undertaken the same journey on several occasions and just hoped the weather would stay dry. Muddied tracks were the very devil for holding everyone up, especially the carts which rolled at the rear carrying supplies. Fortunately, Sir Tony would be with the faster fore-runners who would spy out the ground for obstacles and enemies. He took two horses with him. Having found himself in funds since his master had paid him for services rendered over the previous months, he purchased a decent bay hackney for three pounds which was in addition to his regular mount, a grey courser of which he was very proud.

'Well, Six-toed,' sighed a friend – one of the soldiers he knew well – 'Off we go again. Why can't his lordship stay in one place for at least a couple of months? Why must he always be on the move?'

'It's his nature, I suppose. But he pays our wages, therefore we go whither he goes. Anyway, cheer up! Middleham's not such a bad place.'

'Anything further than Nottingham's alien to me. It's the back of beyond as far as I'm concerned.'

***

They reached the back of beyond at the end of August and Lord Warwick immediately sent out demands for men to see off the threat of uprising from the Lancastrians, who had gathered under the command of a distant relative of Lord Warwick – Humphrey Neville of Brancepeth. There was a poor response, which was worrying for the earl as he wasn't used to being thwarted, particularly on his own turf. Six-toed had all his information directly from a member of the earl's inner circle. Having worn the earl's livery since he was ten years old, Tony was fully trusted, to the extent that his loyalty had been recently rewarded with his knighthood. From what he gathered, it seemed few men in the north were prepared to fight directly for the earl, but were the king to request it, they would willingly take up arms on his behalf. Therefore, Lord Warwick had to swallow his pride and sent his brother, George, newly returned from London, to bargain with the king to give him assistance. Edward agreed to cooperate and support his cousin's campaign against Humphrey Neville in return for a certain amount of "liberty" – such as a visit to York on 10th September. Lord Warwick had no choice but to agree and the king returned to the great city in a royal state – procession, trumpets, flags and crowds out to welcome him. From York, he moved of his own volition to Pontefract Castle where he proceeded to hold court and encourage men to take up arms against the Lancastrian insurrection.

Christ! thought Sir Anthony, *Things move so fast, I can hardly keep up.* They were on the move again, this time further north chasing Humphrey Neville's forces which, it can be told without too much detail, were finally well and truly routed. Indeed, the king went to York in person to see the beheading of Humphrey Neville to great shouts of acclaim from the baying crowd as his unfortunate pate dropped onto the ground, was retrieved, spiked and exhibited in the customary manner on the city wall. King Edward returned to Pontefract. Sir Anthony Tanner remained in York with his master, and watched and listened as events unfolded. He could see immediately where things were going and thought it would be advisable to seek permission to return to London. His master agreed, in fact, positively encouraged it. Six-toed Tanner spurred on his horse, regretfully having to sell his hackney, of which he had become quite fond, but on which he made a small profit. He covered the two hundred mile journey south in six days and arrived in Greyfriars on 5th October.

***

'The king's back!' Pom returned to Sir Tom's room on Thursday morning with the normal supplies of food, but burdened also with a very large stock of news.

'What do you mean "back"?' asked Sir Tom.

'He's on the outskirts of the city, near Cripplegate. They say he has at least a thousand men at his back!'

'Fuck me! Who else is with him?'

'I haven't got all the details.'

'Do you think Sir Anthony's with him?'

'Hardly! He's Warwick's man.'

'Is Warwick not with the king?'

'I have no more details than the fact that Edward IV is approaching London and will surely be let in. Perhaps, Monty Pickle will know more.'

'I doubt it. The man seems to have little interest in anything important. You are both a great disappointment to me sometimes. I rely on you for information about the outside world.'

'You talk as though you were incarcerated in the deepest dungeons of this place, instead of being given free rein!'

'Once a week in the Bankside stews is not sufficient to keep me up to date. My whorelets are hardly reliable sources. I wish Six-toed was here. He'd tell us what's been happening. Has there been any sign of Lord Wenlock? Is he back from Calais? Our wine stocks are down!'

At that moment, Monty Pickle came through the door.

'Good morning Monty,' said Pom, 'What news we've had!'

'News? What news?'

'I told you!' said Sir Tom triumphantly. 'The man never knows anything important.'

Monty bristled, 'I know the king has ridden down from Pontefract Castle and is outside the city gates! He has a retinue of noblemen with him and –'

'Christ, Monty! How did you find that out?'

'I met Sir Anthony as I was coming here and he stopped me for a word. He's on his way to Greyfriars.'

'Good! Sir Anthony's back then. Let's hope he visits soon. So, Monty, who are these noblemen with the king?'

'As far as I remember all their names, there's the Earl of Arundel, the Earl of Essex, Lords Dynham –'

'Dynham? Don't remember him –'

'Howard, Hastings, the Duke of Gloucester and the Earl of Northumberland.'

'That's quite a retinue!' said Sir Tom with a grimace.

'Ah yes. I forgot, the young Duke of Buckingham's there too!'

'No, not another Buckingham!'

'Indeed. Humphrey Stafford's fifteen-year old grandson, Henry.'

'Little bastard, he'll be just like his grandfather, you wait and see; grasping and greedy.'

Pots and kettles, Sir Tom! thought Monty, but did not say it.

Malory sighed, 'So the king's back with the usual crowd of hangers-on; Lord Warwick's somewhere but we know not where and we might expect Six-toed at any minute. I hope he brings cash with him!' He picked up some papers, 'Is there any more news to relate from either of you? If not, we've wasted enough time this morning. Let's get on. Did you finish your quota of pages last evening, Monty?'

'I did, Sir Tom, and have made some notes.'

'Nothing that's going to muddy the waters, I hope?'

'No, just minor issues. Mostly concerned with –' and there he halted as they heard footsteps approaching and then Sir Anthony Tanner entered the room, boyishly handsome and infusing the air with energy.

'Sir Tom, Mr Appleby and Mr Pickle, good morning!'

'Six-toed, welcome back. Have you got my money?' Sir Tom was ever one to come straight to the point.

'I have, Thomas, and will come to that presently. I'm here to tell you all the latest news.'

'Mr Pickle said you told him that the king is just outside the city, Sir Anthony,' said Pom – pouring a glass of claret and handing it to the newcomer. Mr Pickle was feeling distinctly uneasy and had gone a little pale when he saw Sir Anthony enter the room.

'Well, I've just come back from Westminster, and can tell you he's now inside the city gates and received a very cheerful welcome from the city fathers. What you won't know either is that their lordships, the Archbishop of York and the Earl of Oxford, who'd been sent by Lord Warwick to follow the royal forces, are both stuck outside Cripplegate waiting to be admitted. King Edward has sent the message that when he wants to see them, he'll send for them. So there they sit, not knowing which way to go!'

'Where does that leave the Earl of Warwick?' asked Pom.

'In the shit, I suppose!' growled Sir Tom, topping up his glass. 'He's allowed the king to slip through his fingers. I suppose you know all about that, Tony?'

'I do and will tell you as soon as you've carved me off some of that fine-looking bacon, Pom!'

Pom set too with his dagger, hacking at the flitch and cutting off a generous portion. Anthony Tanner attacked his platter with relish, 'I haven't eaten since yesterday evening,' he said with his mouth full, 'This is fine bacon, Pom. I'll have some of that cheese too, if I may.'

Malory said, 'Help yourself, but while you eat, tell us what's been happening in the north, and how the king has been able to slip from Lord Warwick's clutches and return to London.'

Ten minutes of Sir Anthony's chewing and reviewing saw the inhabitants of the Newgate cell fully appraised of the events in the north. Finishing his food, Tony Tanner belched, wiped his mouth with the back of his hand and sat back with a sigh of contentment. Sir Tom immediately asked him if he could have his money.

'I have fat purse for you and a message from Lord Wenlock via Lord Warwick. He says he's arranged for a consignment of wine to be sent from Calais within the next two weeks; just as soon as his pirates have refreshed their supplies! I like the energy of the old man and the way he has no qualms about harrying our enemies in the Channel, just like the old days when the Earl of Warwick took personal command of our pirate fleet.'

'I'm relieved about the money, but not so sanguine about the return of the king. What will it mean for us who've always been loyal to Lord Warwick? We could all end up in the fucking Tower!' observed Sir Tom.

Monty shivered and went pale.

'My informants inside Westminster tell me the king is being careful to speak well of his cousin and his brother, George, as though nothing has happened, and they all remain friends. But others around him are less forgiving, as you'd expect.'

'I imagine little Fuckingham Buckingham's whispering in Edward's ear!' snarled Sir Tom.

'Henry Stafford's just a boy. No one takes much notice of a fifteen-year old.'

'I wouldn't underestimate anyone with that name; bastards all!'

Tony Tanner sighed, 'Really, Sir Tom, you should try and forget this long-standing hostility you have towards the Staffords. I'm still not sure where it comes from, it was certainly many years ago it all started and Humphrey Stafford's long dead.'

'And good fucking riddance too! But I'll never forgive or forget. Still, moving on, is there anything else we should know?'

'Only that King Edward has dismissed Sir John Langstrother as Lord Treasurer; he was given the office by Lord Warwick. The Bishop of Ely, William Grey's taken it over. And all Lord Warwick's Welsh offices have been taken back, and given to King Edward's brother, Richard.'

'This is normal, offices change hands all the time,' said Sir Tom blandly, 'I wouldn't read anything into that.'

'But the fact that Lord Anthony Woodville has turned up, using his dead father's title of Earl Rivers, tell us quite a lot about how the king still views his in-laws. Maybe you've forgotten how Woodville escaped from the battle of Edgecote – when his father and young brother, John, were caught and executed by Lord Warwick? Lord Warwick won't be pleased to hear a Woodville still hangs around Westminster like a bad smell!'

'You seem to have been able to glean a great deal of information from your contacts, Tony?' observed Sir Tom.

Sir Anthony tapped his finger against his nose and raised those fine black eyebrows which had such a devastating effect on many a young woman. 'I just listen, that's the job of a spy. I give nothing away, but take everything in!'

That sounds like very good advice, thought Monty, as he looked at this force of nature. He wondered how on earth Robert Stillington imagined such a colourless person as himself could ever fulfil the same role. But other considerations crowded into his mind as he looked at Tony Tanner, leaving him feeling very uncomfortable.

'What are your plans now, Six-toed? Will you remain in the city or return to Lord Warwick?' Sir Tom looked up from busily counting out the money from the purse and distributing it into piles.

'I'll try and pick up as much news, gossip and official information as I can, and then ride back to Yorkshire. I hope the king will continue to view our mutual lord with a benign eye, unless those caitiffs round him successfully pour their poison in his ear!

'Well, thanks for the cash, we can at least be assured of provender for the next few weeks and I can afford a decent bath with extras in the Stews on Saturday.'

'You may see me there, Sir Tom. I have a fancy for young Bessie, if she's available. Some relaxation before the long ride back!'

'I don't doubt she'll be available to you, Tony. Who could resist your charms?' said Sir Tom with more than a little acerbity prompted by jealousy. 'Just remember, I've booked Plump Poll every Saturday for the next two months.'

'I would never encroach on another man's territory, Sir Tom! Believe me. Bessie will suit me fine!'

***

As soon as Sir Anthony had disappeared down the stairs, Malory picked up his papers and looked quizzically at Monty.

'Are we ready for work? Or has all this court of King Edward business crowded out any thoughts of the court of King Arthur?'

'No, indeed not, Sir Tom. In fact, it all resonates, doesn't it?'

'Resonates? What do you mean?'

'Arthur's court, knights vying with each other for the king's attention; feuds and jostling for favours. Although, there are no giants or roasting babies!'

'Not yet, but murdering children is not unknown in court circles!' said Pom darkly. 'What happened to the real Prince Arthur in the time of King John? He was said to have been murdered by his uncle, the king!'

'That's all well and good. Stop distracting us, Pom, and clear up this shambles that Sir Anthony has left. I must say, for all his good looks, he's a messy eater!'

They worked on for a full hour and even Sir Tom, generally never fully gratified, expressed some satisfaction at their output. 'We are really coming along, Monty. Let's hope there are no further interruptions for the next week or two. Perhaps, the king will get a grip of the country and come to terms with Lord Warwick. Then we can all settle down to what really matters – getting my book finished!'

***

But Monty couldn't settle down after this encounter with Sir Anthony Tanner. He now faced the dilemma as to what to tell Robert Stillington when he made his report to him. Should he admit to the Lord Chancellor that Six-toed had visited Sir Tom and discussed affairs of state? Perhaps, Stillington already knew; perhaps, he had spies placed at the gates of Newgate watching who went in and who came out. If so, they would know Sir Anthony had visited someone and would then question the guards, including Fat Gregory. Therefore, if Monty failed to mention the visit, then Lord Robert would presume his would-be source was unreliable to say the least – maybe even lying. The most sensible thing would be to tell him and hope that there were no serious ramifications for Sir Tom or Sir Anthony. After all, Sir Anthony wasn't an outlaw; he wasn't on any wanted list. He was an honest retainer of the noble Lord Warwick who was, as Six-toed had just reported, presently viewed as a loyal subject by King Edward himself.

And so, on the appointed afternoon, he took a wherry to Westminster, clambered up the green-slimed steps – mindful that a careless footing could be lethal – and within minutes found himself in Stillington's chamber. This was his first meeting with the Lord Chancellor in his guise as "spy" and he exhibited signs of nervousness which his lordship took to be a natural reaction rather than a devious one – at least he would give Monty the benefit of the doubt.

Stillington came straight to the point since he had no intention of wasting any more time than was necessary. In truth, he didn't see this man as productive of anything interesting. It was just satisfying to know he had a spy in Malory's cell. Some little gems might result, but he wasn't expecting much.

'Good day, Mr Pickle. You have news for me? Sir Tom has been behaving himself? I hope not!'

'There's been nothing untoward, my lord. We've been hard at work on the manuscript and it has come to –'

'Try to avoid any exposition of *Le Morte D'Arthur,* if you will. I'm not interested in Knights of the Round Table at present; more interested in Knights in a Small Newgate Cell. Just stick to useful facts like who has visited.'

Monty drew a deep breath, 'Well, Lord Robert, Sir Anthony Tanner arrived from the north two days ago.'

'Ah, one of Lord Warwick's espials! Interesting.' Monty was undecided whether the Lord Chancellor had prior knowledge; he seemed genuinely interested as though it was new to him, but the scribe had by now decided to trust no one and continued with his report as he had rehearsed it.

'I don't know about that, my lord. He had come from Lord Warwick and just reported what we all now know, how the king has returned to London and everything is back to normal.'

'You may say that! Normal? That's not so. But never mind, Sir Anthony didn't mention Margaret of Anjou or King Louis of France, by any chance?'

'Margaret of Anjou?' said Monty in amazement. This was the first time anyone of such magnitude had been mentioned by his interrogator.

'The previous queen is always in our thoughts, Mr Pickle. If you pick up any mention of her, or any other of our continental enemies, you must come directly to me.'

'Sir Anthony made no mention of such people. He simply reported events from the north. How Sir Humphrey Neville had been executed for his treason.' Unfortunately, he gulped as he said the word and the Lord Chancellor looked at him with a frown. 'There's nothing else you have to report then; nothing untoward in Sir Thomas' behaviour?'

'Nothing out of the ordinary, my lord.'

'These are very slim pickings you've brought me. I hope you'll do better next time, Mr Pickle.'

'I can only report what I see and hear, my lord. I can assure you, we have been hard at work on Sir Thomas' book. I'm only there during weekdays. I have no idea what he does or who visits at the weekend, apart from his priest on a Sunday.' Monty had his fingers well and truly crossed at this point since he knew full well what Sir Tom did on Saturday mornings.

'Yes, this business of his own private Mass, most unfitting. Why is he allowed such privileges, I ask myself?'

That's not the only privilege he's allowed and it's this office that has authorised it! thought Monty but did not say it. What he did say was, 'It seems to me Sir Thomas is not in a suitable place to involve himself in any state business, my lord. Neither does he seem interested. He's obsessed with the completion of his *magnum opus* as he calls it.'

'I'll *magnum opus* him one day! The man's been a thorn in the side of the state for years. The number of felonies he's committed and many more we never hear about, I'm sure. I'm certain he's up to some mischief, it's in his nature!' He looked sourly at Monty, 'Well, Mr Pickle, just do your best, although what you've brought me hardly justifies your journey. Good day to you!' and picking up a paper from his desk, he nodded a curt dismissal. Sighing inwardly with relief, Monty hurried out of the room as fast as dignity and his trembling legs would allow.

***

Life in London and specifically Newgate continued peacefully enough for the next few weeks. Sir Tom, now in funds, made his weekly excursion to enjoy the pleasures of the Stews. Plump Poll seemed to be far more interested in what Sir Tom had to say than was normal and his vanity was tickled that she should hang onto his every word as though he was the fount of all knowledge. Even her questions were sharper, and she was less fixated on people and more on events and his opinion of affairs of state.

'You know, Pom, she's quite an intelligent woman once you get past her professional skills. Of course, she can talk while giving me pleasure – which is a bonus. A clever whorelet is all I've ever looked for in a woman.' Pom didn't deign to mention Lady Elizabeth who was rarely referred to these days. That genuinely good woman remained loyal in that she sent small but regular sums of money to her husband; monies which were the proceeds of rent and fees from his midlands estates, and monies which paid for his whorelets.

News from outside was relayed to Sir Tom by Pom and Monty, the later having also sharpened his ears to state affairs because they would be chewed over by Sir Tom, and discussed at length. Living in the precincts of Greyfriars, Pom has easy access to Lord Warwick's officials and was on good terms with many of them. They were free with their information and consequently, Pom received regular reports of their lord who remained in the north. By the beginning of November, Monty had made three visits to Stillington's chambers, managing to tell him nothing, or at least very little. He reported on the progress of *Le Morte*, the absence of visitors – for Sir Anthony had disappeared back to Yorkshire and not been heard of for weeks – and the fact that there had been no sign of letters or mangled verse emanating from Sir Tom's cell. He felt he was playing the game well; his lordship became increasingly frustrated. He had abandoned his idea of using Jack Worms as an agent of information. In fact, when Jack had recovered from his injuries and returned to see Lord Stillington, he had been told there would be no further investigation into the matter of paper supplies. The Lord Chancellor realised it would be very difficult to associate the stationer with the offending verses, since it was true that most of the shops in Paternoster Row bought supplies from the same source. Besides, the origins of scurrilous verses, which had not been uncommon in the last decades of upheaval, were notoriously difficult to uncover and his spy network could be more usefully allocated to members of the nobility closely associated with the king. That needed professionals who knew what they were doing, and Jack Worms and Montmorency Pickle did not fit that description. As far as the latter was concerned, it comforted Stillington to know that there he kept a link at least to the old reprobate in Newgate, however useless it was.

As for Plump Poll, who he had commandeered to fulfil a similar role, he considered her a success as her contribution had been more fruitful. A shrewd harlot who knew her business well, she understood that immediately after a man enjoys a state of ecstasy, he often becomes talkative and confiding. Poll had related several conversations stemming from Sir Tom's libidinous state, mostly connected with his avowed loyalty to Lord Warwick. She played the game as far as Robert Stillington's requirements were concerned. She listened to her client while he lay musing in his bathtub; asked pertinent questions – casually and not too searchingly; let the man ramble on about the state of England and its current woes. Admittedly, some of her resulting accounts she made up to titillate the Lord Chancellor – just for the fun of it, for she liked to see men who thought too much of their own importance foolishly excited. In his post-ecstatic state, Sir Tom would occasionally mouth indiscrete malevolent thoughts, which could be interpreted as seditious on the grounds they were directed at senior members of the nobility. But Poll carefully filtered her accounts to Lord Robert to protect Sir Tom, of whom she was fond. After all, he had been good to her; generally not too demanding; mostly quickly and easily satisfied; sometimes bad tempered, although, unlike some of her regulars, he had rarely struck her. For her "services to the state", she received a small payment from the Lord Chancellor who intended it also as a means to keep her mouth shut about his own regular visits to Bankside. But it was unnecessary. Stillington should have known, as Sir Tom certainly did, that discretion was the watchword of the Bankside pimps and whores, who never discussed their customers' business or predilections, however perverse. The adage, "don't bite the hand that feeds you", was certainly in play down in the Stews on the south side of the Thames.

***

The Sunday sessions with Pom resumed and Monty picked up the threads of Malory's previous existence outside the confines of prison. Pom had reached the beginning of the year '51 when, in March, Fuckingham Buckingham has come to the end of his patience, and a warrant was issued for the arrest of Sir Tom and Pom Appleby – 'with eighteen others – we weren't the only ones in his sights – but no doubt we were his chief target!'

'So, Sir Tom made his first appearance in court?'

'No, Monty, nothing came of it and do you know why?'

'No.'

'Lord Warwick came to the rescue, although it was all kept very quiet. Remember the local feuding between the two noble lords? The earl wasn't going to let Humphrey Stafford incarcerate his retainer. He stood bail for Sir Tom, although he didn't put his own name to the bond. I don't know what the process was, but the warrant was never followed up. What it is to have friends in high places!'

'Yes, I was thinking about Lord Wenlock who seems to hold Sir Tom as a great friend – the wine and money as well. How has that come about?'

'That's for another time, Monty. Let's stick to events in order,that will help you when you come to write it up, surely. Although, I'm no writer.'

'You're right,' nodded Monty, 'Carry on, Pom. What happened next?'

'Sir Tom was still living on his estate in Newbold Revel and, as usual, we were very short of cash. Two farmers in a neighbouring village near Cosford owed him money and wouldn't pay up. So Sir Tom and I, and a few friends, rode to his farm and repossessed some livestock.'

'Livestock?' said Monty.

'Seven cows, two calves and 335 sheep to be precise –'

'335 sheep! How many of you were there? How did you manage a flock that size and nine cattle?'

'There were seven of us on horseback and with dogs. We took their cart too. It was as smoothly executed droving as you've ever seen! We got them all safely back to Newbold Revel, where Sir Tom had arranged to sell them on. He got thirty-eight pounds in all, which more than covered the debt. Unfortunately, Billy Rowe and Will Dowde, the two farmers concerned, reported it as theft, and that's how it went down on the warrant.'

'But Sir Tom still had not been arrested?'

'Well, not yet. But that was when he made his first big mistake.'

'Oh yes, what was that?'

'He picked a fight with the Benedictine brothers of Monk's Kirby Priory. The trouble with Sir Tom is that he was – is – quick to take offence. It may have been some trifling matter; he told me afterwards, "It was all the fault of those fucking brothers! They should have paid up." But I was never sure what it was all about. Later he told me it was "a gambling debt", but I doubt it. Anyway, we waylaid the two defaulters, had a skirmish with them and cracked their shaven pates. As a result, the Abbot of Axholme, which was the mother-house of Monk's Kirby, made a huge fuss which resulted in Henry VI, king at that time, taking action against Sir Tom; the Duke of Buckingham became personally involved.'

'What do you mean "personally"?'

'I mean the duke took to his horse, and with a small unit of fully armed men, came after Sir Tom and me to arrest us. The king directed the Earl of Warwick to join the duke, but Lord Warwick chose not to. Buckingham gathered sixty mounted local yeomen at his manor house in Atherston – conveniently situated between his main house at Maxstoke and most of his retinue at Stafford, and came in search of us.'

'Were you in hiding?'

'Certainly not! While his grace was away from his estates in Stafford, we took the opportunity to plunder his deer park at Caludon. After all, he'd left it mostly unguarded and the beasts were there for the taking. We always thought he was lax in the security of his parks. Remember the story I told of the one hundred men who took beasts from his property in Kent? Well, we thought it was worth a try, so we broke down the walls, and drove out six fine does, which we had butchered and sold for a good profit. I forget how much we made. However, the duke alleged we'd done five hundred pounds of damage in the process, which was an exaggeration.'

'Are you saying that while Buckingham was out looking for Sir Thomas, having left his park unguarded because he had taken his men with him, Sir Tom robbed him?'

'That is the truth, Monty. Our friend had such a violent hatred of Buckingham that it was as much an act of spite as of seeking profit. He wrecked his dove-cote while were there! I think that upset the duke more than the loss of his deer.'

'Where does all this malevolence come from, Pom?'

'I'm sure it was the Harcourt business which sparked it. The fact that Humphrey Stafford was responsible for the deliberate ransacking and burning of Stanford church, with us in it, as well as the home of Sir Tom's great friend, Robert Harcourt, had a serious effect on him and he vowed vengeance ever after. There is also his loyalty to the Earl of Warwick. But I've told you all this before.'

'Yes, I remember. So what happened then? Did the duke arrest Sir Tom?'

'Yes, he did. We were betrayed by one of our own villagers in the end. We were living quite openly in Newbold Revell, off-guard thinking we were safe, when suddenly, five days after breaking into his park, on the night of 25th July, our house was surrounded, and half-a-dozen of the duke's men broke in and dragged us from our beds! We received some rough treatment, as you can imagine. The duke wasn't too scrupulous in his regard for the laws of arrest! We did fight back and cudgelled a few heads, but they easily outnumbered us. We were forced to walk for two days behind Buckingham's small army; almost twenty miles, hands tied and taken to the Warwickshire sheriff, Sir William Mountford, who was staying in his manor in Coleshill. He was a little more forgiving and told us we would spend the night there "where we would be treated as gentlemen – although we didn't deserve it!" I remember him saying that. He was quite a gent himself.'

'So what happened next day?' asked Monty, now totally transfixed by this story, which could have come from one of Malory's more outrageous French romances. To his intense disappointment, Pom rose from his seat, 'That's for another time, Monty. You will hardly believe it when I tell you. It has much that Sir Thomas' stories might include, except perhaps the chivalry!'

'Oh, how disappointing. Must I wait a week?'

'I'm afraid so. But it will be worth it, believe me!'

***

As the year '69 ended, the atmosphere in London remained tense and expectant. King Edward had drawn back the threads of power and in his insouciant way, continued to live as a successful monarch – diverted by hunting and women, and particularly, enamoured of his two daughters, Elizabeth, aged three and Cecily, nine months. There was yet no son and heir, and the Duke of Clarence, as next male in line, retained that position.

As far as the king's approach to his cousin, the Earl of Warwick, was concerned, he held out the hand of friendship by inviting the earl and Clarence to a Great Council in Westminster in October. Still in the north, the two noblemen declined, untrusting, and demanding assurances and guarantees for their safety. Messengers wore tracks on the roads as they galloped up and down between Westminster and Neville strongholds in North Yorkshire. It wasn't until the last week of November that Lord Warwick agreed to ride to London.

'The city is heavily guarded, Sir Tom!' said Pom cheerfully depositing his usual basket of food on the table, 'I've been in the market and all they are talking about is what the king will do when Lord Warwick meets him.'

'No sign of Wenlock or Tony Tanner, I suppose?'

'I haven't heard a thing, although Lord Wenlock is certainly not in Calais; but I'm sure it won't be long before he returns there, he is the king's lieutenant out there, after all.'

'If he keeps sending the wine, Pom, I don't care where he is! But I'd like to hear from Six-toed Tanner. He always knows what's going on. You say the gates to the city are well guarded? Is that to keep Lord Warwick in or out, I wonder?'

'They say – and it's market gossip only – that Lord Warwick will attend the council in two days.'

'I'd like to be a fly on the wall when that takes place, Pom. You've no idea how frustrated I feel that I can't be involved in all this, just stuck in here impotent and that's not a word I would chose to describe myself, as you will appreciate.'

'Indeed, Sir Tom,' Pom said with a broad grin through his beard, 'Plump Poll would agree with you, I'm sure.'

'That's the only outlet for my energies these days, Pom – my whorelets and the book. God's teeth! Who knows what I could have achieved in statecraft if I'd been free!'

'Well, I'm the only one who would ever say this to you, Sir Tom, but you did rather stymie that possibility when you focussed your ire on his Grace, the Duke of Buckingham.'

‘Don’t mention that name again, Pom. I’ve always told you he was the root of all my misfortune.’ Pom knew it was fruitless to remind his master that he was the author of his own misfortune – and that of his servant too; unlike Malory, Pom was always prepared to take responsibility for the situation his past actions had brought him to.

‘Anyway,’ continued Sir Thomas, ‘talking of whorelets, walk down to Gropecunt Lane and find young Meg. I’ve a mind for a tumble.’

‘It is well after ten in the morning, Sir Tom, and Mr Pickle will be here at eleven. He’s always prompt too.’

‘Well, I suppose you’re right. It might be a close fit – ha! Just my joke! I’ll wait ’til this afternoon.’

‘A wise decision, sir!’ said Pom relieved that he wouldn’t have to walk up to Cheapside. Although he always went armed with his old sword these days, he was apprehensive of encountering any young bucks who were wandering the city looking for trouble – or more likely seeking opportunities for robbery. The streets were always dangerous in London, but with the heightened tension, more rogues and villains were abroad, while decent folk stayed indoors unless it was necessary not to. Gropecunt Lane, one of the main centres for London’s brothels, was the natural haunt of whores, pimps, thieves and every kind of cutthroat imaginable. It was an unhealthy place to wander for a middle-aged portly man not fast on his feet or well-practised in arms. Pom wished his master would curb his appetite mid-week and save it for Saturdays. Then visits to Gropecunt, Popkirtle and Cock Lanes in Cheapside would not be necessary.

He was saved further instructions by the arrival of Jack Worms who brought in a ream of paper, fresh quills and a large bottle of ink, ‘Good morning, Sir Tom. Pom! I find you both well, I hope?’

Pom nodded and smiled; Sir Tom grunted, ‘Morning to you, Master Worms. I’m well enough. Pom tells me the streets outside are dangerous, but I don’t suppose you have much trouble in Paternoster Row. Quiet place, I imagine!’

'We have our moments, Sir Tom,' said Jack, thinking of the terrifying visit by Jasper Percy. 'But you're right, we're generally not troubled by villains, not like they are around the Inns of Court or the Steelyard. We're too close to St Paul's and Greyfriars'. Most people treat them with respect, especially when Lord Warwick's in residence!'

'As he will be soon, according to Pom here, who's picked up some gossip.'

'Well, that'll be an interesting meeting, the king and Lord Warwick, I mean. I wonder what they'll have to say to each other, given the events of the last few weeks!'

'Christ knows! We won't, stuck in here. Now, I suppose you want payment?'

'That is the case, Sir Tom,' said Jack firmly. He knew from experience that Malory would always play games with him – try to defer settling by claiming he was waiting for cash to arrive from some mysterious source.

'We are in funds, so you're lucky,' and he groped inside the drawer of the table and drew out a purse from which he extracted a few coins, 'I think you'll find that's right, Master Worms.'

Jack checked the amount and nodded, 'All in order, Sir Tom! Good to do business with you.'

'See yourself out. I'm expecting Mr Pickle soon and I don't want him drawn into gossiping with you.'

Jack was used to Malory's brusqueness by now and never took offence. He smiled and said, 'Good day to you, Sir Thomas!' and made his way down the stairs. He passed Fat Greg, who was in his usual position at the bottom of the stairs to Malory's tower room chewing on a piece of bread and cheese, his arse overhanging a small stool. Jack saw Monty coming through the main gate. He waved and said, 'I've just delivered some materials to our man.'

'What kind of mood is he in?'

'Usual, slightly bad-tempered. I think he needs a whore.'

'Don't encourage him, Jack. He's obsessed with copulation! Anyway, I've some news for him. I've just seen a unit of Lord Warwick's men riding up Cheapside towards Greyfriars'.'

'What were you doing in Cheapside – a dangerous place at the moment?'

'I had to get in some provisions. It was quieter, being early. Anyway, it looks as though Lord Warwick will be back in the city before nightfall. That will cheer Sir Tom up, the earl may bring Tony Tanner with him, who's bound to have all the news. Now that's all Sir Tom seems interested in.'

'What about *Le Morte D'Arthur*? How's that coming along?'

'Quite well, although we do have some longueurs when he runs out of ideas. Perhaps Lord Warwick's exploits will fire up his imagination again! I'd better go and report to him. Talking of reports though, do you still visit Stillington?'

'No, he decided I wasn't of any use. I was disappointed that I never got started on the spying business; although I don't suppose I would've been any good at it. How are you doing on that score?'

'I report what I see and hear – but as you know, most of it is trivial and of little use to anyone in Westminster. The Lord Chancellor always seems disappointed and I'm not sorry. I don't wish to put Sir Tom or Pom Appleby in harms' way – but I have to be careful.'

'Both of us have become embroiled in matters which we're not fitted for. Spying is a dangerous business and requires skills neither of us has. Perhaps, you'll be able to extricate yourself – as you say, most of what you hear is gossip and speculation. That can't be of much use to Lord Robert; he could get that from plenty of other sources.'

Monty sighed, 'I hope he'll come to see that and release me from this obligation he thinks I have to him. Until then, I shall just have to watch what I say and do!'

'Well, Christmastide is nearly upon us; something to look forward to! What will you do on the holy day?'

'Stay at home, as usual. I suppose you'll visit your sister?'

‘I’m not sure what I’ll do; but in view of all the excitement we’ve lived through these last nine months, I look forward to some peace and quiet!’

***

There was an absence of Jack Worm’s “peace and quiet” at Christmas in the year ’69. Instead, it was one of the most memorable Monty would ever spend. Sir Tom, more relaxed and convivial than normal had asked him how he would be spending the holy day.

‘You’re very welcome to come here, Monty,’ he said, ‘I know it’s a prison cell, but we can make it comfortable – bring in a few more chairs – plenty of coals, and above all, I’ve hoarded a stock of wine and food which will see us drunk and replete for days. It’s an offer you can’t refuse, or have you other plans? These mysterious relatives of yours, for instance, will you be visiting them?’

‘No, Sir Tom, I won’t. Can I think about your offer? I was wondering what Master Worms will be doing; he has a sister –’

‘Fuck it! Monty. He hardly ever sees her. Anyway, I’ve invited Jack so there’ll be the four of us. We can play at Hasard, anything you like!’

This made Monty hesitate even more. The idea of this holy day spent in overindulgence and gaming was not what he was used to. His normal routine was to attend mass and an evening service, treat himself to a few extra coals and purchase a bottle of cheap wine. Then he would settle to work to earn the money to pay for his indulgence.

‘Jesus! Your hesitation is nothing other than insulting. What’s the matter with you, Mr Pickle? I’m offering you warmth, food and as much wine as you can sink! I know how you’d spend the day otherwise, so don’t pretend you have a more attractive offer!’

‘You can’t possibly know what I do on a holy day, Sir Thomas,’ said Monty stiffly.

‘I can guess! Pom’s told me how frugally you live, like one of my hermits in *The Morte D’Arthur*! No wine, no succulent food and above all, no women!’

‘Women?’ Monty was immediately on the alert, ‘If you intend to import some whores on Christmas Day, then you can count me out!’

‘Don’t be ridiculous! Everyone knows my whorelets abandon their abandon and take a rest. No, this will be an all-male affair. We may talk about women, but anything else will have to wait a day or two.’

Monty reflected on this unexpected and risky offer. It was true he never enjoyed the season; it served to accentuate his loneliness and isolation. The thought of a warm room, good food, and the pleasant company of Pom and Jack Worms – with the added spice of Sir Tom’s disregard for formal courtesy in language and opinion – suddenly began to appeal. After all, it would only be for one day.

***

The afternoon of December 26th. Monty was aware of a rhythmic banging which seemed to be coming from outside his body – or maybe just inside his head. He was also conscious that he could not swallow owing to a mouth as dry as any desert in Biblical Egypt. His lips were also desiccated and unable to form themselves into normal communication with his tongue which was stuck to the roof of his mouth. He lay spread-eagled on the floor of Malory’s Newgate quarters, face up, mouth wide open, and throat parched through long and persistent snoring.

He became aware that someone was moving about and cussing loudly: ‘Fuck it! Fuck it! Where’s my fucking hose?’ and carefully raising himself on an elbow, Monty saw Sir Thomas crawling across the floor, eyes shut, hands feeling their way around the room for his undergarments. The room was bathed in weak December sunlight and Monty squinted at its feeble rays which came through the bars of the cell and was decorated with a million motes of dust.

'What day is it?' he croaked.

'The next fucking day to Christmas Day! God help us all! Pom! Pom!' Sir Tom yelled, his mouth close to Monty's ear and half-deafening him, 'Pom! Come and find my hose. How can a man eat his breakfast with his bollocks exposed?'

There was a scuffling and someone yawned, evidently stretched themselves and immediately fell off the bed.

'Christ Almighty!' said Pom, as he sprawled across the floor, 'Do you have to shout, sir? Let me try to stand up and I'll look for them. They'll be where you last left them. Jesus! What a night!'

'Of course, they will, you fool! That's what I can't remember – where I last had them.' Sir Tom was standing by now, but swaying unsteadily. His red-rimmed eyes lighted on a body stretched in front of the fireplace and covered in a heap of clothes. The fire was well and truly extinguished, and offered no comfort. Sir Tom pawed at the clothing and gave a shout of triumph, 'Got them! Let's see, who's this underneath?' He pulled at the remaining pile to reveal an unconscious Jack Worms, whose head was perilously close to the centre of the fireplace.

'Pom, get this man woken up and then we can all have breakfast. I suddenly feel hungry!'

In truth, Sir Thomas Malory had the supremely useful knack of fast recovery from any drinking bout because of years of practice. This session had lasted well over twenty-four hours – an excessive amount of wine had been consumed. Providing the evidence, an empty roundlet lay drunkenly crooked on its trestle, along with numerous empty vessels which lay around the room like nine-pins knocked over in a bowling lane. Coming around because of all the shouting, Monty pulled himself to his feet by means of a table leg, all six legs wobbling slightly. To his great embarrassment, he discovered he was stark naked and he took immediate steps to locate his clothing. Grabbing the first pair of hose he came across, he found he was in contention with Jack Worms who had also begun to recover and seek his garments.

'These are mine, I think!' said Monty with some vigour and pulled them out of Jack's hands. There's nothing like having one's genitals exposed to the general gaze for boosting a man's capacity for abrasiveness.

Several minutes of rummaging, stumbling and cussing saw the four men fully dressed. They stood blinking at each other, like bears that had just come out of their long winter sleep and were wondering where they could lay paws on some honey. Pom, ever practical, and like his master practised in the arts of such recovery, stirred his legs, took some money from Sir Tom's drawer, gathered up his basket and disappeared down the stairs. Through the open door, they heard him curse as he tripped over the sleeping hulk of Fat Gregory, who had evidently passed out at some time during the revels.

Jack and Monty made attempts to bring the room to order – they placed the chairs the right way up, tidied the bed and cleared the table of the debris of food. Sir Tom sat back in a chair with his eyes closed, as though in a reverie. 'What a night!' he said with satisfaction.

'What night?' asked Jack, 'I can't remember any of it.'

'It'll all come back eventually, believe me!' said Sir Tom.

'I rather hope it doesn't!' muttered Monty. 'At what point did we take off our clothes?'

'We were playing some games of Hasard, losers had to strip because someone dropped all the fucking money on the floor. I suppose it's still there? Judging by the state of us, it seems as though we all lost at some time or other!'

Monty sighed inwardly with relief. He'd half thought it might have been the consequence of some awful bawdy game of comparison – the sort of "comic" pastime practised in the Stews among the customers, or among young boys coming into puberty.

The room had gone quiet as the three men began to reflect on their Christmas Day. Jack Worms broke the silence, 'Does anyone know what the time is? I haven't heard any chiming recently, only the clanging in my head!'

'Christ! Does it matter?' said Sir Tom bad-temperedly, 'It won't alter the fact that I need my fucking breakfast. Where's Pom with the food? While we're waiting, I'll tap the roundlet and we can get started!'

Monty went white and suddenly felt very sick. He had memories of the time he had vomited into Sir Tom's fireplace and was determined to fight the urge to throw up again. He sat down in a chair and said faintly, 'I'll stick to water, if you don't mind, Sir Tom.'

Jack Worms nodded, 'And so will I!'

'What a couple of milk-sops you are! Can't take your drink evidently!' he poured himself a glass full of Burgundy and proceeded to gulp back the liquor. 'It's the best cure for a headache!'

'We'll take your word for it sir,' muttered Jack.

At that moment, Pom entered with a basket of bread and meats. 'I nearly broke my neck on that fat article lying across the top of the stairs. It's a wonder he didn't roll down and kill himself!'

'What was he doing there anyway?' asked Jack.

'If you remember, you were going to invite him to join us, but on second thoughts, decided his bulk would take up too much room. We sat him outside and left the door wide open so he could be part of our companionable crew, but in his own space. I've no idea when he succumbed,' explained Pom, who by now appeared comparatively sober; undoubtedly the effect of the crisp December air.

'What time is it, Pom?'

'I think it must three of the clock, Monty.'

'Fuck! It can't be,' exclaimed Sir Tom. 'It's not dark enough.'

'Three o'clock in the afternoon, Sir Tom.'

'Good God! Have we slept the clock round?'

'It would seem so.'

Sir Tom shrugged, 'No matter, we had a splendid time, didn't we?' and he looked round, a happy smile on his full lips.

‘If you say so, Sir Tom,’ said Monty, ‘I need time to think about that.’

Monty’s memories of the previous day were returning slowly. He recalled how he had arrived at Newgate directly after mass, walking there in the company of Jack and Pom who had both been at the service. True to his word, Malory had provided a glowing fire, a table laden with food and full glasses, and had even “borrowed” a couple of chairs from the prison keeper. ‘Roger Clyfford won’t miss them. Anyway, he’s absent for a few days.’

For the first few hours, they had sat and drunk moderately, following Sir Tom’s expert guidance that they should “pace themselves for the hours to come.” Monty, now very wary of exposure to what Sir Tom considered “reasonable drinking” was careful to moderate his intake, despite exhortations from the old knight to “get it down, Mr Pickle! Get it down!” He also made sure he took plenty of food, but by mid-day, he was beginning to feel uncomfortable. What with having to visit the privy every hour to relieve his bladder, he began to think he would never last until he could safely make an excuse and go home where he could empty his bowels in private. The thought of performing such an intimate natural requirement in the presence of others weighed heavily. *It shouldn’t,* he thought, *everyone has to shit and most people are casual about who they do it in front of. I’m just used to going unobserved. I hope I’ll be home before the urge comes on me.* But there was no going home for Mr Pickle, and in the end, he was forced to use the communal bucket and accept Malory’s “humorous” gibes. Fat Greg was deputed to empty the contents every so often, in return for helping himself to food and drink; a large amount which he consumed in silence seated on his stool just outside the door.

Conversation was broad-ranging, but generally came back to the current situation at court and the presence of Lord Warwick in the capital. ‘What do you think the earl will do?’ asked Jack. ‘Things haven’t really changed; the Rivers family still dominate –’

'With another Fuckingham Buckingham!' growled Malory, 'I wish Tony Tanner was here, we'd have good company and information. I expect, he's away spying somewhere – there are a lot of spies about – spies spying on spies!' and he burst into laughter, and rocked backwards and forwards in his chair.

Now, Jack Worms, unused to excess vinousness in the daytime, had reached the point in his drinking which made him bolder than usual. He became talkative and excitable, unusual for the young business man who prided himself on his self-possession, 'Monty and I have done some spying, although, we weren't very good at it.' Monty was sufficiently in charge of his faculties to appreciate this monumental indiscretion.

'Spying?' asked Sir Tom, 'Spying on who – on whom?'

'On you, Sir Tom, isn't that funny!' and Jack laughed. Monty was at a loss as to what to do. There would be no shutting Jack up now, and Sir Tom would be like a dog with a bone and not let it go. There was a long silence and the three men stared at Jack who was oblivious to his blunder.

'What do you mean spying on me. On whose authority?'

'The Lord Chancellor's. He –'

'Fuck me! Robert Stillington? He has the nerve to send a couple of gullible fools to take notes on my affairs in the hope of having my head – which his office has always wanted.' For a rare moment, he was speechless. Then, to Monty and Jack's amazement, he threw back his head and gave a great shout of laughter. 'I've not heard anything so funny all year! Tell me, how often do you report to him?'

There was nothing else for it but to confess; Monty stepped in and gave a brief account of their connection with the Lord Chancellor, and the man's expectations and their responses. Also, how he had been incarcerated in the Tower for a weekend. Sir Tom was impressed that his scribe might have suffered at the hands of torturers, until Monty described how he had been rather well treated.

'So you see, Sir Tom, Jack's no longer involved and I have really had nothing to tell his lordship. I did mention that

Sir Anthony Tanner visited when he was in the city, but then he knew that already. Sir Anthony hardly makes himself invisible.'

'Do you tell Stillington about my peccadilloes – my whorelets? That must get his pulses racing!'

'Of course not! I don't know what you get up to when I'm not here, neither do I want to know. I just pass on information about what we do here – which is mostly working on your manuscripts.'

'I'm sure he's really interested in that! Tell me, does he fall asleep or is he hanging onto your every word?'

'Sometimes he seems distracted and rushes me along.'

'I bet he does! You must be a great disappointment to him. Now listen, here's what I'm going to do. I'll liven up your accounts for him, can't have the Lord Chancellor bored to death. I'll think up some contrivances to keep him occupied, even send him down some wrong tracks. Leave it to me. I'll settle some old scores with the man!'

Monty's heart sank. This was an unintended consequence of his honesty; detailing his relationship with Lord Stillington had been designed to bring everything out into the open, to allow Sir Tom to take precautions against indiscretion. The last thing Monty wanted was to be drawn even further into a web of intrigue. His head began to ache and he sipped at his drink, feeling quite depressed.

Sensing the mood was changing from conviviality to gloom, Sir Tom looked across at Pom, 'Let's forget all this nonsense. Get the dice out, Pom, we'll play at Hasard. I hope you've all brought your money!'

And the afternoon proceeded downhill from there. Monty lost 3s 7½d which, along with everyone else's money, found its way under the bed. After that, his luck continued to take a downward spiral, and he forfeited his doublet, shirt, hose and boots. He knew nothing after seven in the evening until he woke and found himself stretched out stark naked the following afternoon on the rush-covered floor.

***

Two days later, Monty and Jack were discussing their most memorable Christmastide. Both were still pale and sickly-looking, though had returned to their work. They sat in the nearest tavern to Jack's shop and sipped gingerly from their pots of ale; alcohol was now just about tolerated by the pair, although Monty had taken longer to recover than his friend, who had the advantage of a youthful intestinal system. Their conversation naturally centred on Jack's indiscrete revelations.

'I suppose I shouldn't have let it out, but I really don't know what Lord Stillington expected from us. It's not as though Sir Tom's in the forefront of conspiracies. How can he be, incarcerated as he is?'

'Well, in your case, the Lord Chancellor obviously realised almost from the start that you could provide very little useful information, not being on the spot. I can't say I'm sorry that Sir Tom knows. It's been a real strain trying to feed news to Stillington without landing our friend into trouble. But now, I have the added strain of wondering what games Sir Tom has decided to play with the Lord Chancellor. It's a nightmare. Sometimes I think I'll just pack up and leave London. Go back to Wiltshire and join the local priory! I already live like a monk, might as well take advantage of the safety of a cloistered life!'

'Don't do that, Monty. We've only just got to know each other and I consider you a good friend. I'd miss you and so would Sir Tom – and Pom. He tells me how much the old curmudgeon likes you – as much as he likes anyone! Besides, he'd be lost without your skills. That book of his will never be finished if you leave.'

'Well, that is one reason to stay, I suppose. I have become very embroiled in *Le Morte*, I will confess and would like to see it completed. Believe me, it is a worthwhile project.'

'There you are then – an excellent reason to stay.'

'There are other things which worry me though.'

'And what are they?'

'One of them is the uncertainty.'

'Uncertainty? What are you uncertain of?'

‘The uncertainty of who’s ruling the kingdom. The “arse-lickers” round the king as Sir Tom calls them, and the ambitions of the Earl of Warwick and his son-in-law. I can see it all coming to a bad end.’

‘That’s all well and truly outside your control, Monty. You should only worry about things you can influence. Anyway, in this case, I think you’re being too pessimistic. Look! The king’s back in London securely on his throne; Lord Warwick’s coming to see him to kiss and make up; the French are no longer much of a threat, and we have good relations with the Duke of Burgundy. Everything seems back to normal!’

Monty smiled and looked back at Jack over the rim of his tankard, ‘When you sum it up like that, it does sound as though we could be in for a long period of peace and prosperity. Thank Christ for it. That’s all I’ve ever wanted, so I hope you’re right!’

But Jack Worms was to be proved wrong in his assessment; Monty was to be very disappointed, and Sir Thomas Malory implicated in plots and counter-plots which neither of them could foresee.

Chapter 7

In which we follow Six-toed Jack Tanner into the flat lands of Eastern England;
Lord Wenlock puts in another appearance; Pom reveals much more, and the
Lord Chancellor's secretary gets a bloody nose.

Tony Tanner dismounted from his courser, stood with the reins in his hand and sniffed the Lincolnshire air; he was in a county he had never visited in all his wide travels. Late January, the weather was cold, with a keen and perpetual east wind blowing in from the North Sea, but it was fortunately dry. He pulled his cloak about him, grateful for its thick wool. He thought about his mission, which was not an unusual one; it was to meet an acquaintance of Lord Warwick, pass on documents and receive others.

'Anthony, there are great stirrings in Lincolnshire; a long-standing dispute over land between two powerful county families – the de Burghs and the Welles – has come to a head. Briefly, the situation is this: it's our intention to capitalise on these skirmishes and make something of them.' The Earl of Warwick had called Tony to his apartments in Greyfriars, where the nobleman paced up and down – tense and energetic as always. A tall, slim man of forty-one, Lord Warwick had a face with regular features, but which was now beginning to show its years; marked by a restless life spent almost entirely on the move. His auburn hair, streaked with grey, was cut short – as was his pale grey beard.

'In what way can I serve you, my lord?'

'Letters and documents, the usual thing. They're all under the seal of the Duke of Clarence and concealment is vital. The least you know of our intentions, the safer you are. Get them to Lord Richard Welles; you'll find his estates in the south-east of the county. Where he is at present, I've no idea. The last I heard, he was planning a serious attack on de Burgh's manor in Gainsborough and is probably moving towards the town as we speak. Thomas De Burgh is the king's master of horse and Edward won't take an attack on one of his servants lying down, however much that young man tries to resist trouble. It's my guess, he'll become involved in some way. But, as I say, it's not necessary for you to know anything else. Just get these documents delivered and bring us the reply.'

It was over 150 miles from London to Gainsborough and Sir Anthony achieved it in four days, some nights sleeping rough for a few hours on the side of the road. Hidden among bushes and intensely uncomfortable, he was attended by the usual night-prowling foxes, which coming upon him, briefly exchanged a stare and then disappeared into the shadows. Sometimes he heard wild-boar squealing and snuffling, but thankfully they kept their distance once they had sniffed him out. On the morning of the fourth day, as he approached the town, he could see smoke and smell burning. De Burgh's manor was only half-a-mile outside; the land being so flat, Tony could clearly judge where the flames were. 'So Lord Welles has carried out his threat and is in the process of sacking his enemy's manor house. Well, my watchword is discretion. I'll wait until the dust settles, and then ride in and seek out Sir Richard, or at least find someone who knows where he is.'

Huddled in his cloak, he sat under a tree for an hour watching from afar movements around the town. At one point, several carts laden with household goods passed him on the track. Enquiring where they were going, the carters were reluctant to talk, although Tony noticed they all wore the same badge – a black lion rampant on a gold ground. Whether these were de Burgh men rescuing his belongings, or Richard Welles men purloining good and chattels from the raid on the manor, he couldn't tell since the insignia on chests and sleeves were strange to him.

Next, he saw a unit of men-at-arms coming towards him and deciding he should take the initiative he stood in their path, 'Good day to you! I'm a stranger here. What's to do in the town?'

The leader of the troop reined in and looked down at him. 'No place for fucking strangers here! What's your business in the town?' he said brusquely.

Tony was tempted to say, 'None of yours!' but instead was more placatory, 'I just happened to be looking for a bed for the night on my way north to Doncaster.'

'Well, don't try the manor house, there are no beds left. We've taken them all!' So, these were Lord Welles' men.

Tony nodded and said, 'Tell me, who's your chief?'

'What's your interest?' asked the man suspiciously.

'When I see the remains of a property burning to the ground, I wonder what the cause was, that's all. Common curiosity.'

The soldier mounted next to him broke in, 'We fight for Sir Richard Welles and have just given Thomas de Burgh a bloody nose, and not before time.'

Not wishing to hear the antecedents of the quarrel, Tony said more robustly, 'Well, I know Sir Richard, at least my chief does,' and he pointed to his sleeve, and showed the armband of the Earl of Warwick. 'While I'm in the district, I'd like to pay my respects on behalf of the earl. I'm a close retainer, Sir Anthony Tanner.'

There was a distinct shift in atmosphere and the leader became conciliatory, 'Beg your pardon, sir, but you can see the situation. There are many cracked heads up there,' and he nodded towards the town, 'and we're not popular – very unpopular now. We're careful when we meet strangers on the road under normal circumstances, but today we're especially watching out for ambushes.'

'Quite right too!' said Tony, embracing the mood, 'But look, I appreciate you're leaving the town, but perhaps you could offer me an escort back to Sir Richard if you could spare one? Get me through the town in one piece?' He jingled his purse.

Within minutes, Anthony was riding through Gainsborough flanked by two men-at-arms. The town itself was untouched, silent, the streets empty of people; but as he reached the outskirts, the acrid smell of burning thatch, wood, metal and dung hit his nostrils, and almost made him retch. As he rounded a bend, he saw a sight of devastation. A large building – clearly the manor house – stood with its roof caved in; wooden beams were smouldering, and barns and huts were charred cinders. Hay ricks destined for winter fodder were giving off sparks which fluttered in the air and extinguished as they hit the damp ground. There were the remnants of household effects, those considered not worth plundering; among them some children's toys: a little hobby horse and a wooden doll. It was a sight Anthony had seen before – the aftermath of battle or feuding. He never got used to it, and always considered the sacking and pillaging of property a complete waste of resources. It was simply a venting of hatred, benefitting no one.

Passing through the manor grounds, they came to a small shabby tent and Sir Anthony was presented to Richard Welles. A rough-spoken man, small and rat-like, about forty-years of age, he stood in full armour drinking from a fine silver goblet. *Plundered, I suppose,* thought Tony. He bowed and introduced himself. 'I have messages for you from Lord Warwick and am to wait for a reply.'

Welles grunted, took the package, unsealed it and began to read the contents. 'I'll need an hour to respond. I'll arrange food for you and fodder for your mount.'

'Thank you, Sir Richard. I would be glad to be underway before nightfall.'

Welles nodded and called one of his servants, 'See to this man's needs and bring him to me in an hour.'

Anthony walked outside and breathed in the dank, fetid air. The sooner he was on the road, the happier he would be.

***

As he set off back to London from Gainsborough, Anthony mused on the current situation the Earl of Warwick and his son-in-law had placed themselves in. They had captured the king, held him under "house arrest", then realised that arrangement could not continue since they had no support from much of the nobility. They needed their acquiescence to recall parliament through which they could run the country. At the same time, they were faced with an uprising in Yorkshire which required the king's resources; the only way to achieve that was to let Edward go. It was a demeaning situation for the earl and the duke, and even Tony Tanner, a stalwart supporter, was surprised at Richard Neville's seeming reluctance to admit defeat.

Why doesn't he just make up with King Edward and cooperate? What is it about the man that makes him so perverse? The king had always pardoned his opponents in the past, he's not a vindictive man. He and Lord Warwick have a long history together; after all, the earl helped young Edward to the throne and has been loyal for almost ten years. Perhaps, it was the business of Edward marrying Elizabeth Woodville, a widow with no dowry and a circle of greedy siblings. That was a miscalculation on the king's part, he thought, *but it can't be undone and forever opposed. Lord Warwick should accept the situation and move on.* Sir Anthony's thoughts then moved to the problem of France and Burgundy. The earl favoured an accord with King Louis XI, with whom he got on very well; King Edward inclined to Burgundy – Edward's sister, Margaret, had just married Charles, Duke of that territory. That was a sticking point. There was also the fact that, before the earl knew that Edward was wedded to Elizabeth Woodville, Richard Neville had been keen to negotiate a marriage for his king to Louis' sister-in-law and had set negotiations in train. It had been a bitter and embarrassing blow when his plan was stymied by what he considered the reckless decision Edward made, "on the insistence of his loins, not political sense", as Lord Warwick had fumed afterwards.

As he cantered along, Tony Tanner also considered his own position. Was he backing the losing side? What would happen if Lord Warwick tipped over the edge into treason by taking up arms against the king? What if he lost?

No! Surely it wouldn't come to that! he reassured himself, *that's too much of a gamble, even for a risk-taker like the Earl of Warwick!* But nonetheless, the thought had embedded itself in his mind and he chewed on several possibilities as he covered the next twenty miles until he came to his intended resting point.

***

'Good news, Sir Tom! I've just seen Lord Wenlock's servant and he says to tell you his lordship will visit at midday today!'

'Christ! I shall be very glad to see him again!'

'And not just because he'll bring badly-needed cash, I hope?' Pom looked sternly at his master.

'Not at all. What do you think of me, Pom? You make me out to be some kind of grasping knave! Shame on you!' Pom's silence spoke volumes. 'Now,' continued Sir Tom, 'make sure we have plenty of that good wine he sent and some food. Take this purse and buy supplies. Before you do that, bring in extra coals and –'

'Sir Tom, can I remind you I haven't got two pairs of hands and I am not a scullion!'

'But fuck it! Pom, who else am I to ask?'

'That fat lump at the bottom of the stairs for a start. He could do with the exercise. Get him to hump buckets of coal up the stairs. I'm not getting any younger you know!'

Malory was very much taken aback by this outburst. 'You've never complained before, Pom; I've always –'

'Taken it for granted I'll fetch and carry for you. Well, up to a point I will. But I resent you barking out orders as though I'm some kind of minion.'

'Me? Bark? I've never barked in my life! I am the most considerate of employers. Ask anyone; ask Monty Pickle.'

'You bully him worse than you do me. No, sir, I need a little more respect from you please.'

Sir Tom stood with his eyebrows raised and his mouth open. Pom had never been anything less than an obliging servant; in return, Malory fed, clothed and housed him. Surely that was enough for any man. And they'd been through so much together – as fugitives, soldiers, outlaws, prisoners. There was no situation they had not shared. For the first time, Malory could think of no suitable reply. He shrugged, looked sulky, and then, thinking better of it, tried to give a thin smile and said, 'Jesus Christ, Pom! I've run out of words – which as you should know is very unusual!'

'I've made my point, Sir Tom. We'll say no more about it!'

'Fuck it! I'll tell Fat Gregory myself to fetch the coals – and that it's his job from now on!'

A small but significant victory! thought Pom and gave a little sigh of satisfaction. 'Now, sir, will we put off Mr Pickle today if Lord Wenlock is visiting at midday?'

'Certainly not! Remember how Robert Stillington is so interested in my visitors. Let Monty tell him the Earl of Warwick's right-hand man visits Sir Thomas Malory and see what he makes of that!'

***

'Did you hear that the inquiry into the accusations of witchcraft against Lady Jacquetta is to be held on 20th?' Lord Wenlock stretched out his long legs in front of the blazing fire stoked up with coal delivered by the sweating and puce-faced Gregory. 'The little lead image has been passed around I believe!' and he looked straight at Sir Tom, and winked. 'Even though it's expected she'll be exonerated, it's done its work. Whoever thought it up has succeeded. The seeds of suspicion have been sown.'

'Indeed, Lord Wenlock. I imagine that was the plan and a very clever one too.'

Monty Pickle sat at the desk, ostensibly reading through a page of script, but really absorbing this interesting conversation. Lord Wenlock continued, 'We've been back in London for two weeks and it's all I've heard people talking about. That and this outbreak of feuding in Lincolnshire.'

'But these local conflicts happen all the time, my lord!' said Malory.

'This is more serious, and the earl's involved – indirectly,' Lord Wenlock said hastily, 'He's not actually taking part in any of the trouble.'

'Just capitalising on it, I presume!' laughed Sir Tom. Monty pricked up his ears.

'Richard Welles is in conflict with Thomas de Burgh over land – isn't it always that – and, according to reports, is prepared to fight for it. Welles is a second cousin of Lord Warwick, so he's bound to support him on the grounds of family if nothing else.'

'I thought Welles supported the Lancastrians?'

'He did, not sure whether he still does; but he's no friend of the king's.'

Monty's ears positively twisted on their bases. Lancastrians! The name Jasper Percy came into his head. *I'm not so stupid as not to see the possibility of a connection,* he thought. *In these strange times, that could be significant.*

'I think Lord Warwick sees this situation in Lincolnshire as an opportunity.'

'For what?'

'I'm not sure, Tom, but things have been building up between the king and the earl since we've returned to London.'

'I thought all the quarrels between them had been resolved and they were friends again,' said Pom.

'So did we all, but nothing's really changed – the Rivers faction is still in control and Lord Warwick can't do a thing about it. The Duke of Clarence is a tactless moody young bastard and doesn't help keep the peace. He definitely has his eye on the throne and doesn't care who knows it. I personally think they're both playing dangerous games.'

Sir Thomas frowned, 'Strong words from you, Lord Wenlock!'

'I speak as I find. I've no intention of being dragged into any foolhardy adventures. Anyway, I'm off to Calais very soon. I've duties to perform, so will be well out of it.'

'Out of what? You can't leave it there! What are the duke and the earl planning?'

'Fuck it, Malory! I don't know. Warwick doesn't confide in anyone these days. All I know is, I don't want to be involved in anything treasonable!'

'You've not mentioned that word before, Lord Wenlock!' Pom looked decidedly uncomfortable, as though a draught of very icy air was suddenly swirling around the room.

'Don't get me wrong, I'm sure neither of them has that in mind. It's just that the earl is sometimes so reckless and Clarence still acts like a schoolboy. That can be dangerous for their associates. I'm glad I'm off to Calais.'

'Does that mean our wine supplies will continue uninterrupted, Lord Wenlock?' asked Sir Tom.

'It's always good to know your priorities, Thomas! And the answer is "yes" it does. How could I not keep my old friend supplied? I will always be in your debt. By the way, I have a purse for you as usual. I hope it'll keep you going until I get back.'

'I'm sure it will and you know how grateful I am,' Sir Tom was almost effusive in his thanks.

How very unusual! thought Monty, *I really must get to the bottom of how Lord Wenlock comes to be in Sir Thomas' debt; most intriguing!*

Sir Tom continued, 'One thing I would know, Lord Wenlock, have you heard any news of Sir Anthony Tanner?'

'Six-toed? The last I saw of him was at Christmas which he spent in Warwick. I know he's in the earl's special favour and has been involved in the disturbances in Lincolnshire. But I've said too much, Thomas,' Wenlock stood up and stretched, clearly determined not to reveal anything too confidential. 'Much as I'm enjoying the company and the fire, I must be off back to Greyfriars'. Lord Warwick is hosting some sort of supper for friends and acquaintances. His usual policy of "casting his bread upon the waters". It's always worked for him – it's why he's so popular. I sometimes wonder what would happen if the bread and meat ran out! How many would stay loyal?'

Malory nodded, 'A good question, Lord Wenlock. But the earl has maintained his reputation for largesse for decades. It's not likely to disappear overnight, I'm sure.'

'I expect you're right. By the way, I forgot to ask you, how's the book coming on? How far have you got with it? The earl himself asked me the other day.'

'If I tell you it runs to almost nine hundred pages and we have reached –,' he turned to Monty – 'where exactly are we Mr Pickle?'

'Page 474, Sir Tom.'

'There you are, half way!' said Sir Tom triumphantly, 'A milestone.'

'Well done! When do you hope to have it finished?'

'Possibly in six months, barring interruptions, illness and acts of God!'

'God will act as he thinks fit, as He always does! Anyway, keep at it. I'm sure it'll be a great success! How will you – how will you –'

'Get it out? That's what everyone asks me. It'll be copied out like every other manuscript, according to sales. That is why I have my helper here – Mr Pickle.' Lord Wenlock looked across at Sir Tom's scribe, who thought he detected a wink but couldn't be sure. Monty stood and bowed low. He was never sure of the protocols due to a baron as he had only ever met one, and that was the man standing before him.

'Good work, Mr Pickle! You must find it all very interesting. Sir Tom doesn't work you too hard, I hope?'

'I never over-tax any of my servants!' protested Sir Tom. Pom and Monty involuntarily and simultaneously raised their eyebrows, and wide-eyed, exchanged exasperated glances.

***

‘You tell me Lord Wenlock actually used the word “treason”?’ Robert Stillington sat forward in his chair and stared hard into Monty’s face.

‘Only in a general way, Lord Robert.’ Monty squirmed slightly in his seat. He knew this would be a difficult interview – treading a fine line between outright lies and a simulacrum of the truth. ‘I’m sure you know better than anyone how hostility still exists between Lord Warwick and the Duke of Clarence, and the king’s relations, despite all King Edward’s efforts. Lord Wenlock only repeated what everyone else is saying.’

‘How has this business in Lincolnshire anything to do with what Lord Wenlock was suggesting? Did he mention plots against the king?’

‘Absolutely not. All he said was that he would be glad to sail to Calais and get on with his work as lieutenant. I don’t think he likes the thought of conspiracies – who does, if it comes to that, my lord?’

‘Plenty of people. Really, Pickle, you are so naive! I wonder why I’m using you at all. Still, if what you say is true, it sounds as though Baron Wenlock is becoming disenchanted with Lord Warwick and if that’s the case, then it’s good news for us. Nothing was said about the earl sending troops to Lincolnshire to help Lord Welles?’

‘Nothing of that sort, my lord.’

‘Very well! Slim pickings again, Mr Pickle,’ and Robert Stillington looked sternly at his “agent”. ‘Do better next time and see if you can’t pump Sir Thomas for what he knows, anything at all. Nothing passes that sly old dog. Just because he’s shut away in Newgate, it doesn’t stop him meddling in matters outside. I’d give anything to know what goes on in his head!’

And so would I, Lord Robert, thought Monty, but did not say it. He left the room, satisfied he had given nothing away which could possibly incriminate anyone. ‘I’m just not cut out for this!’ he said to himself as he picked his way carefully down to the Westminster quay side, ‘It’s just like manoeuvring up and down these slimy steps – treacherous!’

***

Saturday morning down in the Stews and Plump Poll had had a busy week. Her pimp and landlord of *The Unicorn,* Master Roberts, had procured several new customers because of the tension in the city streets which seemed to make men more libidinous than normal.

'Perhaps, they think they should take their pleasure while they can, for walking the streets is risky and their time on earth may be cut off – as might other parts of their bodies!' She smiled as she thought of the stupidity of men who only cared about satisfying the contents of their hose. She knew her power well and used it. The number of minor nobles who frequented the Stews would surprise the majority of decent London folk. These so-called "betters" were no different when their hose was off and they were writhing under her skilful hands. Robert Stillington, for example. Pompous fornicator! In church all day Sunday; fucking like a rabbit on Monday and Friday; and he expected extras for free. This business of spying on Sir Thomas, for instance. She gave Stillington nothing; but the state he was in by the time she's finished with him, she could have made him believe anything – the King of France had visited Malory's cell and shared a merry hour with the man! As it was, she gave him tiny and insignificant information which, when he chewed it over later, found it of no use to him at all.

Now she was waiting for Sir Thomas to arrive and take his weekly bath – "with extras" which he would pay for. She had the hot water ready, and perfume and petals to sprinkle across it. He was an old goat – but he was her old goat, although she knew she shared him with young Meg from Gropecunt Lane, but that was business after all. Meg gave him youth and energy – Poll soothed and comforted him.

As he lay back in his bath, the old goat said, 'Ah, Poll! You've no idea how much I look forward to these visits.'

'You should be grateful to the king for letting you out like this. There's not many prisoners have that kind of privilege!'

'Privilege? It's my right. After all, I've never been found guilty of any crimes. I'm permanently on remand, waiting for my case to be heard! Fuck that! Just find the soap for me again, there's a good woman!'

Smiling, Poll duly performed her regular duty, and she and Tom became absorbed in satisfying his bodily needs for a few minutes. Then, satiated, in his usual forthright manner but to her surprise, he asked, 'Poll, do you have children?'

'A daughter and two sons, sir.'

'And do they live with you here at *The Unicorn*?'

'Oh no, sir! They live with my mother out at Epping. I wouldn't want them here and I don't want my daughter to do what I do, unless we meet with great misfortune.'

'So what do you want her to be, Poll?'

'Respectable, sir! Marry a yeoman farmer, or a tradesman – blacksmith, something of that sort. I have some money put by towards a dowry for her. I've been saving for that very purpose. On no account do I want her to end up a strumpet like me!'

Sir Tom mused on these statements. He wondered how realistic Poll's intentions were. Possibly they could be achieved, if the children stayed well away from their mother.

Christ! That's sad! he thought, *The poor woman must miss them.* He took her hand, gazing at her through watery eyes, red-rimmed because the steam. He went on, 'I should tell you, Poll, I view you with the utmost respect – never mind what you do – "thank God for it!" I say.'

Polly was touched by this rare demonstration of humanity from a man she respected most for his forthrightness and lack of sentimentality. She smiled, 'Thank you, sir, I appreciate that. Now, in return, I'll tell you what I told the Lord Chancellor yesterday!' and she proceeded to entertain her client, not only with details of her "report", which was nugatory as usual, but with more hilarious descriptions of Lord Robert's frolicking. Under all other circumstances she was a model of discretion when it came to her clients' business, but Stillington had tried to bully her into spying on one of her regulars and she resented it deeply. She would not be manipulated by that overweight son of a whore.

'You have done well and I won't forget it!' Sir Thomas leaned back in his tub. 'Most satisfying, Poll! Stillington's a hypocrite of the first order. But did he really ask you to –' and he lowered his voice and pretended to sound shocked.

'Indeed, he did, Sir Tom. It was a first for me, I can tell you!'

'I don't think I fancy it myself, Poll. I hope you charged him for it.'

'I did, sir – sixpence!'

'I'm sure he thought it was worth every penny. Now, enough of the Lord Chancellor and his concupiscent proclivities – that means acting like a goat, Poll. Could I have more hot water? And – oh dear! I do believe I've lost the soap again. Careless of me!'

***

'The answer to your question, why is Lord Wenlock in Sir Tom's debt, is because seven years ago in the winter of '62/'63, Sir Tom saved the baron's life while they were engaged in the capture of four great castles in Northumberland.' Pom sat back in his chair as Monty poked the thin embers of his fire. It was a wet Sunday afternoon in late February and Pom Appleby was making one of his regular visits, keeping his promise to expand on his master's previous escapades.

'Were you there too, Pom?'

'I certainly was and a very hectic time we had of it! We were trying to retrieve these fortresses from the Lancastrians who held them. Lord Warwick took it upon himself to visit each of the castles personally and oversee our siege arrangements. You must have heard of the earl's "great ride" – a circuit of forty-five miles every day for over a week, from one castle to the next, to ensure his men were well-victualled. It was a great feat and did much to enhance Lord Warwick's military reputation. Sir Tom was included in the earl's party on two of the eight days. That was where we first met Anthony Tanner. He was nineteen and reckless with it. We'd already heard the story of his toes and what with his good looks, he was someone we were unlikely to forget. Lord Warwick was taken with his energy and willingness to take risks. Tony's been a loyal servant ever since. Have you noticed he wears the Warwick ring? I think it was in Northumberland where Tony began spying for him. Anyway, on our second circuit, one of the look-outs in Bamburgh Castle put his sights on Lord Wenlock. Sir Tom's eyes were much sharper then, and he spotted the man and his intention. He pulled Lord Wenlock from his horse just before the bolt found its mark.'

'A lucky escape for his lordship!'

'And a lucky piece of work for Sir Tom. When Wenlock discovered what had happened, he expressed himself forever in his debt and promised he would "always see him right", which he's been doing ever since – money and wine as you will have observed!'

'It shows what an honourable man the baron is, Pom. He could easily have let it go – forgotten about it. Especially as Sir Tom was – is – a prisoner and out of sight.'

'That's not Wenlock's way. It's also fortunate for Sir Tom that he has been moved to Newgate – on the earl's London doorstep. Lord Wenlock lodges there when he's in London and, of course, Sir Tom doesn't hesitate to remind his benefactor that he's here. But I think John Wenlock likes Sir Tom's company, and it's no chore for him to walk across the road and spend a convivial hour with our mutual friend.'

Monty nodded, 'Last time we spoke on these matters, Pom, you left me hanging in the air when you had both been captured in July of the year –' and he consulted his notes, ''51 and put into the charge of the sheriff of Warwickshire.'

'Yes, Sir William Mountford – well-meaning but naive! Whether he had some residual loyalty to a fellow county-man, or was too kind-hearted, I never worked out, but instead of putting us in the cells in Coventry Castle, as would have been sensible given Sir Tom's reckless reputation, he arranged horses for us and we were escorted to his own manor house in Coleshill, a twelve-mile ride. We arrived quite late at night and, again carelessness on his part, instead of being locked in the cellars as a couple of felons should have been, he housed us in a first-floor chamber – well appointed as I remember, with windows which overlooked the moat. That's when the fun began!'

'Fun?'

'Never one to miss an opportunity, Sir Tom paced the room clearly thinking of ways to escape. Then, looking out of the window he said, "Fuck me! Pom, we're only twelve feet from the ground." He poked at the wood around the window, "Look at this – shoddy work! We can easily prise it out in its entirety and both of us are thin enough to get through" – I was a lithe young man in those days! – "all we have to do is launch ourselves off the sill outside, jump into the moat and swim across! The whole thing could have been designed for us to get out! Who knows, perhaps Sir William wants us to escape."

"Why on earth would he want that?"

"I've no idea – these so-called gentlemen have strange ideas. Perhaps, like me, he hates the Duke of Buckingham and wants to see him stuffed!"

"We've no money or dry clothes, sir! What happens when we reach the other side?"

"Don't be such a fucking milk-sop, Pom! It's a warm July night; we'll dry out soon enough. As for money, that's not important; what we need above all things are our horses. But I'm certain our friends in Newbold know where we are. Remember, we've always sworn to look out for each other. William Hall, John Sherd and his brothers, John Masshot and the rest will have followed us, and I bet they're somewhere nearby, unless by bad luck they were captured too."

"Sir William didn't mention any of them as we were riding here."

'Quite! As I said, I'd put money on it – if I had any – that they've tracked us here. They're probably waiting for us to be moved tomorrow and will take the opportunity to get us away. But we won't wait for that! Now, take your boots off and tie them round your neck with something, then follow me." He swiftly loosened the frame from its setting in crumbling mortar and pulled the whole window out and laid it on the floor. "That'll teach Mountford to cut corners on carpenters!" He poked his head and shoulders out, and looked down. There was the sliver of a moon. "I can just see the moat directly beneath us. Perhaps it's shallow enough for us to wade across."

"I hope not!" I said, "I don't want to jump in and break my neck on any rocks!"

"For fuck's sake, Pom, be quiet! Just follow me," and he eased his body through the space and onto the sill, which was wide enough for him to stand upright. Then he launched himself, legs first. I heard a splash and a whoop of success, "Come on in, Pom – the water's lovely!" He was making a racket, which I thought very risky, and would surely wake the guards and dogs which Sir William must have had posted, but evidently not – since nothing stirred, apart from the corvids in a nearby rookery; disturbed, they ruffled their feathers and cawed with annoyance. Now, I am a poor swimmer, can barely keep afloat, but where Sir Tom goes, there go I. So I took my chance and a deep breath, and plunged in after him. The moat was deeper than I imagined and I only briefly touched the bottom before bobbing up like a cork to the surface. By Christ, I remember the water was cold! I could just about see Sir Tom's head yards in front, one arm flailing and the other keeping hold of his boots. Manfully, I followed my master over the fifteen yards, and was relieved to see him reach the other side and begin to clamber up its side. When I joined him, I found him lying on his back breathing heavily but, to my amazement, I saw he was grinning all over his face. As he recovered his breath, he started to laugh out loud, "Fuck it, Pom! What an adventure! I'll dine out on this for years! Now, we must –'"

Monty could not contain himself any longer, 'Pom, you do realise that your escape via the moat is recorded in *Le Morte D'Arthur*? One of the Knights of the Round Table did it!'

'I'm not surprised. Who was it?'

'Sir Lancelot.'

'Did he actually swim a moat?'

'Not exactly, but he used a sheet and let himself out of a window.'

'What was he doing locked in a castle in the first place? Not robbing anyone I take it?'

'Certainly not! He wasn't locked in; he was just resting for the night in a garret over the gate house. Climbing out of the window was faster than running down the stairs. He went to the aid of a knight threatened by three others.'

'No swimming involved then? I vaguely remember Sir Tom telling me afterwards that, if he ever needed a good escape in one of his stories, our retreat from Coleshill would come in useful!'

'Well, it immediately rang a bell with me. But I interrupted you, what happened next?'

'Robbery was what happened next, Mr Pickle! Sir Tom was right; ten of our friends had tracked us to Coleshill and were keeping watch for an opportunity to set us free. They must have seen our escape, for they were upon us almost immediately and with our horses.

"We're short of ready cash, boys!" said Sir Tom, "And I know where we can lay hands on some. We'll ride to Combe Abbey and see what we can retrieve from those fat, overfed monks!" We rode fast through the night, covering the twenty miles to the place and arrived in the early hours, just as the monks were rubbing the sleep from their eyes and walking towards the chapel for early morning prayers. We took them completely by surprise and with a knife at the throat of one of the stragglers, we forced the abbot to take us to where the money was kept. We took eighty-six pounds in cash, plus some nice silver ornaments.'

'Robbing the church!' said Monty, horrified.

'As Sir Tom always said, "they have too much of everyone else's money and do nothing for it. Praying doesn't fill empty bellies!"'

'Those are Luddite sentiments, Pom!'

'As far as Sir Tom's concerned, it's just natural justice.'

'Sir Tom doesn't like abbots very much, does he?'

'No. I think it's closely connected with his hatred of the Duke of Buckingham, who was on very friendly terms with the abbot.'

'So did you get away with the money and the ornaments?'

'We did indeed, and not only that, we returned the next day with one hundred men this time and had a real mêlée with the monks.'

'One hundred! That was excessive surely – that's a small army! Why did you do it when you had already taken their cash and belongings?'

'Sir Tom felt he had an obligation to his men – all locals from Newbold Revel and thereabouts; we'd done well by them. Sir Tom was very popular in Newbold – generous in helping his neighbours and they would have done anything for him. On the other hand, the Abbot of Combe was not popular. None of villagers had any liking for the fat greedy man, who tried to bleed the local labourers of cash and kind. Sir Tom told them he was sure there was more money to be had and that he wanted to reward them all with a share in the spoils. Anyway, we took the monks unawares again, they certainly weren't expecting a second attack and with those numbers. Sir Tom all but defrocked the abbot, he had him in his great chair and with a knife at his throat, told him to undress. He had him down to his under garments – fat and fleshy he sat, his chins wobbling with fear until he told him where the money was.'

'That seems unnecessary – to humiliate the man!'

'Sir Tom didn't think so and neither did the rest of us. The monks had a hard time for a little while. One or two of them tried to retaliate, but received cracked heads and a lot of harsh words which, on reflection, should probably not have been used on holy men.' He picked up his notebook and studied it, 'Let me see, I wrote it all down. In the end, we left with forty pounds cash, rings, silver belts, coral, amber and jet rosaries, and a small but valuable psalter; at least Sir Tom said it was. Oh yes, and we purloined their bows and arrows.'

'And just rode off?'

'We did. It was necessary that we scatter to the four winds, once the spoils had been divided. Sir Tom and I laid low for a month in different locations. Everyone in the district was willing to hide us; Sir Tom's reputation for fair dealing was solid; besides, no one likes greedy monks!'

'So, what happened next?'

'Simple! We were caught and brought to the assizes. The details are long and tedious – we were betrayed in the end – the same old story – by some jealous caitiff from another village, for hard cash; we came before a court in Nuneaton and ten of us were charged with a long list of offences, except for the attack on Buckingham's deer park, which was strange because he tried to have us for the ambush against him as well. He was one of the justices, which was against the law, seeing as how he had a direct interest in that case. But, when you're a duke, these niceties don't matter. It was just another reason for Sir Tom to hate Fuckingham Buckingham as he's always been known to us!'

'How did Sir Thomas come to be in prison in London?'

'That's another story, too complicated to tell, or for me to remember all the details, but in October of that year, we were moved from a lock-up in Nuneaton to a cell in the King's Bench Prison in Southwark here in London, and where we spent the next eight years in various other prison cells – more or less.'

'Without trial?'

'Yes, every time our case came up, we asked for it to be heard by a jury of our peers, that is twelve true Warwickshire men. Each time the Chancellor's office said they couldn't find anyone willing to travel from our county to London. Bear in mind, it's not cheap making a hundred-mile journey, what with overnight stays, and the hire of horses and fodder for them, as well as sustenance for the travellers. So there we stayed, moved about from one jail to another in various states of discomfort. It wasn't always like it is here in Newgate, Monty.'

'Well, from what I hear, the situation Sir Tom is in is incomparable. I've never heard of a prisoner given so much licence!'

'It's not quite so extraordinary. Some prisons allow their inmates out at various times of the day. The Fleet Prison, for instance, has prisoners housed outside the main building for lack of space. They come and go quite freely on licence.'

'But what about the – the –'

'Whores?' laughed Pom, anticipating Monty's sensitivity. 'Not uncommon for prisoners to be allowed the services of prostitutes. The authorities don't condone it officially, rather they tend to ignore it since it keeps the men more docile; prevents trouble breaking out and, therefore, saves on guards' wages.'

'Fat Gregory's hardly kept busy guarding Sir Tom, I must say!' observed Monty.

'No, the lazy beggar certainly doesn't earn his keep, but Sir Tom finds him useful, especially when they visit the Stews together; Gregory's never in a hurry to get back to meet the curfew.'

'I suppose it helps that Sir Tom keeps on good terms with the keeper, Roger Clifford?'

'Money and the odd roundlet of wine changes hands quite often!' laughed Pom.

Monty was so engrossed in these escapades of Sir Tom that he failed to notice the fire had gone out completely and the room had now become extremely chilly in the late afternoon. Pom shivered and stood up, wrapped his cloak around him, and said he would take his leave. Realising his omission, Monty was very embarrassed and began to apologise for this lapse of hospitality.

'Think nothing of it, Mr Pickle,' laughed Pom. 'We've both been engrossed in the details of my master's extraordinary life! I find it almost as incredible as the stories you and he are putting together. His deeds are on a par with many of his "perfect, gentle knights", although there's certainly nothing "perfect" or "gentle" about Sir Tom! Even as I relate them, if I hadn't been there and witnessed them all,

I would never believe what happened to us! However, lest you wonder what other felonies Sir Thomas and I committed, all I'll say is that there were only a few; mostly connected with escaping bail. But that will be for another time. I can assure you most of our major criminal antics were finished with once we were imprisoned in London.' And with that, he put on his cap and headed for the door.

***

A quiet Wednesday in early March; a damp day with a north-easterly chill to it. The fire in Malory's Newgate cell was blazing nicely, and Monty, the knight himself and Pom were enjoying its warmth.

'This is the point in the story where we move away from Sir Tristram and Sir Percival, and concentrate on Sir Lamorak and Margawse, Queen of the Orkneys, King Lot's wife. I particularly enjoy this section; it has everything – lust and matricide!'

'Matricide?'

'Yes, a man killing his mother. You didn't think it had anything to do with bedding?'

'Of course not! I know what it means, it just seems a little extreme.'

'That's the thing about the French writers; they don't do things by halves. If it's appropriate, then what does it matter if a man kills his mother? Let's look at that section and see if we can improve it. Listen!' and, as usual, he stood foursquare, paper in hand and began to declaim:

"And where Sir Lamorak alit he tied his horse to a privy postern, and then he went into a parlour and unarmed him; and then he went into the queen's bed and – I particularly like the way the French put this next bit – *she made of him passing great joy, and he of her again* –"'

'That sounds very – very explicit, Sir Tom! Do we need the "again"?'

'Don't be coy and don't interrupt, Mr Pickle,' said Malory sternly, 'I'll continue:

"And he of her again, for either loved other passing sore. So when the knight, Sir Gaheris, – you remember he was the son of King Lot and brother of Sir Gawain – *So when Sir Gaheris, saw his time, he came to their bedside all armed, with his sword naked, and suddenly gat his mother by the hair and struck off her head."'*

'I suppose you can't get more matricidal than that, Sir Tom! What does Sir Lamorak do?'

'He confronts the bastard knight, of course! How does this sound?

When Sir Lamorak saw the blood dash upon him all hot, the which he loved passing well, wit you well he was sore abashed –'

'I bet he was – covered in his lover's blood. Anyone would be "sore abashed". I think –'

'Never mind what you think, don't keep interrupting. We continue,' and he drew a breath and read aloud:

"He was sore abashed and dismayed of that dolorous knight" – we like "dolorous knight", don't we Monty?' Monty nodded and Sir Tom continued – '*"And therewithal, Sir Lamorak leapt out of bed in his shirt as a knight dismayed saying thus: "Ah, Sir Gaheris, knight of the Table Round, foul and evil have you done, and to you great shame. Alas, why have you slain your mother that bare you? With more right you should have slain me."'*

Monty was silent for a few seconds and Sir Tom looked quizzically at him. 'I think this is a story for our time, Monty!'

'Really, Sir Tom?' replied the scribe doubtfully. 'In what ways would you consider that to be true?'

But just as Sir Thomas was about to share his thoughts on the relevance of the beheading of Queen Margawse to the current political situation in England, there was a racket on the stairs and the door opened with a bang.

'Jesus Christ!' exclaimed Sir Tom, letting fall the paper; for three men had entered the room, two heavily armed. 'Fuck it! Sir, that's no way to enter a gentleman's chamber. What's to do here?'

Behind Peter Crosby and the two soldiers was the sweating and panting keeper of Newgate, Roger Clyfford.

'I couldn't keep him out, Sir Thomas. He says he has been sent to search your room for treasonable material.'

Malory faced the intruder, 'Who are you, sir? And who sent you? No, let me guess – Stillington? Am I right?'

'Correct! The Lord Chancellor has sent me,' and he fumbled in his pocket, and began to pull out a rolled paper with a heavy seal dangling from it. By this time, the room was very crowded and it was evident to the bearer of the warrant that it was going to be difficult to make a thorough search among so many bodies. 'Outside, you two,' he ordered the soldiers. 'Allow no one else in!' The two bulky men took up positions outside the door. There was no sight or sound of Fat Gregory.

'Now, I can introduce myself. I am Master Peter Crosby, secretary to Lord Robert Stillington. He has charged me to –'

Sir Thomas was by now red in the face, 'Yes, you've already explained – to come here and disturb a peaceful morning's work! How can I be expected to finish my life's achievement with these CONSTANT INTERRUPTIONS!' And Malory leaned forward and roared into Peter Crosby's face.

The young man took a step backwards in surprise and said, 'That attitude won't help you, Sir Thomas. If you'll just allow me to get on with the search, my men and I will leave you in peace to continue whatever it was you were doing. As I said, there's no escaping –'

'That's what prison cells are usually designed for!' said Malory with heavy sarcasm.

'In your case, I beg to differ, Sir Thomas. We all know you've been given excessive licence –'

'By the king himself!'

'Indeed. But, never mind that. As I said, I have a job to do.' His voice became harder, and he turned to Pom and Monty, 'Sit down all of you! I think we should start with the desk.' He made a movement towards Malory's papers and Pom recognised a look of fury in the old knight's eyes. Crosby picked up the quire of paper Sir Tom and Monty were working on, which happened to be tied with string in the corner to keep the pages in numerical order. Crosby handled the bundle roughly and began pawing through it, presumably looking for incriminating seditious content.

'Careful with that, you bastard!'

'No need for that!' said Crosby smoothly and continued carelessly to tear at the pages. Monty thought he noted spite in his action and that he was trying to antagonise Sir Tom; in which case he was successful, because after a few seconds of mishandling of the precious manuscript, Malory leapt at him.

'Fuck you, Crosby, and your master, Stillington! Leave my papers alone!' and he moved towards the secretary, like lightening– surprisingly so for an old man unused to any regular exercise apart from copulation.

Crosby stumbled backwards towards the fire and immediately held out the sheaf of papers as though he would consign them to its flames; an act of gross provocation as far as their owner was concerned. With a cry of rage, his eyes blazing with the *ignis fatuus* behind them, Malory raised his fist and swung it at Peter Crosby, thumping him between the eyes with such force that, as the young man fell to the floor, the papers came out of his hands involuntarily, but were neatly caught by Pom who, with great sleight of hand, placed them under the blanket covering the truckle bed and promptly sat on them. Malory, with considerable prescience, as Monty realised afterwards, grabbed the document which hung out of Crosby's pocket and threw it on the fire. There was an immediate crackle and hissing, followed by the smell of burning wax.

These events took but a minute at best and during that time, Monty and Roger Clyfford had stood, as highly interested observers, mouths open. The keeper then asserted his authority – this was his building after all – and went towards Peter Crosby to inspect the damage.

'Sir, are you all right?' There was genuine concern in his voice, but, as he explained later, simply because he did not want the inconvenience of a fatality in his prison. There would be enquiries which might reveal a certain lax approach to his responsibilities. As it was, Crosby was bound to report the incident to the Lord Chancellor and he would certainly want to follow it up. Quickly, the keeper considered that attack might be the best form of defence.

By this time Crosby had recovered and stood up, swaying slightly. He had a deep cut above his right eyebrow from which the blood was pouring, and making passages down his cheek and onto his neck. The crisp white shirt fastidiously laundered and donned only that morning, was now stained and soiled with sweat and blood. He was giddy and furious.

'Master Clifford, you witnessed that attack? Entirely unprovoked by me. I want this man arrested and brought to the Tower. Bring in the guards, and have them take all these caitiffs away and locked up in an appropriate manner until the Lord Chancellor decides what to do with them.'

'I appreciate your distress, Mr Crosby. As for the "attack", well, I wonder.'

'What is there to "wonder" about? The man Malory put his fist in my face for no reason other than a chronic bad temper and fear that he was about to be found out as a scurrilous traitor to his king and country!'

'Well, sir, I'm not so sure. You were in the process of trying to destroy his property and, without a warrant to enter, you are also trespassing.'

'I showed you the warrant – here it –' and he fumbled in his pocket for the document, but found it was no longer there. 'I had it here somewhere, signed by the Lord Chancellor himself, giving us the right to enter and search!'

'Well, unfortunately you appear to have mislaid it. I must tell you, and in all the activity you may have forgotten, none of us saw it or were able to read it. I believe it remained in your pocket. Perhaps you assumed we'd know what it was; in which case you were mistaken, I'm afraid.'

'What else could it have been – I told you that's what it was! What did you imagine it was?'

'That is not quite correct, Mr Crosby. All you said was that you had come on the Lord Chancellor's order. There was no mention of a warrant. Your paper could have been anything, Mr Crosby. The Lord Chancellor could have sent you with an advance order for Sir Thomas' book!' said Clyfford and I swore he winked at Sir Tom.

'Don't be ridiculous! It was a warrant, it had the king's seal on it. That's why I brought soldiers. Anyway, why on earth would Lord Robert want to order a copy of Malory's vanity project?'

Malory spluttered and his fist clenched again. Roger Clyfford came to Crosby's rescue, 'I grant you, the soldiers do seem excessive under the circumstances, but you are visiting a prison where there is a predominance of felons – you may have thought you needed protection. May I say people do order books before they are ready – pre-scribed editions, I think they're called. They make sure they are first in line when the book is completed. I believe Lord Rivers is interested, isn't that right, Sir Thomas?'

For a rare moment, Sir Tom was slightly confused, but as Clyfford raised his eyebrows and nodded, he growled, 'That's right. I've had enquiries from several of the nobility. In fact –'

From the point of view of his own integrity, which was being stretched well beyond safety, Clyfford had no intention of letting this line of dissembling continue, 'So you see, Mr Crosby, we didn't read your document which unfortunately has been accidentally consigned to the flames – as I see from the evidence of melted wax in the hearth – where you would have had Sir Thomas's life's work if it had not been for his quick, but admittedly, impetuous action. As he says, there are several senior noblemen interested in this work and I don't think they'll be best pleased if it's destroyed before they've even read the prologue! I must remind you again, you were trespassing without a warrant. Even an Englishman's cell is his castle, Mr Crosby. Magna Carta tells us that!'

'Fuck Magna Carta, what do I care about Magna Carta!' fumed Crosby.

'A strange attitude for one working for the Lord Chancellor', replied Clyfford, 'I would have thought it should be uppermost in your mind.' He looked around at them all, 'Are we agreed that none of us were actually invited to read the Lord Chancellor's document? That Mr Crosby entered uninvited, with two armed men, thereby destroying the sanctity of Sir Thomas Malory's home? That he tried to destroy property belonging to Sir Thomas and that, in an effort to protect it, Sir Thomas took very strong – but reasonable – steps?' Of course they all nodded vigorously and murmured agreement. 'Then, Mr Crosby, perhaps you should be on your way; I'd advise you to go home and change your shirt, which is considerably soiled, I'm sorry to say.'

'Not as sorry as you'll all be when I come back with another warrant, Master Clyfford! I wouldn't be surprised if the Lord Chancellor has your job.'

'I'm afraid that's not in his power, Mr Crosby. I serve the sheriffs of London who are directly responsible to his majesty. I'm sure the Lord Chancellor will not want to trouble the king with such trifling matters, particularly now when there are many other very important issues for him to attend to.'

'Those "important issues" are the very reasons I am here, sir,' said Crosby through gritted teeth. 'It is a matter of treason at its highest.'

'I find it incredible that anyone should think an ancient knight, solely concerned with literature, should be involved in any matters of state, let alone treason! I'm sure the king would find it amusing if he were told. Look around you, sir, what do you see? A man and his secretary preparing romances,' he looked across at Malory, 'and based on the old French, Sir Thomas, as I understand it.' Malory nodded, completely speechless as he watched the keeper in action. 'If the whiff of the French language constitutes treason, then we all deserve beheading or a whipping at least. Never a day passes that I don't use some French word or phrase to enliven my speech! N'est pas, Chevalier Malory?'

By this time, Sir Tom was almost purple in the face for want of laughing out loud, and Monty and Pom were both crossing their legs; controlling their mirth was having a desperate effect on their bladders.

Crosby was feeling dizzy. The severe blow to his skull and Clyfford's sophistry were having a dire effect on his health and temper. He could see there was no point in remaining here any longer. He had been thwarted, attacked and his shirt ruined. He had lost the day and it would be better to withdraw with whatever dignity he had left. Without a further word, he walked to the door and headed for the stairs. His two guards fell in behind him and they walked slowly down the steps to the bottom, where Fat Greg, buttocks overlapping his stool, had resumed his usual spot. As he passed him, Crosby lashed out viciously with his arm and, taken unawares, Gregory fell off his seat and went sprawling over the stone floor.

'Fat villain!' spat Stillington's secretary spitefully.

***

As they left, Pom rose and slowly closed the door. There was a moment of complete stillness, then the four of them burst into riotous laughter and clapping; for a full five minutes, they could not contain themselves.

'Fuck me, Roger! What a performance! I take my hat off to you!' Sir Tom was, by this time, pumping Clyfford's hand up and down, and the keeper was also beaming.

'Careless of him not to show us his warrant and very quick thinking of you, Sir Tom, to consign to the flames.'

'Of course I knew what it was, but you were quite right, we had no sight of it and his visit was void – indeed, illegal.'

'You did fetch him quite a wallop, Sir Tom!' said Pom.

'Nobody threatens my paper-work! You know as well as I how many years it has taken me to prepare *Le Morte* and I won't allow some upstart secretary – especially the Lord Chancellor's upstart secretary – to interfere with it. Once I could see him heading to the fire, I had to take action.'

'We mustn't be too complacent. My guess is Lord Robert will try and achieve retribution for our treatment of Peter Crosby,' said Clyfford.

'Well, sir,' said Pom, 'I hope it will cause you no trouble!'

'Probably not. As I told him, I do not answer to the Lord Chancellor. But we'll have to wait and see what he does. In the meantime, I think we all deserve a drink. Have you any of that excellent Burgundy you were serving last time I visited?'

'Jesus! I was forgetting my manners, Roger! Pom, tap the roundlet. I think we can manage a bit of a session. Work can wait for a while; we need to celebrate a great victory against pompous arses! Let them do their worst, I say!'

***

There were ramifications. Within the hour, Crosby had rushed home, changed his shirt, gone back to the office and presented himself to the Lord Chancellor.

'Are you telling me you allowed Malory to punch you in the face and throw an official document into the fire?' Lord Robert looked with fury at his secretary who stood before him in a clean, crisp shirt, a nicely developing black eye and with a sheepish expression.

'They plotted against me, Lord Robert. The keeper was most devious and I warned him his job was at stake.'

'You and I both know that can't be the case. You should have saved your breath. But I'll be revenged on Malory and his Newgate rabble. This is what we'll do,' and he leaned forward to share his strategy.

'Now, put that into action and you'll go some way to redeeming yourself in *my* book, Crosby!'

***

Two days later, a Friday, Monty Pickle entered Newgate's main gate and headed towards the tower room just in time to see Fat Gregory and Pom manhandling a large wooden tub up the stairs. Puffing, panting and cussing, the two men were obviously having trouble and Monty resisted asking them "what's to do?" until he followed them into the room.

Setting down the tub, breathing heavily, Pom said, 'Don't ask me to do that again, Sir Tom!' and Fat Greg leaned against the door jamb speechless and puce.

'What's this all about, Sir Tom?' asked Monty.

'Stillington's fucking revenge, Mr Pickle! He's persuaded the king to revoke my licence to leave Newgate, which means I can't take my weekly bath down in the Stews. It was an act of pure spite! But if I can't go to the Stews, then they can come to me. Just like Meg on a Wednesday, Plump Poll says she'll do home visits on Saturday mornings. She can entertain me here.'

'Can I stop you there, Sir Tom?' said Pom slowly, looking bemused, 'Have you thought who is to run up and down stairs with buckets of hot water to fill this damn thing? It won't be me, I can assure you!'

Sir Tom frowned, 'Then Gregory can do it!'

Gregory looked slyly at Sir Tom, 'Only if you pay me extra.'

'Very well, say a groat a bucket.' Gregory narrowed his eyes, trying to look as though he was taking his time to assess the offer, before nodding quickly in case Sir Tom changed his mind.

'By the by, Sir Tom, have you considered how you are to empty the thing? The water will have to be bailed out back into the buckets and taken down the stairs again,' Pom was always practical, 'You surely weren't thinking of pouring the water out of the windows? You couldn't anyway, as they don't open.'

'Of course, I know that! Gregory's groat will cover filling and emptying; don't keep putting up objections.'

Gregory frowned and thought, fleetingly, that he might haggle – but "a bird in hand" was a good maxim, and he decided to stay silent.

Malory continued, 'The thing's here now and I intend to use it tomorrow. I want you to get word to Poll today and tell her to be ready to come across for eleven tomorrow morning.

Give her the wherry fare and tell her to look respectable, otherwise the guards might challenge her. Tell her pimp, I'm prepared to pay her extra for the inconvenience.'

Pom looked put out at the idea of a journey across the Thames which would take up some of his free time. 'This is all very inconvenient, Sir Tom,' he observed.

'Damn right it is. Stillington's got a lot to answer for and I'll have my revenge, believe me!'

Monty was regarding these transactions with the utmost interest. It struck him how pig-headed Sir Thomas could be when he thought he was being thwarted, particularly by officials and how he personally would not want to get on the old knight's wrong side. He also considered how much room this wooden object took up in Malory's cell.

'Perhaps we could turn it upside down when it's not in use and make an extra table of it. That would be helpful,' he suggested.

'Not a bad idea,' agreed Pom.

Wrenching his mind back from the necessity of these unwanted arrangements, Sir Thomas turned his attention to Monty. 'Mr Pickle, we've wasted enough time here this morning. Let's continue where we left off yesterday. Remind me – Stillington's retribution has completely put it out of my mind!'

Chapter 8

Tony Tanner returns to Lincolnshire; Jack Worms seeks information; Pom gets a shock and Monty uses his wits to escape an unforeseen situation.

It had been a good week for hard riding. The early March weather had been crisp, clear and dry, and journeying from north Yorkshire to meet with Lord Warwick's troops in Coventry had taken Sir Anthony Tanner less than a week. He had been kept up to date with most of the events which had taken place since he was in Lincoln and the earl had returned to London. Lord Richard Welles and Sir Thomas Burgh had been summoned to the capital by King Edward to answer for their behaviour. The king was forced to take this local disturbance seriously because he was told by one of his spies that the Lincolnshire commoners were demanding the release of Henry Lancaster, otherwise Henry VI, who still languished in the Tower; there were obviously seeds of rebellion being sewn in the county. As soon as Welles reached London, the king gave him an audience and a pardon, but kept him under house arrest. At the same time, in the very early days of March, Edward ordered Lord Warwick and the Duke of Clarence into Warwickshire "to raise troops to help the king put down rebellion in Lincolnshire", which he declared "he would later oversee in person".

According to secret information which was channelled to Sir Anthony through Lord Warwick's network of spies, it was Clarence who was master-minding the fomenting of this rebellion. On the day Lord Welles was pardoned, 3rd March, Clarence, still in London, sent word to Welles' son, Robert, to unleash the rebels in Lincolnshire. On the same day,

Edward at last prepared to ride out from London to deal with matters himself, but Clarence forestalled him by writing a note asking for a meeting. With his army behind him and Lord Warwick raising troops in the midlands, Edward could see no risk; he certainly still trusted his brother. A family meeting was arranged between the two brothers and their mother at the York's London home of Baynard's Castle on 6th March.

Arriving in Coventry, Tony Tanner went straight to the apartments of Lord Warwick. Well recognised by the guards, they didn't hesitate in letting him through the tight cordon of soldiers round and inside the castle walls. Within minutes, he was outside again with clear instructions.

'Jesus Christ!' he swore, 'I've ridden almost two hundred miles in five days, now it's back to Lincolnshire to liaise with Robert Welles. Up and down, east to west! It's a good job I'm young and fit! I could have done with a day's rest. But, those are my orders and the earl treats me well enough.' He twisted the small silver ring on his little finger and thought of the purse of silver he would receive when his task was complete. Lord Warwick was always true to his word, and paid all his retainers and soldiers on time and in full.

Jack's mind wandered as he cantered out of the precincts of the castle, 'I wonder what those caitiffs in Newgate are up to? I'd give anything for one of Master Robert's strumpets to be soothing me in a bath of scented water! What day is it? Ah, Wednesday. Meg will be visiting the old whore-master.' He sighed and turned his horse's face eastward and prepared to ride to Lincolnshire – *a dreary, flat place,* he thought, *one where the wind never stops blowing!*

***

There was nothing dreary or flat about the atmosphere in the Newgate cell; it was purposeful. Thomas Malory was working at his table and Monty on the upturned bathtub. Now and then the scribe was forced to stand up, and walk around the room to get rid of the cramp, to Sir Tom's annoyance.

'Will you stop bobbing up and down, Mr Pickle? It's most distracting!'

'So is this arrangement, Sir Tom? I take it you've never tried working on the base of a bathtub? No! I thought not. There's nowhere for me to put my legs.'

'Try working standing up then!'

'Then I get a back-ache. I think we should come to a different arrangement. Why don't we use the tub to set out the manuscripts as we complete them? That way we separate them from those which have to be worked on and I can continue working side-by-side with you as we did before.'

Sir Tom thought for a few seconds and to Monty's relief, nodded, 'Yes, I agree. It is better when we sit together!'

'There's a great deal of commotion in the streets round St Paul's, Sir Tom.' Pom entered the room having been out collecting the laundry from their washerwoman. 'It's said that the king and the Duke of Clarence are going there to make an offering together in a show of friendship.'

'Friendship, my arse!' growled Sir Tom. 'The king must be mad or stupid not to know what his brother's about! Lord Warwick's gone to Coventry to raise troops; Lord Wenlock's back in charge of Calais, and the Duke of Clarence is as slippery as they come.'

'It's said the brothers had a convivial evening with their mother at Baynard's Castle last night and are now bosom friends. Clarence says immediately after he has been to St Paul's, he's travelling westward to join his wife who's expecting a child in the spring. No one's exactly sure where she is.'

'This is all gossip, Pom. We need someone like Tony Tanner to tell us what's really going on. I wonder where he is. Last we heard, he was heading to the far north. Anyway, wherever he is he's bound to be in the thick of it! I wish I was.'

'Perhaps you could get an hour's dispensation to go to St Paul's and see the king's procession with his brother. It would be a loyal gesture on your part and the king couldn't object to that. We could ask Roger Clyfford, he's on duty now.'

‘That’s one of your better ideas, Pom. Go and ask him. Perhaps he’s like to join us. We could visit a tavern or two –’

‘I don’t think he would condone that, Sir Tom. Anyway, we’d have to take Fat Greg with us, and it would cost you a fortune to keep him in food and drink – which he’d expect in return for extra work.’

‘Yes, you’re right. But just getting out for an hour or two would give my old bones a great deal of pleasure. As you say, it’s not as though I’m asking to visit Gropecunt or Pokeskirt Lanes! See what you can do.’

***

Tony Tanner was in the thick of it, as Sir Tom had surmised. He reached Lincoln to find the city in a state of emergency and immediately wrote to his master a description of what he observed:

“Lord Robert Welles had been busy doing His Grace the Duke of Clarence’s bidding and very successfully. As soon as I arrived I noticed the streets were crowded with armed men clearly preparing for an uprising. There was a large crowd of citizens clustered round the door of a church and, fighting my way through I saw a notice pinned up which Sir Robert Welles had signed, summoning all able men to the standard of Lord Warwick and the Duke of Clarence. As you know, last month rumours were put about that the king was coming to hang anyone in the county convicted of treason. The same threat is being used, but this time the people are aware that the king has taken command himself, has left London and is heading to Lincolnshire with a large force. Men have seen my livery and I show them the Warwick ring; they ask me what they should do and I tell them they should muster all the men they can and fight for you my lord. I have also completed the task you gave me and visited Sir Robert Welles at Grantham and given him one of your silver rings as a token of your support for his cause.

I am putting this note in the hands of a skilled rider I can trust who will be with you in two days. As you ordered, I will proceed to Yorkshire immediately to find Lord Scrope of Bolton, Sir John Conyers and Lord FitzWalter and pass on your order that they stir an uprising in their county. Thus the king will be assailed on two fronts. The last report of the king's progress was that he had reached Fotheringhay."

Certain that he could do no more in Lincoln, and that Lord Warwick would undoubtedly be able to raise at least twenty thousand midland men and join the Lincolnshire army, Tony traded in his courser for a fresh younger horse and turned his face to the north yet again.

***

'It's good to get out, Monty!' Sir Tom started to take a deep breath of London air and then thought better of it. The stink of the city was universal, covering rich neighbourhoods and poor ones in equal measure. The wind blew foul odours from the river to the land and back again; an intertwining of stench which contained vapours from every sphere of human and animal activity.

'I always forget how gut-wrenchingly bad the air of the city streets is, Monty!' laughed Sir Tom. 'Like Pom, you're obviously well used to it. I always thought the Stews and the river-crossing were bad enough. St Paul's is no better; monks' turds stink just as badly as villains'. We're all equal in the sight of God as far as our bowels are concerned!'

'Indeed, Sir Tom, but one becomes inured to it.'

'Inured to manure! I like its ring, Monty; jot it down, we may use it sometime.' Malory was like a magpie with words and phrases – he purloined them whenever and wherever they sparkled, and took his fancy. Monty had a half-filled notebook of such stolen gems and several had found their way into the *Morte*.

Malory began to get impatient, 'Now, when is the king coming? We should get closer; I can't see a thing,' and he put his elbows to the fore and jabbed his way forward. Monty and Pom followed in his wake, ignoring the curses of others. Malory's scribe hated crowds and was looking about him cautiously for the slightest sign of a dagger or other sharp weapon. There were cutpurses too and he clutched at his doublet pocket where he had hidden his purse, protecting it from the quick slash of a blade which could skilfully detach that object from its anchor on a belt, the owner unaware of its loss.

'Come on! Here's a good spot,' and Monty felt himself tugged hard by the collar and propelled next to Sir Tom, with Pom on his other side, 'we can see the procession from here. They're coming from Baynard's so they'll come up Paul's Chain to join the South Chain and then on to the entrance to the cathedral. We'll have an excellent view!'

They stood waiting for half-an-hour. Fat Gregory lagged at the back of the crowd, chewing on his finger nails and wondering what all the fuss was about. Keeper Clyfford had given him strict instructions not to allow Sir Thomas to visit any whore-house, ale-house, tavern or inn – specific descriptions designed to thwart any attempt by Malory to confuse his guard. He was also to return him to the cell when the service or celebration – whatever it was – was over; Clyfford was no clearer than anyone else what the royal visit to St Paul's was all about.

The crowd was becoming restive when suddenly they heard drums and trumpets from down the street. Soon the advance guard appeared; a small contingent of soldiers in the king's livery. Behind came the king with the Duke of Clarence beside him. Edward was several inches taller than everyone else and towered above them all, sitting bolt upright in his saddle, finely dressed in red velvet. Monty's mind went back to a similar procession he had observed when the previous king, Henry VI, had made the same journey to the city's most prestigious cathedral. *What a contrast,* he thought, *No wonder Henry lost his crown! It's all in the eye of the beholder. A king means certain things to his people – and size and strength are two of them. Edward has it in abundance.*

‘There’s Clarence, next to the king!’ shouted Malory above the general din. ‘He looks very shifty, doesn’t he?’

‘Why don’t you shout a bit louder so the king can hear, and have us arrested and hanged?’ scowled Pom, who had never wanted to come in the first place and would rather have been resting his short legs in front of the fire.

‘Christ, Pom! You’re an old misery! I’m enjoying this. I’d give anything to know what was said at Baynard’s last night; even more to know what’s going on in Clarence’s head.’

The procession reached the portals of the cathedral and to a flurry of trumpets, Edward and his brother dismounted, walked up the steps hand in hand – like a couple about to wed – and went in through the enormous oak doors. The soldiers took position up the steps and the doors were firmly closed. A select number of nobility and gentry had been invited, and were already in their seats.

‘I should have been there,’ grumbled Malory, ‘stalwart Yorkist that I am!’

Pom looked at Monty and muttered, ‘when it suits!’

The crowd was beginning to disperse, not willing to wait an unspecified time for the congregation inside to emerge. ‘Let’s get to a tavern quickly before everyone else does,’ said Sir Tom.

To Monty’s surprise, Gregory had appeared alongside and overhearing his prisoner, said, very sharply for the fat man, ‘Back to Newgate for you, Sir Thomas.’

‘Surely you’d like to join us in a drink to celebrate this accord between brothers?’

‘You know your words confuse me, Sir Thomas. Keeper Clifford has given me orders and I must follow them or it’s my job – he’s told me that. “Master Gregory,” he said, “on no account is Sir Thomas to visit a whore-house, an inn, a tavern or a – a –’

‘An ale-house or hostelry?’

‘That’s it, Sir Thomas, an alehouse, although he didn’t mention no hostelry.’

'There you are then – let's find one immediately and all have a drink. What do you say?' and he looked around beaming.

Pom frowned, 'You know exactly the spirit of Master Clifford's instructions to Gregory, Sir Tom. Don't drag the man into trouble. Let's get back and open some of Wenlock's wine. Who wants to be jostled in a crowded tavern? I don't!'

'There's nothing I'd like better! Fuck it, Pom! We're free for a couple of hours. Let's make the most of it!'

'Orders is orders, Sir Tom!' Gregory was looking anxious and Pom determined. After a couple of minutes argument, Sir Tom lost the day and the four of them fought their way back through the crowds, the old knight grumbling and complaining until they arrived back in Newgate, and he accepted the inevitable – there would be no more licence that day.

'Well, apart from a breath of freedom, I didn't think there was much to make a fuss about. The king looks well. Clarence, as I said, shifty and who knows what the outcome will be.'

It wouldn't be many days before they found out.

***

Worms' Books, like others in Paternoster Row, was a place where customers came unfortunately not always to buy, but rather to browse and gossip. Jack knew he must tolerate these time-wasters, speculating that at some point they would decide to purchase their writing materials from him, or buy a pamphlet or ballad sheet on impulse. The subject of conversation in recent early April days had been about the king and Lord Warwick's activities in the midlands. No one had any idea what was afoot, it was all guesswork and had little basis. Where the green shoots of facts were few, rumour seeded itself easily in poor soil.

On this Thursday morning, 12th April, two gentlemen stood in his shop, one of them leaning casually on his workbench, to Jack's annoyance, voicing his view that, 'There'll be another civil war within days, believe me!'

'Don't talk rubbish! The king's ridden out to meet his brother and cousin to overcome these flatlanders in Lincolnshire. They're all working together.'

'Me talk rubbish? I tell you, Richard Neville and George Duke of Clarence have a different view of things!'

'Oh, and you know what they think, do you?'

'It's obvious they're up to something; it's posted up on all the tavern doors. Haven't you read what they're saying? That Warwick and Clarence are traitors?'

'That's old stuff and has been around for a month. It's just the Woodvilles making trouble. We should wait and see what real news comes back to London. What do you think, Jack?'

Jack looked up, *'I think you should buy something and clear out of my shop,'* was what he would have liked to have said. Instead he shrugged, 'I don't pretend to know what's going on. It seems to me that nothing's changed, whoever's king; life follows its regular pattern. For myself, I get up, have a shit, come to work, go back home, eat, occasionally get drunk and go to bed.' This rather bleak account of a sadly familiar mundane existence stopped the gossipers in their tracks for a second.

Then one nodded, 'Yes, well, we all lead regular lives. But it does matter who's on the throne! Look at all the trouble we've had with the sainted Henry. He was no good at all – lost all our lands in France for a start!'

Fearing he was going to be subjected to a long and intricate history lesson, Jack put down his bradawl and took up a sharp knife with which to cut some fine leather. 'Listen, gentlemen, I don't want to seem impolite, but I do have some urgent work to do. As much as I would like to chat, I don't think we can possibly speculate on what's going on a hundred miles off. I prefer to wait, and hear from anyone who's been there and seen for themselves. Now, I really have to get on with this; it is very intricate – requires complete silence!'

Taking the hint, the two men nodded and walked towards the door. One looked back and said, 'It doesn't pay not to be concerned with what's happening, Master Worms. We're all affected in one way or another!'

'You may well be right, Master Thompson, but at this particular moment, this fine binding needs my undivided attention; more than I can give to the serpentine affairs of state!'

***

Jack was not as uninterested in national events as he had demonstrated to his two time-wasters. In fact, he was as fascinated by the machinations of the nobility as anyone. It was just that he hated misinformation, which seemed to be the currency of the gossip which gripped London now. Taverns were full of "experts" on English politics and their ramifications, but Jack knew where he might find the clearest and most accurate exposition of events, and that was Newgate Jail.

Closing his shop for an hour as St Paul's bells tolled midday, he hurried through the narrow alleys round the cathedral and into Newgate Street. Within three minutes, he was climbing the stairs to Sir Tom's room.

'Ah, Master Worms! Good day to you!' said the old knight affably.

'Good day to you too, Sir Tom – Monty – Pom!'

'We haven't seen you for a while? Still spying for Stillington?' Sir Tom said with a hint of malice.

'The only place I could glean any useful information is from you, Sir Tom. That's why I've come. I've had numerous customers talking complete –'

'Bollocks? Yes, I've heard some of it from Pom and Monty. Most ridiculous is that the French are about to invade! Lord Wenlock found that very amusing I can tell you!'

'Have you had any news from the baron?' asked Jack.

'Now, Jack, are you asking as a spy or a friend? Will you take anything I say straight back to the Lord Chancellor? Can I trust you?' and he winked at Pom and Monty.

'Of course, you can trust me. Anyway, Stillington didn't want me as an espial; he said I would be of no use, I'd look too shifty and he's right. I'm no good at lying.'

'I'm glad to hear it, Jack! You know our friend here –' and he pointed at Monty – 'our friend here is still visiting the noble Robert with trifles I feed him?'

'Yes, he has said so. He also told me Lord Robert's had you barred from visiting Bankside.'

'Yes, and I intend to pay him back for that; something I'm still working on! Now, what can we do for you? As you see, we're very busy,' and he swept his arm towards the upturned bathtub on which were balanced numerous small bundles of manuscript tied with different coloured string; Malory's "system" for organising his sections.

'I've really come to see if you've heard anything from Six-toed Tanner recently? The gossip-mongers in my shop are putting out all sorts of versions of what's happening outside London. I wondered if he's been touch with real news.'

Sir Tom ran his hands through his greying hair until it stood up round his face like a halo, 'We've heard nothing since Lord Wenlock was here. Like everyone else, we're in the dark.'

'Do we even know where Six-toed is?' asked Monty.

'Here!' and the door flew open to reveal the man himself, 'A fortuitous entry but I must confess I've been eavesdropping – like a good spy – and waiting for the right moment to surprise you.'

Sir Tom went pink with pleasure and grabbed Tony Tanner's hand, 'Fuck me! Tony, but it's good to see you. Sit down – Monty, give him your chair! Drinks, Pom – the best we have. The Newgate Five are together again!'

'The Newgate Five?' Monty frowned, obediently standing up to give Tony his seat. 'Makes us sound like one of your felonious gangs, Sir Tom!'

'More like a band of brothers, Mr Pickle. By the way, Tony, I don't think you've met Master Jack Worms – stationer of this parish. Jack Worms – this is my good friend, Sir Anthony Tanner, soldier and – and other things.' Jack bowed slightly and looked quizzically at the newcomer. Monty had told him a few details of Sir Anthony's life and occupation and he was curious as to what an informant looked like – having himself failed to make the grade in Stillington's eyes. He had to agree with everything Monty had said about the young man; Tanner had the piratical looks and the swagger necessary for a man of fortune.

Malory continued, 'Now, Tony, tell us everything – where you've been, what you've been up to and what's happening outside this god-forsaken city.'

'First things first, Sir Tom. Pour me a glass from that jug, Pom. I haven't had a decent drink in days!' Pom dutifully obliged and Tony Tanner took a sip of Wenlock's best and gave a sigh of pleasure, 'That's what I call the real stuff! Now, where to start? Where was I going when I left London last? I've been to so many places I've lost track!'

'The last I heard was from Lord Wenlock who said you were in Lincolnshire – although he wasn't giving anything away. What were you doing there?'

'What I always do – supporting Lord Warwick.'

'Well, are you going to get on and tell us what's been happening, or do we have to get you drunk or beat it out of you?'

'Neither. I've come straight here from Manchester where I left Lord Warwick and the Duke of Clarence. They've sent me on important business, but I thought I'd call in and give my friends the latest news. It'll be all over the city within days and you might as well hear the truth of things before the rumour-mongers get to work on them.'

'This sounds serious, Tony,' said Malory, 'Monty, go down and tell Fat Greg to bring up more coals, and tell him not to allow anyone else in under any circumstances – not even Keeper Clyfford himself!'

The fire was banked up, seats and stools were found for everyone, and attention was all on Sir Anthony Tanner, whose handsome face showed signs of weathering from hard riding.

'Well –' and Sir Tom looked expectantly at his visitor, 'Go on then, don't keep us in suspense. Get to the point!'

'Lord Warwick and the Duke of Clarence are on the run from Edward's army. The last I heard, they were heading for Warwick to collect their wives, and then make a dash for the coast and take ship to Calais.'

'Running away! Why?'

'It's a long and complicated story, and I'm not sure of all the details myself. All I know is, these events started when Sir Robert Welles called off his rebellion in Lincolnshire because the king had his father Richard Welles in custody and threatened to have him executed unless Sir Robert capitulated. There was a skirmish just outside Stamford, when Welles and some of Clarence's men had to run for their lives from the king's men, and I'll come onto that in a minute.'

Malory leaned forward looking puzzled, 'So how was Lord Warwick implicated – he wasn't there, was he?'

'No, he was still in Coventry trying to raise the twenty thousand men he needed to carry out his plan, which was to confront Edward. He was also relying on the men from Lincolnshire – possibly another twenty thousand of them. Sir John Conyers was poised in Yorkshire waiting to help and Lord Warwick was convinced his friend King Louis in France would back him against Edward.'

'So what went wrong?'

'Edward had Richard Welles and his brother-in-law, Thomas Dymmock, brought from Lincoln to London. When they arrived, he threatened to have them beheaded unless Welles sent word to his son, Robert, to submit immediately. Meanwhile, Lord Warwick was having trouble raising men. Even in loyal Coventry, there was little support for the adventure. Word had inevitably got out that this was a bid for the crown and Lord Warwick was backing Clarence for king. The duke's not at all popular and we couldn't muster half the number of men we needed.'

'I always thought my old home county was totally loyal to Lord Warwick,' Sir Tom looked gloomily over his glass.

'Well, I got around the city taverns listening in and I can tell you there was no enthusiasm for Clarence. Then a messenger arrived from Sir Robert Welles that "he was considering changing his mind" when he heard of the king's threat to his father. He thought he might submit and stand his army down, although he hinted he was going to make a bid to rescue his father, who had been brought from London with Edward's army and was still under arrest.'

'So what happened then?' asked Pom, warming his backside at the fire.

'It all became a bit confused until reports dribbled in of this battle close to Stamford. Edward entered the fray, and unleashed his ordnance and Welles army was routed. "Lose-coat" it's being called because his men threw off their livery as they were running away – at least that's the story! Anyway, Welles was captured. Unfortunately so was a cache of incriminating correspondence between Clarence and the rebel leader. You wouldn't believe it, but of all unlikely places, it was discovered in the helmet of a slaughtered Lincolnshire yeoman wearing Clarence's livery! No one knows how it got there, but could anything have been more careless?'

'What about the fight then?' Sir Tom, who had been listening intently, leaned even further forward in his chair, 'Were there many losses, much bloodshed?'

'For a short, sharp encounter, losses were high and they say a few thousand Lincolnshire men were killed, but there are no exact numbers for either side. It was very bloody by all accounts and since he'd been unable to persuade Welles' son to submit to him, the king carried out his threat, and Richard Welles and Thomas Dymmock were summarily beheaded in full view of both armies as they were engaging. Afterwards, Sir Robert remained Edward's captive.'

'So, it was a bloody encounter with executions! My Knights of the Round Table aren't the only ones with a blood lust, you see, Monty!'

His scribe frowned. *Real beheadings are nasty messy affairs; bits of bone and brain splattering everywhere. Decapitations in "Le Morte D'Arthur" are generally quick and clean; there's no comparison!* he thought, but did not say it. Instead, he looked at Tony Tanner's face, grown red with warmth from the fire and the excitement of his tale; he listened intently as the young man continued.

'With no army raised, we set out from Coventry towards Burton-on-Trent and then on to Derby. The Earl of Shrewsbury, who'd left Coventry earlier ostensibly to raise men to our cause, turned traitor and instead rode to find the king who was also heading northward and offered him his army of three thousand. There was also a report that Lord Warwick's brother-in-law, John de Vere, Earl of Oxford declared he was off to France to join the Lancastrians at Anjou.'

'So bad news all round with these fucking capricious magnates. I told you: never trust a nobleman – except Lord Warwick, of course. How did he take this news?'

'As ever, in his stride. I heard him say, "Well, at least we know where we stand with Shrewsbury; I was never certain of him – our family quarrels stretch back some long ways; as for de Vere, he ever was a turncoat."'

'What happened when you reached Burton?' asked Sir Tom. 'When was the next real action?'

'The rebellion which I'd helped set up in Yorkshire came to nothing and was put down almost as soon as it started. We were on our way north to Chesterfield –'

'Where's Chesterfield?' asked Jack.

'In Derbyshire. Anyway, it was there we heard it had failed and then things really started to unravel. We knew the king was only twenty-five miles east of us and travelling fast enough to block our entry into Yorkshire. We arrived in the town to be met by Edward's Garter King of Arms, who delivered two summonses for the Duke of Clarence and Lord Warwick to appear before the king. It was all very – very – I can't think of the right word. Probably "bloody" would describe it best because the herald, who was looking very stern, said, "The game's up, my lord! Robert Welles has spilled his guts and paid the price." Then suddenly, he threw a heavy bag at Clarence, which fell at his feet with a soggy thump – I was standing close enough to hear. There was no need to open the thing – it was evident what it contained –'

'Robert Welles' head, I suppose? "Head in a bag", Monty! It might come in useful. Make a note. What did Lord Warwick do then, Tony?'

'It was obvious to us all the king knew everything, so the earl played for time by sending fruitless messages to King Edward via the herald. After several attempts to acquire full pardons, and being refused, in the end, he asked for safe-conducts. Finally, the king ran out of patience; the essence of his final terse reply was that even his ancient enemy, the French, wouldn't ask for such sureties! If the pair were as innocent as they protested, then they should have no fear of him; if guilty, they could expect a degree of favour and pity for their long friendship's sake. It was at that point they decided to make a run for it.'

'So what was their plan then?' asked Sir Tom, literally on the edge of his seat.

'To head for Manchester where Lord Stanley was waiting with his army. They were going to insist he kept his promise of aid whenever we needed it. So off we went at full gallop, managing to evade the herald and his men.'

'And did Lord Stanley stand by his word?'

'Unfortunately not – he sent a message he was otherwise engaged in a clash with the king's brother, Richard of Gloucester and couldn't – or wouldn't – help.'

'The bastard!' Sir Tom got up out of his seat and began to pace the room. 'Where's the sense of honour?'

'He's always been a trimmer,' said Sir Anthony.

'What's a trimmer?' Jack Worms whispered to Monty behind his hand. He had been sitting transfixed by Tony's tales of battles, treasons, heralds and back-stabbing. *Sir Thomas should write this up rather than wasting time with trifling French romances. This is the real thing!* he thought.

'A trimmer is a fucking turncoat, a deceiver and someone who can't be trusted,' said Sir Tom with the vigour he customarily showed when agitated. 'The Stanley have a poor record for loyalty – it should be burnt into their family escutcheon: "No Honour". I'm getting so worked up here, I need another drink. Pom, break open that new roundlet and fill up the jug!'

Monty squirmed on his stool. The last thing he wanted was to be included in one of Malory's drinking sessions. He had other work to do when he went home; a commission had landed on his doorstep from one of his regular clients; the work was required urgently and it would pay well. He was just about to wave away Pom's hand, which had the jug poised over his glass, when Sir Anthony saved the day.

'It was at this point that I left Lord Warwick's party. We heard there was a general proclamation abroad for our capture, with the offer of generous rewards. We were – are – outlaws, and Lord Warwick pulled me aside and gave me a specific task here in London. When it's completed, I'm to meet him in Calais as soon as I can take ship across the Channel. I think it would be better for me not to reveal any more of the business. I have no wish to implicate any of you in Lord Warwick's immediate affairs, apart from yourself, Thomas, and possibly Mr Appleby here. It's better for your own safety, Jack and Monty, that you know as little as possible, particularly considering your association with Robert Stillington, Mr Pickle. For now, all I will say is that Warwick, Clarence, and their wives and daughters should have arrived on the south coast seeking to join Lord Fauconberg's flotilla, or assemble a small fleet of Lord Warwick's own vessels in the Channel. For, as I said, he's destined for Calais where he has firm friends and allies – Lord Wenlock for one. That's all I'm prepared to tell you.' He sat back in his chair, looking as a man relieved to have rid himself of a great burden of information.

***

Monty had been following this tail of treason with his mouth open in amazement. So it was true, what Lord Wenlock and Sir Tom had reasoned – Lord Warwick and the Duke of Clarence were after the throne, but had failed in their attempt. He wondered what Robert Stillington would make of it;

surely, he had received the news by now? Would he think that Monty knew about such a plot, but had failed to pass the information on? Would he send his men round again, this time with real menace? The thought of the rack was always in the back of his mind – now it pushed its way firmly to the front. He dared not ask searching questions, lest the answers be even more incriminating. Sir Tom was not so coy, 'Well, fuck me, Tony! This is a to-do in no mistake. What happens now?'

'As I said, I'd rather keep this between us Tom – and Pom. I don't want Master Worms or Mr Pickle to be put at risk. Perhaps they could leave us for an hour?'

'Certainly! Mr Pickle, Master Worms – you heard the man. Take an hour for your dinner, Monty, and then come back. We'll resume work at one o'clock.'

Monty left with mixed feelings. Grateful that Sir Anthony was concerned for their safety by not involving them in further conspiracies, but also intensely curious as to what Lord Warwick's intentions were, he walked to the door followed by Jack who was looking annoyed at being unceremoniously dismissed. 'At least Sir Tom didn't tell us to "fuck off"!' he muttered as they walked down the stairs.

As soon as they had gone, Tony Tanner resumed his account. 'As I said, King Edward had offered the two noblemen pardons if they stood their men down, but the stakes were too high – Lord Warwick knew he would be in an impossible situation if he threw himself on the king's mercy. He has a plan and is sticking to it.'

'What do you mean?'

'Although I'm not privy to the details, it's my guess he's going to France to seek help from King Louis, eleventh of that name – a great friend and admirer of Lord Warwick. Louis considers the *milord* as a brother. I'm going with him as soon as I can take ship. One of the reasons I'm here is to beg shelter for a couple of days, at the most. I can't stay at Greyfriars – Stillington and his bullies will be watching the place for anyone going in and out. Some of the servants have already ditched their liveries and gone elsewhere. All I need is somewhere to sleep for a night. Can you manage that?'

‘Jesus Christ! Of course we can!’ Sir Tom had gone pink with excitement. The idea of subterfuge, conspiracy – anything mischievous – was meat and drink to him. Pom had long since realised that the old knight’s obsession with tales of quests and damsels in distress came from a deep-seated need for action. For a man with those latent energies, to be shut away in a prison cell was an exquisite form of torture. The whoring, drinking and gaming were side-shows, mere distractions.

‘I thought you would and I’m grateful. As I said, I have some serious business to attend to in London. My horses are stabled across the road in Greyfriars – I still have friends there who will never give me away. I also have money! One of the benefits of working for a man of probity is that I’ve always been paid on time. I can certainly contribute to my keep –’

‘We wouldn’t hear of such a thing, would we, Pom?’

‘No, Sir Tom!’ But Pom looked less keen than his master. He was working out where the bear-traps were in this arrangement. One of them was that there was an inspection of the cells at lock-up and, lax as Master Clyfford was in the supervision of Newgate’s resident rogue, lock-up was one area he was very sharp about. Roger Clyfford didn’t want Sir Tom entertaining his whorelets throughout the night and, therefore, every evening without fail, the duty-guard was sent to check the room had only one occupant. Pom generally left the building at lock-up, unless he had pre-arranged permission to stay; the same arrangement applying to Sir Tom’s few regular visitors. This left the question, where to hide Sir Anthony? The privy was curtained off, but it was a very confined space; generally, Sir Tom and Pom were comfortable taking a shit without recourse to the curtain. Still, Tony Tanner would have to squeeze behind it whenever anyone entered the room. Fortunately, visitors were few and Fat Greg only struggled up the stairs when he was called. In any case, the guard was easily fooled and Pom decided he would have to ensure Gregory was on duty while Six-toed was with them.

All this flashed across his mind and he was not paying much attention until he caught the words "passing information to Stillington" emanating from Tony Tanner's lips. His heart sank as he could see Sir Tom's eyes lighting up with glee. This was more mischief for him to enjoy – probably at Monty Pickle's expense.

'Of course, as you appreciate, we have our own resident conduit to Lord Robert – Mr Pickle himself has been appointed as spy-in-chief to the Lord Chancellor. It couldn't be better.'

'That's why I'd rather discuss this between us, Thomas. But now I would appreciate some food if you have any. I've been on the road for days and I'm famished!'

'Certainly, certainly! Pom, organise it for our guest. You can't imagine how pleased I am to have you staying here! It's been a dull existence for the most part. We can even furnish you with a whorelet. Would Bessie suit? I'm sure we can arrange a home visit. You know that Plump Poll now supplies all my wants on the premises?'

Pom was exasperated. As usual, with anything out of the ordinary, Malory was treating the whole situation as a sort of huge diversion. He seemed to have blocked out the thought that he was poking about in a dung-hill of treason and likely to smear the rest of them with its excrement. He sighed and wondered where all this would lead them, apart from in the shit. Meanwhile, Sir Thomas was busy filling the jug from the roundlet and as he did so he looked across at his visitor and asked, 'So, Tony, what's the plan?'

***

Monty and Jack were also busy, having no choice other than to repair to a tavern to chew over Six-toed Tony's remarkable account. Speaking in a low voice, Jack asked, 'What do you make of all this, Monty? Do you believe the Earl of Warwick and his son-in-law guilty of such treason?'

'I can't think why Sir Anthony should make up such a story. After all, he was witness to it all.'

‘We only have his word. He could be exaggerating.’

‘As he said, by tomorrow, word of this will be all around the city. I’m sure Robert Stillington already knows. His spy network must be very efficient.’

Jack grimaced, ‘He certainly didn’t think that of me. Tell me, Monty, how much information do you give him? Do you think he trusts you?’

‘As little as I can! I don’t exactly subvert the truth. Most of what I give him, he knows already. He just wants someone inside Newgate. I don’t think he trusts me. What he does know is that at any time, he could have me arrested and sent to the Tower. I’m sure that one day he’ll ask me to do something against Sir Tom – plant evidence or make false witness against him.’

‘So what are you going to tell him about Tony Tanner’s visit? Have you thought?’

‘I don’t know. It depends whether he knows already. It’ll be no good me lying and saying that I haven’t seen the man if he does. As Sir Anthony said, Stillington’s men are watching the area. They’re bound to post spies around Newgate as well as Greyfriars’. It’s most likely they’ve already spotted him. They may even be waiting to arrest him when he leaves the prison. One thing I’m glad of though –’

‘What’s that?’

‘That I don’t know what Lord Warwick’s business is that Tony’s mixed up in. At least I can’t give anything away.’

‘It was thoughtful of Tony to exclude us from his plots. Like you, I certainly have no intention of getting myself involved in these great matters of state. When are you next visiting Lord Robert?’

‘At the beginning, he wanted me to report as and when I saw “anything interesting”. But since I’ve been giving him so little, he now calls me in when he wants information, or reassurance that Sir Tom’s not up to something. With all this going on, I’d be surprised if I didn’t get a summons from him tomorrow at least!’

‘So I suppose you will have to think out a strategy to answer his questions.’

'He's inclined to try and play cat and mouse with me. I've developed some methods to counteract him though!'

'Jesus, Monty! You're beginning to sound like a real spy! You're not going to tell me you enjoy it?'

'If you want the truth, I'm always scared shitless when I see him. He has this way of leaning across his desk and scowling at me. I expect him to call in the guards and have me in chains at any time. He knows I have a guilty conscience!'

'That's because he's the top lawyer – if the Lord Chancellor can't spot a villain, there's no hope for us!' said Jack, cheerfully sipping his ale.

'I'm no villain!' said Monty spiritedly. 'Just a man who has stupidly got himself involved with a rogue.'

'Ah, yes. Sir Tom. How's his book coming along? I bet he's annoyed at all these distractions.'

'Not a bit of it! Didn't you see his face light up in glee when Tony Tanner arrived? He's so contradictory! Grumbling about interruptions, but seemingly enjoying diversions. But he's quick enough to keep me focussed if I seem distracted. I hope we can settle to a couple of hours this afternoon before I go home. Did I tell you I have another commission? Paying well too!'

'Good. I hope you'll be spending the proceeds in my shop!'

'These things are usually beneficial to us both – I'll always need supplies.'

'Well, since you say you're in funds, what about filling this pot up again?' and Jack pushed his tankard in Monty's direction.

***

Pom had walked in the direction of the Greyfriars' kitchens and now stood uncertainly at their doors. As far as he was concerned, this was another fine mess that Sir Tom – and his companion in crime, Tony Tanner – had placed him in. As soon as Sir Anthony had crossed the threshold of Sir Tom's Newgate residence, Pom knew there would be distress, difficulties and danger. While his master might thrive on those three uncomfortable conditions, Mr Appleby did not. By and large, he enjoyed his time in Newgate. In truth, Sir Tom could be extremely vexing, but he had become inured to his master's eccentricities over their forty-year acquaintance. Peace and quiet was now all he craved, and he thought he had found it within the confines of their prison cell. But recently, he had been dragged into matters about which he knew nothing and cared less. True, he had spent a lifetime following a man with no conscience and a capricious view of the world. He had committed crimes at Sir Tom's behest; had extorted money and valuables from his fellow countrymen; had attacked and robbed members of the nobility and the clergy. But this was the first time he had been involved in treason.

Hearing Sir Anthony's account of the debacle in the midlands and the Earl of Warwick's flight to France, he knew that Sir Tom was "on the wrong side".

'Stillington will know of all this and, as I stand here, his men are probably spying on me.' He felt extremely uncomfortable. 'I'm ill-suited to subterfuge! Fuck Sir Anthony!' It said much about the depths of Pom's irritation that he cussed. He always felt Sir Tom did enough of that for them both. 'I should never have been brought into this. It's enough I spend my life fetching and carrying for Sir Tom, without playing conspirator for his friends.'

He had been deputed by Sir Anthony to pick up "a very important bundle", content undisclosed.

'You know all the kitchen and stable staff in Greyfriars', Pom, don't you?' Mr Pickle and Jack Worms had left and Tony Tanner looked across at Pom with raised eyebrows. It was a rhetorical question. The man knew that Pom was well-acquainted with most of the servants in Lord Warwick's residence, lodging as he did just outside the main walls of the place and close to the stabling block.

'I do indeed, sir,' replied Pom waiting for the next question, request or order.

'Tomorrow could you pick up a small bundle of papers for me? I've arranged for one of the earl's humbler clerks to have it delivered to the kitchens. Take your basket, walk across the road and just go into the kitchens as though you were taking delivery of some produce or other. Plenty of people visit Lord Warwick's kitchens, as we know. It's how he's built such a reputation for *largess*. You will go quite unremarked on; there's no risk! Besides, everyone knows you there!'

If there's no risk why even mention the word? thought Pom, but did not ask it.

'Put it in your basket; get them to cover it with bread or something – nothing that's likely to get smashed or spilt – like eggs or milk; something solid like bread or vegetables. I'm sure Sir Tom will be grateful for any extra provender you can bring back. It'll be a welcome addition to your stores and you won't have to pay a penny for it.'

'I like the sound of that, Tony!' growled Sir Tom, 'Pom, just do as the man says and act like a good servant.'

The next morning he was outside the Greyfriars' kitchen trying not to look guilty. He pushed open the door to see the familiar sight of boys, young girls, women, and sturdy men rushing here and there preparing, cooking and serving food. If a melange of sound can be described as a "cacophony", then the smells from the various rooms were its equivalent. His nose was assailed by everything, from the earthy smell of raw vegetables, the pungent aroma of malt and yeast in preparation of bread, and the mouth-watering tang of roasting meat turning on huge spits over great fires. Despite the flight of their lord, many of Warwick's retainers were still at work, although Pom noticed their numbers were reduced. Yet, the customary file of people waiting in line for the gift of such meat, which Lord Warwick had ordered for anyone who could show they were in real need, was as long as ever. Pom had known of this procedure for years, it was well-attested to throughout the city. How they were selected was down to the temper of the kitchen stewards. On some occasions they would be generous, cutting thick slices of roast and boiled meats which were skewered by the recipients onto their daggers. Then, with a piece of bread in the other hand, they would start chewing at the food before they had even left the place. At other times, the *largess* was more thinly spread and allocated with less sympathy. There was a fine line of want between the lowly kitchen staff doling out the food, poorly paid but always within reach of sustenance, and those unemployed and on the wrong side of that line. The former viewed the latter with contempt as Pom had sometimes witnessed.

Suddenly, he was aware of a young woman tugging at his basket, 'I'll fill this for you Mr Appleby; just wait there.'

And before he knew what was happening, she had taken the large wicker basket from his hand and disappeared into the throng of people. Within minutes, she had returned and, with a smile, thrust it back loaded with bread and some root vegetables. 'We've had a delivery of nice leeks – late in the season but still firm; you can make good soup with that. I've also put in a few little extras!' and she smiled at him again – all gums, no teeth.

Pom was feeling distinctly on edge, but managed to take the basket from her without dropping it, whispered a hoarse "thank you" and turned towards the door again. Within a minute, he was outside the Greyfriars' walls and on his way back to Newgate. When he reached the foot of the guard tower, he saw that Fat Gregory's stool was empty; the man was nowhere to be seen. This was not unusual; Gregory was possibly the most incompetent guard in the whole of the London prison system, which was fortunate given the liberties Sir Thomas took with it. Pom made his way slowly up the stairs, the basket was heavier than usual and he wondered exactly what this bundle contained that increased the weight so much. Arriving at the door, to his surprise, he found it shut. Now, this was very unusual, for although the cell was of a good size, Sir Tom preferred the door to be always left ajar at least, 'We need fresh air, Pom!' he would say as he wedged it open with a log or a large lump of coal.

He knocked at the stout studded door but, hearing no answer, hesitated. Perhaps, Sir Tom and Sir Anthony were in private conversation; should he enter uninvited or not? The question was decided for him when he heard Sir Tom say, 'Mr Appleby, please join us!' The formality was certainly strange, and Pom turned the large iron handle and pulled the door open. What he saw made his guts feel as though they had dropped to his feet.

***

'Come in, Mr Appleby!' The summons came from Robert Stillington who stood leaning on the bathtub. Mr Peter Crosby and two burly guards, halberds ready, were looking on. Sir Tom was standing at his desk, hugging some of his manuscript to him, looking furious. There was no sign of Sir Anthony. Pom was also quick to notice that the room had been well and truly searched. The table and chairs had been moved violently, the curtain to the privy was drawn back to reveal the bucket – fortunately unused. The bathtub was covered in a blanket on which were arranged those parts of Sir Tom's *magnum opus* he considered complete. Some of them seem to have been disturbed, but at least no attempt had been made to consign them to the fire. Lord Robert continued to lean on the tub staring in perplexity at Sir Thomas.

As Pom entered, Stillington changed his focus of interest, 'Ah, Mr Appleby! I see you have been out purchasing provender. Would that be from the Greyfriars' kitchens? We all know of Lord Warwick's generosity towards the poor and needy, although I wouldn't put you in that category, Sir Thomas?' and he turned to the old knight who stood remarkably silent, 'Nothing to say? Well, I haven't got time to waste. Guard! Take the basket and put it on here. Let's see what good stuff the earl has provided today.'

Before Pom could utter a word of protest, one of the guards grabbed the basket and put it on the bathtub. Sir Tom immediately made a move to grab his papers, but Stillington nodded to the other guard who just as quickly prevented him with his halberd. Rolling up the exaggerated sleeves of his velvet gown, Lord Robert delved into the basket, flinging out small rolls of bread, and the untrimmed leeks which spread their dirt all over the precious manuscripts. Sir Tom gave a cry of pain, as though the Lord Chancellor had driven a dagger through the heart of his only child, 'For fuck sake, man! Have a care.'

'There are more important matters to me than a speck of dirt on a few scraps of insignificant paper. Now, let's see. Ah! I think we have found our treasure!' and he pulled from the bottom of the basket a bulky square parcel tied up with string, and sealed. 'Whose seal is this? Let me guess – the bear and ragged staff of Lord Warwick. Well,' he said smugly. 'This is interesting. Why would a package be nestling inside a basket full of the means of making soup? I presume leek soup was planned for supper this evening, Mr Appleby? And very nice too! But not so nice flavoured with sealing wax, so let's see what's within this exciting looking package. Is it unusual herbs, perhaps? A little scarce pepper – so expensive it has to be wrapped and sealed in case villains like me get their hands on it!' He carefully cut the seal, damaging it as little as possible and then proceeded to untie the knots in the string. 'I never cut string, Sir Tom; so wasteful!'

Pom found he was holding his breath. He looked across at his master whose face had taken on the inscrutable look of an ancient sphinx – Sir Tom had once shown him a picture of the mythical being. He could gauge nothing of what Malory was thinking as they watched to see the contents of the packet exposed and to feel the inevitable consequences. What they all saw was totally unexpected. A large and obviously succulent piece of pork lay open on the table, its cloth wrapping slightly bloodied, but otherwise a perfect slab of pink flesh surrounded with creamy fat and bronze skin.

'Very generous of Lord Warwick, don't you think, Lord Chancellor? That's a fine piece of meat, eh, Pom? Plenty of skin for crackling, I'd say!' said Malory, looking over Stillington's shoulder. There was no hint of triumph or glee in his words. Stillington on the other hand was completely taken aback.

'What is this?' and he poked at the pork with the end of one of Malory's quills.

'Don't do that!' said Sir Tom sharply. 'You'll ruin the tip – they cost money!'

Pom saw one of the soldiers give a smirk to the other, and Stillington noticed it too. Now inflamed with anger, he took a step towards the man as though to strike him, thought better of it in consideration of the halberd, turned on his heels and faced Sir Thomas. 'I don't know what's going on here, but something stinks in this room!'

'It can't be the pork, Lord Robert! That looks perfectly fresh to me. Perhaps one of your men needs my privy. If that's the case, please feel free. After all, we're all men together here!'

As though the fates decided to intervene at that precise moment, there was a knock on the door and who should enter but Plump Poll.

'Good morning, Polly. What a welcome sight! My lord, are you acquainted with my good friend and barber, Mistress Polly Fisher – one of the few women with such skill? She sees to my every need and very business-like she is too! Particularly handy where troublesome orifices are concerned – noses and ears, I mean!'

Poll looked slightly bemused, but she was well used to Sir Tom's humour and, although she was very surprised to find the Lord Chancellor in a room in Newgate, she took it all in her stride – curtsied low and said, 'Good morning, my lord.' As she bent down her eyes caught sight of a hand poking out from beneath the tub and waving with a certain amount of style, before withdrawing into the internal cavern beneath the blanket.

Staring back at Poll, Lord Robert was dumbstruck, recognising defeat when he met it. Nodding curtly, he snapped his fingers, 'We're finished here!' he said through his teeth.

You certainly are, Lord Robert! thought Pom.

'You wouldn't like Mistress Fisher to give your nostrils a quick trim, Lord Chancellor? A shave even? We can provide the hot –'

‘I want neither trimming nor shaving, Malory! Let me tell you this before I go. I know that caitiff Anthony Tanner has been here and I know he’s up to his neck in plots against his majesty with his two traitorous masters, the Earl of Warwick and the king’s brother, who should know better. I also know you are their creature too and I’m warning you that I shall be keeping watch on everything that goes on in this den of thieves and spies.’

‘Well, it certainly won’t be difficult for your spies since I’m obviously not going anywhere – not even Bankside, where I know you enjoy a little dalliance with the whores yourself –’

‘How dare you associate a senior officer of the crown with the pox-ridden residents of the Stews! I could have you for slander, sir!’

‘That’s very demeaning to Barber Poll here, Lord Robert. I’m sure she’ll testify as to your presence across the river – regular presence, I believe. But perhaps you’re just like the Bishop of Winchester who, as we all know, is Bankside’s landlord; just visiting to ensure his properties are maintained and proprieties upheld. I know nothing of anyone’s peccadilloes of course; the business women in the Stews are the most discreet in the land. In fact, they would make very good spies, being able to keep their mouths shut. I daresay they have many a valuable secret which would be entertaining in the telling. Isn’t that right, Polly?’

‘If you say so, Sir Thomas, but I wouldn’t know anything about that kind of business. I just cut men’s hair and shave them – from wherever they require!’ and she laughed, and Sir Tom laughed and even Pom managed a smile.

Peter Crosby had been silent throughout these proceedings. He had accompanied his master, who insisted he undertook this search personally and would serve the warrant himself, making sure it was read by Malory before they set to work. Crosby felt this to be a punishment for his mishandling of the last visit and had not been looking forward to being the butt of Malory’s malicious humour. They had served the document, witnessed it read and then proceeded to almost ransack the place, although there was precious little to disturb. They had been through the drawers, cupboards, larder – even the coal bucket and log basket had been emptied – dust all over the floor which was soon trodden into the rushes strewn across the room. With a ceremonious flourish, Stillington had thrown back the curtain hiding the privy, but there was no handsome spy lurking there, on or off the bucket. By the time they had finished, the place was a mess. The bathtub which served as a table was immovable and at the end of their labours, Lord Robert leant on it heavily with his back against it, making it rock on its uneven surface, 'You should get a carpenter to have a look at this table – it must be very difficult to work at wobbling as it does. Just an observation,' and he gave the tub a vicious kick.

'I certainly will, my lord, thank you for the advice. Now, if that is all, I would ask you to leave so that my man here can clear up the mess you've made and get on with making our dinner – something with pork and leeks, I guess – am I right, Mr Appleby?'

'You certainly are, Sir Tom! Once I've got the fire going again. Like you say, we'll have a nice piece of crackling too.'

'An excellent way to end a not very pleasant morning; I wish you good day, Lord Robert – Mr Crosby. Careful on the stairs, they're very worn in places!'

As the visitors disappeared down the stairs, a muffled shout came from beneath the bathtub, 'For fuck's sake get me out of here!' and the hand which had so insouciantly waved at Poll began to scrabble for a hold on the wooden edge of the tub which had been propped up on three small logs, hidden by the blanket, to allow in some air. Hence, the "wobble" observed by Stillington.

Between them, Sir Tom, Pom and Poll managed to lever the bath up far enough for Tony Tanner to crawl out, puffing and cussing, 'God's bones, Thomas! Do you know how cramped I was in there – curled up like a baby in the womb!'

'But a perfect hiding place, you must admit,' observed Sir Tom, 'The fact that our friend was leaning on it made it more piquant,' and he and Tony burst into fits of laughter.

Pom was less amused, 'Never mind "piquant", Sir Tom! Can someone explain what's going on? I was almost floored by the fact that Lord Robert was here when I thought I had treasonable letters in my basket. This isn't funny at all and I don't take it kindly that you all consider it so.'

Sir Anthony clapped him on the back, 'Quite right, Pom, and we don't take it lightly. However, be assured you were never to be put in danger.' He turned to Plump Poll who had been listening intently, 'Now, Polly, you will appreciate these are very important and dangerous matters in which you are now unfortunately involved. I know you serve Stillington in your own manner, but I also know your loyalties are with Sir Tom and consequently my master, the Earl of Warwick, is that not so?'

'Yes sir, they are – with Sir Thomas, I mean. I'm not very interested in great matters of state – statesmen, yes – but their official business is their own affair.'

'Yes, I've heard that you have a reputation for great discretion – that is why you are successful at – at what you do –'

'Poll has other qualities too, Tony!' protested Sir Tom.

'Yes, you've told me often enough of her practical skills.' Polly blushed at these compliments to her trade.

'So we can rely on you keeping very, very quiet about this, at least until I'm out of the country? Once those letters are in the right hands, Stillington and the king have no real evidence against the earl.' He looked at her intently with his deep cornflower-blue eyes and smiled; her heart thumped and her knees began to buckle.

Turning back to Pom, he said, 'Now I'll explain. As far as this enterprise was concerned, it was a ruse to put Stillington off the scent – and it certainly worked. I primed one of my contacts in Westminster, who reported directly to the Lord Chancellor his "concerns" that there were murky dealings about to take place between Newgate and Greyfriars' this morning; hence his arrival here at exactly the right time. But the letters had already been delivered to me and are here in my pocket,' and he took out a thick innocuous looking bundle with no sign of a seal. 'The king is desperate to get his hands on these documents. Do you remember me telling you how the Duke of Clarence carelessly left incriminating correspondence in a yeoman's helmet after Lose-Coat? Well, it occurred to Lord Warwick that there were also letters which could cause him great trouble if they fell into the wrong hands. That was my task, to collect them from his secretary in Greyfriars' and take them to France.'

Pom scowled, 'So I was a lure? You put me through all that terror to trick the Lord Chancellor!'

'And very well you did it too, Pom. Look, don't be put out; I'm sure our master would want you to have a token of his appreciation for your help,' he pulled at the silver ring on his little finger. 'Take this – Lord Warwick doesn't give these away lightly. When I explain he'll replace it for me, I know. It may be too small, but a good silversmith will stretch it for you. Or you can put it on a string and wear it round your neck as a talisman.'

Pom hesitated. He was still angry at having been so badly frightened and unnecessarily. He had been through many situations where he was genuinely scared, but capture for treason, with its accompanying threat of torture was another matter. Still, there was no harm done and recognition from one of the mightiest noblemen in the country was not to be sniffed at. He held out his hand and Tony placed the small silver band in his palm. Then he shook Pom's hand heartily, 'Let's all have drink, and perhaps we can enjoy the pork which the Greyfriars' kitchen have so kindly sent. The thought of that crackling is making my mouth water!'

***

The only thing making the Lord Chancellor's mouth water was the spittle he was producing when he considered how he had been duped. As soon as they arrived back in Westminster, he made out another warrant for the detention of Mr Montmorency Pickle. 'Crosby, get that man in the Tower; he knows something and we'll get it out of him somehow!'

***

There were windows and moonlight in the room. Monty noticed how the moon shone through the bars of the windows and made odd patterns on the wall opposite; strange how things of no consequence pushed their way to the front of his mind. He was surprised. He thought he would be in complete darkness with just the sounds of dripping water on stone walls and floor, and the faint cries of prisoners in agony. Instead, he was sitting on a plain wooden chair, his hands and feet tied, looking round a small airy cell. There was no furniture, just a brightly burning brazier and a small table. However, what drew his eye immediately, and made his heart flutter and a pulse in his head pump, was the array of butchers' knives which lay on the table in a muddled heap. He was aware how silent it was; apart from the beating of his own heart which pumped away in his chest, he could hear nothing, which was almost as unnerving as cries of agony would have been. Rooms in the Tower were obviously well insulated for sound.

Crosby and his men had dragged him from his bed at four in the morning, having broken unceremoniously through his door, mounted the stairs to his bedroom where they had ripped off his blankets. A warrant had been thrust into his hand, a candle lit and Monty forced to read the document aloud; Crosby had learnt his lesson. With his hands tied, Mr Pickle was marched at a quick pace from Number 3, Stinking Lane down to the riverside, where a wherry was waiting. So terrified was Monty that he could remember hardly anything of the river journey to Tower Wharf, except the blackness of the water and the eerie sight of mysterious objects floating alongside the small boat. Apart from the splashing of the oars, everything was conducted in a blanket of silence until they reached the bank, where he was lifted onto land and told to "get a move on!" up the steps and through a postern gate into the Tower.

His state of terror increased fourfold when he was marched towards dark stairs which could only lead to one place – the deepest dungeons. But to his relief, his guards hustled him into this small room on the ground floor, forced him onto the chair and anchored him to it close to the brazier. Such was the heat the fire was throwing out that one side of Monty's face became at first pink, then deeper red. He could do nothing to relieve the itching and irritation, and wondered if this was some form of novelty torture he had not heard of; death by slow roasting. Perhaps, like meat on a spit, when he was well done on one side, he would be turned around, just like the little children roasted by one of Sir Tom's giants. To his great relief, one item was missing; there was no sign of the rack in this room. Indeed, nothing could really identify the cell as a place where exquisite pain might be administered, apart from the pile of knives. Monty observed that many of them appeared to be rusty – or was that old blood?

He was torn between wishing someone would come and put him out of his misery, or that he be allowed to enjoy the last few minutes of his life as painlessly as possible. He thought he had been in the room for at least an hour before someone arrived. In fact, it was all of thirty minutes, but time goes very slowly when one is anticipating the possibility of bodily torment. Then he heard voices outside and the door opened. To Monty's surprise, Robert Stillington entered, followed by Peter Crosby and a small man in a leather apron.

'Good morning, Mr Pickle. This is very inconvenient for us all. I don't like losing sleep, especially in this fashion.'

Monty had already rehearsed what he would say to his jailer; he was determined not to appear feeble. Although he had never been tested, he had rehearsed this moment in his nightmares, when he would wake in a sweat, touched by the shadow of the rack. 'Lord Robert, I have no idea why I'm here or why you should be here either!'

'I have made a personal commitment to the king that I will root out all spies and traitors,' he looked witheringly at Monty, 'however insignificant they are! Crosby showed you the warrant? We have done everything correctly. You have been apprehended because we are sure you have information concerning the whereabouts of Sir Anthony Tanner, recreant and traitor. And don't say you don't know. The man has been seen hanging around Greyfriars' and Newgate.'

'Why haven't you arrested him then?'

'Because he's been too quick for my incompetent men and given them the slip. He's also had help from other villains – Sir Thomas Malory for one and probably you. When did you last see him?'

'Who are we talking about?'

'Don't play for time. Tanner, of course!'

'Last Thursday.'

'Where?'

'He visited Sir Thomas' cell.' Monty knew that Stillington already had all this information and it was no use lying.

'What did he talk about?'

'He just gave us a report of all the events in the Midlands, and how Lord Warwick and the Duke of Clarence were making for France.'

'Running like curs with their tails between their legs. Of course, Tanner will try and join them. Did he say anything of letters or document?'

'No, as I said, he was just telling us what is common knowledge; I really can't help you any further, my lord. Could you please move my chair away from the brazier? My face can't take much more of this heat.'

'You're going to feel a lot more than a little heat in a minute. You realise you are consorting with caitiffs up to their necks in treason. Shit sticks, Mr Pickle! That makes you guilty by association. Tell me again, what were Anthony Tanner's intentions?'

'I tell you again, I don't know! I left the room before Sir Anthony. I presumed he would be leaving immediately afterwards – if as you say he was following Lord Warwick and his men to France.'

'You failed to come to me with this information – that Tanner was visiting Malory in Newgate. We had an arrangement, Mr Pickle. I'll tell you now; this is why we're here. I am not impressed with people who let me down. If you refuse to tell me anything that I believe you are hiding, then matters will have to take their course.'

Monty was suddenly aware that he had wet his hose which caused him almost as much anguish as Stillington's beady eyes on him and his burning cheek. There was a tell-tale puddle on the floor which Crosby noticed. 'I think Mr Pickle is in some discomfort already, Lord Robert. It seems he has lost control of his bladder.'

'Are you that frightened then, Monty?' The Lord Chancellor's voice became silky, 'Anticipation is almost as bad as realisation I'm told. That's one of the side benefits of torture. You would be surprised how many men – and women – tell us all we want to know before we've even shown them the array of implements we have to hand for the administration of pain. Anyway, I've wasted enough time with you. Let's bring matters to a conclusion – guard, heat up a knife – the smallest and most pointed. We'll start with his eyes.'

Monty froze, then from back of his mind, for an unaccountable reason, he thought of Sir Tom and how he had caught him with Meg one afternoon. A chain of consequential thoughts ran through his head.

'I will say something to you, my lord: S.T.E.W.S. and P.O.L.L.Y.' He spelled them out. 'Your butcher here surely can't spell and will, therefore, have no idea what I'm talking about, so I'm sparing your reputation – for the moment. Obviously, your secretary will understand, but then I'm sure he knows already of your secret visits to B.A.N.K.S.I.D.E but is too loyal to give you away.'

'Whatever are you talking about, you fool? What do you know? You're no threat to me. Don't you realise you're already my prisoner and I can silence your mouth forever and immediately; tip you down one of the oubliettes where you will never be seen or heard of again. Forgotten, in fact! Just my little joke – oubliette – forgotten; are you with me?'

'Answer this, Lord Robert, what am I?'

'What are you? A traitorous caitiff! What else?'

'No, what do I do to earn my bread?'

‘You’re just time-wasting. You can’t put this off!’

‘I acknowledge you’re firmly in charge here, but humour me for a little. What am I?’

‘You’re a scribe – and not a very good one, I gather. Anyway, what’s that got to do with anything? Let’s get on with it!’ and he nodded to the man in the apron who moved to the table and began rummaging through the pile of knives.

‘A scribe, yes, one who writes for a living. Now, as well as helping Sir Thomas with his great work, I have been compiling an account of his life and his doings – with his consent, of course. Much of it is very titillating, very revealing and includes very frank accounts from some of the ladies known to you in the S.T.E.W.S. They have been less than flattering about your performance, my lord. They also talk about your predilection for, shall we say, *very* young men? Tell me is it true you’re suffering from L.I.C.E. – in an awkward place?’

Stillington’s mouth formed a thin straight line, and his cheeks flushed almost as red as the side of Monty’s face, ‘Shut your mouth! I tell you, I’ll have you disembowelled before you can blink – but of course, you won’t be able to blink since he’s about to take those eyes of yours out of their sockets.’ And he nodded to the guard who had stuck a gimlet-like tool into the red-hot coals of the brazier.

‘Before you start carving me up, there’s something else you should know.’

‘If it’s about Sir Anthony then you’d better be quick!’

‘No, not about Sir Anthony, but about what I’ve noted down and put in a short but interesting document. It’s all about you! And if I don’t appear outside the gates of this Tower unharmed by noon, notices will be pinned up in all the usual places giving chapter and verse of your activities in the S.T.E.W.S. The king will no doubt be shown copies and will be as shocked, as will every other respectable person, that the Lord Chancellor and the Bishop of Bath and Wells indulges himself in unnatural practices and has caught the crabs in the process! I believe the punishment for such perversion was meted out to one of our previous monarchs – if my knowledge of our past serves me right.'

There was silence. Monty looked at Crosby who was trying not to smile. The torturer, oblivious to the chattering of a captive, was testing the gimlet for its potency. Stillington had gone white – with a mixture of anger and fear. 'You're bluffing!' he hissed.

'Can you afford to take the risk? I can see the crowds now knotted around the Standard at Cheapside, or crowding the doors of St Paul's to listen to some fellow reading out the details of your congresses with Polly – and the boys. Remember the accusations against the two duchesses? They are still talked about and believed in many quarters. However much you deny it, the phrase "mud sticks" comes to mind.'

'That whore will take a whipping – or worse if it comes out, have you thought of that?'

'Plump Poll's safe enough. Her discretion is appreciated by many a "nobleman". It would be an awful warning to all of them as to what can happen if she decides to abandon her principles and confess all publicly. So what's it to be? Will you release me and keep your dignity – and your position? Or risk all for nothing, because I can assure you I know nothing. As far as Sir Anthony Tanner is concerned, he's a fast mover and probably already heading towards a ship to take him to France. You'd be better off searching for him on the south-east coast than wasting time with me.'

There was a long silence, 'Pickle – you won't get away with this. You –' and he waved at the man with the gimlet in his hand, 'Leave that and untie his hands.' The man took up a large dagger and sawed through the rope. But immediately, Stillington grabbed hold of Monty's left hand and, with strength fuelled by vicious anger, laid it flat out on the table. 'Hold down his other hand and chop off the little finger of this one!' The man obliged, bringing the knife down with speed and accuracy.

'Now, pick him up, take him to the gates and leave him to find his own way home!'

***

'The villain!' Sir Tom thumped his fist down on the table. 'Leaving you with a bloody hand and no money in your pocket to get home with. Tell me, was it painful? Did you bear it all with the fortitude of a Sir Lancelot?'

The Newgate Four sat in Malory's room, the jug circulating and Monty nursing his bandaged hand. It was early Friday morning, and Monty had come directly to Newgate walking the mile and a half from the Tower in a daze of pain and weariness. He had almost fainted when at last he reached Malory's room, where Pom had immediately ministered to his injury and then gone to find Jack Worms to ask him to join them.

'I can't tell you whether it was painful. I fainted before the knife came down; so I didn't feel a thing!'

'Oh, how unsatisfactory!' Sir Tom looked disappointed.

'Sir Tom!' protested Jack. 'Have some sympathy for our friend.'

'Yes, yes, but sympathy's all very well, I wanted some first-hand material for the book. An account of what torture is really like would have been an asset – help the sales no end!'

'Well, if it helps the pain was excruciating once I was walking back here. People thought I was drunk as I was weaving through Cheapside.'

'It's surprising you arrived all in one piece. Stillington must have been livid that you have so much filth on him! Where is this document – in case we really have to use it?' asked Sir Tom eagerly.

'That's the point – there is no document. I made it all up on the spot.'

'On the spot! Well, fuck me, Mr Pickle, you're full of surprises!'

'It was something Stillington said to me which put the idea into my head.'

'Oh yes, and what was that?'

'He said "anticipation is almost as bad as realisation".'

‘So all this business of you letting the world and his wife know about Stillington’s perversions was a lie! But he doesn’t know it. Oh, how fucking marvellous! The man threatens you with all sorts, and you threaten him with exposure and win the battle! By the way, has he really got the crabs?’

‘He was scratching his genitals all the time he was asking me questions. I just assumed. Polly had already told us he caught head lice down in the Stews and is bald from having his hair shaved off as a consequence.

Pom said, ‘But Monty’s poor finger,’ and he took the bandaged hand, which was covered in dried blood.

‘I see it’s your left hand, so there’s no real damage done!’ said Sir Tom cheerfully.

‘What you mean is Monty’s still able to write,’ said Jack tartly. ‘Really, Sir Tom, sometimes you are too callous!’

‘Callous? Me? Look, Jack! I’m a realist. Tell me, who among us really needs his little finger? Possibly for removing earwax, or clearing other tiny orifices – I mean one’s navel, what do you think I meant?’ and he looked innocently around at his friend’s faces, which were exhibiting disbelief and despair. ‘Monty, look on the loss of your finger as a kind of talisman –’

‘How can something that doesn’t exist be considered a talisman?’ asked Pom.

‘Well, a kind of invisible trophy then.’

‘That’s no different. You can’t have an invisible trophy. Anyway, “invisible trophy” is an oxymoron,’ said Pom with some relish.

‘Who’s the etymologist here?’ growled Sir Tom irritably, ‘If I say it’s an invisible trophy, then it is! What I mean is this can only enhance your reputation. Sir Anthony Tanner has certainly traded on his title “Six-toed Tanner”! How about “Nine-digit Pickle”? I think it has a ring to it, don’t you?’ and he looked around at the three men with satisfaction.

With some spirit, Monty said, ‘I didn’t bite off my finger because of severe hard weather while on active service in the wild northern fastnesses. I had it removed during interrogation for treason – doesn't have the same romantic ring, Sir Tom.'

'Nonsense – your stump is a symbol – is that better, Pom? Is a symbol of your rejection of vicious and unfounded allegations, and the egregious treatment meted out under pain of death by the state. I think that's rather good and worthy of noting, Monty!'

Jack nodded, 'We're certainly all agreed that Monty has been egregiously treated and very clever in protecting himself. I imagine he has heard the last of Robert Stillington.'

'The man's like piles, pitiless and persistent, as well as malevolent – lovely word that – rolls round the tongue like this Burgundy!' said Sir Tom, 'I wouldn't be at all surprised if he wasn't plotting something else against you, Monty – against all of us. We seem to be the focus for his ire at the moment and should be on our guard.'

Monty was aware that his hose was still damp from his accident, and he thought it was time he went home and adjusted his nether-garments. He agreed with Sir Tom's last words, and would be extra diligent on making sure he was not followed home and perhaps re-arrested, although the more he thought about it, the more unlikely this seemed. The Lord Chancellor could never be certain if and when Monty would use what he had against him. Neither did he know where the "document" was placed. By the time he had reached his front door, he was beginning to feel more cheerful, despite the ache in his hand and the dampness round his legs.

Chapter 9

The Newgate Four chew over events; Malory gives readings to selected audiences;
Tony arrives from France with astounding news;
Monty hears of Sir Tom and Pom's felonious activities in East Anglia.

Late spring and early summer were cold and wet. The city roads and alleys of London were clogged with the usual mud and detritus, but life for the citizens was made a little more bearable by cool breezes which wafted away the worst of the city's stench. Life in Newgate settled to a rhythmic routine. Malory now insisted on calling himself, Pom, Jack and Monty the "Newgate Four".

'We are a band of brothers, after all,' he declared, 'and, like the Knights of the Round Table, must have a solid identity.'

'I imagine I'm anything less like one of Arthur's knights,' said Jack Worms, 'I would never be able to fewter a spear – and I hope it will never be necessary for me to learn!'

'We should try to obtain permission to go to Smithfield when they have another tournament. A fine sight the joust! Have you never been?' asked Sir Tom of nobody in particular.

'I tried to go when Lord Anthony Scales and Anthony the Bastard of Burgundy met there in "friendly" single combat four years ago. But the crowds were too great and I gave up in the end. I heard the whole thing was marred by Lord Scales using foul tactics!'

'Yes, everyone knows now that he used a hidden sharp point to stymie Burgundy's horse and bring it down. It was never proved, but no one doubts it. Bastard Woodville!'

muttered Sir Tom. 'But if there ever was a chance to see another tournament, we should take it. They're getting fewer these days; too much real fighting going on! No need to pretend anymore.'

The four were sitting in Malory's room having enjoyed an excellent dinner, provided and cooked by Pom, who sat back in his chair with the contentment of one who has done a good job.

'Tell me, Pom, what's happening over in Greyfriars' now the Earl of Warwick's in France. Has the place been shut up? What's happened to all his retainers?'

'The place is still operating, Monty, although many of Lord Warwick's men have returned to the midland counties, those that aren't with him in France that is.'

Malory frowned, 'Richard Neville was lucky the king hasn't confiscated any of his property. Edward has been remarkably merciful, pardoning everyone who opposed him – except me, of course! I always look for my name on the list of pardons when they're posted. I've clearly been forgotten!'

'We all know you like things as they are, Sir Tom!' said Pom cheerfully. 'Where else would you find peace and quiet to finish your book? But as far as Lord Warwick's lodgings are concerned, the only people who have suffered are the beggars at his gate. The meat, bread and ale supply has begun to dry up as there's not so much money coming in. I had it directly from the Treasure's clerk that he's barely able to pay the wages of Greyfriars' household. That's why they're drifting back to the midlands. The place is nothing like it has been, I can tell you!'

'What will Lord Warwick do next, I wonder?' mused Jack. 'Do we think he's gathering an army in France and preparing to invade?'

'Probably! Fuck me, it's very frustrating not knowing what to expect.' Silence fell, but suddenly from easy conversation, Malory's tone changed to one of briskness. 'We've speculated enough. Monty, there's work to be done. Jack, fetch me some supplies – string and ink particularly.'

'As always, I'll ask the same question – can you pay me? Is Lord Warwick still paying your annuity, and are your wife and Lord Wenlock sending you hard cash?'

'Yes and no! The Warwick estate still honours its pledges. But I haven't heard from Lord Wenlock since he returned to Calais two months ago and I'm beginning to worry that I won't be getting funds from that source for some time. I'm hoping Six-toed Tony will turn up at some point when we're least expecting him and bring me a purse full of cash. As for Lady Elizabeth – she is faithful and sends me regular sums from the estate when she can.'

'Your wife is a saint, Sir Tom!' observed Monty, wondering to himself if his own wages could be covered in the future.

Jack looked doubtful, 'Well, if you're sure you can meet the cost, I'll fetch what you need.'

'We are the Newgate Four – and stand four-square with each other, Master Worms!'

Band of brothers we may be, but I'm not your banker, Sir Thomas! thought Jack, but did not say it. Instead he turned towards the door, 'I'll be back later.'

When he had gone, Sir Tom picked up a sheaf of papers and waved them at Monty, 'We must make up the time we've lost during the events of the last month. Your damaged hand will be no impediment to your ability to write. By the way, are you going to keep the stump covered like that, or allow everyone to see it?'

'I prefer to keep it disguised with this piece of stuffed leather, Sir Tom.'

'I think it looks fucking ridiculous! More like a pre-pubescent prick than a finger. You should exhibit the wound as one who has been through the torture chambers in the Tower and survived more or less intact! Be proud, Mr Pickle! Show your stump!'

'It does nothing but remind me of that dreadful night whenever I look at it. I have no wish to relive those hours.'

Sir Tom shrugged, 'I know if it were me, I would flourish it. But it's entirely up to you what you do, I suppose. Now, changing the subject I've had an idea – a rather brilliant one.'

'Oh?' said Monty doubtfully. The old knight had shared some of his "brilliant ideas" with him in the past and they generally turned out to be dross. 'Better than the last one, I hope, which was to have copies made in French. Just as well you – we – decided it would be too expensive!'

'I admit that was a little ambitious. But this one's more feasible. I intend to get some reaction to our work from a range of people we know – from the more intelligent and discerning – to the illiterate and – and – dotardly – is there such a word?'

'Not sure, but do you expect any of the latter to be waiting in line to buy your book?'

'Of course not, but they could always have it read to them. We need their view of how good the stories are when delivered orally. I thought we could ask Pom to find us some of the scullions across the road in Greyfriars' – according to him, they've precious little to do now the earl's gone onto the continent. Then there's Polly and my whorelets. They're not as stupid as others think them – Polly can read and write quite well. I've told her some of the stories in *Le Morte* and she was particularly captivated with Sir Lancelot – most women will be I'm sure. In fact, I want to start with her. This story of Anglides for example; we're well on with it and I would like her to hear it. I find it most affecting.'

'I agree; it has all the features of a captivating romance – a loyal wife and mother, a wicked king/uncle, a flight to safety and a revengeful nephew.'

'Neatly summed up, Monty. Now, next time Polly visits – which is this Saturday morning as usual – I'd like you to be here!'

'Certainly not, Sir Tom! I've no wish to sit in while you dally with Plump Poll in your bath tub. There are limits to what a master should expect of his scribe and you know it.'

'I wasn't expecting you to provide me with an audience – although Poll and I are not shy! No, come along at mid-day;

we'll have dinner and then settle down to reading her the story. It will all be very comfortable – I'll certainly be in a positive frame of mind if Poll has done her work with –'

'Can I stop you there, Sir Tom? What you and Polly get up to is of no concern of mine; neither do I wish for details. I'll be here at twelve o'clock; please make sure you are both fully dressed and the bath is empty!'

'I can do no more than oblige you, Mr Pickle!' said Sir Tom and began to laugh, much to Monty's irritation.

***

Malory was in his element, with a captive audience, one of whom had just indulged his every physical whim and was now sitting attentively, glass in hand waiting to be regaled with the story of the Lady Anglides.

'What you must remember, Poll, is that Mark, King of Cornwall, is a cowardly scoundrel of the first order. He always runs away when he's challenged and certainly refuses to face Sir Lancelot or Sir Tristram.'

'I presume these are your great heroes you're always talking about, Sir Tom; the ones you based on yourself?' Did Monty imagine it, or had Poll winked at him.

'Well, yes, but they take no major part in this tale, so let's get on. The story so far: King Mark's brother –'

'Prince Boudwin – the one who he murders –'

Malory stopped in mid-sentence and looked at Polly with surprise, 'How did you know that Poll?'

'I was looking over some of your notes while you were dressing. I've read the beginning of the story already.'

Malory looked put out, 'I see. Well, I was hoping to read you the whole thing, but if you're already acquainted with the major characters, I shall proceed from where you finished reading. Where did you get to?'

'The end of Book 10 Section 34, when the Lady Anglides gives her dead husband's bloody doublet to their son, Alisander; how he is made a knight and how she charges him to revenge his father.'

‘Fuck it, Poll! You’ve almost read the whole thing!’

She laughed, ‘I’m a fast reader, Sir Tom, and you take an age to get your hose on these days.’

‘Well, I’ll start at the beginning of Section 35 – is that all right?’ There was heavy sarcasm in the question, which Poll ignored.

She held out her glass, ‘Fill this up for me and please get started. I have another customer to visit this afternoon.’

Malory looked even more put out. Pom filled up her glass and she sat waiting expectantly. Sir Tom cleared his throat and began to declaim:

“‘Now I require thee, and charge thee upon my blessing and upon the high order of knighthood that thou be revenged upon King Mark for the death of thy father.’ And therewithal she swooned.”

Poll put up her hand. ‘If I might comment, Sir Tom?’

He sighed, ‘If you must!’

‘I’m not certain a great lady who has no qualms about handling the bloody doublet of her murdered husband would swoon like that. I think she’d be made of sterner stuff.’

‘Swooning ladies are integral to French romance, Poll. They are what we call a “trope”. You know nothing of the structure and style of that kind of writing.’

‘I know what makes sense in a story. I thought you asked me here to give an opinion.’

‘Yes, but not on matters of literary style. Can we continue?’

‘If you say so, Sir Tom.’ And she sipped at her wine and looked at him with amusement in her green eyes.

“Then Alisander leapt to his mother and took her up in his arms and said, ‘Fair mother, ye have given me a great charge –’”

‘I thought you said she was unconscious?’

‘She’s come round,’ growled Sir Tom.

‘I see. But there’s no description as to how her swoon was ministered to. No ladies with bowls of rose-water –’

‘Bowls of rose-water? Fuck it, Poll! What are we to do with “bowls of rose-water”? This is a story of knightly deeds, not a herbal on dealing with faints!’

Monty wondered whether Poll was being mischievous and deliberately bringing up trifles, but the woman’s face remained inscrutable as she leaned back calmly in her chair.

‘Can I go on?’

‘Please do!’

“So the feast was ended and the constable, by the advice of Anglides, let purvey that Alisander was well horsed and harnessed. Then he jousted with twenty fellows that were made knights with him. But for to make short tale, he overthrew all those twenty, that none might withstand him a buffet.”

As though expecting an objection or comment, Sir Tom paused. He was not disappointed.

‘Sir Tom, two things strike me here. The first is the feast which hasn’t been mentioned before –’

‘This is the feast to celebrate Alisander’s being dubbed a knight if you remember what you read earlier.’ There was a hint of triumph in Sir Tom’s voice.

‘No feast has actually been mentioned though. Anyway, that aside, the second thing is this business of the young man overthrowing twenty knights at the joust – which evidently takes place after this feast. Am I right?’

‘Yes,’ said Sir Tom slowly, wondering what was coming.

‘Isn’t that a bit unlikely; a young and tender boy, upset to see his mother swoon yet getting the better of twenty knights, especially after a full meal? Might it not make him sick, such violent exercise just after eating?’

Although he recognised Poll’s comments as probably mischievous, Monty felt the urge to intervene here. Mistress Fisher was making a point on which he had often challenged Sir Tom; the oft-mentioned great waves of armoured and well-horsed men lounging round wells waiting to be thrown out of their saddles by a singleton; one often young and inexperienced. He drew a deep breath. 'I have often said the same to you, Sir Tom. It's all very inflated and, as Poll says, "unlikely".'

At that point, Sir Tom lost his temper, threw down the manuscript and shouted, 'For Christ's sake! How many times must I tell you to suspend your disbelief? These are fucking STORIES and made up for entertainment. They're not manuals of war – as I've also told you so many times.' He looked at Poll, 'I don't think you're giving this fair consideration, Polly. I thought I'd find you a discerning and thoughtful listener. Instead, all you've done is carp and criticise, and we've only completed fifteen lines!'

'Well, Sir Tom, I think I found reading them for myself more, shall we say, rewarding! It's not that I don't enjoy the sound of your voice, but as I say, I'm a quick reader and when I'm casting my eyes over the pages, I can absorb the meaning more smoothly in my head as I'm going along. But I do think these points I'm raising – and Mr Pickle here agrees with me –' and she smiled at Monty, the lines around her eyes wrinkling quite attractively he thought, 'are valid. You have to admit some of it is wildly unlikely, even for just a "fucking story"!'

Stung with extreme frustration, Sir Tom picked up the papers and threw them on the desk, 'All right! I give in. I'll admit this was not one of my better ideas, Mr Pickle.'

Polly went on, 'I'm not saying I haven't enjoyed the stories. In fact, I was going to ask you if I could read more of them – perhaps from the beginning. Could I take a copy back with me to –'

'Take a copy with you?' Sir Tom's grey cheeks flushed carmine, 'I'll tell you, Mistress Fisher, I don't allow these manuscripts out of my sight. The only person who takes them home is Mr Pickle here and then only in small sections. There are many scoundrels who would like to get their hands on my work and claim it as their own!'

Monty doubted this; there had never been any suggestion that anyone else would want to counterfeit the work. But Sir Tom was right; he would never allow the full manuscript into anyone else's hands. The idea of Polly taking a copy into the Stews and entertaining her clients with her cleverness would be torment for him.

'I think this experiment can be said to have failed, Monty. Poll, I wish you good day!' It was as abrupt a dismissal as he could possibly have made.

Poll shrugged and said, 'Same time next Saturday, Sir Tom?'

He frowned, torn between the anticipation of next week's pleasure and enragement at her present perverseness. But the desire of the flesh overtook the desire for revenge, 'Very well – take your money and get out now!' Poll took the pile of coins which had been left on Malory's table as usual, nodded good day to Monty and headed for the door.

'If this experiment has been deemed a failure, are you rethinking the idea of presenting *Le Morte D'Arthur* to the Greyfriars' kitchen staff?' asked Monty tentatively; fearing a deluge of invective against all would-be critics. He was surprised.

'No, of course not! They're bound to be more appreciative. Pom will arrange for a couple of them to come over sometime soon. But let's forget all about that for now. We should move on to our next section which is –?' and he looked quizzically at his scribe.

'Section 44, the Tournament at Lonezep, Sir Tom: *Of the third day, and how Sir Palomides jousted with Sir Lamorak – and other things.* That sounds very intriguing. Another one of your "hooks" I presume.'

'Good! I'm glad something pleases you!

***

To Monty's great surprise, as Sir Tom had predicted, the audience of the three scullions was extremely appreciative. Two lusty youths and a decrepit old man, they seemed thoroughly to enjoy Sir Tom's declamatory style and didn't interrupt once. Only towards the end did their exuberance overcome their manners, and they whooped and shouted in Section 36 when Sir Tom came to the point in Alisander's story where he and Sir Malgrin "rashed together with their shields like two boars or rams".

'That's very good, Sir Tom – we know how rams and boars do fight – tooth and claw!'

'Rather an inapposite description, my lads! But I know what you mean,' said Sir Tom. They were even more struck by Section 38 and how the hero was delivered from Morgan le Fay by the means of a damosel.

'We like the bit about the damsel and Sir Alis – Alisan –'

'Alisander. Yes, I suppose you would.'

'We did, sir. Especially the bit about how "he kissed her and did to her pleasance as it pleased them both at times and leisure".'

'So you remember that word for word then?'

'Oh we do, sir, and I know I speak for us all, when I say we'd like the time and leisure to do our women pleasance. Are there any more details of what that is exactly? I'd like to think I could fuck as good as any Knight of this 'ere Round Table.'

'Sir Alisander wasn't actually a Knight of – Oh! Never mind!' and Malory shrugged. He would be grateful for an attentive audience for his work at least, even if it failed to grasp its finer points.

They stayed for an hour; their enrapture fortified by several glasses of Malory's poorest quality wine. It was gratifying to Sir Tom how as they were leaving, they each shook his hand, grinning. One declared it "the best afternoon I've spent since they chopped off that fornicating Lollard's bollocks and burnt him at the stake at the Cheapside Standard!"

***

The summer months passed uneventfully to Monty's relief. He heard no more from Robert Stillington; clearly the

Lord Chancellor had decided the Newgate scribe was of little use as a conduit of information, as well as being a permanent threat to his reputation. Besides, the traitors were all abroad in France where, although probably plotting with the French king, they were on the wrong side of the Channel to cause any immediate concern to the king. That was not to say rumours of their actions were not circulating the streets and taverns of London. News was dribbling back to England and disseminated in the usual ways, mostly by word of mouth. When a story broke, it took a matter of hours before it was all around the city in some form or another. Gossip, both malicious and uninformed, drifted across London like the ever-present smoke from thousands of its small fires. A piece of news attested to be from the Warwick camp itself, chewed over and debated upon on one day might, on the next, be discarded as a complete fallacy. Counter-stories were deliberately put about by the king's officials to scotch any idea that the earl and the king's brother might have claims of any kind. However, in July, news arrived which shocked everyone, including those at home who were well versed in the machinations of both the Lancastrian and the Yorkist factions. This included Sir Thomas Malory and Mr John Appleby. It was the latter who heard the rumour first; doubted it as completely impossible; then, having made deeper enquiries and had it confirmed from an utterly reliable source, was forced to accept the truth of it.

'Lord Warwick has met with Margaret of Anjou in Angers, in the presence of King Louis. Not only that, the betrothal has been announced of the earl's younger daughter, Anne, to Margaret's son, Edward Lancaster!'

He sat back with the look of satisfaction which anyone might exhibit who has been first with such explosive news. For a time, Sir Tom was speechless, an uncomfortable and rare condition for the literary knight. Then he said, predictably, 'Fuck me! Say that again!'

Pom obliged.

'That's something I would have never expected in all my years! She hates him; blames him for the ills done to her husband, the unfortunate Henry and all the other villains she surrounded herself with – Somerset, Percy and of course, Fuckingham Buckingham happily slaughtered at Northampton. On the other hand, Warwick has never forgiven her for killing his father at Wakefield – or his uncle, the Duke of York, who she treated so vilely – paper crown and all. Pom, if you'd asked me to make up the most impossible story this would be it – that Richard Neville Earl of Warwick would sit down across a table from Margaret of Anjou, our erstwhile queen, and make conversation, let alone arrange to marry his daughter to her son! It makes Merlin's magic credible! It's unbelievable. Are you sure you have this right? Who's your source?'

'That's another surprise, Sir Tom. When I arrived at my front door last night, just before the curfew, a man was waiting for me. He was so muffled up I had no idea who he was; I was preparing to defend myself from, as I thought, some caitiff set to rob me, but speaking low he told me not be alarmed. It was Sir Anthony Tanner, Sir Tom.'

'Six-toed Tanner has shown up again! That's risky for him!'

'Yes sir, hence his large cloak and a hat, which completely obscured his face. As soon as he showed himself, I let him into my lodgings; he asked for a bed for the night and he remains in my house this morning.'

'Is he coming to see me?'

'No, sir. He still thinks Stillington might be watching you, although I told him of Mr Pickle's misfortune and the fact that Lord Robert seems to have abandoned trying to use him as a spy.'

'So what's he doing here?'

'Trying to gauge the mood of the city I think, sir. Lord Warwick's told him to be back in France in three weeks after he's completed "some other business"; he says he'll have left London by the time I arrive home tonight. He didn't say where he was going.'

'Well, he obviously can't go wandering around the streets asking how people feel about his master, Pom!'

'He's relying on us and others still loyal to the earl to describe the atmosphere towards his master and the Duke of Clarence. He had sad news that the Duchess of Clarence lost the baby she was expecting, during the sea voyage to Harfleur. It was a boy and would have been Lord Warwick's first grandchild –'

'And a future king of England if he has his way! It's obvious to me he's preparing for an invasion, and possibly soon. Did Tony say anything to hint that might be true?'

'He hasn't been involved in these high-level talks, but is always one of the first to know what's been said and agreed afterwards. One thing he did mention was that the Duke of Clarence isn't happy about this proposed betrothal between Anne Neville and Edward Lancaster. The one piece of news I haven't told you is that it's likely Lord Warwick has agreed to rescue Henry Lancaster from the Tower and place him back on the throne – Henry VI will return! You can see what that means for the Duke of Clarence!'

Sir Tom was silent for a moment while he digested this monumental piece of news. Then he said, 'Jesus Christ! I can see why George would be put out! Edward Lancaster, he who was Prince of Wales, will become Henry's heir again and so Lord Warwick's daughter Anne will one day be queen and any male offspring she produces heir to the English throne. That puts the Duke of Clarence right out of the picture!'

'Sir Anthony says it's clear that the earl knows exactly what he's doing. He's been very clever and manipulated things to his own great advantage. One way or another, one of his daughters could become queen, and a future grandson king. If Edward Plantagenet dies without issue, then Clarence becomes king, as has already been arranged.'

'Fuck it, my head's going around in circles, Pom! This is speculation though; Edward IV still occupied the throne when I last looked! Lord Warwick has many hurdles to jump – an invasion to organise and finance, and an unknown reception here in England. You know how we feel about the French. Any hint of a bastard French army on English soil will stymie his cause. Margaret's none too popular either! When is this all to take place, does Tony Tanner know?'

'It's all in the planning stages, but obviously if Lord Warwick and Clarence are to make a move, it will have to be before the winter storms set in – especially considering it'll be a long Channel crossing from the Harfleur area.'

'Not from Calais? What does Lord Wenlock think of all this – has he sent me any money by the way?'

'Lord Wenlock's still in Calais, but has just been dismissed as its lieutenant. Apparently, the king no longer trusts him. Tony visited him in secret on his way to England and his lordship helped to find him a ship to take him across to Sandwich. He told me Lord Wenlock felt badly because, when Lord Warwick was running from the king's army and tried to cross to France, Lord John had to turn the earl away from Calais when he requested assistance for his daughter, Lady Isobel, who'd gone into labour. Wenlock had orders not to let Lord Warwick land in Calais under any circumstances. In fact, the garrison fired on Warwick's ships. All Wenlock could do was to send in some decent wine for the lady!'

'I wish he'd send some here! Did Tony say if we could expect a shipment?'

'He knew you'd ask and the answer is "yes". Lord Wenlock never forgets his friends. I have a purse of monies for you too, Sir Tom. I took the liberty of writing to his lordship to thank him! It's only courteous; he's so generous to you. Tony will deliver the letter for us. Anyway, I thought you might forget to write one – being so busy.' There was a slight edge to his voice. Pom had a great admiration for Lord Wenlock and it had long been a puzzle to him why the nobleman should be so assiduous in his generosity to a crusty old fellow who could be extremely selfish and bad-tempered.

'You don't have to tell me my manners, Pom!' growled Sir Tom, 'Of course I'll write to the noble lord myself. He may be able to tell us much more of what's going on across the water, especially as he's no longer working for King Edward.'

‘Tony says he’ll have to be very careful; the king is making sure Calais is a haven for shipping in the Channel. Many of Lord Warwick’s ships have been seized from our southern ports.’

‘Let’s hope it doesn’t affect our supplies of Wenlock’s best, Pom. So – what now?’

‘As I told you, Tony will return to France in three weeks to tell Lord Warwick that London is as it always is – sturdily independent and that support could go either way. I did tell him the city is enjoying a brief spell of stability – much of the troubles in the country are outside London in the provinces and counties. Tony already knows there are rebellions brewing in Yorkshire again – at Lord Warwick’s instigation, although that’s my guess, not what he told me. I have a feeling that was where Sir Anthony is riding to today.’

‘I see. So it’s a waiting game. Still, we’re going nowhere, Pom. Life will be unchanging for us, as always. But at least we now have the means by which we can exist in some comfort. I’ll look forward to this delivery of wine – did Tony indicate when we might see it?’

‘No, but we both know Lord Wenlock is a man of his word. You’ll just have to be patient Sir Tom!’

***

By and large, events in the wider world escaped the full attention of those who lived patiently within the walls of Newgate and the narrow streets around it. Little news arrived from France; Malory and his friends were as well informed as the rest of the citizens of London. There were rumours of uprisings in Yorkshire, but these were met with shrugs of resignation. ‘They’re always revolting in the north over something – must be the persistent rain which makes them restless.’

‘Wolves, that’s what it is! You would likely be agitated all the time if you were always threatened with wolves!’ said a man to no one in particular. He was standing with a group around yet another posting on a tavern door; this time it called for every good man to rise and save his king from the northern hordes.

'That may be so, but there's no cause for them to make war on our king!' said another.

'How can wolves make war on the king?'

'Don't be foolish – I meant the Nevilles. I did hear that they're involved!'

'They're all Nevilles up there – it's a great family spider's web. They all marry each other you know.'

'All nobility does that – it's to keep the likes of us from polluting their blood!'

'Polluting? What do you mean?'

'Poisoning it! They reckon if they mix their noble blood with our common blood, the sky will fall in or some kind of disaster will strike the land. It stands to reason we must keep to our own. They lay with their ladies, we fuck our women. It's simple!'

'I think we're getting away from the real problem here,' said a man who had kept quiet up to that point, 'I'm sure Lord Warwick's behind this latest trouble in Yorkshire!'

'Oh, you know that for certain, do you? What are you, a spy or something?' and the small crowd looked at him suspiciously.

He shrugged, 'No, I just work things out for myself, instead of being influenced by other people's ideas,' and he looked witheringly at the notice pinned up in front of them. 'The king would do well to take this threat in the north very seriously. Think about it – Lord Warwick's in France, probably talking to the French king at this moment and plotting an invasion.'

'Bringing a French army here! You jest! Lord Warwick's no traitor – I've tasted his roast beef and I can tell you, he loves the common man and would never sell out to the French! You should watch what you're saying!'

The man began to look as though he wished he'd kept his mouth shut. The mention of the French and their monarch had, as usual, struck a nerve with this small, but representative group of English citizens.

'I'm only suggesting that you look at the facts! It's an open secret the Duke of Clarence enjoys being heir to the throne –'

'Until King Edward has a son. That can't be far away; we all know what a lusty monarch he is!'

'Yes, I agree. It's unlikely that the duke will become our king!'

'Thank Christ for that!' said a man fervently. 'He's a man with a boy's brain. He's no king!'

'You're probably right; so, even more reason to take these events in Yorkshire seriously. I prophesy something serious will come out of them and very soon.' There was something portentous in the manner of the man's declaration, and the small crowd looked at him – some nodded in agreement, some curling their lips as though dismissing his words as a fantasy.

There seemed little else to say after that and the group began to fragment. Men went their own ways, but the stranger's words resonated with some of them and they had cause to remember his prophesy – sooner than they could imagine.

***

Tell me, Monty, how far has Pom got with my life-story? There seems to have been so many interruptions to the smooth rhythm of our days, I've lost track as to whether he still visits you on a Sunday.'

'As you say, sir, we have had fewer opportunities to proceed.'

'Well, where had you got to, Pom?'

Monty, Sir Tom and Pom were together in Malory's rooms on a warm day in mid-August. Monty felt life had taken a gentler turn since the horrific events earlier in the year, and, apart from the loss of an "unimportant digit", as Sir Tom insisted on describing it, he had felt few ill-effects. Progress with *Le Morte D'Arthur* was steady and regular, in fact for some time, Malory had been satisfied the book itself was complete; it just needed the final touches of light proof reading and a search for anomalies. 'Your area of expertise, Mr Pickle!' commented Sir Tom cheerfully. 'You have a remarkable facility for picking over the bones!' This was a rare compliment from one who was generally miserly with his praise.

There were few interruptions now that Anthony Tanner had disappeared, whether to France or Yorkshire, no one was certain. Undoubtedly, he would reappear at some point when least expected. Lord Wenlock had kindly replenished the dwindling wine stocks and Lady Malory had sent the quarterly remission of fees from her husband's Warwickshire estates. She never appeared in person, clearly unwilling to make the long and arduous journey from the midlands. Neither did Sir Thomas' son ever visit his father. Malory insisted it was "pressure of work", but Monty thought Robert Malory could not face the shame of his father's continual imprisonment. That extended captivity was occupying Monty's thoughts that morning as soon as Sir Tom mentioned his "life-story". The old knight was right, Monty and Pom has made little headway, although not for lack of interest on the part of the scribe.

Pom scratched his head, 'As I remember I told Monty how you were incarcerated in various prisons in London for a few years until May of '54.'

'Ah – yes, bringing us to the Norfolk period! It's all coming back to me. The good old duke of that fair county arranged bail for me for almost six months, and we decided to leave London and take our chances in East Anglia. Great days, Pom! Do you remember how, as usual, we found ourselves with no money and you took it upon yourself to find the means whereby we could eat! As I recall, you went in for horse thieving in a big way! Even had an alias!'

'I certainly did, Sir Tom; I was styled "John Addesley" – but I didn't choose it – I think it was a misspelling of my name on the charge sheet!'

'Do you remember the tally of beasts?'

'To the letter, sir! Five horses; not all at once but over a few weeks in May, June, and July. First there was a decent bay and an aged grey – they were from the Abbot of Titley in Great Easton.'

'Ah yes, another abbot stuffed! I was proud of you, Pom!' said Sir Tom with relish.

'Then I robbed a vicar – which pleased you almost as much. I took his fine white horse, and a week later a sorrel and a young bay from two other men in his parish of Gosfield – it's funny, I can remember the horses perfectly, but not their owners!'

'I know you came to find me in Thaxted where I'd taken lodgings. Someone reported you were there and I was accused of harbouring a fugitive!'

'We've been harbouring each other for forty years, Sir Tom! But I suppose we shouldn't have broken into John Green's house – do you remember that?'

'I certainly do! But he owed us £4 6s 8d for one of the horses. As I told the sheriff, Green was a bad payer.'

'The sheriff was sharp and knew all about your reputation, Sir Tom! He obviously didn't believe it and sent out a posse afterwards. But I will say – the break-in was a well-planned operation.'

'So remind me what happened,' Monty said, appalled at these revelations of hanging offences so casually admitted.

'We were clever and waited until Sunday morning and everyone was at mass. I'd done the ground work and discovered Green was storing his brother's goods in his house, so there were good pickings. It was a pity we were interrupted.'

'Yes, we didn't expect William Green to come back because he'd forgotten his missal. It was sheer bad luck! I was just getting to grips with the implements to force an entry when he saw you and raised the alarm: "Malory! Malory!" I had no idea you were that well known in the district!'

'I've always been proud of my infamy, Pom! It was a pity he turned up when he did; Jesus Christ! We missed our chance with some chests and coffers full of decent stuff.'

Monty had remained silent through this reminiscence. He had heard the story before, but it was interesting to hear Sir

Tom's account which lacked any show of remorse or shame. The only regret the man had was because he hadn't succeeded in robbing one of his neighbours. Really, Malory was nothing but a scoundrel at bottom.

'It was prison for us from then on, Mr Pickle,' Malory turned to Monty, 'The posse caught up with us and we were arrested in Thaxted; then sent to Colchester Jail. The sheriff of London tried to have us transferred for "legal reasons" to the King's Bench prison, but we resisted, didn't we, Pom?'

'That was a low point, Monty,' said Pom. He looked disapprovingly at Sir Tom, 'I was never happy the way you attacked the jailer as you did; he was only doing his job. You see, Monty, we managed to get hold of some daggers, swords and those wicked langue-de-boeufs, and made our escape.'

'Ah yes! The ox-tongue spear; a handy weapon and we certainly put the shits up the guards when we emerged armed with them! I've never seen men run so fast! But, Monty it's remarkable how our friends always came to our rescue; this time they smuggled in the weapons under the guards' noses. These county jails are very lax in their security.'

'But you didn't have to beat the poor jailer up. He was willing to let us go without a struggle!' Pom protested.

'I only tapped him, Pom! I needed to show the others we meant business. It's all very well waving sharp weapons about, but you must show you're willing to use them for it to have any effect. Anyway, I did slip some cash into his pocket – "for his trouble".'

Monty intervened, 'I think this was the point we reached when we last spoke, Pom. I'm uncertain as to what happened next.'

'Not much. We were caught again, and it was the beginning of a long and tedious imprisonment in London for us both. We went backwards and forwards to the King's Bench court, with nothing ever resolved.'

'I was bailed several times and for large sums. The most was two thousand pounds, so they obviously considered me to be a prisoner of some status!' said Sir Tom proudly.

'They were misled then,' said Pom sourly. 'We didn't have a pot to piss in and were living in dire circumstances in poor cells in the King's Bench Prison. That was when one of your "friends" complained to the courts that you had defaulted on a loan he made you, which caused us all kinds of problems as I remember, in the year '57.'

'Ah yes, Grisly Greswold! He said he'd lent me £4 9s 8d which I should have repaid the previous Christmas. I'd forgotten all about it, but the bastard had me shut up in Ludgate debtors' prison and then up in front of the justices.'

'Unlike most of the other charges, this one actually concluded. The judges –'

'The fucking justices – which included Grisly himself, would you believe, Monty, found against me and I had to pay £4 13 0, including 3s 4d costs! Because I couldn't pay, I was sent back to Ludgate. If it hadn't been for Lord Fauconberg –'

'Lord Fauconberg – Lord Warwick's uncle that was?' remarked Monty.

'Indeed, sadly missed – a great gentleman and soldier. He stood my bail later in the year, with some other friends.'

'How did they come to stand your bail?'

Sir Tom tapped the side of his nose, 'Ways and means, Mr Pickle! I know men who know men!'

Monty didn't really understand what the man was talking about, but it was evident that Malory was not going to expand on all his past devious activities or attachments. *Clearly,* Monty thought, *I'm never going to get to the bottom of all the serpentine twists of this man's life.*

Pom continued the tale, 'The bail was set for three months, to end on the last day of December as I remember. In fairness, Sir Tom surrendered himself in person and on time.'

'The first and last time I'll ever do that!' said Sir Tom robustly. 'It was only because it was Lord Fauconberg's money.'

'What happened next?' Monty asked.

'A whole year in the King's Bench Prison; that's what happened next!'

Pom laughed, 'Until I helped you escape and we went back home.'

'Careful, Pom, don't mislead Mr Pickle! It wasn't quite like that; there were no dramatic escapes with sheets down the walls like Lancelot, or jumping through windows like at Coleshill – you've heard all about that, Monty? It was one of my better exploits!' Monty nodded and Malory continued, 'As I remember, I walked through the gates of the prison unchallenged. The King's Bench Marshal, William Brandon, was quite liberal in allowing prisoners to partake of some fresh air, if they didn't stray too far. I strayed one hundred miles up Watling Street as far as Warwickshire, where my friends kept me safe from re-arrest for a while. But by January of '60, I was back in the King's Bench and then transferred here to Newgate, but again, not in such salubrious quarters as you see around you,' and he waved his arm at the modest accommodation as though he was a duke showing off his palace.

'No indeed, Sir Tom. But we should tell Mr Pickle how pleased you were in July of that year when there was a very special event.'

'Indeed, Fuckingham Buckingham met a gruesome end at the battle of Northampton! I thought they should ring all the church bells. It did me the power of good when I heard of it.'

'What is the root of this antipathy to the duke, Sir Tom?' Monty thought this an excellent time to get to the bottom of this mystery.

'His arrogance! When he torched the village church – with Pom and me inside it – in revenge for a slight –'

'Not so much a slight as a murder, Sir Tom!' protested Monty.

'Pom and I hadn't murdered anyone – neither had our companions, apart from Harcourt. It was an unnecessarily harsh response to a private quarrel. Anyway, my instincts have always been with Lord Warwick – and Buckingham and he were never friends. Therefore, since "my enemy's enemy is my friend", I have always followed Richard Neville.

Besides I hate everything Buckingham stood for – creeping round Queen Margaret. He deserved what he got in the end.'

Monty wondered if he had really got to the bottom of the business. There were plenty of other dukes and earls who could be accused of similar behaviour, but they didn't seem to warrant the hatred Malory evidently felt towards this magnate. However, perhaps Sir Tom himself had forgotten where the roots of this intense dislike originated. Monty considered it would be best to avoid the subject in future.

'Are you listening, Mr Pickle?' Malory's voice crackled with irritation. 'You asked to hear about significant events in my life – do me the courtesy of listening! Christ, you seem to be in another world and it was obviously more interesting than this one! Were you thinking of women?'

Monty started, and shook his head dumbly, 'I beg your pardon, Sir Tom.'

'Right, perhaps afterwards you'll share your internal musings with Pom and I! Now, where were we?'

Pom continued, 'The same July Buckingham was killed, in the year '60, we were all let out of the Tower following the great siege of the place by Lord Wenlock. That was when we were asked to join the Yorkist army under Lord Warwick. We fought at St Albans, where unfortunately that same lord was forced to withdraw, but we were there when King Henry was deposed and brought to London tied to his horse. What a sorry sight that was!'

'He was a useless king. I will admit, Edward's much more suited to the role – tall and upright. The women love him, and he loves the women I'm told!'

'Too much, sometimes,' said Pom acidly before continuing. 'When Edward Duke of York became king, all his supporters were granted pardons.'

'What a day that was, Pom! I can't tell you, Monty, what a pleasure it was taking the king's pardon to the King's Bench justices and waving it in front of their noses! Twelve years in and out of their pox-ridden jails, moved pillar to post across London and never having my day in court.'

'You were almost held in contempt at one point – telling one of the justices "to go and fuck himself"! It was as well I dragged you out before you were arrested again.'

'Can you blame me? Those caitiffs had me by the bollocks for years. Anyway, we weren't dragged back to Newgate, instead we made our way to the nearest tavern and drank ourselves witless, until we were too fuddled to fuck anything; which was a pity, but we made up for it over the next few days!'

'So, did you go back home to Warwickshire?'

Pom went on, 'We did, Monty, but as I remember it, Sir Tom, although we found ourselves back home among friends and family, it wasn't long before you were, shall we say, bored with domesticity.'

'God's bones, Pom, I was greatly out of the habit of being a family man. Lady Elizabeth had grown old and worn –'

Pom bristled, 'You were very harsh to your wife. For some of the years you were in prison – and now – she has kept you as well as if you had been in your own manor house – all the comforts you need and far better than the rest of the poor sods incarcerated with you. And there is the succession of whorelets you've brought through their gates. Lady Elizabeth surely heard rumours of them, but when you came home, there were no recriminations.'

'That's because she no longer cared for me!'

'Can you blame her?' cried Pom, evidently very exercised on Lady Elizabeth's behalf.

'Pom, you were there; you could see. She was not at all interested in me, only our son, Robert, who did very well for himself when Edward became king. As far as I was concerned, it was very ironic that he was made Lieutenant of the Tower of London! Perhaps they thought our family was so imbued in the penal system, he would need little training for the job.'

'I still say you treated her badly, and continue to do so!'

'She's happy enough – grandchildren, furs and a comfortable manor house. Anyway, she takes no interest in my writing.'

'That's because you don't share it with her!'

'She's a woman and wouldn't be interested in a work of such literary merit!'

Monty felt he had to intervene, 'Sir Tom, I have women clients, women who are very interested in matters of the world, literate and capable of understanding more difficult concepts than thronging, wrasting and rashing!'

'Are you saying my work is trivial, Mr Pickle?' There was a definite note of menace in Malory's voice and Monty realised he had pricked a nerve.

'Not at all, sir, but women make up half of our society; many can read and will be interested in a romance like *Le Morte D'Arthur*. Some great ladies are accumulating libraries – while their menfolk are off killing each other. I would say you ignore that market at your peril when it comes to selling your book!'

Malory was silent; then he grunted, 'Hmm, but I still say it wouldn't do for Lady Elizabeth; it's too – too – explicit in some sections!'

The hypocrisy of the man! thought Monty, but did not say it.

As often occurred when there was any awkwardness which needed to be mollified, Pom came to the rescue. 'Monty, as I've already told you, it was at this point that Sir Tom and I felt ready for further adventures, and that was when we found ourselves up in Northumberland with Lord Fauconberg and the Earl of Warwick!'

Monty was relieved the conversation had been diverted and nodded, 'Yes, I remember; Lord Warwick's amazing ride round the four castles!'

Malory opened his mouth, evidently intent on relaying the tale in gory detail, but Pom, realising time was passing and no work had been done on the manuscript, hastily intervened again and said, 'You have all the details in your notebook, I believe, Monty. Now, perhaps we should fill the jug and take a glass of Burgundy before you both proceed with your task. I think I heard the Abbey bells chime the hour.'

Sir Tom stretched his arms over his head and yawned, 'By Christ! You're right, Pom. We've wasted enough time.' He looked accusingly at Monty, 'It's your fault, distracting me with my life-story. I know it is of great interest to you, but I never intended it should interfere with my work. So, let's get on, shall we?'

Monty nodded, picked up a paper and charged his quill with ink, sighing inwardly with frustration at this irritating and complicated man.

Chapter 10

Jack in distress; Tony Tanner arrives with news from France;
The king leaves the country; Lord Warwick enters it;
Sir Tom receives unwelcome news but rescues a damsel in distress;
Gregory also comes to the rescue; the manuscript is finished.

'Sir Tom?'

'Mm?' Malory was deeply absorbed re-reading a passage concerning Sir Tristram and Sir Palomides' ride to the Humber bank, and finding a ship wherein lay the body of King Hermance. Before Monty could express his thought, Malory said, 'Listen to this, Monty; I think it's rather good:

"So thus they rode until that they came to Humber bank, where they heard a cry and a doleful noise. Then were they in the wind where a vessel hilled over with red silk came, and the vessel landed fast by them. Therewith Sir Tristram alit and his knights. And so Sir Tristram went afore and entered that vessel. And when he came within he saw a fair bed richly covered and thereupon lay a dead seemly knight, all armed save the head, was all be-bled, with deadly wounds upon him, the which seemed to be a passing good knight."'

Privately, Monty thought it was no better or worse than the rest, but Malory obviously considered it of enough worth to read out to him. On those occasions, his scribe was expected to give a favourable response. This time Monty felt the urge to challenge – perhaps it was all this charging and couching which over-dominated the action in the stories. He also had a major concern about the whole work and had determined to bring it to the fore as soon as an opportunity arose. He felt this was it and drew a deep breath.

'Sir Tom, there's a point I'd like to bring to your attention –'

'Yes, I'm sure there is, but what do you think of the opening to Section 59?'

'Oh – it's very – very – anticipatory.'

'Anticipatory? What does that mean?'

'It means your reader is left wondering who this dead knight lying in the bowels of a ship could be. Have we met him before, or is he a new character? Your reader will be induced to continue to turn the pages to find out. So, an excellent literary device!'

'Yes – I agree – anticipatory; a good word, Monty, and one I shall use myself when the need arises.'

'But to get back to my point –'

'Very well, as long as it doesn't take up any time. What is it?'

'Some of these strange words, sir. In the section you've just read, for instance; what does "hilled over" mean?'

'Covered! Any fool knows that!'

'I managed to work that out, but at the expense of my concentration as to what was coming next. Then, there are those terms directly connected to the joust, the tournament and chivalry in general. Have you considered that some of your readers, the ladies, for instance, won't have a clue what they mean? I didn't know what "abrayed" meant, or a "hough" was. Fewtering was something right outside my experience or knowledge until you explained it.'

'Well, you only have to ask and I'll tell you.'

'But what about your readers who don't have that facility, Sir Tom? Here's a suggestion: why not add a glossary to explain the meaning?'

'A glossary? You mean a list of unusual words at the back? No, I don't think so; it would be patronising to my readers.'

‘I’m not so sure. I think many of them would be grateful not to have to show their ignorance and ask the meaning. They could simply turn to the back and find out for themselves.’

‘This book is aimed at the nobility who have all the chivalric knowledge necessary to decipher a few unfamiliar words.’

‘Doesn’t that rather narrow the scope of your readership, Sir Tom – limit the market, as it were? Can I remind you that you did take the trouble to try the stories out on non-noble audiences, small ones admittedly, but who were, by and large, impressed. They would surely need help in this regard,’ Monty said smoothly.

There was a silence from Malory. He disliked any idea which had not come from his own head, but privately he wondered if his scribe wasn’t right. He really needed as wide a readership as he could get; anything which dissuaded it from buying the book was to be avoided.

‘I admit the idea has merit, Monty. I’ll think about it, but if I agree then I rely on you to arrange it coherently. Probably best in alphabetical order.’

‘My thought too, Sir Tom!’ Monty had already foreseen that, should Sir Tom agree, he would automatically pass it to someone else to organise. It could only be himself. He had already begun his suggested list of characters – in his own time.

It was mid-September. Outside, early frosts were having their biting effects on leaves half-hanging from branches now tired and anxious for winter rest from which they could fuel a spring-time renewal. Their papery burden deepened into hues of carmine, gold and umber, before succumbing and falling to the earth, where they were trodden carelessly into the permanent detritus of the paths, alleys and streets of the capital by its inhabitants. Inside, a good fire was blazing in Malory’s grate, to the extent that the door had to be left ajar for draughts of cool air to enter. Fat Gregory was on duty, lodged in his usual position on his stool at the bottom of the stairs, his back leaning against the stout grey walls; semi-dozing in a most un-sentry like way. He was brought to life by the entry of Jack Worms who, in his customary courteous way paid some respect to Gregory's office by mumbling incoherently whether it was permissible to ''o a'oft'. Gregory was unacquainted with nautical terms; his only experience of water-borne transport was when he escorted Sir Tom across the Thames from Blackfriars Wharf to Bankside. Even if he had that knowledge, he would not have understood the incoherent babble which came from Jack's mouth. Nodding lazily, Greg resumed his dozing as Jack walked slowly up the stairs. Again, using due deference, he tapped on the door of Malory's room.

'Ah, Mr Worms – come with my supplies! But what's amiss? Why the bandage?' The stationer appeared before his three companions with a heavy linen cloth tied around his jaw and head.

'You look as though you've prepared yourself for burial before your time, Jack!' and Malory began to laugh. 'Would you like some pennies for your eyes?'

'Is 'ot fuuy,' muttered Jack, 'is 'oothache! 'ack 'ooth!'

''Oothache? Ah – a rotten back tooth! Is that all?' Sir Tom was immediately unsympathetic, 'I've lost a few in my time. In fact, I've only half of what I started out with; fortunately what's left is all at the front! If it's that painful, it needs to come out. What do we think, Pom? Shall we use your skills on him? I've never had any complaints after you pulled mine out.'

'Oh, 'o!' and Jack shook his head vigorously, the part of his face not obscured by the cloth showing distinct alarm.

Monty was more compassionate, 'Have you tried a rosemary mouthwash?'

''Es, 'ut is 'o oose.'

'Mouthwash?' Sir Tom scoffed. 'Don't be fucking ridiculous! Of course it's "'o oose". What he needs is some good Burgundy before and after Pom gets to work. Gregory!' and Malory roared down the stairs. 'Get up here! We need your bulk.'

Jack was even more alarmed and prepared to leave promptly, but Malory grabbed him by the arm, 'Oh no! What can't be cured must be extracted. Believe me, you'll thank me for it afterwards. Now, lie down on the bed.'

Jack continued to resist and Malory signalled to Pom and Monty to grab the poor stationer, and force him onto the truckle. By this time, Fat Greg had roused himself sufficiently to mount the stairs; he now stood staring at the sight of three men wrestling with a fourth, trying to lay him flat on the small bed.

'Don't stand there with your mouth open, you fool, sit on his chest!' Monty was now also alarmed; Gregory was twice the weight of Jack Worms and would surely have crushed his ribs to splinters, to say nothing of the bed. The scribe felt this whole exercise was typical of Sir Tom's bull-at-a-gate approach to everything.

'If we must use force, I think Gregory would be of more use holding down Jack's shoulders.' He leaned over the recumbent stationer, 'Will that be all right, Jack?'

Jack Worms looked pleadingly at Monty and shook his head as vigorously as the bandage would let him, ''O, 'o!'

'Take no notice, Pom! I'll get his jaw open; Mr Pickle, you get his legs; Gregory, for Christ sake, keep his shoulders still. I'll turn his face to the window – that'll give us more light. Now, Pom, have you got the pincers?' Jack's eyes rolled up into his forehead.

'Yes, Sir Tom; if you could just get his mouth wider, I'll have a go!'

'He said it was a back one; it must be on the right where the bandage is. Have a look and see what's going on in there.'

Malory had wrenched Jack's jaw open with relish and, with surprising strength for an old man, his hands were now in complete control of the poor man's mouth; Gregory had his ham-like hands on each of Jack's shoulders and was bearing down with his full weight; Monty lay across Jack's legs and Pom peered into the cavity. Then, with a cry of success, he said, 'There it is! I can see it; it looks nasty! Black as the ace of spades. I just hope I can get it all out in one piece and it doesn't snap off; if that happens, it'll be a disaster because it'll surely turn bad and give him a lot of trouble later. Still, here goes!' and he opened the pincers and placed them round the offending molar. Then deftly, seemingly without any assistance or heavy pulling, he unscrewed the tooth and out it came, followed by a great spurt of blood. Pom looked triumphantly at the rotting object between the claws of the pincers, 'A clean pull. Not a bad job though I say it myself!'

'That was well done, Pom! I expect that's a relief, eh, Jack?' But Jack had passed out and was lying unconscious with his mouth open, dangerously close to drowning in his own blood. 'Get him up before he chokes to death and give him a good pull of wine, Pom,' Malory stood up and wiped his bloody hands on his shirt. 'In fact, pour us all one, including Fat Greg here,' and he nodded at the guard who, docile as ever stared unblinkingly at the black stump now lying on the table among Malory's papers. Jack had come around, and was groaning and mopping his mouth, from where the blood continued to drip; at the same time, with shaking hands, sipping cautiously at his drink.

Malory was more concerned at the effect of the comingling of bodily liquor with good Burgundy, 'Christ, Jack! That's Wenlock's best! Have a care!'

Jack said nothing, but colour was coming back into his cheeks and the wine had a warming effect.

'That was skilfully done, Pom!' said Monty. 'You've obviously had a lot of experience. Tell me, who pulls yours out?'

'I have been known to do it myself; but if the tooth is difficult for me to get at, I'll find an old soldier; they're very experienced. I rarely use the barbers – they charge too much for a simple job. No, I'll pay an old warrior sixpence, and he'll do the job cleaner and quicker than anyone.'

Gregory downed his drink and held out his glass hopefully. Malory shook his head, 'You'll be lucky Greg, that's enough! Now back to your stool you go or I'll have Master Clyfford on my back.' The guard was just about to back out of the room when they heard the bottom gate open and footsteps on the stairs. Then the door was pulled open wide and Sir Anthony Tanner appeared in the doorway.

***

Looking round the room, Tony Tanner took in the scene: the blood-stained cloth, Jack Worms with his head in his hands; Monty patting his shoulder; Pom carefully cleaning his pincers and Malory sitting back in his chair with a self-satisfied look on his face.

Tony frowned, 'What have I missed here?'

'We've just extracted Master Worms' tooth for him, Six-toed. But never mind that; what brings you to London? What's the news from France? You know the king's in the north? Where are Lord Warwick and the Duke of Clarence?'

'One thing at a time, Tom!' laughed Sir Anthony. 'First how about pouring me some of that fine wine – and how are you set up for some food? I'm starving – I've been riding almost non-stop for two days,' he turned to Jack. 'Better in than out, as they say,' he said cheerfully.

Pom immediately set about satisfying the needs of their latest guest, and soon Tony, with his mouth full of chicken and bread, began to satisfy their need for news. 'Firstly, yes, of course I knew Edward was in Yorkshire – he's in York now. As for Lord Warwick, he's just left France for England; I came across two days ahead of him to alert Greyfriars of his imminent arrival in the country – and of course to visit my old friends!'

'So, Lord Warwick's sailing for England – is he bringing Margaret of Anjou?'

'No, she's waiting in France. I suppose to see how things work out and whether the Earl of Warwick will free her husband from the Tower. You know of course that Warwick has come out for the Lancastrians?'

'Yes, Pom reported to us what you told him back in the summer. I must say I was as shocked at the news as anything I've ever heard – since – since –'

Pom helped his master out as usual, 'Since Lady Elizabeth told you she was pregnant?'

'Yes – that I suppose; anyway I was full of amazement. Fuck it, Tony! How can anyone change sides like that?'

'Well, if you'd been in France this summer, and heard all the negotiations and plotting, I don't think you would be surprised that this was the outcome. Anyway, King Louis is backing the earl and the duke for an invasion, and they have men ready and waiting on this side of the Channel. With Edward in the north, this is the perfect time to strike.'

'Strike?' Sir Tom looked quizzically at Tony Tanner, 'You mean make a bid for the throne?'

'Yes, what else?'

'By Christ! So that really is in the wind, is it? We can expect the two noblemen in the city at any time.'

'They're landing on the south coast within the next few days, weather permitting. Then heading to the midlands on their way north to confront Edward; I'm on my way to meet them in Coventry. Then we'll see.'

'It must come to a fight, Tony!' said Sir Tom.

'I suppose it must. But whatever happens, I'm for the Earl of Warwick and I hope you are too!'

'Jesus Christ! Of course we are – all loyal to the core – aren't we?' and he threw a challenging look at Pom and Jack.

Monty exchanged glances with Jack Worms; the latter was still in no position to speak, so Monty answered for them both, 'I must say, I would really like to hear the justification for trying to dislodge an anointed king, Sir Tom – no disrespect, Sir Anthony.'

Malory was brusque as usual, 'God's bones, Mr Pickle! We've been over the reasons innumerable times. King Edward has seen fit to take himself off to the north and abandon his capital; he's surrounded himself with arse-lickers like – like –'

'Like the Lord Chancellor, Sir Tom?' said Tony Tanner with a knowing look at Monty.

'Yes, like that fawning cur Stillington. Let's hope he loses more than his position when Warwick's in charge.'

'Will he be in charge though? Wouldn't Margaret of Anjou want to take back power on behalf of her husband, Henry? We all know he's not capable of ruling the country.'

'I'm sure they'll come to some mutually beneficial arrangement. The main thing is to get the matter settled quickly,' said Tony, 'With the king of France behind them, I'm certain of their victory. Now, tell me, what's the mood in the city? You get out and about on the streets, Pom; tell me, are the people still for Lord Warwick?'

Pom nodded, 'Mostly they still are. Some merchants and gentry support him; King Edward owes them money and anyone who offers to settle his debts will have their gratitude I'm sure.'

'Is the city safe for you, Tony?' asked Malory, 'Where will you stay tonight?'

'Now the king's in the north, the city's been emptied of many of his spies and soldiers who have gone with him. I've found discrete lodgings in Greyfriars tonight; tomorrow, as I said, I'm heading for Coventry.'

'So you don't wish to partake of my bathtub again?'

'If it's all the same, I'd rather not! Thank you for the food and wine, much appreciated. I must get back and see to my horses. They also need sustenance before we set out on the road again. Those poor beasts have travelled too many miles with little rest. A man's horse must always be first in his thoughts – we're useless without them.'

'That may be true for you with the freedom to travel where you will; for us poor bastards locked away in here, a horse is of no use at all!' grumbled Sir Tom.

Within two weeks, that "poor bastard" locked up in Newgate and his friends, were about to have their lives turned upside down, as were others of their acquaintance.

***

'He's gone! He's gone, Lord Robert!'

'Who's gone?' Robert Stillington put down his quill and scowled at the interruption. 'If you'd just stop shouting –'

'The king – the king's left the country and gone – gone – somewhere.'

'Left the county? Rubbish! He's in York sorting out the rebels. Where did this come from? I hope you're not spreading rumour and speculation, Crosby! There's been too much of that already.'

'Indeed not, my lord, I heard it from one of King Edward's officers in the palace just now. He was on his way to see you himself, but was waylaid and asked me to tell you. The king has taken ship from the Yorkshire coast with just a handful of men and is sailing – probably to Burgundy.'

'Why should we think he's fleeing? He has an army at his back. He's probably made a spur-of-the-moment decision to visit his brother-in-law, Duke Charles on important matters of state.' The Lord Chancellor knew this could not possibly be true but was completely stuck for any other explanation of his sovereign's actions.

'There's no army at his back anymore, my lord. Lord Montague's decided to fight with his brother, the Earl of Warwick and has deserted the king. Lord Warwick and the Duke of Clarence are riding towards London from the midlands. I believe George Neville, the Archbishop of York, is riding ahead and will request the gates are opened to let them all in.'

The Lord Chancellor stood up and thumped the table, flushing red with anger. 'Jesus Christ, Crosby, I knew the villain had arrived in the country with his so-called supporters, but I thought he was riding north to make some accommodation with King Edward. Now it seems the bastards are all making a bid for the crown. You'll be telling me next, Margaret of Anjou is with them waiting to take it back for that pathetic excuse for a king, Henry Lancaster. Why wasn't I informed of all this earlier?'

'King Edward's agents have all ridden with him. There are very few left to disseminate news to London. Which brings me to another serious matter, my lord; this news has got out into the streets and there's real trouble brewing. People are upset.'

'Upset! Upset! I'll give them "upset"! We'll all be "upset" in a minute. You know what this means, don't you?'

'I'm not too sure, my lord,' said Mr Crosby tentatively, although he had a good idea.

'It means our heads – that's what it means! I've had this post for three years, but George Neville held it before me. He'll be after it again and some revenge thrown in.'

'So what should we do then?'

'Make a bolt for it, that's what. Get ourselves out of Westminster and claim immediate sanctuary in St Martin's. Don't forget I'm its Dean as well as Bishop of Bath and Wells; I still have my church connections, thanks be to God!' and he crossed himself vigorously.

'Couldn't we just go across the cloisters into the Abbey and claim sanctuary?' asked Crosby.

'No! St Martin le Grand is safer for us – out of the way. I can't see George Neville bothering us anywhere near Newgate Street – too close to the prison, for a start! Let's hope we don't end up there. There'd be nothing worse than having that scoundrel Malory for a neighbour! By the way, when I say "us", Crosby, I really mean "me"; you'll have to shift for yourself. But first, what I want you to do is burn all the papers – anything that might not read well as far as the next incumbent is concerned; in other words, anything that's incriminating.'

'Maybe it's not my place to say it, my lord, but King Edward is still our sovereign and you are still the Lord Chancellor. Now he's gone abroad you're really in charge of the country – at least as far as law and order are concerned. What about the Great Seal? Who's to have custody of that? The country can't be run without it after all. Wouldn't it be a good idea to take it into sanctuary with you; keep it safe until the king returns? You are its official custodian after all.'

'Certainly not! If George Neville and his brothers are approaching London, then it's time to take evasive action. I'll leave the Seal in the office with you. This is the first place they'll come to. Wait here until somebody arrives to claim it and then –'

'But wouldn't that be rather reckless, my lord? How will I know who to hand it over to? Anybody could claim it.'

'Don't be ridiculous! They'll have a warrant. These are not barbarians at the gates; they'll have it all planned out;

they've had plenty of time while they're on the road; after all, there's no one following them according to you.'

Peter Crosby could tell his master was getting extremely agitated and testy. It would be of no use to argue. 'Very well, my lord, leave it all to me; I'll take care of everything! Should I come and report to you in St Martin's?'

'Of course not! Once I'm in there the sanctuary rules apply. My presence must be inviolate for forty days at least.'

So, what will happen to me? thought Peter, but didn't say it. Instead he began to gather up some of the papers on the desk in preparation for burning. Lord Robert grabbed his hat and gown and headed for the door. 'Will your – er – housekeeper be going with you, my lord?'

'My housekeeper? Good heavens no! I'm off for a few weeks peace and quiet. Now, get on with the job and make sure you burn everything – everything!'

'Very good, my lord,' said his secretary smoothly. Once Stillington had disappeared through the door, Crosby took his place in the imposing seat behind the Lord Chancellor's table and looked across its broad expanse. Immediately in front of him was a highly decorated box, open and revealing the Great Seal with King Edward's likeness etched on it; this chief symbol of royal authority was attached to a simple blue ribbon. Slowly he picked up the perfectly round metal object which weighed heavily in his hand. *I wonder how much it's worth,* he thought, but carefully replaced it with a sigh.

Then he stood up and collected every document he could find, parcelled them up, and placed them in a leather satchel which he took outside and hid in an innocuous-looking corner cupboard in a shadowy area of a small blind passage off the main corridor. There was a possibility they would come in useful – one day.

***

Peter Crosby gained no advantage from his forward planning, for he never returned to claim his cache. Five hundred years later, the Palace of Westminster was undergoing one of its frequent bouts of maintenance. During a tea-break, two builders discovered an old cupboard set within the recess of a wall in an isolated section of the corridor, where they were stripping off old mortar and whitewash. With workmen's experience of hitting upon secret places, in anticipation of finding something "to their advantage", one put his hand inside and drew out a leather satchel which, although somewhat dried out, was almost as pristine as when it had been placed there, apart from a thin covering of dust and old cobwebs. Imagining a hoard of coin, jewels or other valuables, they were disappointed to find just a thick bundle of letters and documents and, as far as they could tell, all in Latin. Their excitement and expectations were diminished considerably.

Eventually, the satchel and its contents came into the hands of a distinguished antiquarian whose meagre juices were set flowing by the discovery of this treasure trove of fifteenth-century documents from the Lord Chancellor's office. Fifty years later, they found their way into the new British Library, where they were safely stored away in vaults deep in the building. They had come full circle, from one hiding place to another.

***

Shortly after Peter Crosby had delivered the news to the Lord Chancellor of the king's flight, Pom arrived in Newgate in a fluster with the news, 'He's coming back!'

'Who's coming back?' Sir Tom put down his quill and scowled at the interruption.

Pom was flushed and breathless from excitement and bounding up the stairs with a full basket of provisions. 'Lord Warwick, Sir Tom! He's almost outside the city walls.'

'When's he expected, Pom?'

'In about two days they say. George Neville is ahead of him paving the way for the rest. The other news is that King Edward has taken ship for Burgundy; he left Yorkshire on the second of the month.'

'What's today?'

'The fourth of October, Sir Tom. There's more news too and it will certainly please you – and you, Monty!' Monty raised his eyebrows, 'Stillington's gone into sanctuary – at least I think that's what he's doing. I met someone who said he was taking his lordship's belongings to St Martin Le Grande around the corner.'

'I'm reminded of rats and sinking ships, Pom!' said Sir Tom with extreme relish. Monty could almost see the man licking his lips, 'Justice is coming our way at last! Let's hope Lord Warwick has the man's head, eh, Mr Pickle?' Monty looked at his damaged hand with its missing finger and was inclined to agree.

'So what do we expect to happen now?' asked Pom. 'Do you think these rumours of Lord Warwick making amity with Margaret are true?'

'Well, it seems to me that if Edward has really fled the country then it leaves the way free for Lord Warwick to either place the Duke of Clarence on the throne, or have Henry released from the Tower and re-crowned as Henry VI.'

'But Edward is still the anointed king whether he's over the sea or not!' protested Monty. 'No one can overturn the Lord's anointed surely?'

'Monty, I keep telling you – you're very naive! Our country's kings are frequently tumbled from their thrones, anointed or not – Edward II, Richard II, Henry VI! It seems to me the test of a successful monarch is how long he can keep his arse on the thing!'

Pom frowned, 'So, what do we think – Clarence or Henry for our next king?'

'I think the Earl of Warwick will have Henry Lancaster released from the Tower and set up as king, but with Clarence, George Neville and himself running things,' said Sir Tom.

'Margaret won't like that!' observed Pom.

'She'll be happy her son will once again become the Prince of Wales and heir to the throne.'

'Clarence won't like that either!' said Pom.

‘Whatever happens, it seems to me there will be much more trouble to come,’ observed Monty gloomily.’

‘Jesus Christ, Mr Pickle! Let’s be more cheerful please. Stillington’s shivering in St Martin’s, uncertain of his head; our friend Lord Warwick is on his way to bring peace and calm to the kingdom; we’ve nearly finished *Le Morte D’Arthur* and we still have a decent supply of Wenlock’s best. I suggest we open some of it and drink the health of all those preparing to take over.’

As usual, Sir Tom had his way, and whatever Pom and Monty felt privately, they obediently raised their glasses “to the new custodians of the kingdom”!

***

‘I have great news, Sir Tom! Something I’m sure you’ve been waiting for.’ Roger Clyfford stood in front of Malory holding a parchment.

‘You’re going to tell me I’m free to visit Bankside once again!’

‘Not only Bankside, but anywhere else you wish to travel to! You’ve been granted your freedom!’

It was the day after the news that Robert Stillington was no longer Lord Chancellor. Monty, Jack, Pom and Sir Tom were all much the worst for the quantity of drink they had taken the day before in celebration of that fact, among other positive news. Monty had never become used to the thumping headaches he always suffered after many large glasses of Burgundy. Manfully, he tried to keep pace with the others, but always succumbed – either throwing up in the street on the way home, or experiencing disorientating dizziness as his bedroom ceiling involuntarily raised and lowered itself as he lay on his bed. He was in a familiar fragile state this morning as he and Sir Tom were struggling to concentrate on a particularly difficult passage in Book 16, Section 4. The hermit Nacien was explaining to Sir Gawain and Sir Ector the substance of their visions.

‘This seems a very long and unnecessarily complicated section, Sir Tom,’ observed Monty wearily.

‘Complicated? What do you mean?’

‘Well, it just goes on and on. I think the reader might become a little – a little –’ Monty hesitated.

‘Bored? You were going to say “bored” weren’t you, Mr Pickle?’

‘Well, yes I was. It does rather drag, unlike the rest of it of course,’ he said hastily.

Fortunately for Monty, it was at that point Master Clyfford came into the room waving his official-looking document. At the mention of freedom Malory seemed to freeze. He became remarkably still and quiet; his normally pink cheeks – from wine, not healthy living – became almost ashen grey. ‘Did you say “freedom”, Master Clyfford?’ his voice had dropped to a hoarse whisper.

‘I certainly did, Sir Tom, and may I be the first to congratulate you on your imminent release. In fact, you can go whenever you like!’

‘Go? Whenever I like?’ repeated Sir Tom faintly.

‘Certainly, I have your release papers here – signed and sealed. You’ll be able to return to the bosom of your family in Warwickshire and pick up your life as a gentleman – and no recriminations.’

There was a silence. Pom looked at Monty, his eyes and mouth wide open in amazement. Sir Tom shook his head with a look of puzzlement and said, as though to himself, ‘The life of a Warwickshire gentleman? In the bosom of my family?’ Then he seemed to come back to life, ‘Certainly not! Fuck it, I can’t think of anything worse! Look here, Clyfford, I’m not leaving London or Newgate. You can tear up that paper; I’m staying where I am! Why on earth would I want to go back to Newbold Revel? What’s there for me other than a parochial prison? It would be worse than being shut away in the cellars here.’

‘But, Sir Tom,’ protested Clyfford, ‘You’ve been ordered to be let out – all the supporters of Lord Warwick and the Duke of Clarence are being freed from every jail in London.’

'On whose orders?'

'The Archbishop of York, Lord George Neville, who's now Lord Chancellor. Sir Geoffrey Gate has been deputed to arrange it.'

'Sir Geoffrey Gate? Who he?' asked Sir Tom.

'A very important man. He was once Governor of the Isle of Wight,' said Clyfford.

'Where's the Isle of Wight?' asked Monty.

'Never mind that!' said Sir Tom vigorously. 'Although his name may be suited to the task, this Gate man should mind his own business! He should have asked me first if I wanted to be freed.'

The Keeper of Newgate looked aghast, 'Surely, Sir Tom, you want to be out of here as soon as possible. As I said, you could go right now if you wish.'

'But I don't wish; I've work to do – a book to finish. Where on earth will I find peace and quiet to do that? In Warwickshire? I don't think so; my wife in one ear – bastard tenants in the other. I'll not get a moment to myself. No, I wish to stay in this room for as long as it takes me to complete my great work! Anyway, I've paid you for it until the end of the year – three months in advance.'

'But I'm not running a hostelry here, Sir Tom!' protested Clyfford. 'It's not in the rules that I should accept paying guests. This is a –'

'A prison? Yes, I know it is, and a very well-run and comfortable one; I can testify to that. No, I'll stay here if you don't mind. I'm doing no harm and pay you generously. I know very well the authorities have no idea exactly what our arrangement is. Perhaps they'd like to, eh?' and he stared with raised eyebrows at the keeper, who was beginning to frown and look a touch anxious. This was outside his experience and unheard of – a prisoner who didn't want to be released.

Pom stepped in, mediating for his master in his usual calm manner. 'Look, Master Clyfford, you have rather sprung this on my master. It's come as a shock, the idea of leaving this room which he has inhabited for almost two years.' He looked hard at Malory as though warning him to keep his mouth shut.

'Sir Tom has told me that his work is almost done – he and Mr Pickle here are in the process of preparing it for copying and bringing it to the attention of those members of the nobility who are very interested in reading it. We wouldn't want to disappoint them, would we?'

'How would we be responsible for that?'

'Well, if Sir Tom has to uproot from here and travel back to Warwickshire anything could happen to the manuscript – it could be stolen or blown away in the wind –'

'I'd have thought that most unlikely, Mr Appleby,' said Roger Clyfford stiffly.

'Maybe so, but there's always a risk with loose papers – I'm sure you've experienced such problems yourself.'

'There are such things as paper-weights!' said Clyfford. Pom could see Malory getting very fidgety and he continued. 'My point is that there are two things to consider here: firstly Sir Tom is right – he has paid you in full for the room up to the end of the year – you shook hands on a gentlemen's agreement; secondly, his work is of great importance – national importance – and it would be a pity if it was your fault it never saw the light of day. Just think – you could be responsible for the loss of a major contribution to vernacular English.'

Now Master Clyfford was not a stupid man, but neither was he a particularly well-educated one; he'd never visited Oxford or Cambridge, let alone attended either of their universities. He had no idea what Pom Appleby was talking about, but he certainly did not relish going down in history as one who had deprived the nation of a piece of great literature. Admittedly, he had no idea what *Le Morte D'Arthur* was about and any scraps of the work he had overheard never stimulated his interest or imagination enough for him to ask for more. He knew knights and ladies, jousting and magic were involved, but he preferred the Bible and the bawdy bits of Geoffrey Chaucer which his brother, who had a cherished copy of sections of *The Canterbury Tales*, occasionally let him read. There was also the question of the cash which Malory had given him for the renting of the gate-house room.

He had plans for the nest-egg of which it was part. Those plans would have to be postponed or cancelled if he threw Sir Tom out and had to return the money. It seemed to him, in the minute it took to absorb Pom's words, that it would do no harm for Sir Tom to remain where he was for the time being. After all, he had never been officially charged in the first place – just arrested and awaiting a "hearing" which had never taken place because the officers dealing with it were "too busy".

However, he didn't feel he should capitulate too easily; Malory was a man who would always take advantage of a perceived weakness.

'Mm,' he murmured. 'It could be that you might stay – until Christmas only, when our agreement comes to an end. That should give you time to finish the work.'

Sir Tom bristled, 'And who are you to tell me when?'

Pom stepped in again, frowning at Sir Tom, 'That's very generous of you, Master Clifford, and we accept the offer – don't we, Sir Tom?' and he frowned again at his master, this time fiercely nodding his head behind Clyfford's back. Malory set his lips into a thin line and looked vexed, but he nodded back in agreement and held out his hand to the keeper. They shook on it and Roger Clyfford turned to go, still bemused how it could be that one of his long-stay prisoners was now a long-stay guest.

Before he left he said, 'You may have the room, but not the services of Gregory Hapgood. He'll no longer be running up and down the stairs with hot water for that damn tub, or coals for the fire; he's a prison guard after all and I still have legitimate inmates here who need to be guarded. You can make your own domestic arrangements from now on!' And he turned on his heels and left.

'Well, that was a surprise!' said Monty to no one in particular. Jack Worms had been very quiet during these exchanges. Now he said, 'Poor Master Clyfford, he didn't seem very happy! I wonder what's prompted this sudden release of prisoners by the Lord Chancellor.'

'Well, it's obvious; Lord Warwick's going to need all his supporters close to him during the weeks and months to come,' said Sir Tom. 'I'm certainly one of the more important of his followers. I wouldn't be surprised if I wasn't first on Gate's list. I wonder who else has been released.'

'You do realise you'll be able to get around the town and find out for yourself now, Sir Tom?' said Pom.

'More important, I can reacquaint myself with Plump Poll down at the Stews. In fact, we'll go this afternoon, Pom – perhaps you'd like to come with us Jack – you too Monty – we could make a foursome!'

Monty shuddered, and said nothing. Jack looked at the scribe, 'Sir Tom, I think, Mr Pickle and I have much to do this afternoon. We'll leave you to it if you don't mind.'

'Please yourselves; the offer was well meant!'

'I'm sure it was, but work calls for us both.'

'Letgames!' Malory said with a laugh.

'What's a "letgame"?' asked Monty.

'According to Master Chaucer, "a hinderer of pleasure" and I think it's appropriate in both your cases. You'll never know what you've missed.'

'I'm prepared to risk it!' said Jack with a laugh, 'now how about this money you owe me for supplies, Sir Tom?' He took out his notebook, 'According to my reckoning it amounts to 4s 6d and is well overdue!'

***

Things moved swiftly over the next few days. The Duke of Clarence, the Earls of Warwick and Shrewsbury, Lord Stanley and Jasper Tudor Earl of Pembroke entered London through Cripplegate and were met by cheering crowds. The Newgate Four found themselves at the back of the mob as the noble procession rode to the Tower where, according to the account that reached them from the front, Lord Warwick would enter and kneel before Henry Lancaster.

'Can this really be true?' muttered Jack Worms to Monty, as they struggled in the jostling crowd.

'According to Six-toed Tanner, that is now the plan – for Lord Warwick to reinstate Henry as king again.'

‘Jesus Christ, Pom! I can’t see a thing here!’ grumbled Sir Tom. ‘This is a waste of time. Let’s head back to Newgate and wait for news there.’

Unfortunately, the crowd also began to move in a general westerly direction and the four were in danger of being swept along involuntarily. ‘I suggest we try and hire a wherry to row us back the mile or so to Blackfriars’ Wharf. Has anyone got a sixpence?’ said Sir Tom. Monty felt in his doublet pocket and produced the necessary coin. The four men struggled through the throng and eventually found themselves on Tower Wharf where there were a few other hopeful passengers waiting. The wherrymen were busy and it was at least thirty minutes before they could clamber into one of the sturdy single-sailed boats. The wherryman pulled on the oars – an abnormally taciturn man for his trade who accepted their fare without a smile. As they ploughed up the river, Monty noted the usual detritus floating on its surface. A dead horse passed them by on its side; close to the boat he could see that its mouth was wide open and its great teeth exposed in a rictus grin. Monty wondered if it was an omen or fate’s judgement on the state of the nation. The stink of the Thames was almost unbearable, and he marvelled how the river-folk put up with it day in, day out. It was with great relief that he clambered out of the boat and onto Blackfriars’ Wharf.

To their dismay, they found the crowds in the streets leading to St Paul’s were even denser than those near the Tower. ‘For fuck’s sake! Why so many people?’ Sir Tom asked a spectator who had his elbow in his face. The man said, ‘Lord Warwick and King Henry are coming to St Paul’s for a mass. Everyone wants to see Henry VI. We all thought he was dead, but no – he’s going to be king again!’

‘How long will that be?’ asked a fellow standing next to Jack Worms.

‘Days – weeks? Who knows?’ muttered someone else, ‘depends if he manages to hang onto his crown this time. What I want to know is, when will that hag of a wife of his arrive in the country – and how many French troops will she bring with her?’

'You should be careful what you say, neighbour,' warned another, 'you never know who's listening.'

'Where's King Edward's queen, that's what I'd like to know. I thought she was pregnant with another royal bastard!'

'She's taken sanctuary in Westminster Abbey with her children.'

'You seem very well-informed, sir!' said Sir Tom, 'how do you know this?'

'I keep my ears and eyes open, that's how.'

There was a sudden murmur through the crowd and voices calling, 'They're coming!'

'I can't see a thing, Pom. This is even more of a waste of time; let's get back home! I've got work to do, and so have you, Monty.'

'I'd really rather stay and see what happens, Sir Tom, if you don't mind.'

'I do mind – look, the crowd's too big – besides, I'm not used to crushes like this. You never know who's standing next to you with a weapon – cutpurses, pimps!'

You'd know all about them, Sir Tom, thought Jack, but didn't say it. Instead, he found himself agreeing with him. 'There are too many people here to see anything. Someone will come and tell us what happens I'm sure. Anyway, I need to get back to the shop. I may have no customers but there are still manuscripts to bind, and Dick Addlepate shouldn't be left on his own with the glue-pot; I'm heading back to Paternoster Row.'

'Good luck with that, then,' laughed Pom. 'If you can fight your way through the crowds without getting a knife in your gizzards I'll be surprised!' But Jack had already disappeared, swallowed up by the throng of people. Reluctantly, Monty decided that Sir Tom was right – there was too much of a crush and, not a tall man, there was no chance he could crane his neck over the crowd and view the proceedings outside the cathedral.

The three men pushed and elbowed their way through the throng and eventually found themselves in Newgate Street and the main gate of the prison. It was a new experience to simply walk through it towards the guard-tower door without seeing Fat Greg sitting idly on his stool at the bottom of the stairs. The unfortunate man had been directed to other duties and was not happy. Sir Tom had paid him for his "extras" and the money had gone some way to mollifying Gregory's dissatisfied wife, who felt she was recompensed for being married to a block-head when he'd brought home an enlarged purse at the end of each week. She had bought herself a respectable hat and a pair of second-hand shoes with the proceeds and was looking forward to purchasing material for a new gown. When Gregory came home and told her of the new arrangements she had lashed him with her tongue, then flown at him with a skillet. The poor man had no defence, other than to give her a good buffet round the head, which silenced her into a massive sulk for a day or two at least – a relief to the bewildered man who also felt cheated by Keeper Clyfford's new orders. Now, forced to stand for hours by the cells with his halberd, a weapon which he had long-since forgotten how to wield effectively; he found it very heavy and it made his arms ache. He had also developed large red and painful growths on the sides of his big toes because of prolonged standing in flimsy ill-fitting boots. Above all, he missed the comradeship of Malory's cell; the odd glass of Burgundy had gone down very well, and sometimes he even felt part of the fellowship that was the Newgate Four. He had no understanding of what they discussed, nor could he appreciate their jokes, which he knew were sometimes at his expense. But they were a jolly crew and, in winter especially, Sir Tom always had a good fire. Now Greg was isolated; no one spoke to him and life had become miserable at home and at work. He had thought he might ask Sir Tom if he needed a bodyguard or an extra hand; he would have given anything to be other than what he now was. But even Gregory, simple as he was, could see that Pom Appleby was all that Sir Tom required in the way of a servant.

***

As soon as they entered Sir Tom's room, the knight made straight for his table and his precious manuscripts.

'Monty, I want to consider aspects of the story of Lancelot and Queen Guinevere in Book 18, Section 25.' He picked up a quire of papers and thumbed through it, evidently already having marked where he meant. 'This section on "stability" and how true love is likened to summer:

"For in many persons there is no stability; for we may see all day, for a little blast of winter's destruction, anon we shall deface and lay apart true love for little or nought, that cost much thing; this is no wisdom nor stability, but it is feebleness of nature and great disworship, whomsoever useth this."'

Monty looked over Malory's shoulder at the page, 'Is there any particular reason why you want to look at this?' It was unusual for the old knight to alter work that had already been completed, but when he first read it Monty thought this was an unduly abstruse passage, although Sir Tom had not accepted his suggestion to simplify it.

'To tell the truth, this word "stability" came into my mind when I heard how the king had fled and Lord Warwick was filling the void. That, coupled with my new status as a "free man" and the suggestion that I should go home to my wife. I had a sudden feeling of remembrance – a yearning for the past. I thought perhaps Roger Clyfford was right – I should return to Warwickshire and my family.'

Pom and Monty looked at Malory in surprise, 'You aren't really thinking of leaving London, Sir Tom?' asked Pom.

'Of course not! The feeling passed as soon as it entered my head! No, we stay and complete our work. But this business of loyalty and the wisdom of stability are extremely relevant at present. I want to add a small section just before the end of this particular book and would like to hear what you both think. I've been working on it in my head for the last two days. Listen:

"Wherefore I liken love nowadays unto summer and winter; for like as the one is hot and the other cold, so fareth love nowadays; therefore all ye that be lovers call unto your remembrance the month of May, like as did Queen Guinevere, she was a true lover, and therefore she had a good end."

His audience was silent for a minute. Then Pom said, 'Well, if my opinion is of any value to you Sir Tom, I think it is rather – er – poetic!'

'Christ, Pom! I should hope it is. That is what we've been about all these years – strong explicit words written as rhythmic prose. But what do you think of its substance? Does it ring true? You notice I continue with the analogy of summer and winter and how love blossoms in the summer of our years, but old age withers it.'

Monty could see there was more to this than mere poetical fancy. Sir Tom was clearly thinking back on his own past; the word "remembrance" had given that away. There was also the reference to "a good end". Was he looking at his own mortality for the first time? Pom Appleby had always said the man thought himself immortal, but the abrupt change in his circumstances may have made him consider that aspect of his life again.

'What do you think Monty?' asked the knight.

'It seems an opposite addition, Sir Tom. But we know that Queen Guinevere doesn't meet "a good end". Even though she enters a nunnery she still dies.'

'I disagree. She may die, but it is of love – or is it *for* love? And there can be no finer end than one person dying for love of another, surely.'

This is a rare side of Sir Tom, thought Monty, *Touching on his own sentiment; how surprising!* He nodded, 'When you put it so eloquently, Sir Tom, I'm forced to agree.'

'Good, then we'll add it and make ready to continue with Book 19 tomorrow and learn about Sir Meliagaunt.'

'Just remind me who he is, Sir Tom,' said Monty.

‘A new knight for the story, Monty!’ Monty sighed inwardly; yet another one to add to the list of dozens. Was there no end to them? He supposed this one would do his fair share of jousting, aventring, and fordoing! It really had been necessary to start compiling a glossary of names as well as one of terms. Whether Sir Tom would agree to its inclusion was another matter. Monty knew he would have to pick his moment.

Malory continued, ‘Meliagaunt is the son of the King of Gore – Bagdemagus. He lives in a castle seven miles from Westminster and lusts after Guinevere, but does nothing about it while Lancelot is around. Eventually, he takes her prisoner. But read it through tonight, Monty; you’ll find out how he goes about it and what happens. We can discuss it first thing tomorrow. I think it reads rather well!’

‘Can’t wait!’ said Pom.

***

A week later, Pom, Monty and Jack Worms were standing in the street in front of St Paul’s again, but this time with a good view. They were waiting for yet another procession of noblemen and the King of England, Henry VI, back on his throne after nine years’ absence.

‘This is just to parade the man in front of the citizens,’ said Jack, ‘To show them he’s really alive and with a crown on his head; then they’ll take him into the cathedral for a mass.’

‘Where’s Sir Tom?’ asked Monty.

‘Writing his will!’ replied Pom.

‘Writing his will? This is something new,’ laughed Jack. ‘He’s not preparing himself for the Grim Reaper, is he?’

‘He’s not ill?’ asked Monty anxiously.

‘Nothing like that,’ said Pom reassuringly. ‘You remember the conversation we had the other day, Monty – when he was reading bits from *Le Morte* and talking about going back to Warwickshire?’

‘Which he said he never intended doing under any circumstance,’ said Monty.

‘No, but it made him think about the future, especially since he’ll have to make new arrangements by the end of the year – unless Roger Clyfford’s prepared to allow him to stay. He’s also worried about the manuscript and what should happen to it, now it’s almost completed. He says he’s going to make explicit orders for its safety and eventual publication. I believe we three are all involved somehow.’

‘Involved “somehow”? What do you mean?’ asked Jack suspiciously. ‘If I know anything about Sir Thomas Malory, it’s that “somehow” means nothing straightforward – it’s bound to cost us money or time – probably both!’

‘I don’t know the details. He says he’ll let me see it “sometime”. “I don’t expect to expire tomorrow, Pom!” he said to me, “But in the event of me dying suddenly, before I go I want to set my affairs out to my satisfaction.”’

‘I suppose it’s something we should all think about doing,’ observed Monty with a frown.

‘As I say, let’s hope Sir Tom doesn’t try to commit us to anything onerous or expensive!’ said Jack. ‘Now, I can hear cheering – the procession must be on its way!’

As it turned out, the three men wished they hadn’t bothered. King Henry was a great disappointment – although the extremely shabby blue gown he had been wearing when rescued from the Tower had been replaced with one of expensive velvet in a deeper shade of royal blue, and he had a rather elegant coronet on his head. Excessively thin and old-looking even at the age of forty-eight, he seemed bemused, as though he wasn’t quite sure where he was or what he was doing. The Newgate Three had excellent views and noted how proudly and almost disdainfully the Duke of Clarence looked down on the crowds from his horse. The Earl of Warwick was greeted with the usual cry of, ‘À Warwick!’ which seemed to please him greatly.

As the king and noblemen dismounted in front of the cathedral steps, Jack shouted, ‘Look! The Earl of Oxford has placed himself in front bearing the Sword of State and the Archbishop of York has the royal seal round his neck!'

'I don't think Sir Tom would have been too impressed, especially with King Henry, who's hardly regal,' observed Pom. 'My master's asked me to describe "in detail" what we see, but as we're outside the cathedral doors and have no means of entry there's nothing to tell; all those guards up the steps – obviously there to keep us riff-raff out! I suggest this is the only glimpse we're going to get. I'm going back to tell him he was wise not to have struggled into the streets!'

Monty and Jack could do nothing else than agree with him and the three men pushed their way to the back of the crowd and towards Newgate again.

'Is the Earl of Warwick lodging at Greyfriars',' asked Monty.

'No, he's staying with King Henry at the Bishop of London's palace at Lambeth. Clarence has gone to Le Elber – Lord Warwick's father's London lodgings on the river. I don't know where the likes of Oxford and the Earl of Pembroke are staying. Greyfriars' is busy, though. The usual line of supplicants has gathered at the doors of the earl's kitchens since he returned. It must cost him a fortune.'

'Well, now he's in charge of the country's coffers that won't be a problem for him,' laughed Jack.

'Well, my Greyfriars' sources tell me there's no money in those coffers. Trade has come to a halt while there's this serious trouble with Burgundy. You'll have noticed the cranes at the docks are inactive – no goods are coming in or going out until these disputes are settled. I'm told that it's Lord Warwick's priority to get to grips with the matter. He can't afford to upset the city merchants; he'll rely on them for loans to run the country.'

Monty rarely thought about how the country's requirements were paid for; he had enough problems with his own budget; money, or the lack of it, was a constant source of worry. In fairness, despite his early misgivings, his employer had been mostly honourable in paying the correct amount and on time, but the Greyfriars' monks had recently seen fit to put up his rent – with no warning – and he was now expected to pay an extra sixpence a week. He had put the word around to his old clients that he was still available for work, but some of his regulars had gone elsewhere thinking him thoroughly occupied by his work for Sir Tom. Jack Worms promised to put the word around that his friend was free for any kind of legal commission, but there had been no response. His fortnightly payment was due in a couple of days, which would buy Monty some time to arrange matters so that his rent was paid in advance. He would have to pare away some of his more unnecessary expenses, although what they could be was difficult to decide. *Thank God for Sir Tom's generosity in feeding me!* he thought, *A return to a diet of cheap bread and cheese would be most unwelcome. Let's hope it continues after Christmas.* For Sir Tom was not the only one relying on the sympathetic ear of Master Roger Clyfford; Pom, Jack and Monty were all hopeful of existing arrangements being maintained in 1471.

***

Life continued much as before except news was now readily available – Sir Tom just had to walk out on the streets and join the bystanders at standards and tavern doors where information was posted almost as it happened. Perversely, given he was now a free man, Malory seemed to prefer the seclusion of his old cell to the bustle of the local streets. He continued to make his weekly visit to Bankside, where Plump Polly was always delighted to see him and they made free with the soap together. Young Meg visited on Wednesdays, but now it was together with her new pimp, who insisted on accompanying her to her various clients. She reacted badly to this intrusion into her working arrangements, but as the man exhibited many scars and injuries from old conflicts, and carried an exceptionally large knife, she could do little but acquiesce. Sir Tom was incensed when the man insisted he "would stay" while she got on with the job. It was not that he was embarrassed by an audience, rather the opposite – he was quite proud of his sexual prowess and not at all shy in sharing it. No, it was the arrogance and bullying nature of the man which angered him; he felt protective of Meg, who had told him she was "passing fifteen summers as far as I can remember", and he could not bear to think of her in thrall to this foul man's aggression. He started to ponder what he might do about it and had the beginning of a plan. But for now, he just put up with the grinning ape whose dirty breeches sullied his fine embroidered footstool and who made lewd and unhelpful comments while Meg and he went at it. At the end of the session, Sir Tom was forced to hand over the money to the rascal and he knew that Meg wouldn't see a penny of it. Meg, who had been a vibrant and good-humoured young woman, was beginning to look wan and thinner than he had ever remembered. She had lost her buxomness and her mop of dark curls was now lank and lifeless. He decided he must act.

Life outside was complex as the new rulers reset the process of government. One event which did draw Sir Tom outside was the welcome beheading of the Earl of Worcester John Tiptoft. Lord Warwick had been in charge for a month when he ordered a unit to set out to capture "this bastard executioner!" as Sir Tom described him. The story of his crime was soon told. In April of that year, while Lord Warwick and the Duke of Clarence were preparing to sail from France for England, King Edward sent word ahead to the ports of the south coast and Calais to oppose them and seize their vessels. Ships were taken and more than twenty captives were summarily tried as traitors on the quayside of Southampton and immediately executed in the town centre on the orders of the Earl of Worcester. Anthony Tanner had been there and told Malory and his friends exactly what had happened.

'The cruel bastard had them hanged, drawn and quartered and then beheaded. If that wasn't bad enough, afterwards they were hanged up by their legs and a stake made sharp at both ends; one end was put in at the arse and hammered in through the body, then turned right-way up and their heads placed on it. All the corpses were stuck in the ground in the centre of the town. The townsfolk were very angry and there are great mutterings against the Earl of Worcester. They feel he's gone well beyond what the law says and it was an unnecessarily cruel and vindictive act.'

That anger never abated and now Warwick's soldiers had found Worcester hiding at the top of a tree in Huntingdon Forest. He was given a fair trial, even though overseen by Lord Oxford, whose father and brother Worcester had consigned to death eight years previously. On October 15, he was found "guilty as charged" and condemned to be led on foot from Westminster to Tower Hill, a four-mile journey through the narrow streets of the city and their jeering, hostile crowds.

'We must be there to see it, Pom,' said Sir Tom. 'It's been a long time since I've seen a good execution, and I can think of no one more deserving of it. We'll set out before dawn and bag a place.' Monty declined to go, and Jack Worms was away on business in Kent, so the Newgate Two set out together just after curfew was lifted. They took a wherry to Tower Wharf and walked up the hill to the place of execution. Crowds were already forming and it was only by dint of elbows, curses and threats with a small dagger that Pom could lead his master to a prime spot behind the ropes guarded by a quantity of soldiers, whose duty it was to protect the noble lord from being torn limb from limb before his official beheading.

But there was a serious hindrance to the proceedings. The mood of the crowd, which had built up to enormous proportions, became extremely dangerous as soon as Worcester was led out from the prison gates. Cobbles, bricks, rotten vegetables – anything which came to hand – were thrown at him and the guards. One soldier was felled by a massive corbel which had become detached from the Tower wall. The unfortunate man was killed instantly and one of his brothers-in-arms picked up the body and threw it over his shoulder, preparing to make a retreat. The rest of the unit was forced to make a cordon around the prisoner and hustle him back inside the Tower. The crowd remained watchful and suspicious until a notice was pinned up which made the bloodthirsty onlookers even angrier. The execution would be postponed until the morrow.

'Fuck me, Pom. We'll have to do this all over again. I'm not so keen on these early starts!'

'Do we really want to come back again?' asked Pom, who had never felt much interest in executions, having seen plenty in his time. Admittedly, this was a man who deserved everything he got and he was certainly not sorry he was going to meet a grisly end.

'We certainly must – this man had men impaled. Hammering stakes down their arses, even if they're already dead, is not only barbaric, it's disrespectful! I haven't included that in *Le Morte* and there are plenty of shocking episodes in it to satisfy anyone's blood lust! No, I want to see him squirm before they hold up his head.'

As it turned out, the next day the man was brought to Tower Hill with a huge body of armed guards, all of whom had spent the night with Tiptoft in the Fleet Prison three miles away. How they managed to smuggle the man in and out again without being noticed was remarkable, but there he was at ten o'clock the next morning, shaven-headed and collarless, trying not to shiver with either cold or fear.

Later, back in Newgate, with great relish Sir Tom related the nobleman's last actions and words to Monty. 'Arrogant and unrepentant to the last, he declared on the scaffold that all he had done was for the good of the state. An Italian priest reproached him for his cruelty, but Worcester would have none of it. Then he requested the headsman to do his job in three strokes – "in honour of the Trinity".

'And did he?'

'No, the man did it in one – a clean strike – one for the Devil! There was such a roar when the head was held up. But I swear there was a smile on Worcester's face! The cruel bastard!'

Monty was silent. Part of him relished the fact that this man, who had ordered other men to do acts of extreme violence against their fellow humans, had received a just punishment – an eye for an eye, or a head for twenty or so heads. But, as usual when he heard any tales of vicious retribution he wondered how it was all justified. Blood begat blood and nothing was ever solved by it. Sir Tom, though, was still enjoying the whole affair. 'Good riddance. They should have put a pointed ash stick up his arse and stuck his hat on the tip when it came out of his skull.'

'You can't say fairer than that, Sir Tom!' was Pom's final comment on the matter.

***

The days approaching the end of November were tense. Master Clyfford had given no word that he had changed his mind and Sir Thomas was becoming increasingly bad-tempered as the year wound down to its end. Pom was becoming increasingly concerned at the lack of certainty about their future, and sought out Jack Worms and Monty in the tavern closest to St Martin's.

'Has Sir Tom approached Master Clyfford again on the subject?' asked Monty.

'Not since the last time, when the keeper told him he hadn't changed his mind and confirmed we had to be out by the second day of Epiphany, which is in a few weeks' time.'

'Would it help if I spoke to Master Clyfford and put it to him that it would be foolish to upset a mutually beneficial arrangement? After all, the keeper was making a nice little pot of money on the side.'

'Are you suggesting blackmailing the man?' asked Jack, 'that doesn't sound like your style, Monty!'

'No, but it wouldn't hurt for him to be reminded it's not only he and Sir Tom who will lose out – your business will suffer and my income certainly will. Pom will also have to move – if Sir Tom is forced out.'

'Anything's worth a try, Monty!' sighed Pom, who was in the rare situation of feeling slightly panicked; normally the ups and downs of Sir Tom's life made little inroads into his mindfulness; he took them in his stride. This time he had the feeling that matters were different. His master's life's work was coming to an end and Pom realised this was be a defining moment for the man. What would Sir Tom do when the last correction was made and the manuscript deemed completed? For almost fifteen years Sir Thomas had been absorbed in *Le Morte D'Arthur*. In the last two years the work had become a way of life for him. Pom wondered if this wouldn't be the end of the man. How else could he fill his days? A move away from all he knew, the place and the people, would be disastrous; perhaps he would never recover – just wither away somewhere unfamiliar and hostile. Suddenly he thought this might be a persuasive argument that he could put to Master Clyfford himself. That was it – he would plead for his master's life.

'Monty, reflecting on it – I think it would be better if I saw Master Clyfford – I can put the case for us all, we've rehearsed it enough times in the last few weeks. Leave it to me; I'll deal with it.'

'Very well, if you think that would work Pom,' said Monty, relieved. He found the keeper a rather stern unfathomable man at times and would have had difficulty estimating how to mine his sympathy.

'Try taking him a roundlet of Burgundy, Pom!' suggested Jack with a laugh, 'that'll be a good start. He's never said "no" to the offer of Wenlock's best before!' Pom nodded and smiled. 'Perhaps I will Jack, perhaps I will!'

Over a second tankard of ale the three men discussed events in the capital, and the latest circulating rumours. The persistent trouble between England and Burgundy was the main talking point in a city which relied for its wealth entirely on trade, especially with the Duchy. There was also news that Edward IV's wife Elizabeth had given birth to a son. 'That surely will induce Edward to return!' said Jack, 'We can't have two Princes of Wales! Edward Lancaster will have to watch his back!'

'When the young man eventually gets here. I don't understand why Margaret hasn't sailed with her son to join

Henry now he's back on the throne,' said Monty, shaking his head.

'We could do with Six-toed Tanner here to bring us up to date. Has Sir Tom heard from him, Pom?' asked Monty.

'Not a word since he left in July. We've presumed he's in France, although he might arrive in London now the earl's established here. I wouldn't be surprised to see him at any time.'

'Let's hope he gets here before Sir Tom's evicted from Newgate!' said Jack, taking a long pull at his ale and then wiping his mouth with the back of his hand.

'If I have my way, that won't happen,' said Pom and Monty noted the determined glint in his eyes.

***

Someone else had a glint in his eye. Sitting at the prow of the good ship *George* out of Bristol and "commandeered" in the English Channel by Lord Warwick's men, Anthony Tanner was anxious to get back to London to his master and the centre of activity. He had come in advance of French ambassadors who were two days behind him and sent by Louis to conclude a peace treaty with the earl. Tony had spent the summer and autumn months in France with Lord Warwick and Queen Margaret, as she had always styled herself, watching her every move – paying handsomely for information as to what she discussed and with whom. Always by her side was the attenuated, carrot-topped Jasper Percy; a spy like himself, but perhaps too physically distinctive to be as effective. Margaret seemed to rely on him almost as much as she did her son Edward, who Anthony took a dislike to on first meeting. The young man was a cruel bully and treated his servants abominably. Tony felt particularly sorry for the Earl of Warwick's daughter Anne, a young woman of fourteen years with a sweet nature, very much like her mother. Her marriage to Edward Lancaster was arranged for some time in late December. He thought to himself, *I shudder at the thought of Lady Anne in the arms of such a tyrant. You would never believe he was the grandson of Henry V, that honourable warrior. Still, these marriages between the nobility are always a matter of expediency – pleasing the father, and in this case, the mother, rather than the children.*

Reflecting on the situation which he would be reporting to the earl, Tony had little substantial news to tell him. It seemed to Six-toed Tanner that Margaret was dithering – King Louis had promised her help with money, ships and men, but she still had not decided as to when to set sail. The "peace treaty" was outside Tony's brief; he was no diplomat. What he was really looking forward to was meeting up with Sir Tom and his friends in Newgate again.

***

'I've called you both in because I have good news – for all of us!' Pom looked at his friends Monty and Jack with a smile and glanced across at Malory. John Appleby was enjoying himself, sitting back in his seat and stretching out his stubby legs to the warmth of the fire.

'For Christ's sake, Pom, stop arsing about and get on with it. I don't pay you to make a show of yourself!' Sir Thomas was never pleased when attention moved from himself to others.

'You hardly pay me at all, Sir Tom! But no matter. My news is soon told. I went to see Master Clyfford this morning and had a very long talk with him.'

'And?'

'Well, we talked a little about the weather and how mild it's –'

Malory was going very pink in the face – his usual response when he was intensely irritated, 'Weather! I don't care about how fucking mild it's been. I want to know what he said. I presume you were discussing future arrangements? I must say, I would have liked to have done it myself, Pom.'

'Yes, and like the last time you would have immediately antagonised the man with your – your –'

‘Directness,’ intervened Monty seeing tact and diplomacy were required.

‘Yes,’ said Pom, ‘your directness. Anyway, to get to the point –’

Sir Tom sighed, ‘Jesus! At last!’

‘To get to the point, Master Clyfford has agreed to let you stay for another six months from the end of December, which he says gives you enough time to make other arrangements for next year. After all, *Le Morte* must be fully completed – you’ve said yourself it only needs a little attention before it is introduced to the world.’ Pom looked round at his friends; if he had been expecting whoops of joy and arms waving in the air he was disappointed. Monty looked relieved; Jack Worms nodded and smiled slightly; Sir Tom pursed his lips and was silent.

‘Well, Sir Tom, a “thank you” would be appropriate!’ said Pom somewhat sourly. He had spent a wearisome hour with Roger Clyfford, pleading his master’s case. He was looking forward to some plaudits from his friends. Then Malory seemed to shake himself as the news was absorbed, ‘Of course, Pom, good effort! It’s a relief to us all I’m sure that we have another six months here,’ he looked at his two companions, ‘don’t you agree?’

‘Of course we do!’ You’ve just taken us by surprise, that’s all,’ said Monty quickly, and rose out of his chair and took Pom’s hand, which he shook hard as he said, ‘Well done! You must have been very persuasive.’

Pom was somewhat mollified and nodded, ‘It took some doing; at first the man was adamant that we should clear out in four weeks’ time.’

‘So what persuaded him otherwise?’ asked Jack.

‘I reminded him that five people had a stake in Sir Tom’s work – we four and himself. The rent Sir Tom pays is not an inconsiderable sum and he would surely miss it if it dried up. I then mentioned Mr Pickle and his investment of time and energy in Sir Tom’s project and Master Worms’ business would lose out if he could no longer supply Sir Tom with his writing materials.’

'Since you told him the book is almost finished he must have gathered that Master Worms' supplies will soon no longer be needed?' observed Sir Tom.

'Yes, but as we've already discussed, Jack will be part of –'

Malory shot him a warning look, stopping him in mid-sentence, 'We needn't go into that, Pom. Sufficient to say, Jack, you will be commissioned to bind the manuscript when the time comes.'

Jack and Monty exchanged glances. *More scheming!* Jack thought, but did not say it. These things always came out in the end. He would be patient and not enquire further at the moment. Instead he thanked Pom for his efforts, which had given him some relief. It seemed the present arrangements would be maintained, which meant that Sir Tom's income and expenditure would not be disrupted and his bills would continue to be honoured.

During the time of these exchanges Sir Tom realised that his servant and friend had achieved the impossible. For the last few months, silently, he had worried himself witless at the thought of having to move out – probably back to the midlands. Master Clyfford had seemed implacable in his demand and Sir Tom could see no solution, other than to succumb to the inevitable. Now they had a life-line. Much could happen in six months; Clyfford might continue the arrangement if Malory made it worth his while. He was undertaking some mental calculations as to whether he could afford to pay the man extra when he heard Pom say, 'And that's not all I got out of him!'

'There was more?' said Monty.

'Fat Gregory can help out with the heavy work again – for payment of course. I reminded Master Clyfford that I wasn't getting any younger; carrying coals and provision up and down the stairs is becoming harder for me. Apparently, poor old Greg's very unhappy now he's back as a full-time guard and Clyfford says he's sick of seeing the man's miserable face every time he passes him. The keeper's only proviso is that we buy the man a decent pair of boots; Greg has suffered with his feet since he was posted on full-time guard-duty. Buying some good footwear for him will be in our interest if the man is to run up and down the stairs on a regular basis.'

'That's a minor issue! Extremely well done, Pom. Will he be a permanent member of my staff?' asked Sir Tom.

'Staff – that's pushing it a little, sir! But yes, although the keeper will need him occasionally for stand-in-duties.'

'Well, he'll have the boots for that job then!' Sir Tom looked around for a response which was not forthcoming, 'stand-in duties – boots? No? Perhaps you're all losing your sense of humour. Anyway, this is all very good news. I wish Plump Poll and young Meg were here to celebrate with us. But no matter! Let's fill a jug and drink to –'

At that moment Sir Anthony Tanner knocked and entered. 'Good morrow, all. Did I hear orders for a jug to be filled? Seems I'm just in time!'

'Anthony! Welcome. We've been speculating as to when you might turn up. God's bones, it's good to see you,' beamed Sir Tom, 'you're certainly in time to help us celebrate some good news!'

'I can always sniff out a celebration – it's one of the skills of my trade! So what is it that has given you such good cheer?' And, as he filled the jug from the tiny barrel and poured the first glass of Wenlock's best, Pom proceeded to tell him.

'You must be very relieved Tom? No one likes an uncertain future!'

'Talking of uncertain future, what's the news from France?'

'Before Sir Anthony launches into his news, perhaps we should invite Gregory up to share a glass with us?'

Malory beamed, 'Good idea! This has the beginnings of real revels. The Newgate Five – six if we include Gregory – we must include him!'

'Why not! Anthony replied, 'the Newgate brotherhood needs its own jolly fat man – just like Robin of the Hood and Friar Tuck!'

'Jolliness is not something we can ascribe to Gregory,' observed Pom. But Fat Greg was called up and invited to participate in a drink as one of the "brotherhood". Somewhat bewildered as to what exactly a "brotherhood" was, nonetheless he had already been informed of the new arrangements by Master Clyfford, and was looking forward to his duties – but more so a new pair of boots. Above everything else he realised this would mean being on better terms with Mistress Hapgood, who could have her new gown after all and might just desist from her sulking and withdrawal of conjugal rights.

The six men drank many servings from the roundlet; Monty, as usual, never keeping up with the capacity of Malory and Pom, who he thought must both have hollow legs. But he paced his drinking, and by dinner time could hold down a decent portion of beef and pie without disgracing himself. However, Gregory showed a remarkable capacity and was still on his feet when Sir Tom himself was beginning to flag during the afternoon. By the end of the session he was the last man standing and saw fit to tidy up the glasses, food and platters strewn around the room. After all, he was now one of Sir Tom's servants and knew his place!

***

December came and went. Christmas was celebrated in Newgate with general abandon and the relief of the postponement of a move remained to enliven the atmosphere. Anthony Tanner and Gregory swelled their number, although the latter had, on occasion, to be reminded of his place when he became unusually boisterous. 'It's just happiness,' explained Monty, 'The man's like an untrained puppy.'

'Just as long as he doesn't piss on the rush matting!' said Jack with a laugh.

Six-toed Tanner spent as much time with his friends as he was able, but there were very serious trade talks going on between the Earl of Warwick and the party of French ambassadors. Matters became crucial in early January when it became clear there was the possibility of war with Burgundy, to the satisfaction of the increasingly angry city merchants, but the dismay of others. The streets became centres of violence yet again, despite the cruel weather which made the frozen rubbish-strewn paths and alleys extremely dangerous for those on foot; horse transport was out of the question unless protective covers were wrapped around hooves. Men came out in anti-French/pro-Burgundian riots, no matter that their champion Lord Warwick supported trade with the French. 'People don't like change, Tom,' explained Tony Tanner one dismal day at the end of January, 'but Lord Warwick still holds onto the ordinary people – shop-keepers, journeymen and the poor who all hate the rich merchants.'

'As long as he keeps handing out the beef and bread he can't fail!' laughed Sir Tom. He was considerably more relaxed than Pom had ever seen him. His work was almost complete and he had recently received a purse of cash from Lord Wenlock who, although far away in Calais, never seemed to forget his obligation to his old friend. Monty was permanently surprised – and impressed – with the noble lord's generosity. After all, it had been almost ten years since Sir Tom had pulled Wenlock off his horse and saved his life. During those years the baron must have provided Malory with nearly one hundred pounds in cash – to say nothing of the consignments of wine.

'How is the great work coming along, Tom?' asked Tony Tanner.

'Almost at the end. We've been looking at the section on the Grail – to my mind it's perfect and I have no wish to change anything, but my friend Monty here found a few simple errors – his eyes are sharper than mine.'

'A great story – I heard it told in France when I was there a few years ago.'

'Well, I've drawn it from the French, but considerably improved it. For instance –'

Pom intervened swiftly, 'Shall I ask Gregory to bring up the provisions, Sir Tom? It's almost dinner time?' He could see that Malory was drawing breath to give a full exposition of his amendments to the Grail story and, as most of those present had heard it many times before he felt he should come to their rescue. Sir Tom was inexorable when he held all the attention in the room and could speak for hours on anything connected to King Arthur. Malory nodded and withdrew gracefully for once; Pom went outside to wake Gregory from his door-side-dozing. He had moved his station from the bottom to the top of the stairs; enormous buttocks still spread over the three-legged stool. Always waiting for orders, he was anxious – sometimes too anxious – to oblige Sir Tom, who he seemed to almost worship. Ready to fetch and carry before he was asked, occasionally he would irritate the old man; but a quiet word in Malory's ear from Pom ensured he never gave way to his temper and snubbed or rebuked Fat Greg. 'The man's doing his very best here, Sir Tom. He's hardly costing you anything and can't do enough for you. What more could you want?' The ex-guard had been a remarkable success, and his own esteem had risen considerably with his new-found usefulness.

The esteem of others who provided services for Sir Tom was not so elevated. Young Meg from Gropecunt Lane grew paler and more wan; her pimp more malapert and vicious. Quietly Malory formulated a plan which he shared only with Sir Anthony, 'Come on Wednesday, Tony, and we'll sort this caitiff out together!'

***

"The caitiff" was approaching the Newgate tower with a tired and reluctant Meg in tow. The young woman sported a purple eye and a bleeding lip. The pimp, who went by the name of Simon Clapp, wasn't relishing this visit to the occupant of the Tower Gate; he had formed an intense dislike of Sir Tom the first time they met, and as insensitive to others' feelings as he normally was, he knew the antipathy was reciprocated. The knight went out of his way to belittle and scorn him. For a start he insisted on calling him 'Piper the Pimp'.

'My name is Master Simon Clapp, Sir Tom. If we're to do regular business I'll ask you to use it.'

Malory laughed and said, 'I'm simply emphasising who's calling the tune here; besides, as a writer, I like the alliteration.' Master Clapp had no idea what "alliteration" was and no intention of asking.

This was the fifth time they had attended on Sir Tom, and Clapp was determined not to be demeaned again. As soon as they arrived, pushing past the fat lump at the top of the stairs and entering the room without knocking, he said immediately, 'The price has gone up – it's a shilling.'

Sir Tom who was lounging in his chair with a glass of wine in his hand said nothing – just raised his eyebrows. But as his eyes moved to take in the sorry sight that was Meg he immediately saw the bruises to her face. 'What's this then? Can't keep your fists to yourself? I thought you'd have had more sense than to damage the goods!'

'It's all they know; she got impudent with me, that's all. It's only on the surface, nothing permanent. Now, do you want to fuck her or not? I have other clients less fussy.'

'I may or may not – doubling the price is risky. Anyway, I'm not so sure I want to put money in the pocket of a reprobate like you.'

Clapp shrugged, 'Please yourself; we'll go then. But I should charge you for the inconvenience of travelling all the way from Gropecunt Lane. Time's money – shall we say thrupence?'

'I'll say nothing at all except to tell Meg to step over here,' and Malory stood up and beckoned to the girl. Clapp nodded, 'So you've changed your mind – I thought you would. Pass over the cash and you can have your half-hour. Perhaps you'd offer me a drink while I wait.' Simon Clapp knew he was pushing his luck, but he was never shy of coming forward.

'There'll be no drinking. Just leave the girl here and piss off back where you came from!' Sir Tom's rheumy eyes glinted as he looked the man up and down. Now, Simon Clapp was no weakling. Protecting his kind of business required strength and speed. He had learned his trade from his father, who had learned it from his. In fact the Clapps formed a dynasty of pimps who had operated round Pokeskirt and

Gropecunt Lanes for sixty or more years. Simon would sometimes boast that his great-grandfather pimped for England at Agincourt, where he managed to stay out of the action by hiding in the baggage train with the boys and trollops until the battle was over, then emerging to show off a trophy from some dead Frenchman's body which he searched out for that purpose. Aside from their ignominious martial history, the Clapps prided themselves on keeping their hand in when it came to seeing off rivals or awkward customers. Simon was no mean street fighter; his method was mostly below the belt or the stab in the back. He looked witheringly at Sir Tom and thought, *No contest – I'll rough him up and leave him as a warning to others not to cross the Clapps. But I'll give him a chance first – don't want to be accused of starting it.*

'You don't get it, do you? I bring the whore, you pay the money! Now, do you want to –?'

'No, it's you that doesn't get it, Piper the Pimp! Meg will remain here and you will leave. You're never laying a hand on her again!' Malory signalled to the girl, who stood wide-eyed and stiff, like a rabbit petrified by the stare of a weasel. 'Come over here, Meg. Don't be scared.'

'– Don't fucking move, whore!' muttered Clapp through his teeth, which were in surprisingly good condition for a man of middle-age. His immediate reaction was to go for his knife; he'd show this old flea-bag he wasn't to be challenged. He had just got his eye in to centre the tip of the knife at Malory's throat when he felt a blow to the back of his head which lifted him up a little, before he fell over and sprawled out on the rushes.

'Nicely done, Tony!' Malory said. Anthony Tanner, who had stepped out from behind the curtain concealing the privy, put down the small iron pan which Pom used to heat up the pottage. He picked up the knife as they heard a groaning from the body and Clapp put out his hands to heave himself onto his feet.

'What shall we do with him?' asked Six-toed.

‘Throw him out – Gregory can conduct him to the main gate and give him a few buffets on the way!’ By this time the pimp was on his feet, rocking slightly but managing to stay there. Anthony grabbed his arms and, holding them behind his back propelled him towards the door. This opened outwards and Fat Greg, who had remained outside, was standing behind it. The door rebounded from him as Clapp went through; at this point Anthony had to let him go. Trying to avoid the heavy door as it swung towards him, the pimp tottered to the top of the stairs; unfortunately for him Greg’s stool was in the wrong place. Simon Clapp tripped over it and tumbled head first down the stone steps.

***

Pom had been sent out for the morning. Sir Tom had been uncharacteristically evasive as to why he wanted to be alone. ‘I – er – er – just want a word with Tony Tanner; nothing serious, but I’m sure you have things to do; people to see?’

‘Won’t Mr Pickle be coming in sir?’

‘No, I’ve told him not to bother today. Things are coming to an end and I suggested he spend his time at home looking over the final text for stupid mistakes.’ Pom wasn’t stupid and knew his master was up to something. Of course, it was Wednesday and he must be expecting a visit from young Meg and that creature Clapp. Whatever the reason Sir Tom didn’t want Pom there. But he could always use time to himself. Perhaps he would visit Jack Worms and bring himself up to date with shop gossip; besides there was a bill for materials to pay.

Sir Tom wanted no witnesses to his dealings with Clapp. Although he was sure Pom would never disapprove of his intended strong-arm methods, the business had now become personal between Malory and the pimp. All that was needed was Tony Tanner’s strength and speed to back things up.

Unfortunately when Pom arrived at Jack Worm’s shop he discovered he had come without his purse – to Jack’s disappointment. ‘I’ll go back for it,’ he said and leaving the shop Pop turned towards Cathedral Place and Newgate Street again. He reached the main prison gate and was heading off towards the steps to the tower when he heard a bang and a cry. As he hurried towards the stairs he saw Fat Greg leaning over an object sprawled out at the bottom.

'What's to do, Gregory?' asked Pom, hurrying toward the man whose bulk was completely obscuring whatever was lying on the ground.

'He fell down the stairs, Mr Pom. I think he's dead.'

'Who fell down the stairs?' As he was leaning over the inert body of a grubbily-dressed man, Pom heard Sir Tom and Jack Tanner coming down the steps towards them.

'I think the pimp's dead, Sir Thomas!' Gregory had assumed the position of expert, since he was the only one of them close enough to assess the possibility of life. Malory pushed him out of the way and knelt beside the body. Pom and Tony looked down at Simon Clapp, who lay with his neck unnaturally twisted and thin streams of blood issuing from his nostrils and left ear. Sir Tom nodded, 'I believe your assessment's correct, Gregory! The man's no more – good! A tidy end, that's what I like. Now the question is what to do with him?'

Pom was silent – quite shocked at Sir Tom's matter-of-fact approach, 'How did this happen, Sir Tom. Did he fall, or was he pushed?'

'Pom! I'm surprised you could even ask. He fell and if anyone's to blame, it's Gregory here – leaving his damn stool in the wrong place.'

Gregory looked suitably guilty and shuffled from one sore foot to another. 'I suppose you're right, Sir Tom. Will I get the blame? It was an accident.'

'Of course it was and no one will blame you at all, Greg,' said Sir Tom reassuringly, patting the man on the shoulder, 'all you have to do is get rid of the body for us. Any ideas?'

For the first time Gregory Hapgood found himself the centre of everyone's interest and, to his great joy it looked as though they were all relying on him to provide them with a solution to their problem. This was a first; all his life he had taken orders – in the early days from his army sergeant, then Keeper Clyfford and always Mistress Hapgood. He looked round at the three questioning faces and wrenched his brain into unaccustomed movement. It grinded slowly into action, like an old clock which had been starved of oil and silent for years, but now greased, was being asked to gear itself up again.

'Well!' said Sir Tom, becoming impatient as Gregory furrowed his brow into various frowns and twisted his plump mouth into weird expressions, 'what can you do?'

Gregory was by no means disingenuous; he was not playing to the audience, but genuinely seeking a solution. Suddenly he said, 'We've got the jail fever –'

'My God, when? How long?' cried Sir Tom.

'Three days ago – six have gone since yesterday.'

'Why wasn't I told?' Sir Tom was going very red in the face, 'we should have been informed so we can take precautions.'

'You're quite safe up here, Thomas,' said Tony Tanner reassuringly, 'I wager these were poor bastards in the filthy dungeons and cellars?'

Gregory nodded, 'Yes, sir.'

'Anyway, you'll take the necessary measures against it – won't you Pom?' and the servant and dogsbody nodded soothingly. Then Tony asked Greg, 'But what has this to do with the disposal of Clapp's body Master Hapgood?' Gregory seemed to grow even larger, expanding with pride at this gratifying use of his full title, 'Well Sir Anthony, I've been put on burial duty – part of my Newgate duties as arranged with –'

'Yes, yes! We know about the arrangements with Master Clyfford, but what has this to do with our current predicament?' asked Malory.

Greg had no idea what a "predicament" was, but nonetheless continued with his hard-won chain of thoughts. 'Keeper Clyfford has told me to bury them in quicklime after sunset today and I'm to dig the hole in the prison grounds this afternoon.'

‘I see – so you can provide space for an extra body? Excellent idea Gregory! No one will want to go near seven rotting corpses, especially the keeper!’

‘Will there be no words said over the graves by a priest?’ asked Tony.

‘No one bothers with that when it’s only prisoners,’ said Pom, ‘my guess is they won’t even be named.’

‘What do we do with this wretch in the meantime – while Gregory’s digging the grave?’ asked Sir Tom.

Gregory was in full command, ‘I’ll find an old winding sheet, wrap him up and carry him to where the others are stored – in the cellar underneath here; there’s no guards to see – everyone’s shit scared of catching the fever. That’s why we throw the bodies in at night when there’s no one about. The keeper likes to keep it quiet when there’s been an outbreak.’ This was one of the longest speeches the guard had ever made and reflected his new-found confidence.

‘I’m sure he does!’ said Sir Tom sourly, ‘what about us poor bastards who are living here.’

‘Your choice, Sir Tom, as I remember,’ said Pom with unusual acerbity, ‘we could have moved to the countryside of Warwickshire and breathed in some clean air – but no! You wanted London filth instead!’

‘Don’t bring that up – you know why we stayed.’ He turned back to Gregory, ‘Good, that’s settled. Can you manage this caitiff on your own or should Sir Anthony give you a hand?’ Tony Tanner shook his head vigorously, ‘Forget that! There’s no chance I’m going down into a cellar full of jail fever.’

‘Don’t worry, Sir Anthony,’ said Greg cheerfully, ‘I can manage him!’ and with one movement he had Simon Clapp draped across his left shoulder, steadying the body with his right hand.

Sir Tom nodded approvingly, ‘Good man! Report back when it’s all completed, Gregory – there’ll be a drink waiting for you. By the way, you can keep all his clothes and anything else you find on him, although I’ll keep this,’ and he waved a fat leather purse which he had extricated from Clapp's belt as skilfully as any seasoned cutpurse.

Gregory's heart swelled with pride as he took his burden and turned from the stairs towards those which led to "the chamber of death" as it was known. He had never felt so happy!

***

The three men returned to Malory's room where Meg stood, still transfixed and now shivering with fear. 'Christ! I'd almost forgotten about you, Meg!' Sir Tom suddenly became almost tender towards the young woman and immediately took up one of the blankets from his bed and draped it round her shoulders. 'Come closer to the fire. Pom, pour her a drink! Pour us all one.'

Pom obliged and Meg took the glass. Trying to avoid the cut lip she held it to her chattering teeth.

'Well that bastard will never trouble you again, Meg!' said Sir Tom, looking at her with great satisfaction. To his surprise she burst into a flood of tears. 'But, sir! What am I to do now? Simon was my pimp – how am I to go about making a living on my own?'

'The same as you did before, Meg. You seemed to be managing very well before Piper came calling!'

'Well, I had my mother looking out for me. It was when she died it all went wrong – when Simon came along and took over her business. I had no choice but to go with him. Is he dead, sir?'

'Yes, he is and good riddance!' said Sir Tom with relish. This produced a further burst of tears from Meg, who threw her dress over her face, exposing her bare thighs to Jack's fascination. Malory remained unperturbed and said, more sharply, 'Now listen to me Meg. I've got this all worked out. It's been my intention all along to extricate you from Clapp –'

'Extricate sir? What do you mean?'

'Get you out of the situation – set you free; well at least from his bullying.'

'But where am I to go? I can't go back to Gropecunt – they'll all know soon enough that Simon's disappeared and they may think I had something to do with it. Besides, there are plenty of other pimps down there who'll try to take me on, some worse than he was. I'll be back in the same situation as I was before! Oh dear, oh dear!' and she sobbed for a full minute into her thin grubby gown.

Malory looked appealingly at Tony Tanner, 'For Christ's sake say something to the girl, Tony. You've told me often enough how you have a way with women! Tell her my idea and see if you can't cheer her up. Fuck it! Anyone would think I didn't have her interests at heart the way she's carrying on!'

'She's confused, Thomas,' said Tony and gently he took Meg's hands out of the folds of her dress and away from her face. Stroking them soothingly he said, 'Listen to me Meg, Sir Tom has it all planned for you. You're to go across the water and be looked after by Mistress Fisher and her pimp Master Roberts. I know them both well and I can assure you they'll be very kind to you!'

'Yes, Plump Poll is prepared to take you on and keep you safe. Master Roberts is a fair man and won't cheat or harm you.' Sir Tom took out the fat leather purse he had stripped from Clapp's belt. Spilling the contents on the table he was gratified to see at least three gold nobles as well as a selection of coin which must have amounted to twenty-five pounds or more.

He gave a whistle of pleasure, 'Well, this is unexpected. I thought he might carry some of his earnings with him, but not all of them! Now, Meg, here's one pound for yourself. I'm going to give Sir Anthony five more for him to give to Plump Poll – to Mistress Fisher – and three to Master Roberts. They'll certainly make you welcome after that!'

'Am I to go to France then sir?' asked Meg, sniffing and wiping her nose with the back of her hand. The attentions of a good-looking knight of the realm, together with the gleam of cash on the table, had distinctly lightened her mood.

'France? Why France?'

'You said "across the water"; will I go on a ship sir? I don't like the water – I once went on a wherry and –'

Tony laughed, 'When I said, "across the water" I meant to the south-side of the river, you goose! But you will be travelling on a wherry for a short time – just to get you across to Bankside.' Meg became subdued again, looking apprehensive. Tom Malory, becoming bored with the whole situation, thought it was time to wind up the conversation which was never going to be interesting. 'Sir Anthony, I put young Meg in your charge. We can call her "your damosel in distress". You are her knight errant!' he grinned, but Tony Tanner looked very doubtful. Young Meg might have needed rescue, but a snot-ridden, red-eyed, pale and skinny girl was certainly not his idea of a romantic distressed lady. However, along with the demand Thomas held out two nobles, 'Fair shares Tony! You were excellent today.'

Struck by this uncharacteristic generosity, Tony Tanner nodded his thanks and turned to the damosel in question, 'Come Meg, finish your wine, wipe your face and we'll find a wherry to take you to a new life.' It was the closest he could get to a fulsome Arthurian conclusion.

After they left, Malory divided the spoils from Simon Clapp's purse, 'Five pounds for you, Pom, and the rest for me.'

'But what about Gregory? He's literally taken the burden from the rest of us – risking his life in that fever-ridden cellar and hiding the evidence of manslaughter. Surely he deserves something.'

'His wife will grab anything I give him – it'll be wasted on wimples.'

'Well, if you're worried about that why not persuade him to spend it on himself; if anyone can you can.'

'Very well, I'll give him five shillings – that's a small fortune to a man used only to receiving groats.'

When Gregory returned late in the night to report that all had been accomplished, Malory gave him 13s 8d and told him not to tell his wife, 'Spend it on something you really desire.'

'I'll take it with me next time we visit the Stews, Sir Tom, and have one of Plump Poll's specials – in fact I'll have it twice.'

'And if there's anything left over you can buy me a drink, Gregory!' said Sir Tom. Pom shook his head and sighed.

***

March 1st. London was in a ferment and more so than usual. The standards and market crosses were crowded with people looking for recent news. It varied in content and intensity as it was passed mouth to mouth, like a faithless lover's kisses. The rumours became wilder as the day went on and liquor was consumed.

'Margaret's landed at Southampton; Warwick's ridden to meet her and bring her back to London. She has ten thousand Frenchmen behind her!'

'I heard it was twenty thousand and King Louis provided the ships and men.'

'They'll slaughter us all when they get here – no one trusts that French vixen Margaret; she'll be wanting revenge!'

'This is all fucking made up to confound us. None of that's true, but I've been told on good authority that Edward is moored with his fleet at Flushing on the Netherland coast with thousands of soldiers – just waiting for the tide. The Duke of Burgundy's backed him. The king's coming to get his crown back and a crowd of Germans are coming as well, looking for revenge on the Earl of Warwick for all the trouble he's caused them with their shipping in the Channel.'

'So what you're saying is there'll be another war for the crown using foreigners! If that's the case, I'm leaving the city and heading for somewhere safe – Wales perhaps! I hear that nothing much happens there – other than sheep-stealing.'

The rumours, as all rumours do, had an element of truth in them. The Mayor of London, John Stockton – Mercer Stockton as he was disrespectfully called – at the first hint of trouble took to his bed feigning an ague. When it seemed apparent he would make no further appearances, Sir Thomas

Cook was pressed by anxious aldermen to stand in for him. But secretly Cook was packing up his own belongings ready for a get-away. Such was the breadth of panic in the streets of the capital.

The beauty of isolation in the Newgate Tower was that its occupants could literally rise above the chaos of misinformation seething around them. Sir Tom, usually acutely interested in everything that was happening was presently more concerned that his manuscript was at last finished. On the day the above conversation was taking place round the Standard at Cheapside, he stood in his room looking at a neat pile of manuscripts, threaded together in bundles and occupying the table, a chair, the footstool and the bed. He gave a great sigh of pleasure, but one which was also tinged with sadness, 'It's over! It's done Pom!'

His long-time friend, servant, dog's body and confessor looked at his master and didn't know how to respond. Pom had been worrying about this moment for weeks. The question lurking, but which he dared not voice, was, *What are you going to do with your days now, Sir Tom?'* For he knew there was no answer. Malory had given almost half his life to *Le Morte D'Arthur*, to the exclusion of everything else. The man was fifty-five, still relatively fit and active – at least where his loins were concerned. If Sir Tom had any ideas about the future they had not been shared with Pom. This was doubly concerning since Mr Appleby's life was totally entwined with his master's. It had become worrisome. Where would they go? The inevitable answer was "back to Warwickshire". But on many occasions in the past, when that possibility was mooted Sir Tom had expressed robust antipathy to it, and in his usual forthright way. 'Fuck it Pom! You can forget that. I'd rather be impaled on a Tiptoft spike than return to a rustic existence!'

But now they had come to it. Decisions had to be made. Pom wondered what Mr Montmorency Pickle and Master Jack Worms thought about the matter. Both would be out of pocket as soon as the last page was bound. Although Pom knew Sir Tom had made his wishes clear in his will, he had not yet discussed with any of the Newgate Three what should happen to the manuscript – how many copies should be ordered – who would take care of it. All these loose ends needed attention. Perhaps Monty would be the best person to introduce the matter; the man had a gentle and intelligent approach to Sir Tom. He never argued with his employer per se, but had the knack of bringing him round to his way of thinking – not always, but some of the time. Yes, Monty would be the man.

But Sir Tom had his own ideas. Of course he had been gnawing away at the bone of decision for months. He knew there would be a void when the book was finished, and that it would be impossible to fill. But the answer came upon him one day, like a flash of rush-light in a dark street. All these quests he had been sending his knights in pursuit of; he would go on one himself! Over the next few days he mused on how he might go about it and who would be willing to accompany him. Then it came to him; The Newgate Four could form themselves into a questing brotherhood. The goal: to deliver the manuscript into safe hands – the Grail story in reverse! Malory's personal Grail was the manuscript and his quest was to place it in safe keeping. Anyone who found it would have a spiritual experience! *How fucking clever! How appropriate!* thought Sir Tom. He would say nothing to anyone yet, but wait until he had ironed out the practical difficulties. One problem he did not have currently was that of cash. The money in Clapp's purse had relieved all the pressure in that quarter. Malory owed no one, and had plenty of coin in his own purse.

Two days later, 3rd March, Monty arrived in an unusually excitable state, 'Lord Warwick's back in London Sir Tom; I've just seen a body of his men coming out of Greyfriars' and the earl's standard's flying over his lodgings.'

'Is Margaret with him?'

'I haven't heard, but these rumours of King Edward preparing to land on the east coast are still circulating.'

'Well, Mr Pickle, let's worry about those things we can control and ignore those we can't!' said Sir Tom cheerfully.

Monty was taken aback; this was not Sir Tom's usual style – he was always agog for news from the streets – official and rumour. 'I thought you might be interested. They say the Bastard Fauconberg is in command of the fleet and will remain loyal to the earl.'

'I should think so!' said Sir Tom vigorously, 'he's family after all. That's what matters, Monty when it comes to it – family and friends!'

Monty was even more surprised and wondered where this thought had come from, but did not respond. Instead, looking round the room he said, 'I see the manuscript's ready for copying. Are all these in the right order?' and he stretched out a hand to a pile of scripts on the footstool.

'Christ – don't disturb anything!' said Malory sharply, 'I've spent hours getting them right. They start on the left-hand side of the table and work round to those on the bed. This morning I just want to check with you that they are correctly placed. Then I have the most important work of all to do.'

'And that is?'

'The final words.'

'But I thought we completed it all with the death of King Arthur and Sir Lancelot; how the one was borne away on the barge to Avalon, and the other dying from grief at the death of Guinevere, his body borne away to be buried in the Joyous Gard. I thought that was very touching and well-written, Sir Tom, and an appropriate ending to the saddest book in the whole work.'

'But it doesn't have my name on it.'

'Your name? Surely that will come on the front – as the author.'

'That's not enough. I want the reader to know who I am – that I was a prisoner myself who appreciated what it is to be locked away in dungeons awaiting rescue. Although in my case it wasn't an orgulous knight who came, but a document sent from the Lord Chancellor. I've written out a few words which I think we could insert. What do you think?' And Sir Tom took up his usual stance when he was about to declaim.

Monty sat on the end of the bed – the chairs were occupied – and waited.

'"Who that will make anymore, let him seek other books of King Arthur or of Sir Lancelot or Sir Tristram; for this was drawn by a knight prisoner, Sir Thomas Malory, that God send him good recovery."'

'But surely that suggests the book isn't finished.'

'Of course – well spotted, Monty!' said Malory with more than a little sarcasm. 'My thinking is this: I'll place it after Book 4, when readers are settling down into the story. It will whet their appetite for more, in case their attention wanders. But as for the ending of the final Book 21, Section 13, I have another idea for that, listen:

"Here is the end of the whole book of King Arthur, and of his noble Knights of the Round Table, that, when they were whole together there was ever a hundred and forty –"'

'I told you there were dozens, Sir Tom. I still think we need my glossary of their names!'

'Never mind that – anyway, it's too late. Now, pay attention:

"And here is the end of the death of Arthur. I pray you all gentlemen – and gentlewomen –"'

'So you do agree – literate women will read your book!' said Monty with great satisfaction.

'You made quite a persuasive argument, I'll give you that. But to continue:

"That readeth this book of Arthur and his knights from the beginning to the ending, pray for me while I am alive, that God send me good deliverance, and when I am dead, I pray you all pray for my soul –"'

'Aren't those sentences somewhat – somewhat –'

'Dark is the word you're searching for, Mr Pickle. I don't think so. I want people to pray for my soul; somehow, I think I'm going to need all the help from this the world when seeking my place in the next! But to continue:

"For this book was ended in the ninth year of the reign of King Edward the fourth –"'

'But we're in the first of Henry VI's reign, or his fortieth if you include when he was king before.'

'Mr Pickle, we can't afford to confuse the reader – especially those in the future who won't care a fuck about such niceties! No, let's leave it how it is. Did you know Edward became king exactly ten years to the day tomorrow – the 4th March? Funny how I remember that, but can't think what I had for dinner yesterday. But, I digress. This is the final sentence in the book:

"By Sir Thomas Malory, knight, as Jesu help him for His great might, as he is the servant of Jesu both day and night."

'Clear enough, eh? By the way, I've laid all my instructions concerning the manuscript in my will. Pom is to execute it for me. He knows my wishes already.'

'There's nothing you want to tell me, Sir Tom? You aren't ill, are you?' Monty said, now concerned at the contents of this addition to the text and the turn the conversation had taken.

'Well, if you must know, since the book was finished I've felt rather – rather –'

'Empty?' said Monty frowning.

'Exactly that! It's made me consider my life in the future and it all seems rather bare at present, although Pom and I have started to make plans – which would include you too Monty – and Jack and possibly Tony if he's available.'

'Listening to talk on the streets, I rather think Sir Anthony's going to be very, very occupied in the next few weeks, Sir Tom. All these rumours of Edward returning to claim the crown back, and Margaret landing in the south to do likewise. It sounds as though war's approaching yet again.'

'You're probably right. Lord Warwick will have much use for our young friend at present. A pity – I always enjoy Six-toed's company. But to return to our work. Do you agree that I should include these little additions?'

'Indeed sir, I think they are an excellent idea!'

***

Two days later, Malory called Gregory to him. It was a Saturday and Fat Greg was looking forward to his visit to the Stews with Sir Tom. He tapped respectfully on the door.

'Come in, Gregory!' Malory was seated at his table and half-dressed.

There's going to be no visit to Bankside this morning, thought a disappointed Greg.

'I'm not in good enough spirits to visit Mistress Fisher today, Greg; but that doesn't mean I don't want you to go. While you're there, ask her to visit me on Tuesday next – can you remember that? Repeat it back to me.' Gregory obliged and then, concerned at his master's unusually subdued demeanour said, 'Is there anything I can do for you, Sir Thomas? Do you need any more coals before I go?'

'No, thank you. Master Appleby has seen to all my requirements this morning. I'm rather tired and besides, I want to take a final look through my great work,' and he nodded towards the towering pile of papers now occupying a good deal of floor space.

'Very well, sir, if you're sure.'

'Don't hurry back, Gregory – unless the keeper has work for you?'

'No, sir, I'm not needed until tonight,' and he left Malory perusing a sheet of paper. *There's something up if Sir Tom feels too tired to visit Plump Poll,* thought Gregory as he plodded down the stairs, *Perhaps he's sickening for something? But that can't be it – I've never known him ill.*

Arriving at the *Unicorn*, to his relief, he could remember word for word his message for Pauline Fisher, who was equally surprised by Sir Tom's absence. 'Do you think the old man's not well, Greg?' she asked.

'He's not himself, Mistress Fisher,' he said. The fact that Plump Poll was a whore made no difference to Gregory's respect for her; he would always give her due deference. As far as he was concerned, she was more of a lady than his wife could ever be – with her kindness and generosity towards him.

'Hmm,' she said, 'Tell him I'll see him on Tuesday. Now, what little services can Bessie do for you today? First I should take off those new boots – they look as though they're crippling you!'

***

Gregory wasn't the only one who noticed that Sir Tom was out of sorts. Monty continued to call on the old man every day, although the work was considered "completed". Malory had paid him until the end of March, an extra four weeks and the scribe therefore felt it incumbent on him to offer any service he could to Sir Tom, who was still his employer. Monty noticed some of the vigour had gone out of Thomas Malory and to his relief, the old man's use of oaths, imprecations and blasphemies had all but disappeared.

Sir Tom now seemed to relish companionship more than he had ever done. The three of them would sit round the fire and, a glass of Wenlock's best in hand, Pom would tell more tales of their colourful past and Malory would also fill in some of the gaps, which Monty eagerly set down. He was particularly lively when he talked of his days in the King's Bench. 'I would turn up to find there was no jury from Warwickshire – as it was my right to be heard by my own county men; so I was sent back again. I couldn't count the numbers of trips to the King's Bench I made over the years. A complete waste of time and money; even the judge was bored with it all by the end – "Not you again, Sir Thomas!" he would say. By the way, talking about being bored – what are you going to do with all this stuff? Do you think people will be interested,' growled Sir Tom, waving towards Monty's notebook.

'You know very well your reputation goes before you; too much false modesty, Sir Tom,' laughed Monty, 'I'll write it all up into book – like you've done with the French romances.'

'You'll show it to me first or I'll want to know why! How do I know you won't paint some picture of me that's not true?'

'Your stories are almost as unbelievable as the tales of Arthur and his knights!'

'Well I suppose so; I've been fortunate in some parts of my life; less so in others. Fifteen years of incarceration was not what I had planned as a young man.'

'What were you going to do as "a young man"?' asked Monty.

'It's such a long time ago it's difficult to remember. Like all young men, win my spurs I suppose; do great feats of daring and bravery! Become a baron or an earl. Yes, I would have liked to have been Lord Malory and had a handsome tomb – lying as a stone effigy with my sword and spurs at my feet in St Mary's Warwick,' he sighed. 'But it's not to be. Who knows where this poor old body will end up! Pauper's grave, I expect. Let it not be the prison lime-pit, Pom!'

'Sir Tom! Sir Tom,' said Pom reprovingly, 'this is too gloomy. Why don't we take a walk this afternoon – visit some old haunts in the city?'

'What "old haunts" do we know, Pom? If you mean the London jails, we can take a tour and I can show you the best means of escaping from them all! No, I think we should avoid the London streets now; dangerous places back alleys and footpaths. I hear everyone's gearing up for a fight – or planning to leave; they say even the Lord Mayor Thomas Cook's packed his bag and pissed off!'

'Do we know where all the Lancastrian noblemen are?' asked Monty. It seemed strange to call anyone associated with Lord Warwick a "Lancastrian".

Pom, as usual the source of all current knowledge said, 'Lord Warwick's here; Clarence has gone off to rally troops in the south-west with the Earls of Devon and Somerset; Oxford's doing the same in the east and Jasper Tudor's in Wales. One thing I heard this morning from my source in Greyfriars' was that Lord Warwick has had many important men arrested, including the Duke of Norfolk and the Archbishop of Canterbury. You'll be pleased to hear that among the others is the Earl of Wiltshire John Stafford, Sir Tom.'

'Music to my ears! Let's see how a Stafford likes prison! But I still say we're safer here than out on the streets. You can hear the row from here – people roaring and shouting, 'À Warwick!'

'Well, at least they're shouting for the right side,' said Pom.

'But for how long, Pom, how long?'

***

On 13th March, Pauline Fisher washed her face, wiped under her arms and paid close attention to her nether regions. She put on her cleanest gown and least-worn shoes and took a wherry across the Thames to Blackfriars'. From there, she made her way through the narrow streets and alleyways which led to St Paul's, where she made an offering to the Holy Virgin, before diverting off to the left and Newgate Street. She worried about Sir Tom throughout the journey; he had never missed a visit to her; surely, he must be ill. Fat Greg escorted her up the stairs, knocked on the door and then, on Malory's command to "enter" the fat man held the door open, as though she was a duchess.

'Ah! Poll, good morning!'

'Good day to you, Sir Tom! You are well, I hope?'

'In fine fettle as they say where I come from – Warwickshire, in case you didn't know.'

'Of course I know, sir. You've often spoken of it.'

'Have I? It must have escaped me. Anyway, there was something important I wanted to say to you – now, what was it?' and he seemed to hesitate as his brow furrowed and he forced his mind to remember. 'Ah, I have it – Meg – young Meg. How is she? Has she settled at the *Unicorn*?'

'Indeed she has, sir, and very well. Bessie has taken her in hand and makes sure her customers are suitable. You know that Master Roberts is very fussy about who visits – it makes good business sense because everyone knows he treats his girls well and so they perform better. It means we get a better class of gentlemen. Meg's very popular with one or two of them; they show their appreciation generously, which pleases Master Roberts. No, sir, you needn't have any worries about Meg. We've tidied and fattened her up a little. She's quite a young beauty now.'

'I always thought there was something there – under the grubbiness. And you, Poll, how are your children?'

'Two are still with my mother, sir. But you'll be pleased to hear that the five pounds you sent me has bought my eldest a decent husband – a farrier in Essex. She won't be making her way in the world on her back like her mother! And it's thanks to you sir.'

'I'm very glad to hear that, Polly, and that the ill-gotten gains of Master Clapp were put to such an appropriate use. But what about your future? Surely you won't be able to carry on whoring forever?'

'I have money saved, extra now that my daughter's off my hands. Master Roberts has made me an offer – says I can come into the business with him – if I can find ten pounds. I have £6 6s 8d at present and I think I can make up the rest by next year.'

'I see. Well, one of the reasons I asked you here was that I don't think I'll be making many journeys across the Thames to visit you –'

'I can always do home visits – you know, like we did when you were banned from coming across,' said Poll quickly. 'What fun we had with the bath-tub, do you remember? Here, I've brought some soap,' and she delved into the pocket of her gown and brought out a small yellow cake, 'just in case it was needed!'

Sir Tom smiled, 'We don't have the bath-tub any more, Poll! It took up too much room. It's a tempting offer, but not why I sent for you,' he hesitated, 'now, why was it again? Ah yes, on the table is a purse. Take it; it'll go some way to making up what you need for Master Robert's offer.'

'This is very generous of you, Sir Tom, and not necessary. You've already given me five pounds!'

'No, say no more about it, please. Just use it for whatever you think necessary to make your life easier. You've done as much for me in the past.'

Polly was touched, but also worried. This was a changed Sir Thomas; someone she hardly recognised. He looked tired and worn-out, as though the flame of his life was diminishing. She had no illusions about him; he'd been – how had he once described himself? That was it – a contakour! He'd told her Mr Pickle had called him that and Sir Tom had been greatly taken with the word. He was a man of words – all those words wrapped up in all those papers. And she looked round the room. Pens, ink, paper, string – all for what. The story of a king who had never existed, and his knights who did strange and impossible tasks. Then there were the dwarves, giants, hermits, ladies, wizards and witches, to say nothing of all manner of cruel deaths – beheadings, roastings, gaugings, poisonings – every kind of evilness one could imagine. Above all there was great love – she had been particularly taken when Sir Tom had related to her the story of the love Sir Lancelot had for Queen Guinevere. That night she had gone to sleep dreaming that someone would one day feel the same intensity of feeling for her, and woken up disappointed, knowing it would never happen. She looked at this frail old man in front of her. Where had all these tales come from? What had been the starting point? She wished she had known Sir Thomas when he was a young man. What a rogue and a lover he would have been. Then she thought of Anthony Tanner – perhaps Sir Tom had once been like him – good looking, smoothed-tongued, exciting and mysterious. Yes, she could have fallen for Sir Tom if he had been like Sir Anthony. She sighed to herself, *Oh to have been twenty years younger!* She wrenched herself back to the present to hear Sir Tom say, 'Anyway, I wanted to thank you, Poll, for the good times we had.'

'Had, Sir Tom? We'll have plenty more I'm sure.'

'Perhaps. But now I'm rather tired and I intend to have a little sleep. Before you go though, we'll take a drink together,' and he pulled himself up out of his chair and shambled towards the roundlet propped up on a trestle in the corner.

'Let me do it, Sir Tom,' urged Poll.

'It's a *poor* host who can't manage to *pour* his guest a drink! I can still do the word-play, Poll!' and smiling he handed her a brimming glass. Raising his own he said, 'To old times, Poll, may they always be remembered.'

When she was outside the door she said to Gregory, 'Is your master all right? He seems rather distracted?'

'I'm not sure what you mean, but he does seem to get tired very quickly; he's become quite forgetful too,' said Gregory, 'he calls me in for some reason then can't remember what it was.'

'We all get forgetful in our old age. I expect he'll brace up after a rest. He has been working so hard for so long on his book. Now he's finished he'll be able to rest and get his strength back.' Poll spoke reassuringly, but in her heart, she was very worried.

***

'The King's coming back!' Pom ran up the stairs as fast as his short legs could carry him. Gregory was not at his post, being otherwise engaged on Keeper Clyfford's business.

As he entered Malory's room, his master, who had been lying on the bed half asleep, stretched his arms and yawned, 'Which King, Pom? Edward or Harry – or perhaps it's Tom or Dick?'

'King Edward sir. King Henry's still in London, or have you forgotten?'

'Of course I haven't forgotten,' said Sir Tom testily, 'I'm not in my dotage!'

'Indeed not, sir. But Edward's fleet's off Cromer and heading for the Humber in Yorkshire where he will surely land with his army.'

'So what's Lord Warwick doing about it?'

'Heading his army northwards, as Edward's will surely come south. There must be a fight.'

Malory sighed, 'Fuck it, Pom! I'm not interested any more. All these comings and goings – I can't keep up with it. I'm just glad my work's finished and I can rest a little. To tell the truth I think I've eaten something disagreeable to my bowels. I'm most uncomfortable. I think I'll stay in bed today. There's nothing for me to do.'

'Very well, sir, is there anything I can get you? Any food?'

'Christ no! Just leave me a little wine and water and put some more coals on the fire – I'm feeling quite cold.'

Like Plump Poll, Pom was now extremely worried. His master had been out of sorts for days – in fact for at least two weeks. It had started when he'd put the final touch to *Le Morte D'Arthur*. After the last stroke of the quill he had laid it down and sighed, as though everything had ended. He'd not been the same since.

Pom placed a small tray containing a pewter tankard of water, a jug of Burgundy and a glass beside the old man before making up the fire. It was six in the evening. 'Shall I stay with you tonight, Sir Tom?'

'No, Pom, I shall be well enough on my own. Make sure the privy's empty – I feel very loose about the bowels.'

'Certainly, sir, I'll call Gregory.'

'Perhaps you'd do it – as you always used to!'

'Of course,' and Pom took the bucket and headed for the stairs.

Chapter 11
Le Morte Du Malory

I hear jingling of harness and the clatter of hooves! thought Sir Tom, *Are Arthur's knights assembled here? Have they come to visit?* He lay on the truckle bed in the dark with just enough glow from the fire to make arresting shadows on the walls from which he could determine shapes of men and horses. 'What are they all doing inside my room? Lancelot, Sir Bors, Sir Ector – what do you do there?' he called. No answer came, but the rattle of armour and the shouts of men continued from somewhere within the shadows.

I'm not imagining it – Arthur's Knights are close by. Perhaps, all one hundred and forty have come to take me to Avalon – how fitting that they should escort the man who brought them to life to his final resting place. His mind wondered over the Arthurian legends and stories he had lived with for so long. It was as though he was imbued with their mythology; that his life had begat their lives and he had become one with them. Finding a last vestige of strength, he raised himself up on his elbow and cried out, 'We are one! Take me with you!'

A horse whinnied close by and the tramp of men's feet echoed around Newgate Street. Lord Warwick's soldiers were mustering for their leader's final battle.

***

Gregory found him. Returning from his late-duty for the keeper, he had stationed himself outside Malory's door, ready to respond to the slightest request from his master.

Customarily, he would sit semi-dozing on his stool, yet with one ear to any sound which might come from the other side of the door. Sir Tom normally slept well and hardly ever roused his loyal watcher. Recently, however, Malory's nights had been disturbed by unwanted dreams and he would sometimes shout out; Gregory would respond immediately – soothing the old man back to sleep. Pom continued to spend some nights with Sir Tom, but on those when he was absent he was confident that Gregory would handle matters adequately. On the night of 13th March, when he had returned from emptying Malory's bucket, his master had told him he was "not wanted tonight, John; stay at home. I'm sure you have plenty of your own matters to attend to!" Rather than argue, as his instincts would have had it, he reluctantly agreed.

Just before dawn, Gregory heard a strange, clear cry through the door; one of anguish. He waited to see if would be repeated. *Perhaps it's just another bad dream,* he said to himself, *But it seems different somehow – more – more – final! Yes, that's it – more final.* A strange conclusion for a man not blessed with too many sensibilities. But Gregory had a basic instinct for anything extraordinary. This cry was distinctively different.

He tapped on the door. 'Are you well, Sir Tom? Is there anything I can do?' No answer. He tapped again and called to his master; yet again, no reply. *I must go in,* was his simple conclusion.

The room was dark except for the small glow from the dying embers in the fireplace. Gregory could see nothing until he groped his way to the truckle bed and saw the outline of Sir Tom. The guard had a small piece of candle in his pocket which he lit from the fire. Holding it up, he saw Malory sitting bolt upright supported by his pillows. The old man was staring in front of him, eyes and mouth open, sweat-drenched short grey locks standing on end.

'Sir Thomas, wake up! You've been having a dream sir.' He took Malory's arm and began to shake it gently. The old man's head fell forward and dangled towards the side of the bed. 'Please sit up, sir – you'll fall on the floor!' There was no response and the body continued to make its way downwards. 'Mother of God! He's dead!' Gregory pushed Sir Thomas back on the bed, propping him up on the pillows again and considered the man's face with the tiny light of the candle. There was no movement from eyes or mouth – no recognition. He put his ear to the mouth and nostrils – no breath from either.

What to do? Who to tell? It was close to one o'clock by the chimes of the Greyfriars' bells. Should he wake Keeper Clyfford who was in residence tonight – or walk over to Mr Appleby's lodgings? Surely, Mr Pom would want to be the first to know? He covered the body with the blanket, locked the door and went off to seek out Malory's friend and servant. He would know what to do.

***

It was all over. Pom sat by the bedside of his master whose body lay flat, covered by the well-worn blue blanket. Keeper Clyfford had been roused and confirmed what Pom and Gregory already knew. Pom had sent Roger away, despite the man's offer to keep a vigil. It was still some hours before dawn and the fire was well and truly extinguished. Gregory had offered to bring kindling to restart it, but Pom had waved him away also. He wanted to be alone with Sir Thomas and his own thoughts.

He was no fool; he knew that Sir Tom had been seriously ill for the last few days. Tonight he had almost insisted he stayed, but Sir Tom was adamant he wanted to be alone.

Typical of the stubborn old devil! he thought, *His last night on earth and I'm not there to share it with him!*

What did he feel? What should he feel? It seemed to him he was in the same situation as Sir Tom had described when his *magnum opus* was finished – empty. There was now a great void where his relationship with this man had been. Forty years of friendship, adventure, hardship, tears, poverty, riches and – above all – laughter. The man was a force of nature and, like him or loathe him, he could never be ignored.

One of his literary friends had laughingly told him he had what the Greeks called "charisma" and Sir Tom had bristled, thinking it an insult, until it was explained to him that it meant "gift of grace and freely given". This description had given Sir Tom and Pom a great deal of wry amusement.

He sat in the gloom wondering why he didn't feel anything much yet. He had been half expecting it, but had never really prepared himself for Malory going first. They were the same age, but Pom had always considered the old man to be steelier – more obstinately healthy than he was. He carried less weight and had a body still sinewy and flexible. But of course, he liked a drink – or two – or three, although he held it better than any other man Pom knew. No, it wasn't his style of living that had weakened his constitution, so that the flux had taken him off in the end; it was the finishing of the book. That large hole in his life could never be filled with anything else. It had absorbed him for years; obsessed him to the exclusion of home, family, children – and some grandchildren whom he had never seen and now never would. Pom realised, he himself had an equally large hole to fill. No wife, no children or grandchildren; all that was left was the generous legacy he knew Sir Tom had left him, some instructions for the safe-keeping of the manuscript, his new-found friendship within the Newgate Brotherhood – and a life time's worth of memories.

Alone and in the dark, he began to think of the past and, suddenly overwhelmed by a feeling of the utmost despair, for the first time since a little boy, he put his hands over his face and burst into a torrent of private tears.

***

'Have they confirmed he's really dead? The old boy's not faking it for some devious reason?' Monty Pickle peered through the gloom at the shape of a body covered with the familiar blue blanket. The three men stood round the bed. Pom, somewhat recovered from his outpouring of grief had, in his practical manner, taken steps to organise matters. He had sent messengers to Number 3, Stinking Lane and Jack Worm's lodgings with the news. It was just before dawn.

John Appleby shook his head, 'No, several people, including Master Clyfford, have been in to see him – done the mirror test and everything. Sir Thomas's dead all right and of the flux. It was Greg who found him; he was sitting in his usual place, on his stool just outside the door, when he heard a cry and came in to see what it was. He said he found Sir Tom sitting bolt upright, having shouted something; then he must have fallen back on the pillows and breathed his last. Gregory's most upset, although he didn't want to go home; said he would "find things to do here until he was wanted".'

'Do we know what it was Sir Tom said?' asked Monty.

'Gregory couldn't hear.'

'Something profane I expect!' said Master Worms, and Monty nodded. Pom pursed his lips and frowned.

'What's that terrible smell?' asked Jack Worms.

'You could say it's the smell of sin but, to put no finer point on it, the flux has affected his bowels – he shat himself *in extremis*,' explained Pom.

'Oh dear, how unfortunate.'

'Don't worry, they've sent for a woman for the dead to come in and clean him up for burial.'

'Do we know where he'll be buried and when?' asked Monty.

'Sir Tom would be pleased, and relieved. It won't be a pauper's grave after all, as he once predicted, and certainly not in the prison lime-pit. The Earl of Warwick has persuaded the monks of Greyfriars' to oversee his burial in the abbey churchyard across the road. The mass for his soul will be said in Christ Church. After all, Sir Tom's almost a resident of Greyfriars', being so close for so long. I had no idea that Sir Tom had been taking steps to arrange for his burial. It was when he started thinking about his will; then the conversation he had with us and his wish not to be cast into the prison lime-pit – you remember, Monty? The funeral will probably be the day after tomorrow.'

Monty Pickle fell silent. It had been a great shock when Pom's messenger had knocked on his door half an hour earlier to give him the news. He had gone immediately to Newgate where Jack Worms had already arrived in Malory's room. The old knight's body was stretched out on the bed, and the room was suffused with the terrible smell of a synthesis of excrement and disease.

'He told me once he would probably die of the flux, the pox or jail fever,' said Monty with a sigh, putting his hand over his nose. 'So it was the flux which saw him off then?'

'Yes,' said Pom, 'we had an outbreak last week. At least five Newgate inmates have died from it; the grisly cull of prisoners by disease.'

'Look, no disrespect to Sir Tom, but I'd rather like to get out of here,' said Jack, 'the air's most unhealthy, and I can't really put up with this stink much longer.'

'You're right, Jack,' said Monty, 'we should go. You're very welcome to come back to my lodgings for an early breakfast – I have a couple of bottles which Sir Tom gave me in lieu of cash when he was short once.'

'Wenlock's wine?' asked Pom hopefully. He had no intention of stomaching Monty's gut-rot, even at such a difficult time.

'Indeed, Burgundy purloined from a Spanish vessel. I always check the provenance!'

'Good, that's agreed. I'll fetch some provender from my lodgings and follow you.' Pom heaved an inward sigh of relief. He felt responsible for his friend and master, but, like Jack, could not have abided the room for much longer. His grief was still sharp, but it was a private sorrow which he would suffer on his own. Attending to practical matters was the best way of assuaging the pain of loss; it had always worked well for him in the past. The company of good friends would be most welcome.

As they were preparing to leave, the door opened wide and Fat Gregory entered the room followed by an elderly woman carrying a leather bucket and bag.

'Begging your pardon, Mr Appleby, this woman's been sent by Master Clyfford to lay out the body. Is it convenient for her to do it now?'

'Well, we're clearing out for a while and I'm sure Sir Tom can make no objection, Greg! Come in and begin your work, woman; the quicker the better I would say.'

As they walked down the stone stairway to the main gate, Monty said, 'Sir Tom would have liked to have met that old woman and written her up as a "wizened crone" or some such. He was always looking out for characters to incorporate in *Le Morte*.'

The three men fell silent as they ruminated on the life and work of their friend; they didn't speak until Pom left them to hurry to his lodgings; Jack and Monty walked off to Stinking Lane. As they reached Monty's front door, he realised, to his great relief, it was too early for sight or sound of the miscreant Talbot children, who anyway seemed to have disappeared over the last few days. He found out later that, in despair of her husband, their mother had returned to her family home and taken them with her, leaving Mr Talbot to his ham-fisted carpentry and imprecations. How long they would be away Monty had no idea, but a certain kind of peace and tranquillity had settled over Number 3 which the scribe relished.

Once inside, the host set about lighting a fire and organising the wine. As he did so he said, 'I wonder what Pom will do now, Jack. It's occurred to me he and Sir Tom were like an old married couple. Forty years together – this will be a great shock to him. Perhaps we weren't very sympathetic?'

'You're right, Monty. He'll feel this very badly. I've no idea whether he has a family to return to. We never talked much about it, did we? We know he's not married; perhaps he has brothers or sisters he can go to.'

'I don't think the domestic life would suit him. He's cut from the same cloth as Sir Tom.'

'We'll just have to be his family for the time being – until things are sorted out. There's still the matter of Sir Tom's will and what's to be done with the manuscript. We'll give Pom all the friendship he needs for as long as he wants it – agreed?'

The man himself arrived to share the contents of his wicker basket and the first thing they did was to raise their glasses to "Sir Thomas Malory, knight and gentleman"!

'Not always!' the three companions thought privately, but did not say it.

Jack Worms, with the nosiness and impatience of youth, asked Pom, 'So, what happens now? Has Lady Elizabeth Malory been told?'

'I wrote to her ladyship this morning to tell her what had come to pass.'

'Will she travel to Newgate?'

'Very unlikely, especially as I told her the funeral will be over before she could possibly arrive. They've been apart for many years; I wonder if she would even recognise him.'

'So, who'll be there?' asked Monty. 'Not the Earl of Warwick?'

'I hardly think so, given the situation; he has other things on his mind now. We were lucky he even had time to send someone to contact the monks for us – decent of him when you think what's happening.'

'Indeed!' said Jack, and the three men fell silent for a minute in consideration of the grave state of the nation.

Then Pom said, 'I don't think there'll be many there – some of the guards who really liked the old boy will attend, and of course Gregory. Master Clyfford will come, I'm sure, maybe other jail keepers. Sir Tom's son, Robert, might deign to show himself if he's in London. Lord Wenlock's in Calais – at least that's what I heard. Anthony Tanner will be otherwise engaged with Lord Warwick. I can't see any of the old Warwickshire crowd being able to attend. I've told Polly and she says she'll pass the news round Bankside and to his other "whorelets" as he called them! There'll probably be some of his old regular creditors too – although I'm proud to tell you he died owing no one a penny!'

'It sounds as though the funeral will be thinly attended – just us, some prison keepers, guards, ex-creditors and whores! Not much of a send-off is it!' said Monty.

'It reflects his life I suppose!' said Pom ruefully.

Jack Worms sighed, 'What a man he was! He certainly drank deeply from the cup of life!'

And from its jug! Monty thought, but did not say it.

'A poetic line worthy of the man himself,' observed Pom mournfully.

Seeing his friend was beginning to look excessively sad, Monty said, 'As you've mentioned poetry, Pom, we should discuss what Sir Tom wished to happen to the manuscript. All that work can't go for nothing.'

'Indeed not,' nodded Jack. 'Some time ago, you hinted the old man had left instructions in his will – and concerning us all.'

'He did, and he discussed it with me after he had made his testament. Up to that point he rarely mentioned it – I suppose he considered himself immortal!'

'So what's to be done?'

'Originally, he planned to go himself, but when he realised that would be impossible he told me he wanted the three of us – the Newgate Brotherhood as he called us – to take the manuscript to the heart of the Arthurian story – to Camelot itself!'

Monty shook his head and frowned, 'But there's no such place, at least as far as I know. Is it somewhere in the wilds of the north?'

'No, there is no place *called* Camelot, but Sir Tom always had one real place in mind for it.'

'And where was that?' asked Monty.

'Winchester.'

'Winchester, but that's miles away – a pilgrim's journey! I should know – it's where I come from,' exclaimed Monty.

'Exactly – he knew that, and it was part of his thinking! He wants us to make a pilgrimage and pay homage to Camelot. We are to leave the original manuscript with the monks for them to make a copy and keep until it's ready to be launched into the world. He saw it as his "Holy Grail".'

'Well, surely there's a problem with that!' said Monty, 'Like the Grail, how will anyone know it exists to want to "launch" it as you say?'

'Sir Tom wanted everyone to know it's finished and ready to be disseminated. This is where you come in, Jack, with your contacts. You can put the word around the stationers' guild about this "great work"; get people interested.'

'It'll be very inconvenient for them to travel down to Winchester to buy a copy when they want one,' observed Monty.

'Not at all,' said Jack. 'We booksellers have our methods. How else would the nobility get hold of copies of any book? I told you, many senior noblemen have taken to building libraries as a mark of their "learned" status – although it's always questionable how much of them they actually read. But Good Duke Humphrey of Gloucester was an exception; he had a very large collection –'

'And look what happened to him – a fiery poker up his fundament!' Pom said lugubriously.

'That was politics; it had nothing to do with literature! But I do have the glimmerings of an idea of how we might disseminate Sir Tom's work – using the most up to date methods.'

'Go on,' said Pom.

'Well, once the monks have made a copy of *Le Morte* we could return to Winchester to collect it, bring it back and then make another – for safety should anything happen to the original. We could take the copies to the Rhineland where the new printing presses are. I'm sure the Germans would be interested in putting them into print with their new machines.'

'That would mean us having this huge work copied out again – it would take months.'

'Not so long if we hire help.'

'That would cost money, Jack.'

Pom intervened, 'Sir Tom has left me a nest-egg. I'd be prepared to invest some of it, in recognition of my master's passion for his life's work.' Monty and Jack fell silent in awe of this confirmation of domestic loyalty. 'He also left some money to be used precisely for the copying of the work at some point in the future, "if there was sufficient interest," as he put it in his will. As Jack suggests, it would mean a journey overseas at some time. But when you consider it, you and I, Monty, are now free-agents – unemployed free-agents! What would you say to a sea voyage to Germany?'

Monty hesitated, 'If it was sometime in the future and I could plan for it, I think it sounds an excellent idea, although it wouldn't be cheap.'

'I'm sure there's enough in Sir Tom's legacies to cover it,' said Pom reassuringly.

'I'm not going to be left out of this!' declared Jack. 'As I said, you'll need someone with experience in the book trade. Bringing out a volume requires skill. Besides, I have the contacts.'

'With German printers?'

'No, of course not, but I would be able to find my way around the stationers of Cologne I'm sure; you'll also need help copying the manuscript in the first place. I can organise that.'

'But what about your shop?'

'I'll sell up!'

'And your apprentice?'

'He can come with us, or go back to his father. But let's not get ahead of ourselves. This journey to Winchester; how far is it and how long will it take?'

'It's about seventy miles. Presumably, neither of you are practised horsemen, so on good nags at twenty miles a day it should take three or four days. We'll go the pilgrims' route and can take in some sights on the way – worship at a few shrines if you're so inclined.'

'I think I'd rather just go straight there and back,' said Monty tentatively. 'About these "nags" as you mentioned; you're right, I should prefer an "ambling mare", the sort Sir Tom describes in his book – his hackneys. My riding days are far behind me. In fact I've not sat on a horse for twelve years and that was to ride to my father's funeral.'

'Don't you worry! I have good contacts in that quarter; over the way at Greyfriars there are stables full of beasts of all sizes and temperaments.'

'But I still worry about how these horses are to be paid for, Pom.'

'Don't worry about that either; Sir Tom left you five pounds remember, to cover the cost of your "employment" in the event of his demise. He was true to his word and I can lay hand on that immediately. That will easily cover the cost.' It took a moment for Monty Pickle to absorb what Pom was saying and, when he had, it occurred to him he was being duped. 'Are you telling me that *I'm* to pay for these hackneys to take Sir Tom's manuscript to Winchester – therefore, it will be at my own expense? I can't believe you just suggested that!'

'Well, look at it this way, Monty. He's paid you in full for the work which is now complete, plus an extra four weeks. The five pounds was a pledge in the event of the work not being finished and you being out of a job – which is not the case. As I see it, you're simply tying up some loose ends for him.' Monty fell silent. A visit to the cathedral at Winchester, and to his home territory was not such a bad proposition. He had nothing much else to occupy him. In fact, he had been wondering how he would fill the void now Malory was gone and *Le Morte* finished. There was always Sir Tom's own story to tidy up and in Winchester he might even find material to write a tract or treatise which Jack Worms could bind. His mind wandered along those paths for a moment until he was jerked back to reality by Pom, who said, 'I promised Sir Tom I would take the manuscript to this chosen location – his Camelot – as soon as possible.'

'How soon?'

'As soon as I've been able to organise things; probably ten days or so.'

'Do you think we'll be there more than a few days?' asked Monty, still thinking about the expense and the discomfort of horseback.

'Depends on how hospitable the monks are and how interested in Malory's script. They may not allow it in their library; after all it does contain some saucy references which aren't fit for clerics' eyes! We'll see; at least it'll be an adventure for you Monty, you dull old dog!'

'Not so dull since I met you and Sir Tom!' laughed Monty, now unfazed by a remark he would have bristled at two years before.

'That's true. Between us, we gave you an education, Montmorency Pickle – one you never expected I'm sure.'

'Never indeed! And overall, I'm grateful for knowing the man, even though he was a contakour of the first order!'

'Contakour? That's an interesting word and one which Sir Tom enjoyed; I heard him use it. Where does it come from?'

'It's pure Wiltshire and means "trouble-maker" and "strife" rolled into one. I called him it once and he was most taken with it – not at all offended. It was a word I hadn't used since I left home, but one I thought suited him perfectly – generous, full of life, but mischievous, bloody-minded and –'

'Arrogant and overbearing!' laughed Jack, 'We all put up with quite a lot, but always came back for more – which is the test of the depth of a friendship – the Newgate Five!'

'Some things I won't miss, like his profanities,' said Monty. 'I never got used to them.'

'I think he considered any words which rolled nicely round the tongue were valid – he relished words and their sounds!' said Pom with a sigh of sadness. 'Talking of his generosity, I didn't tell you how Sir Tom set Plump Poll up with money for her future and, according to his will, left Gregory enough for "the most expensive and well-fitting boots a gentleman can afford" as well as some cash. I've never seen a man so proud as when I told Gregory!'

'A man of continuing surprises,' said Jack Worms sadly.

'Anyway,' said Pom, 'he's gone and we'll never hear him even swear again, more's the pity. So let's raise our glasses and drink a toast to him. We can't drink his good health since that is no more, but we can wish him well on his journey to – somewhere! So, here's to the old man – Sir Thomas Malory – wherever he is!'

The three men raised their glasses, 'The old man – Sir Thomas Malory – wherever he is!'

***

At exactly that moment, the old man was deep in conversation with St Peter regarding the appalling state of the celestial gates

***

Post Word

14th April 1471, Easter Sunday, at four on a damp foggy morning, Richard Neville, Earl of Warwick and Salisbury (1428-71) went head to head with Edward IV (1442-83), King of England, Wales, France and Ireland, on a field outside the small town of Barnet in Hertfordshire. This would be the last encounter between two men who had started out as mentor and pupil, become brothers-in-arms and finally arch enemies.

The battle was hard fought in the mist for an hour, until a misunderstanding between Warwick and his Lancastrians caused his men to throw down their weapons, and retreat. The earl was caught by the Yorkists and killed by one of Edward's men; his body stripped and eventually exhibited half-naked in St Paul's. 'The bug which feared us all', according to Edward IV in the final part of Shakespeare's *Henry VI*, was dead and there could be no mistaking it. Edward spent the next twelve years as king in relative peace, until his death from natural causes. His young son, Edward V, mysteriously disappeared and the throne was taken over by Edward IV's brother, the Duke of Gloucester, who became Richard III.

***

In 1485, William Caxton (c1422-1491) produced the first printed copy of *Le Morte D'Arthur* based on Malory's manuscript. In his detailed preface, he makes one fleeting reference to Sir Thomas:

"I have after the simple cunning that God has sent me, under the favour and correction of all noble lords and gentlemen, enprised to imprint a book of the noble histories

of the said King Arthur, and of certain of his knights, after a copy unto me delivered, which copy Sir Thomas Malory did take out of certain books of French, and reduced into English."

Since then, *Le Morte D'Arthur* has been reproduced in literature: prose and poetry; art: sculpture and painting; theatre, film and television.

Malory was buried "under a marble in the Chapel of St Francis at the Greyfriars', near Newgate", according to the Warwickshire antiquarian William Dugdale writing in the mid-seventeenth century. Sir Thomas' gravestone was inscribed:

Here rests Sir Thomas Malory
A valiant knight
Died 14 March 1471
Of the parish of Monkskirby
In the County of Warwickshire

Sir Thomas continues to be excluded from the pantheon of literary giants celebrated in Westminster Abbey. The first writer to be buried there was Geoffrey Chaucer, immediately after his death in 1400; but possibly more in recognition of his position as clerk of the works to the Abbey than for his literary output.

***

The books in the *Malory Trilogy: Rogue Malory, Malory's Quest* and *Malory's Grail*, although following the historical events of the time and Malory's own very real and well-recorded exploits, are works of fiction. They imagine how the original manuscript of *Le Morte D'Arthur* might have been researched, completed and then lost for fourteen years before the fact of it being first circulated as a printed work by William Caxton in 1485.

Subsequently, what has been claimed as Sir Thomas Malory's possible original manuscript of *Le Morte D'Arthur* remained hidden for almost five hundred years until 1934, when it was discovered in the Fellows' Library of Winchester College by Mr W.F. Oakshott, a school master and academic. A full text of the manuscript became available thirteen years later when an edited version by the literary scholar Eugène Vinaver appeared as "The Works of Sir Thomas Malory".

*